Inhaling deeply, she selfishly enjoyed another tantalizing breath warmed by Chris's skin, perfumed by his masculine scent.

Then she pushed herself back to sitting, forcing him to drop his arms.

He studied her intently, his dark eyes boring into hers. "You do know that I'm going to protect you, right? You seem...scared, or maybe worried."

Unable to stop herself, she caressed his face. Her heart nearly stopped when he rubbed his cheek against her hand. Oh, how she wished her life were different, that she had met this man in another place, another time.

He smiled, a warm, gentle smile she felt all the way to her toes.

"Everything's going to be okay, Julie," he said. "We'll figure this out. Together."

"Thank you," she whispered back. Her gaze dropped to his lips, and her mouth suddenly went dry. She automatically leaned toward him. Her hands went to his shirt, smoothing the fabric.

A shudder went through him and she looked up, her eyes locking with his. The open hunger on his face made her breath catch. And then he was leaning toward her slowly, giving her every chance to stop him, to pull away, to say no.

But she didn't.

SMOKY MOUNTAIN TRAP

LENA DIAZ

&

PAULA GRAVES

Previously published as *Mountain Witness*
and *The Smoky Mountain Mist*

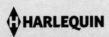

HARLEQUIN

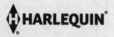

ISBN-13: 978-1-335-42697-0

Smoky Mountain Trap

Copyright © 2022 by Harlequin Enterprises ULC

Mountain Witness
First published in 2017. This edition published in 2022.
Copyright © 2017 by Lena Diaz

The Smoky Mountain Mist
First published in 2013. This edition published in 2022.
Copyright © 2013 by Paula Graves

Recycling programs
for this product may
not exist in your area.

For questions and comments about the quality of this book,
please contact us at CustomerService@Harlequin.com.

Harlequin Enterprises ULC
22 Adelaide St. West, 41st Floor
Toronto, Ontario M5H 4E3, Canada
www.Harlequin.com

Printed in U.S.A.

CONTENTS

Lena Diaz was born in Kentucky and has also lived in California, Louisiana and Florida, where she now resides with her husband and two children. Before becoming a romantic suspense author, she was a computer programmer. A Romance Writers of America Golden Heart® Award finalist, she has also won the prestigious Daphne du Maurier Award for Excellence in Mystery/Suspense. To get the latest news about Lena, please visit her website, lenadiaz.com.

Books by Lena Diaz

Harlequin Intrigue

The Justice Seekers

Cowboy Under Fire
Agent Under Siege
Killer Conspiracy
Deadly Double-Cross

The Mighty McKenzies

Smoky Mountains Ranger
Smokies Special Agent
Conflicting Evidence
Undercover Rebel

Tennessee SWAT

Mountain Witness
Secret Stalker
Stranded with the Detective
SWAT Standoff

Visit the Author Profile page
at Harlequin.com for more titles.

MOUNTAIN WITNESS

Lena Diaz

Thank you, Allison Lyons and Nalini Akolekar.

For my family...George, Sean and Jennifer.
I love you so much.

And in loving memory to the family member
who has passed over the rainbow.
I'll always love you, Sparky.

Chapter 1

Blood, there was so much blood. Julie stood over him, one hand braced on the bed's footboard, the other still holding the gun. The blood soaked his shirt, seeping between his fingers as he clutched at the bullet hole in his side. Air wheezed between his teeth, his startlingly blue eyes blazing with hatred through the openings in the ski mask. The same eyes that had once stared at her with such love that they'd stolen her breath away.

Right before he'd said, "I do."

Julie Webb shook her head, blinking away the memories, wishing she could put the past behind her just as easily. Her hands tightened on the steering wheel as she sat in the driveway, the thin pale line on her ring finger the only tangible reminder of the diamond that had once sat there.

Stop it. He can't hurt you anymore. It's time to move on.

Unfortunately, with most of her assets frozen while the courts did their thing back in Nashville, moving on meant hiding out in the tiny—aka affordable—rural town of Destiny, Tennessee. And with the limited rentals available in Blount County, she'd chosen the lesser of evils, the one place with some land around it—an old farmhouse that had sat vacant for so long that the owner had been desperate to rent it. Desperate equaled cheap. And that was the only reason that Julie had taken it. Well, that and the fact that Destiny was a good three hours from Nashville. She wasn't likely to run into anyone she knew in the local grocery store.

The sound of a horn honking had her looking in her rearview mirror, reminding her why she was in her car to begin with. The moving truck sat idling in the gravel road that ran past the expansive front yard, waiting for her to back out so it could back in. After two days of living out of a suitcase and sleeping on the floor, having a couch and a bed again was going to feel like heaven.

She put the car in Reverse, hesitating when she noticed that her only neighbor had come out onto his front porch. Long, unpaved road, dead end, surrounded by acres of trees and pastures, and she still had a neighbor to contend with. A handsome, sex-on-a-stick kind of guy to boot. Which was going to make ignoring him difficult, but not impossible. She'd had her own sex-on-a-stick kind of man before. And look what it had gotten her.

He flashed her a friendly smile and waved just as he'd done every time he'd seen her in the past two days.

And once again, she pretended not to notice. She backed out of the driveway.

Rhythmic beeping sounded from the truck as it took the place of her car, stopping just inches from the porch that ran along the front of the white clapboard house. It was a much smaller, one-story clone of the place next door. There weren't any fences on either property, so she wasn't sure where his acreage ended and hers began. But clearly he had a lot more land than her rental. The mowed part of his yard extended for a good quarter of a mile to the end of their street.

She didn't care, didn't want to know anything about him. The only way to survive this temporary exile was to keep to herself and make sure that none of her acquaintances figured out where she was. Which meant not associating with the hunk next door or anyone else who might recognize her name or her face, in case any of the news stories had made it out this far. She fervently hoped they hadn't.

The movers had the ramp set up by the time she'd walked up the long gravel driveway. It would allow them to cart the boxes and furniture directly to the top of the porch without having to navigate the steps. That meant everything should go quickly, especially since she didn't have much for them to unload—just the bare essentials and a few things she'd refused to leave in storage.

She risked a quick look toward the house next door. The friendly man was gone. A twinge of guilt shot through her for having ignored him. He was probably a perfectly nice guy and deserved to be treated better. But her life was extremely complicated right now. By ignoring him, by not letting him get involved in any way in her problems, she was doing him a favor.

"Ma'am, where do you want this?" one of the movers asked, holding up a box.

Apparently, the thick black letters on the side that spelled "kitchen" weren't enough of a hint.

She jogged up the steps. But, before going inside, she hesitated and looked over her shoulder at the thick woods on the other side of the road. The hairs were standing up on the back of her neck.

"Ma'am?" the mover holding the box called out. He lifted the box a few inches, as if to remind her he was still holding it.

"Sorry, this way." She headed inside, but couldn't shake the feeling of doom that had settled over her.

Chapter 2

Chris shaded his eyes against the early afternoon sun and watched through an upstairs window as the curvy brunette led one of the movers into the house next door. He didn't know why he bothered waving every time he saw her. Her standard response was to turn away and pretend that she hadn't seen him. He'd gotten the message the first time—she wanted nothing to do with him. Too bad the good manners his mama had instilled in him, courtesy of a well-worn switch off a weeping willow tree or his daddy's belt, wouldn't allow him to ignore her the way she ignored him.

He leaned against the wall of the corner guest bedroom, noting the car that his neighbor had parked on the road. He couldn't remember the last time he'd seen a BMW. Most of the people he knew had four-wheel drives. Come winter, that light little car would slide around like a hockey puck on the icy back roads. Then again, maybe she didn't plan on sticking around that long. Summer was just getting started.

A distant rumble had him looking up the road to see a caravan of trucks headed toward his house, right on time to start his annual beginning of summer cookout. The shiny red Jeep in front was well ahead of the other vehicles, barreling down the road at a rate of speed that probably would have gotten the driver thrown in jail if he wasn't a cop himself, with half the Destiny, Tennessee, police department following behind him.

Dirt and gravel spewed out from beneath the Jeep's tires as it slowed just enough to turn into his driveway without flipping over. The driver, Chris's best friend, Dillon Gray, jumped out while the car was still rocking. He hurried to the passenger side to lift out his very pregnant wife, Ashley. Chris grinned and headed downstairs.

He'd just reached the front room when the screen door flew open and Ashley jogged inside, her hands holding her round belly as if to support it. The door swung closed, its springs squeaking in protest at the abuse.

"Hi, Chris." She raced past the stairs into the back hallway and slammed the bathroom door.

The screen door opened again and Chris's haggard-looking friend stepped inside.

"Sorry about that." Dillon waved toward the bathroom. "Ashley was desperate. She had me doing ninety on the interstate."

Chris clapped him on the back. "How's the pregnancy going?"

Dillon let out a shaky breath and raked his hand

through his disheveled hair. "I'm not sure I can survive two more months of this."

A toilet flushed. Water ran in the sink. And soon the sound of bare feet slip-slapping on the wooden floor had both of them turning to see Dillon's wife heading toward them. Her sandals dangled from one hand as she stopped beside Chris.

"Sorry about the bare feet. They're so swollen the shoes were cutting off my circulation." She motioned toward Dillon. "Let me guess. He's complaining about all the suffering he's going through, right? He keeps forgetting that I'm the one birthing a watermelon." The smile on her face softened her words as she yanked on Chris's shirt so he'd lean down. She planted a kiss on his cheek and squeezed his hand. "Don't worry. I'm taking good care of him."

He raised a brow. "Him? You're having a boy?"

"No, silly. I mean, yes, we might be. Or it might be a girl. We're waiting until the birth to be surprised about the gender. I meant Dillon. I'll make sure he survives fatherhood."

Dillon plopped down in one of the recliners facing the big-screen TV mounted on the far wall. "It's not fatherhood that I'm worried about. It's the pregnancy, and childbirth." He placed a hand on his flat stomach. "Every time she throws up, I throw up. Last week, I swear I had a contraction."

Ashley clucked her tongue as she perched on the arm of his chair. "Sympathy pains." She grinned up at Chris. "Isn't it wonderful?"

Chris burst out laughing.

Dillon shot him a glare that should have set his hair on fire.

"Did you remember to bring the steaks?" Chris headed toward the abused screen door, assuming the food was in the Jeep.

"The chief has them," Dillon said. "I didn't feel well enough to go to the store so I called him to do it, instead." He pressed his hand to his stomach again and groaned as his head fell back against the chair.

Ashley rolled her eyes and plopped down onto his lap. In spite of how green Dillon looked, he immediately hugged her close and pressed a kiss on the top of her head. Dillon started to gently massage his wife's shoulders and she kissed the side of his neck. Chris had never seen two people more in love or more meant for each other. Then again, they'd only been married for close to a year. They were still newlyweds.

"Where do you want all of this stuff?" someone called from outside.

Chris turned away from the two lovebirds and looked through the screen door.

"Those two are enough to make you sick, aren't they?" fellow SWAT officer and detective Max Remington, holding a large cooler, teased from the porch.

"Hey, Max." Ashley waved over Dillon's shoulder.

"Hey, Ash." Max dipped his head toward the cooler and glanced at Chris. "This beer and ice ain't getting any lighter. Where do you want it?"

"Around back, on the deck, well away from the grill. It's hot and ready."

Max carried the cooler back down the steps. Twenty minutes later, Destiny PD's entire five-man-and-one-woman SWAT team was on the large back deck, plus Chief William Thornton, his wife, Claire, Ashley, their

911 operator—Nancy—and a handful of other support staff.

Steaks sizzled on the double-decker grill, which was Max's domain. On one side of him, SWAT officers Colby Vale and Randy Carter chatted about the best places to fish. On Max's other side a young female police intern helped load foil-wrapped potatoes and corncobs onto another section of the grill.

"Two weeks." Dillon grabbed a beer from the cooler at Chris's feet.

Since Dillon was watching Ashley talk to SWAT Officer Donna Waters a few feet away, Chris wasn't sure what he meant. "Two weeks until what?"

Dillon used his bottle to indicate the pretty young intern who was earning college credits for helping out at the Destiny police department over the summer.

"I give her and Max's fledgling relationship two more weeks, at the most," Dillon said. "They have absolutely nothing in common and she's young enough to be his…niece…or something."

Chris shrugged and snagged himself a beer from the cooler. The rest of the team laughed and talked in small groups on the massive deck. The chief and his wife were the only ones not smiling. They were too intent on discussing the best placement of the desserts on the table at the far end. Chris grinned, always amused to see the soft side of his crotchety boss whenever his wife of forty-plus years was around. He hoped someday that he'd be lucky enough to be married that long, and be just as happy. But so far he hadn't met the right woman. Given Destiny's small size, he just might have to move to another town to expand the dating pool.

The sound of an engine turning over had him stepping closer to the railing. The moving truck headed down the driveway next door, then continued up the road. His new neighbor stood in the grass beside her front porch, watching it go. Unless she was deaf, she had to hear the noise in his backyard. Was she going to ignore *all* of them?

He waited, watching. As if feeling the force of his gaze upon her, she turned. Their eyes locked and held. Then she whirled around and raced up her porch steps, the screen door slamming as she hurried inside.

"What's her name?"

Chris didn't turn at the sound of Dillon's voice. His friend braced his hands on the railing beside him.

"I have no idea," Chris answered. "She's been here two days and she hasn't even acknowledged that I exist."

Dillon whistled low. "That's a first for you. Must be losing your touch."

He slanted his friend a look. "Yeah, well. At least I'm not puking my guts up every time someone says fried gizzards."

Dillon's eyes widened and his face went pale. A second later he clapped his hand over his mouth and ran inside the house.

Judging from the way Ashley was suddenly glaring at Chris, she'd obviously noticed Dillon's rapid retreat. She put her hands on her hips. "What did you do?"

"I might have mentioned 'fried gizzards.'"

She threw her hands in the air and shook her head in exasperation. Then she ran inside after her husband.

Chris winced at the accusatory looks some of the others gave him. He shouldn't have done that. He knew that Dillon's sympathy morning sickness could be triggered by certain foods, or even the mention of them. But teasing Dillon was just too easy—and way too fun—to resist.

He supposed he'd have to apologize later.

But right now there was something else bothering him, a puzzle he was trying to work through. He turned back toward his mysterious new neighbor's house, trying to fit the pieces together in his mind. There'd been something about her that was bothering him, the way she'd twisted her hands together as she'd stared down the road, the look in her eyes when she'd met his gaze.

And then it clicked.

He knew exactly what he'd seen.

Fear.

Chapter 3

Judging by the empty beer bottles and bags of trash sitting on his deck, Chris reckoned the annual summer-opening bash for his SWAT unit had been a success. Everyone had seemed to have a good time, even Dillon, once he'd gotten over being mad. They'd probably still be partying if the mosquitoes and gnats hadn't invaded after the sun went down.

He probably should have invited everyone to go indoors. But he'd been too preoccupied to even think of that earlier. He'd spent most of the cookout worrying about a woman he'd never met, who'd made it crystal clear that she wanted nothing to do with him.

After another glance at the house next door, he cursed and forced himself to look away. He grabbed two bags of trash in one hand and a bag of recyclables in the other. Then he headed down the deck steps and around the side yard toward the garage. He slowed as he neared the front. Behind the dark blue BMW next door was a silver Ford Taurus that hadn't been there earlier.

He shook his head. It was none of his business who the woman next door invited over. Judging by the plates on the Taurus, it was from out of town. Maybe some of her friends were helping her unpack and set up the place. Again, none of his concern.

Rounding to the front of his house, he keyed a code into the electronic keypad to open the garage door. After stowing the trash and recyclables in the appropriate bins, he closed the door again and took the front porch steps two at a time. If he hurried, he just might catch the start of a baseball game on TV.

A few minutes later, he was sitting in his favorite recliner with a beer and a bowl of popcorn on the side table. He was looking forward to a relaxing few hours vegging out before going to bed early, even though it was Saturday.

Come dawn, he had a date with a tractor and a Bush Hog and over an acre of brush to clear for Cooper, a neighbor laid up in the hospital. After that, he had his own chores to see to, including repairing some fencing to keep cows from wandering into his yard again from the farm behind his house. Sunday definitely wasn't going to be a day of rest for him. And he'd still have to catch the Sunday evening service at First Baptist or his mom would hear about it and start praying for his soul.

A piercing shriek sounded from outside, then abruptly cut off. Chris jumped up from his chair, grabbed his pistol from the coffee table. Standing stock-still, he listened for the sound again. Had a screech owl flown over the house? Maybe one of the baseball fans on TV had made the noise. Maybe. But he didn't think so. The volume on the television hadn't been turned up very loud. He pressed the mute button on the remote. Still nothing. Everything was silent. So what had he heard?

As if pulled by an unseen force, his gaze went to the window on the east side of the great room. The front of his home was about ten feet closer to the road than his neighbor's. He had a clear view of her porch, dimly lit by a single yellow bulb now that the sun had gone down. Everything looked as it had earlier when he'd dealt with the trash. Two cars were still parked in her driveway. There was no sign of any people anywhere. But he couldn't shake the uneasy feeling in his gut and the memory of the fear he'd seen in her eyes.

Cursing himself for a fool, he headed toward the screen door, gun in hand. His neighbor was probably going to think he was an idiot for checking on her. But he had to see for himself that she was okay. He shoved the pistol into his waistband at the small of his back. No sense in scaring her with his gun out. After jogging down the porch steps, he strode across the lawn to her house.

The sound of breaking glass made him pause before he reached the bottom step. An angry male voice sounded from inside. Chris whirled around, changing direction. He went to the side of the porch, where he wouldn't be visible from the front door, then hauled himself up and over the railing. Crouching down, he edged to the first window, then peeked inside.

The layout of the house was basically a one-story version of his own. He'd been in it dozens of times helping out old man Hutchinson before his family moved him to an assisted-living facility. The front door opened into the great room. The kitchen was to the left, through an archway. Both homes had a hallway that ran across the back, with two bedrooms and a bath. The only true difference was the size and the fact that Chris's home had a staircase hugging the wall on the right.

Boxes were stacked neatly across the left end of his neighbor's great room. A couch and two chairs sat in a grouping on the right. Standing in the middle of the room was a tall, lean man, his face a mask of anger as he said something to the woman across from him. Pieces of a broken drinking glass scattered the floor. But what captured Chris's attention the most was what the man was holding in his right hand—a butcher knife.

Chris ducked down, his hand going to the gun shoved into his waistband. No. He couldn't bust in there pointing his gun. The other man was too close to the woman and might hurt her. What he needed was a distraction, some way to put more distance between the two.

He also needed backup, in case this all went horribly wrong. He didn't want the woman left facing the man with the knife all by herself. He had to make sure she'd get the help she needed, no matter what.

After silencing his phone, he typed a quick text to dispatch, letting them know the situation. As expected, the immediate response was to stand down and wait for more units. Yeah, well, more units were a good thirty minutes away, best case. That was part of the price of living in the country. Like it or not, he had to go inside the house. If he waited, his neighbor could get hurt or killed by the time his fellow SWAT team members arrived.

He shoved the phone into his pocket, then hopped

over the railing and dropped down to the grass. His hastily concocted plan wasn't much of a plan. It basically involved making enough noise to alert the two inside that he was there, and then going all hillbilly on them. If they were typical city slickers, as the BMW and out-of-town plates on the Taurus suggested, they might take the bait and think he was a redneck without a clue. If his gamble paid off, he'd manage to insert himself between the two and wrestle the knife away—hopefully without getting himself or anyone else killed.

Yeah, not much of a plan, but, since he couldn't think of another one, he went with it.

He wiped his palms on his jeans, then loudly clomped his booted foot onto the bottom porch step.

Chapter 4

A hollow sound echoed outside. Julie jerked around to see the sexy guy from next door stomping up the front porch steps.

"Who is that?" Alan snarled, closing the distance between them.

She swallowed, watching the knife in his hand. "My neighbor. I don't know his name."

"Get rid of him."

He edged halfway behind her, his left hand—the one holding the knife—hidden from view. Its sharp tip pressed lightly between her shoulder blades, just piercing her skin. She gasped and arched away, but the threat was still there. Her only chance was to try to appease him. If she didn't, he'd kill her, and try to kill a stranger whose only crime was that he lived next door.

A knock sounded. The tall, broad-shouldered man

who'd given her so many unreturned smiles and friendly waves peered through the screen door, grinning when he saw her standing in the middle of the great room.

"Hello, there," he drawled. "I'm Chris Downing, from the house next door. Hope you don't mind me coming over. I figured it was high time I introduced myself."

"Um, actually, I don't—"

He pushed the door open and stepped inside, his white teeth gleaming in a smile that would have been charming if she wasn't so scared.

She shot a pleading look over her shoulder, then glanced back at her neighbor. "Mr. Downing, this really isn't a good—"

"Chris," he corrected, striding toward her. "No point in formalities between neighbors."

The knife pressed against her spine, a warning that she needed to do something. Fast.

"You sure are pretty, ma'am." His grin widened. "Welcome to the neighborhood." He took one of her hands in his. "And what lovely name did your mama gift you with?" He waited expectantly, his green eyes capturing hers, looking oddly serious in spite of his silly grin.

She could almost taste Alan's simmering anger, his impatience.

"I'm…ah…Julie. Julie Webb. I'm sorry but you *really* need to—"

"Can't remember the last time I met a Julie. Beautiful name for a beautiful woman." His head bobbed up and down while he vigorously shook her hand, pulling her off balance. She was forced to step toward him to keep from falling over.

Alan made a menacing sound in his throat and plopped his right hand on her shoulder, anchoring her and keeping her from moving farther away from him. But her neighbor misinterpreted the gesture. He let go of Julie's hand and offered his hand to Alan, instead.

"Didn't mean to ignore you back there," he said. "Where are my manners? Are you my new neighbor, too, or just visiting?"

The pressure on her shoulder tightened painfully, making her wince. She tensed, fully expecting to feel the bite of the knife sliding between her ribs at any moment. Most people would have read the tension between her and Alan and realized they were intruding. But her neighbor seemed oblivious, his hand still in the air, waiting for Alan to take it.

She could have sworn Alan said "stupid redneck" beneath his breath before he released her shoulder and reached around her to shake the other man's hand.

As soon as Chris's much larger hand closed around Alan's, he gave a mighty, sideways yank, ripping Alan away from Julie. Alan roared with rage and slashed at Chris with the knife. Chris twisted sideways, the blade narrowly missing his stomach. He grabbed Alan's left wrist, both men twisting and grunting with their hands joined crosswise in front of them.

"Get back," Chris yelled at Julie, twisting sideways again.

She jumped out of the way, pressing her hand against her throat. The two men grappled like a couple of grizzly bears. Alan was shorter, but both men rippled with muscles, their biceps bulging as they strained against each other. Chris's extra height seemed to be a handicap, though. He was bent over at an impossible angle. And his hold on Alan's knife hand appeared to be slipping.

"Julie, run!"

Chris yanked Alan again. Alan countered by ducking down, trying to pull Chris off balance.

Julie couldn't seem to make her feet move. She was frozen, her throat so tight no sound would come out.

"I'm a cop," Chris bit out as he and Alan jerked and shoved at each other. "Drop the knife and we can work this out. No one needs to get hurt."

"Work it out?" Alan spit between clenched teeth. "You're the intruder. I can kill you and no one will even question me."

Chris risked a quick glance at Julie. "*Go.* Get out of here!"

She stepped back, ready to do what he'd said. But then she stopped. The room seemed to shimmer in front of her, and she was back in her bedroom five months ago. All she could see was blood, its coppery scent filling the air. It was everywhere. The floors were slippery with it. Her hands, sticky.

No. Don't think about the past. Stay in the present.

She blinked and brought the room back into focus.

"Please." She stepped forward. "Please." Another step. She stared at Alan, willing him to look at her. "Don't do this."

Something in her voice must have captured Alan's attention. His head swiveled toward her. Bloodlust shone in his eyes. Julie knew the exact moment when he took the bait.

He gave Chris a mighty shove backward, catching him off guard. Chris stumbled, his hold on Alan broken. Julie tried to scramble back, but Alan was already lunging at her with the knife. She brought her arms up and turned her head, bracing herself.

Boom! Boom! Boom!

Alan dropped to the floor, inches away from her, unmoving. She stared at him in shock, not quite sure what had happened. Then blood began running in rivulets across the worn, uneven floor, reaching out from beneath his body like accusing fingers, pointing at her. She stumbled backward, a sob catching in her throat.

A piercing scream echoed through the room. And suddenly she was clasped tightly against Chris's chest, his arms wrapped protectively around her. He turned, blocking her view of the body lying on the floor. The screaming stopped, and she was mortified to realize that she was the one who'd been screaming.

"It's okay." One of his hands gently rubbed her back as the other cradled her against him. "He can't hurt you now."

He can't hurt me now. He can't hurt me now. She drew in a shaky breath.

Sirens wailed in the distance. How could there be sirens? She hadn't called anyone, never had a chance to call when Alan had burst into the house. But her neighbor had come inside. Chris? And he'd…shot… Alan? Yes. Those had been gunshots she'd heard. She shivered again.

"The police are on their way," he continued, speaking in a low, soothing tone. "I called them when I saw him through the window holding the knife."

The police. He'd seen Alan threatening her. Wait, wasn't *he* the police?

"I don't… I don't understand," she whispered. "What happened? Who are you?"

He gently pushed her back, his hands holding her upper arms. "I'm Christopher Downing, a detective and SWAT officer from the Destiny Police Department. I called for backup before I came in here." He scanned her from head to toe, as if searching for injuries. "Are you okay? Did he cut you?"

She blinked, her jumbled thoughts starting to come together again. "N-no. I mean, yes, he did. My back. But it's not—"

He carefully turned her around.

His fingers touched her cuts through her shirt, making them sting. She sucked in a breath.

"Sorry." He turned her to face him again. "There isn't much blood. You probably won't need stitches. Did he hurt you, in any other way?"

She frowned, trying to understand what he meant. Then she got it. He was asking whether she'd been sexually assaulted. Heat crept up her neck.

"No, he didn't…ah…do…anything else." She pulled away, rubbing her hands up and down her arms.

The sirens had stopped. Red-and-blue lights flashed through the front windows. She was vaguely aware of a door opening, footsteps echoing on the hardwood. Chris guided her to the couch and she sat down, her gaze automatically going to the body on the floor. Deep voices spoke in quiet tones. Another voice, a woman's, said something in reply.

Blood. There was so much blood. How could one person bleed that much?

She wrapped her arms around her middle.

The couch dipped beside her. A policewoman. She was dressed in black body armor. Bright white letters across the front of her vest read SWAT.

"Hello, Ms. Webb." The woman's voice was kind, gentle. "I'm Officer Donna Waters." She waved her hands at her uniform, the gun strapped at her waist. "Don't let this gear bother you. We came prepared for a possible hostage situation." She patted Julie's hand. "An ambulance is on the way to take you to the hospital to get checked out. But you're safe now. You're going to be okay."

The woman's words seeped slowly into her brain as if through a thick fog. "Hospital? No. No, no, no. I'm not hurt. I don't want to go to a hospital."

"Ms. Webb?"

The now-familiar masculine voice had her turning her head. Chris Downing, the man who'd risked his own life for her, knelt on the floor, his expression full of compassion and concern.

"We'll take your statement after you've seen a doctor. Is there anyone I can call—"

"Is he dead?"

Her question seemed to startle him, but he quickly smoothed out his expression. "I'm afraid so, yes. Do you want me to—"

She grabbed his hands in hers and stared into his eyes. Could she trust him? Would he tell her the truth?

He frowned. "Ms. Webb—"

"Are you sure? Are you absolutely positive that he's dead?"

He had to think she was crazy. But she'd been here before. She'd been the woman sitting on the couch while the policeman told her that he was dead. And then he… wasn't. And then…and then. She shuddered.

"Is he dead?" She held her breath, waiting for his reply.

He exchanged a look with the female officer before answering. "Yes. I'm sorry. Yes, he's dead."

She covered her mouth with her hands, desperately trying to keep from falling apart.

He's dead. Oh, my God. He's dead.

"Someone will take your official statement after you've been checked out at the hospital. But can you tell us anything right now about the man who attacked you? Did you know him?"

"Know him?" A bubble of hysterical laughter burst between her lips. "I married him."

Chapter 5

Chris exchanged a startled look with Donna as he knelt in front of the couch. His neighbor, Julie Webb, had just announced that the intruder Chris had killed was her husband. And, instead of being angry or crying or... something that made sense, she was rocking back and forth with her arms around her middle, eyes squeezed tightly shut. The rocking wasn't the part that was odd. What had the hairs standing up on his neck were the words that she kept whispering over and over in response to him telling her that her husband was dead.

"Thank you, Lord. Thank you, thank you, thank you."

Her callous words didn't seem to match the fragile, lost look in her deep blue eyes, as if she were caught in a nightmare and couldn't find her way out. He instinctively wanted to reach for her, pull her into his arms, tell her that everything would be okay. But the words she kept chanting sent a chill up his spine and started alarm bells going off in his suspicious detective's brain.

If she'd been abused by her husband, which seemed likely given that he'd held a knife on her, Chris could understand her relief that her husband couldn't hurt her anymore. And he'd seen the fear in her eyes earlier today, which lent more evidence to the abuse theory. But he'd also seen many domestic violence cases, and almost without fail, the abused party would defend her abuser. If a cop tried to arrest the husband, or hurt him while trying to protect the wife, nine times out of ten that wife would immediately leap to the husband's defense. Julie's actions were nothing like what he was used to seeing in those cases. The whole situation just seemed...off.

"The chief's motioning for you." Donna kept her voice low. "Go on. I'll sit with her until the ambulance arrives."

He hesitated, feeling guilty for wanting to jump at her offer. He'd created this mess. He should have to stay and deal with the fallout, including whatever was going on with Julie Webb.

"It's okay. I've got this," she reassured him. "Go." She put her hand on Julie's back, lightly patting it like she would a child. Julie didn't even seem to notice. She just kept rocking and repeating her obscene prayer.

As if drawn by some invisible force, Chris's gaze slid to the body of the man who was dead because of him. This wasn't the first time he'd killed someone in the line of duty. Being on the only SWAT team within a hundred miles of Destiny meant he was often called out to help other small towns or unincorporated areas when violence landed on their doorstep. But every time he'd had to use lethal force, the what-ifs and second-guessing haunted him for a long time afterward. He didn't expect this one would be any different.

He wished he could put a sheet over the man, afford him some kind of dignity in death. But the uniformed officer standing near the body was his reminder that the scene had to be preserved until the Blount County coroner arrived. And since Destiny shared their coroner with a handful of other rural counties, that could be a while from now. Two more uniformed officers stood near a stack of boxes on the left side of the room, probably to keep Julie and others from contaminating the scene.

"Downing."

Chief Thornton's gruff voice had Chris finally standing and turning around. His boss stood just inside the front door, still wearing the khaki shorts and polo shirt that he'd worn to the cookout a few hours earlier.

"Powwow, front lawn. Now." The chief headed outside.

Chris followed the chief down the porch steps to where three members of the SWAT team who'd also been at the cookout stood waiting. Max, Randy and Colby were dressed in full body armor just like Donna, back inside the house. It occurred to him that they must have raced like a mama sow protecting her piglets to have gotten here so fast. None of them lived close by, except for Dillon, and he was noticeably absent.

"Is Ashley okay?" he asked no one in particular, assuming the worst. He couldn't imagine his best friend not responding to a call for aid from Chris or any of their fellow officers unless something had happened to Ashley.

"She's at Blount Memorial in Maryville." Max held up his hands to stop the anticipated flood of questions. "When your 911 call came in, Dillon and Ashley were halfway to the hospital because she'd started having contractions. I assured him we could handle—"

"It's too soon," Chris interrupted, worry making his voice thick. "She's only seven months along."

"I know that," Max said. "Like I was saying, I told Dillon not to worry about you, that we had your back. And, before you ask, I spoke to him a few minutes ago. They were able to stop her labor, but they'll keep her there for observation overnight, maybe even a few days. But she and the baby are both fine."

Chris nodded, blowing out a relieved breath.

"You okay?" Max put his hand on Chris's shoulder. "You look greener than Dillon did when you mentioned fried gizzards."

"I killed a man. No. I'm not okay."

Max winced and dropped his hand, immediately making Chris regret his curt reply.

"Tell us what happened," the chief said, impatience etched on his features. "Take it from the top and don't leave anything out."

Chris began reciting the events that had led to the shooting, being as detailed as he could. Since everyone on the SWAT team performed dual roles as detectives in the fifteen-officer police force, they all listened intently, taking notes on their phones or the little pads of paper most of them kept handy.

Dillon was normally lead detective, with Chris as backup. But obviously Chris couldn't investigate a case where he was a primary participant. He wasn't sure who would run with this one.

After Chris finished his statement, the chief motioned to Max.

Max pulled a brown paper evidence bag from his rear pocket and awkwardly cleared his throat as he held it open. "Sorry, man. Standard operating procedure. Gotta take your sidearm as evidence."

Chris knew the drill and had been vaguely surprised that no one had taken his gun the moment they'd arrived. But even after putting his pistol in the bag, the weight of his now-empty holster seemed heavier than before, a reminder of what he'd done, the life he'd taken.

Max closed the bag and stepped back beside Randy. Since Max looked miserable about taking the gun, Chris gave him a reassuring nod to let him know that he understood.

"You said they were arguing when you approached the house," the chief said. "Did you hear what they were arguing about?"

He replayed the moment when he was crouching by the window, trying to remember what he'd heard.

"Seems like they both said something about 'keys,' or maybe it was 'please.' I definitely heard the man mention a gun. But he was holding a knife, so that doesn't seem right." He shrugged. "I was too far away to hear them clearly. I was more focused on what he was doing with the butcher knife and how to get it away from him."

The low wail of a siren filled the air as an ambulance turned down the road and headed toward them.

"About time," the chief said. "I was thinking we'd have to wake up Doc Brookes if it took any longer."

Chris couldn't help smiling. Even though it was only a few hours past sundown, it was probably Doc

Brookes's bedtime. The town's only doctor was getting up there in years. And he made sure everyone knew not to bother him after hours unless there was arterial bleeding involved or a bone sticking out. Unfortunately, with the only hospital nearly forty-five minutes from Destiny, ornery Brookes was who they were stuck with most of the time.

"I'd better move my truck," Max said.

"Ah, shoot," Colby said. His truck's front bumper was partly blocking the end of the driveway. "Me, too."

They hurried to their vehicles to make room before the ambulance reached the house.

"Chief, got a second?" Chris asked.

Thornton looked pointedly at Randy, who took the unsubtle hint and awkwardly pounded Chris on the back before heading toward the house.

As soon as Randy was out of earshot, the chief held up his hand to stop Chris from saying anything.

"I know we still have to process the scene, and get the coroner out here, perform due diligence and all that. But honestly, son, it looks like a clean shoot to me. I can tell it's eating you up inside, but you need to let that go. You saved a life tonight. That's what you should focus on."

They moved farther into the grass while the ambulance pulled into the driveway. The EMTs hopped out of the vehicle and grabbed their gear.

"I appreciate that, Chief," Chris said. "I feel like hell for taking a life. But I know I did what I had to do. That's not what I wanted to talk to you about."

Colby and Max jogged up the driveway, having parked their trucks farther down the road. They started toward Chris and the chief, but a stern look from Thornton had them heading toward the house, instead, and following the EMTs inside.

Still, Chris hesitated. Putting his concerns into words was proving harder than he'd expected.

"Well, go on, son. Spit out whatever's bothering you. The skeeters are eatin' me alive out here."

As if to demonstrate what he'd said, the chief smacked his arm, leaving a red smear where a mosquito had been making a buffet out of him. He wiped his arm on his shorts, grimacing at the stain he'd left behind, before giving Chris an impatient look. "Well?"

"It's Mrs. Webb," Chris said. "The thing is, after the shooting, she asked me whether the guy I'd shot was dead. No, what she asked was whether I was *sure*, as if she thought I was playing a cruel joke on her, as if she *wanted* him to be dead. The guy is, *was*, her husband. And it seemed like she was…relieved…that I'd killed him."

"Well, he did hold a knife on her. Makes sense she'd be happy to be alive and that she didn't have to worry about him attacking her again."

Chris scrubbed his face and then looked down the dark road, lit only by the occasional firefly. Crickets and bullfrogs competed with one another in their nightly symphony. All in all, everything seemed so normal. And, yet, nothing was the same.

"You think there's more to it than that, don't you?" The chief was studying him intently. "Why?"

"Because she didn't ask me just once whether he was dead. She asked several times. And it was more the way she asked it that spooked me. You know how it is. If there's a domestic dispute, a husband beating his wife or trying to kill her, we cops intervene and suddenly we're the bad guys. Happens almost every time. But I shoot Mrs. Webb's husband and she starts praying out loud, thanking God. I don't know about you, but that's a first for me."

Thornton was quiet for a long moment, leaving Chris to wallow in his own thoughts, to wonder if saying anything was the right thing to do. He hated the unflattering picture that he'd just painted of Julie Webb. It didn't seem right, as if he was spreading rumors, gossiping—something his father would have rewarded with an extra long switch applied liberally to his hide. But this wasn't high school. This was the real world, a death investigation, where actions and words had consequences. They mattered. And he couldn't ignore something just because it was uncomfortable.

"How did she seem before all of this?" Thornton finally asked. "If her husband had a history of violence against her, she might have joined a support group and got the help she needed to cut all ties. Maybe she moved here to escape him, thought she was safe. But he figured out where she was, came after her. Seems to me that'd make her mighty grateful that he's never going to hurt her again."

"Maybe." He wanted to believe that was it. But even he could hear the doubt in his voice. He shrugged. "Hard to say what her state of mind was prior to this incident. She kept to herself, didn't even wave. I did get the feeling earlier today, when I saw her on her porch, that she was afraid of…something. And that was before her husband showed up."

"There, see? It's like I said. Her behavior could very well make sense, given those circumstances. And she's lucky you were close by to save her."

"Yeah," he mumbled. "Lucky for both of us."

The chief gave him a knowing look. And it dawned on Chris that Thornton might know firsthand how he felt. Chris had joined the force right out of college, thirteen years ago. But Thornton was already chief by then. There was no telling what horrors he might have faced as a young beat cop, or even in his detective days, what burdens he might have accumulated like an invisible weight that no one else could see. All Chris knew for sure was what *he* felt, which was all kinds of uneasy about this whole thing.

It was bad enough that he'd taken a life. Even worse if there was something else going on here. The "something else" that kept running through his mind was so prejudicial against Julie Webb that he couldn't voice it to the chief, not without proof, something concrete. All he had was a disturbing series of impressions that had begun to take root in his mind from the moment he'd seen her reaction to the shooting.

Suspicions that maybe this wasn't "just" a case of a domestic dispute with tragic consequences.

That maybe Julie Webb knew she was moving in next door to a cop all along.

That she had planned this whole thing from beginning to end.

That she'd just used Chris as a weapon to commit murder.

Chapter 6

Standing in the Destiny Police Department at midnight on a Saturday wasn't exactly where Chris imagined his fellow SWAT team members wanted to be. But not one of them had even considered going home. Max, Colby, Donna and Randy stood shoulder to shoulder with him in a show of solidarity while they watched their boss interview Julie Webb through the large two-way glass window.

Behind Chris and his SWAT team, two more officers sat at desks on the other side of the large open room that was essentially the entire police station. One of them, Blake Sullivan, was a recent transfer and would eventually be a detective and member of their SWAT team. But not yet. For now, he was learning the ropes of Destiny PD as a nightshift cop, which included filling out a lot of mundane reports.

There were fifteen desks in all, three rows of five. And other than a couple of holding cells off the back wall and a bathroom, there was just the chief's office, his executive washroom that the team loved to tease him about and the interview room.

The entire night shift consisted of the two officers currently writing reports and two more out on patrol. Destiny wasn't exactly a mecca for crime. The town didn't boast a strip of bars or clubs to spill their drugs or drunks into the streets. A typical night might mean lecturing some teenagers caught drag racing, or rescuing a rival football team's stolen mascot from a hayloft.

Tonight was anything but typical.

Tonight a man had died.

And Chris wanted, *needed*, to find out what had precipitated the violence by Alan Webb, leaving Chris no choice but to use lethal force. The chief had officially placed him on administrative leave, pending the results of the investigation. He'd expressly forbidden Chris from going into the interview room. But since the chief would've had to fight his own SWAT team to force Chris to leave the station, he'd wisely pretended not to notice him in the squad room, watching the chief interview the witness.

Along with her counsel, assistant district attorney Kathy Nelson.

Plus two administrative lackeys—Brian Henson and Jonathan Bolton—that Nelson had brought with her from Nashville. She'd left the two men sitting at one of the desks on the opposite side of the squad room like eager lapdogs waiting for their master to give them an order.

Chris studied Henson and Bolton for a long moment

before looking back at the interview window. "If she felt she needed a lawyer, why call an ADA? And since when does an assistant district attorney have an entourage? Or drive with that entourage for three hours in the middle of the night for a witness interview, let alone one that's way outside her jurisdiction?"

"Right? Doesn't make a lick of sense," Donna said beside him.

After dodging another barrage of questions like the polished politician that she was, Nelson shoved back her chair and stood.

"Wait, what's she doing?" Max asked.

Nelson motioned to Mrs. Webb. She picked up her purse from the table and stood.

Chris stiffened. "They're leaving."

Donna was clearly bemused. "But they didn't answer hardly any of the chief's questions."

"Screw this." Chris stepped toward the interview room door.

Max grabbed his shoulder. "Don't do it, man. The chief will—"

Chris shoved Max's hand away and yanked open the door.

Julie hurriedly stepped back to put more distance between her and the imposing man suddenly filling the open doorway of the interview room—her neighbor, Detective Chris Downing. With his clenched jaw and hands fisted at his sides, he seemed like a tautly drawn bow, ready to spring.

Before Kathy could say anything, Thornton held his hand out to stop her and confronted his officer.

"I warned you, Chris. You can't be in here." His

gravelly voice whipped through the room. "What do I have to do, arrest you? Lock you in a cell?"

Twin spots of color darkened Chris's cheekbones. His heated gaze flashed to Julie, then back to Thornton. "I need answers. And, so far, you're not getting any. Let me interview her. I'll make her talk."

Julie flinched at his harsh tone. She'd retreated to her chair, but even with a table between them, his anger seemed to fill the room, crowding in on her. Where was the gentle, concerned man who'd knelt in front of the couch earlier this evening, reassuring her that everything was going to be okay?

Kathy didn't move. Her only concession to Chris standing so close was to tilt her head back to meet his gaze. "Are you threatening Mrs. Webb, Officer Downing?"

Thornton aimed an aggravated look at Kathy. "It's *Detective*, not *Officer*. And he's not threatening anyone. Stay out of this."

The shocked look on Kathy's face was almost comical. Julie doubted that anyone, except maybe Kathy's husband, had ever dared to speak to her that way before. She seemed to be at a loss as to how to respond.

"Don't you be questioning my methods, son." Thornton jabbed his finger at Chris's chest. "I was interviewing witnesses when you were knee-high to a mule. Since you're the one who fired the gun, you can't be involved in the investigation. Until this is over, you're a civilian. And civilians have no business questioning witnesses. Now, turn around and—"

"No." Julie jumped up from her seat.

Everyone stared at her in surprise.

She cleared her throat, just as surprised as they were

at her outburst, but she now acknowledged what her subconscious had already known—that this was the right thing to do.

"I want him to stay," she said.

The expression on Chris's face turned suspicious.

"What did you say?" Thornton's question sounded more like he was daring her to repeat her request, a request he had no intention of fulfilling.

"Julie—" Kathy began.

She waved her hand. "Taking a life is a heavy burden that no one should have to bear, even if taking that life was necessary. Letting Detective Downing ask questions about why he was put in that situation is the least that I can do to show my gratitude for his saving my life. So, Chief Thornton, either you allow him to stay, or the interview is over."

While Thornton stood in indecision, Chris firmly closed the door and then straddled the chair directly across from her. He gave her a crisp nod, as if to grudgingly thank her. She nodded in return, just as stiffly—two adversaries facing off before a fight.

The other two gave up their vigil. Kathy sat down while Thornton stared pointedly at his chair, the one Chris was currently occupying. Chris ignored him. After grumbling something beneath his breath about "seat stealers," the chief finally sat down. But the table's small size and Chris's broad shoulders had forced the chief to the end of the table, which had him grumbling again.

Julie waited expectantly. Rather than attack her with a volley of questions, Chris simply stared at her, as if sizing her up. If he was trying to figure out how to intimidate her, the effort was unnecessary. She'd been intimidated since the moment he'd stood in the open doorway like a fierce warrior looking for a dragon to slay.

And she was the dragon.

She clasped her hands beneath the table so he couldn't see that they were shaking. It wasn't just Chris that had her so nervous. Being in an interrogation room again, after all these months, stirred up a host of horrific memories. The past few months had been rough, brutal. But at least she'd survived. Her husband hadn't. And even though she was relieved she no longer had to fear him, she still grieved that it had come to this. There'd been a time once, long ago, when she'd loved him.

He'd been a good man back then—handsome, kind, sweet, helping her move forward after the tragic loss of her family just a few months before she'd met him. She grieved for *that* Alan, the one she'd pledged to honor and love until death do they part. The man who had, or so she liked to believe, loved her, too, once upon a time, until the fairy tale had twisted into a tragedy.

"Mrs. Webb?" Chris's deep voice intruded into her thoughts. "Please answer the question."

She blinked. "I'm sorry. What did you ask me?"

"I'll answer your question," Kathy interrupted. "Mrs. Webb came to Destiny to hide from her abusive husband."

Julie shot the other woman an irritated look. She made it sound like Julie had stayed with Alan through a long, abusive relationship. In truth, before today, Alan had been abusive only once, five months ago. After that one horrific night, she'd filed for divorce and ended her three-year marriage. She supposed she was lucky. Some women ended up caught in cycles of violence from which they could never escape. But Julie wasn't feeling particularly fortunate at the moment. Everything was in turmoil. And Alan had lost his life. There was no way to feel good about what had happened.

"Her husband somehow found out that she was here, in Destiny," Kathy continued. "And he broke into her home and assaulted her. The rest you know. Detective Downing had to use deadly force to protect her."

"How about we let the witness give her own statement," Chris said, closely watching Julie. "Mrs. Webb—"

"Julie, please," she corrected, so tired of the awkwardness and formalities of this never-ending interview. At this point she just wanted it over.

"Julie," he corrected. "Do you agree with the assistant district attorney's version of this evening's events?"

She hesitated, then nodded.

Kathy let out a breath, as if relieved.

"Except for the part where she made it sound like my husband had a history of violence," she said. "Alan and I never had a perfect marriage. But until…recently… he never lifted a hand against me. Something…happened to make him snap." She finished in a near whisper, her defense of Alan sounding weak when she said it out loud. Still, she hated to paint him as a bad person when, for most of the time that she'd known him, he was kind and good to her.

Kathy put a hand on top of Julie's and gave her a sympathetic look. "You're being far too kind to a man who tried to kill you."

Julie swallowed and looked away.

Kathy sighed and turned in her seat to face Julie.

"For the record, are you stating that your husband wasn't dangerous? That you weren't afraid of him?"

"No, of course not. He was definitely dangerous. You know what he did in Nashville."

Kathy groaned and closed her eyes.

"I was wondering why you hadn't brought that up yet." Thornton jumped on her statement. "I ran your husband's name through the computer before the interview. Why don't you tell us your version of the first attack?"

Chris shot a surprised look at his boss. Julie figured he must not have been told what Thornton had found.

Kathy checked her watch, probably calculating how late—or early in the morning now—it would be by the time this was over and she could start the long drive back.

"You might as well tell them," she said. "Now that you've brought it up. Then I'll take you back to Nashville and—"

"I'm not going back."

Kathy frowned. "Why not?"

"I just got here. I don't want to move again. Not this soon."

"You were here to hide out from Alan. Obviously, that's not necessary anymore."

"We don't know if he was the one flattening my tires, salting my yard, and everything else. What if it was his family? I wouldn't put it past them."

"I don't think they're dangerous," Kathy said.

"We both know what they can be like," she said. "I'd much rather stay here until everything is settled. Then maybe they'll finally leave me alone and I can return home and live in peace."

Kathy shrugged. "Maybe it does make sense to stay here, at least until the civil case is over."

"Civil case?" Thornton's voice had risen again and he looked like he was ready to explode with frustration. "This is supposed to be an interview, a police interview. You two need to start talking to *us*, instead of to each other. You need to answer our questions."

"Chief—" Kathy began.

"What did he do to you?" Chris's deep voice cut through the conversation, silencing everyone in the room. His brow was furrowed with concern, his tone gentle, almost a whisper, just like back at the house. "How did he hurt you?"

Her stomach did a little flip. Part of her was tempted to throw herself in his arms and beg him to take her away from the nightmare that her life had become. She must be more exhausted than she thought. Chris had shown his true colors when he'd barged into the room, looking like a bull ready to charge after a red flag. He wasn't really interested in helping her. She'd do well to remember that, and not let her exhaustion and longing for someone to lean on after all these months of being alone influence her decisions.

She straightened her spine and focused on Thornton as she answered. If she looked at the supposed concern on Chris's face one more time she just might shatter.

"The reason I moved to Destiny was to hide from my husband, as Kathy said. He disappeared after posting bail. And there have been some…incidents, annoyances really, that made me wonder if he was stalking me. While it's true that he doesn't have a…*long* history of being abusive, he did attack me about five months ago, which you obviously already know. We were separated. He'd moved out and left the house to me. And then he broke into our home in the middle of the night. He was dressed all in black and wore a mask. And that night, like earlier today, he had a knife. Today, Detective Downing saved my life when he shot Alan. And I deeply appreciate his sacrifice. But there wasn't anyone else around months ago to protect me. So I saved myself. I grabbed my husband's gun, the one he'd left in the nightstand before moving out, and I shot him."

Chris blinked in surprise. "You shot your husband?"

"I did."

Thornton and Chris exchanged a glance. But Julie had no clue what they were silently communicating to each other.

Kathy said, "Mr. Webb was charged with breaking and entering and attempted murder. He had duct tape, a knife and gloves. He attacked Mrs. Webb, pulled her out of the bed and onto the floor. She was able to get away and grab the gun or she wouldn't be sitting here today. She'd be buried six feet under. However, in spite of the overwhelming evidence in the case, the judge went against our recommendations and set bail at one million dollars, which Mr. Webb immediately paid. Then he—"

"He paid a million-dollar bail?" Thornton asked. He and Chris both looked at Julie with renewed interest. "Just how much money did he have? And who's the beneficiary?"

She closed her eyes and squeezed her hands together in her lap. This was what she'd wanted to avoid. Now they would look at her the way Alan's family did.

They'd never believed her side of what had happened and had accused her of trying to kill him for his money.

Kathy said something to Thornton but Julie tuned it out. She just wanted the interview to be over. How had it come to this? As she often did when thinking about the past year of her life, when her marriage had started to fail, she tried to pinpoint that one decision, that one pivotal event that had led to her entire life being turned upside down. But she still didn't know what had happened. One day she was happy, *they* were happy, her and Alan. The next, everything had changed. Alan had become moody, angry, and it continued to go downhill from there. A tear ran down her cheek. Then another. She drew a shaky breath and wiped them away.

"Here." Chris was crouching beside her chair, holding a box of tissues. And in his other hand was a bottle of water, which he held out to her. "They're so busy arguing with each other over there that they didn't even notice I'd left the room to get you the water and tissues."

He jerked his head toward the corner by the window where Thornton and Kathy were standing, having a heated argument. Apparently, Julie had been so lost in her own thoughts, she hadn't noticed anything that had happened over the past few minutes, either.

She wiped her cheeks with a tissue, then took the bottle. He'd already opened it and had set the cap on the table.

"Thank you," she said.

"You're welcome." He gestured toward the corner again. "I think they're going to be at this for a while. Want to get out of here?"

She blinked. "I thought you wanted to interview me?

Or is that your plan, to take me somewhere else and ask me questions without Kathy present?"

He cocked his head, looking every bit the handsome, sexy neighbor again instead of the angry, hardened cop. "Do you trust me?"

"No."

He laughed. "Score one for honesty."

"Sorry."

"Don't be. Never apologize for telling the truth." He glanced at the chief and Kathy, completely consumed in their argument, before looking at Julie again. "I'd like to remind you that I'm a police officer, sworn to protect and serve. And if that doesn't make you trust me, I'll resort to blackmail."

"Blackmail?"

His grin faded, and he was once again staring at her with an intensity that was unnerving. "Like you said before, I deserve answers. So how about we ditch this place and I take you somewhere safe, where no one will bother you? We'll both get a good night's sleep. No questions. No talking unless you want to. Then tomorrow, we take a fresh look at the situation and figure out where to go from there. Sound good?"

"Sounds too good, actually. Why are you offering?"

"Because somewhere along the way this interview turned into an inquisition. The chief and I both want answers, so I don't want Nelson convincing you to leave and never come back. But it's late, we're all tired and you aren't a criminal being interrogated. You're a witness, a victim. You deserve to be treated better than you have been. I'm offering a truce. What do you say?

Will you let me get you out of here?" He stood and held out his hand.

This time it was her turn to glance at Thornton and Kathy. Both their faces were red. Whatever they were arguing about, it didn't look like they'd stop anytime soon.

She put her hand in Chris's. "Let's go."

Chapter 7

Chris glanced at his passenger as he turned his pickup off the highway onto a gravel road. Thanks to his SWAT team, he'd managed to get the witness out of the station without Henson or Bolton being able to give chase. It was hard to follow someone when the only exit door was blocked by three cops with guns. But he was already having buyer's remorse.

The chief was going to kill him for this.

Julie sat stiffly, clutching the armrest as if it were a lifeline, staring through the windshield. Was she also regretting the decision to flee? Wondering if she'd gotten herself into worse trouble than she was already in?

"This isn't the way I go to my house." She leaned forward to peer at the narrow gravel road and trees crowding in that were revealed in the headlights. "I assumed you were taking me home. Is this a back way?"

"Your home is still taped off as a crime scene. You can't go there until it's released."

Her shoulders slumped, but she nodded. "This seems awfully far from town to be leading to a hotel."

"It's called Harmony Haven. You'll see the place over that next rise. See how the sky is lighter up ahead? That's from the security and landscape lights."

"A bed-and-breakfast then?"

He steered around a pothole, surprised the road was in such poor condition. Then again, there'd been a lot of rain this past month, and he hadn't been down this way in quite a while.

"Chris?"

He shook his head. "It's not a B and B. It's a private home on a horse-rescue farm. It belongs to my friends Dillon and Ashley. They're not here right now and I figured they wouldn't mind us crashing for the night."

Any argument she might have been about to give was forgotten as they topped the rise and Dillon's property came into view. Julie stared in wonder at the beautiful vista laid out before them. It pleased him that she seemed so awestruck. He felt that way every time he came here, especially at night because of the way the lights cast an ethereal glow on the place.

With the sweat equity he'd invested to help Dillon get this place up and running over the years, he couldn't help feeling proprietary about it. But with Dillon married now, Chris's visits had become less frequent. Newlyweds needed their privacy, even more so now with a baby on the way. His jaw tightened. If it weren't so late, he'd call the hospital for an update on Ashley. He'd have to remember to call first thing in the morning and check on her.

He pulled the truck to a stop beside the two-story white farmhouse and took a moment to enjoy the view himself. Soft floodlights that Ashley had insisted upon, which were more for ambience than security, dotted a long, pristine, white three-rail fence and acres and acres of lush green pastures that went on forever.

The enormous stable was partially visible behind the house. He parked at the end of the home's enormous wraparound front porch that boasted white rockers and an old-fashioned swing hanging from chains.

"It's beautiful," Julie whispered, seemingly mesmerized as the light breeze teased the swing back and forth, the chains creaking in rhythm with the sound of cicadas.

"I reckon it is." He cut the engine, admiring her profile. The lights from the yard sparkled on the honey-blond highlights in her brown hair. She had a small, pert nose and pale skin with a smattering of freckles across both cheeks. A lock of her hair hung forward and he barely resisted the urge to brush it back.

"Harmony Haven," she whispered, as if testing the name on her tongue. "You said it's a horse rescue?"

He waved toward the stable, the main doors sealed up for the night. "There are a couple dozen horses in there, another dozen or so out in the pasture. Ashley and Dillon run horse camps every summer and adopt out most of the herd. Then rescues trickle in throughout the year and they work on rehabilitating them, regaining their trust. A couple months from now this year's first campers will arrive. There's a bunkhouse farther out for the farmhands and a second bunkhouse for the campers."

"Ashley and Dillon are married?"

He nodded. "Almost a year now."

"Then who's Harmony?"

Chris's smiled faded. "Dillon's baby sister. She loved horses even more than he does, which seems impossible."

"Loved? Past tense?"

"She died a long time ago. Hang tight. I'll help you down."

Before she could ask him any more questions or dredge up memories of the past, he hopped down from the truck and hurried to the passenger side. Although his black four-by-four was suspended a lot higher than the average pickup, it wasn't quite a monster truck. It was just high enough for his six-foot-two frame to be comfortable climbing in and out. But Julie was almost a foot shorter than him, which meant he'd had to lift her up into the truck back at the station. Something he'd realized he didn't mind one bit. She sure was a pretty thing.

She'd just opened her door when he reached her. With a mumbled apology, he put his hands at her waist and lifted her down. As soon as her shoes touched the ground, she stepped back, forcing him to drop his hands. She seemed awkward, uncomfortable as she smoothed her blouse over her khaki pants.

"Why didn't we go to a hotel?" She followed him as he led the way toward the front porch. "Why drive so far from town?"

He stopped with his boot on the bottom step. "There's only one hotel in Destiny. Nelson would have looked for you there."

Her brows shot up. "I didn't know we were hiding from her."

He smiled. "We're hiding more from my boss than

from your ADA. I'm on administrative leave, which means I'm not even supposed to talk to you."

"But you want answers, like you said at the station."

He nodded.

"You aren't too good at following orders, are you?"

"Not when I'm shut out of a case where I had to kill a man."

She swallowed and looked away.

"Look," he said. "I'm not going to force you to do anything you don't want to do. For now, we're just escaping the inquisition back there and getting a good night's sleep. As a bonus, I ensure that Nelson doesn't whisk you off to Nashville overnight."

She stood on the first step, then moved up one more, making her almost eye level with him.

"You seem to think that if Kathy tells me to do something, I jump to do it. What gave you that impression?"

He shrugged. "I think it's more that she drove three hours to come to your rescue. Allowing you to talk anymore to us would have pretty much defeated the purpose in her driving down here. Lawyers don't want their clients to talk. Ever."

He took the stairs two at a time and paused at the door.

When she joined him there, he added, "This place has the best security around. No one is going to sneak up on you while you're here. You're safe."

Her lips parted in surprise.

He shook his head, exasperated. "Did you really think I was buying the picture that Nelson was painting? It's as obvious as the day is long that you're both hiding something, holding something back. And if you moved to Destiny just to hide from your husband, or little high school-type pranks, you wouldn't still be scared."

She stiffened. "What makes you think I'm scared?"

He glanced at her hands, which she was twisting together.

She jerked them apart, her face flushing again.

"I guess the real question is whether Nelson knows whatever secrets you're hiding."

Her expression went blank, as if she'd thrown up a wall. He'd been fishing, but now he knew for sure that she really was hiding something. What could she be hiding that even her ADA friend didn't know about? And why?

She looked at the truck as if debating whether to demand that he take her back to town. Sensing that if he pushed her on it, if he argued to get her to stay, that she'd push back and demand to leave, he remained silent and waited.

"Your friends Dillon and Ashley—they know we're here? You have keys to the house?"

In answer, he separated the keys on his key ring and held up one. "If Dillon is awake, he knows. The security system texted him our picture as soon as we turned down the private road to the farm."

Her eyes widened.

"I'm sure they don't mind," he continued. "But I'll call in the morning and explain the situation."

"Okay, then. I'll stay. Just for the night."

He unlocked the door and waved her inside before she could change her mind.

Chapter 8

Of all the reckless, crazy things that Julie had ever done, sneaking off with Detective Chris Downing was probably the most outrageous and stupid. She couldn't believe that she'd had the gumption to tiptoe out of the conference room, pausing only briefly as he whispered to his SWAT team members, and then getting into his pickup truck.

When he'd handed her that tissue in the conference room to wipe her tears, it was as if they were co-conspirators, the two of them against the world. And she'd been just desperate enough to take the lifeline that he'd offered, tricking herself into believing that he was someone she could trust. He'd been what she'd needed most at that very moment—someone to lean on, someone who would keep her safe, be a friend, if only for one night.

She was such a fool.

They had a truce, more or less, but she knew the limits. The moment she got up tomorrow he'd probably barrage her with questions, and she wouldn't have Kathy here to deflect them. She might as well have stayed at the police station.

As she followed him inside, he paused beside a beeping security alarm keypad and keyed in the security code, disabling it. After locking the door, he set the alarm again and waved his hand to encompass the large open room.

"This is it," he said. "Dillon took down most of the walls to give it an open floor plan. As you can see, the kitchen is on the back left. Feel free to grab something if you're thirsty or hungry."

She nodded, noting the granite-topped island that separated the kitchen from the great room. A straight staircase was in front of them, with a small dark hallway opening behind it on the main floor. The room was an eclectic mix of masculine and feminine touches, with dark chunky wood furniture softened by pastel throws and pillows, and rugs scattered across the hardwood floor.

"Your room is through there." He led her through a doorway on the right, just past the front door. "This is the in-law suite, with its own private bath. Ashley's expecting her parents to stay here for a few weeks after the baby is born. So I'm sure she's already got it stocked with everything you could possibly need—shampoo, toothbrushes, stuff like that. But if there's something else you need, let me know. I can check upstairs."

"I'm sure I'll be fine." She hesitated by the four-poster bed. "I didn't even think about packing a bag when I left my house."

"We wouldn't have let you anyway."

Her gaze shot to his in question.

"Your house is a crime scene," he reminded her.

"Oh." She twisted her hands together, then remembered him noticing her doing that before when she was nervous and she forced her hands apart.

"We'll call Donna in the morning. She's one of the SWAT officers. You met her, just after…"

"I remember," she said, thinking back to the kind woman who'd sat beside her on the couch, while Alan lay on the floor not far away. She swallowed against the bile rising in her throat and rubbed her hands up and down her arms.

Looking uncomfortable, Chris shifted on his feet. "She can get you whatever you need from the house."

She nodded. "What about you? You'll need a bag, too."

He shook his head. "I stay here sometimes when Dillon and I brainstorm cases, or when we have to get an early start during hunting season. Don't stay nearly as often as I used to. But I've still got stuff in a guest room upstairs." He waved toward the doorway to the great room. "If you want, we can see if Ashley has a nightgown that will fit you. I'm sure she wouldn't mind. You two are close to the same size, although you're a bit shorter."

"I don't want to impose any more than I already have."

"You're not imposing. Trust me. Ashley and Dillon would give the shirts off their backs to someone in need."

Trust him. She wished it were that easy. But she'd given her trust before, and it had nearly killed her.

She forced a smile. "I'll be okay without borrowing any clothes. Where will you stay? The guest room you mentioned upstairs?"

His gaze dropped to her hands, and she realized she was twisting them together again. She tugged them apart and tried to keep her expression neutral. She didn't want him to know that she was already getting scared again. It was stupid, ridiculous, to be worried about anyone finding her way out here. But Alan had found her. And that meant that anyone could. So what was she going to do? Going home to Nashville didn't seem like a good option. But neither did staying here. She hadn't been thinking clearly when she'd told Kathy that she wasn't leaving. She should go somewhere else. But how could she leave without a destination in mind?

Chris was studying her. What did he see? Again, she tried to keep her expression neutral, to hide the doubts, the questions, even the fear roiling through her mind.

Finally, he said, "I like the couch down here just fine. If you need anything, just holler."

The couch. This house was huge, probably had four or five bedrooms upstairs, and he was taking the couch. Either he was an old-fashioned Southern gentleman and truly wanted to be close by if she needed him, or he suspected something and didn't want to let her out of his sight. She thought about arguing with him, to try to get him to go upstairs. But that would probably only make him suspicious, if he wasn't already.

"Thank you," she said.

He tipped his head as if he were wearing a hat, but continued to stand there.

The silence drew out between them.

She motioned toward the cell phone on his belt. "I'm surprised your boss hasn't called you by now."

"Ringer's off. What about Nelson?" He waved at her purse. "I assume you've got a cell phone in there. But she hasn't called you."

"Ringer's off."

They both smiled.

He motioned toward the clock on the bedside table. "The sun will be coming up sooner than you think. I reckon we'd better get some sleep while we can." He tipped his head again. "Good night, Julie."

"Good night…Chris."

His smile broadened, and then he stepped through the doorway. He'd just grabbed the doorknob when she called out to him.

"Chris?"

He glanced back in question.

"Tomorrow, when news of my husband's death spreads, when Kathy tells his family what happened, they'll demand justice. They'll accuse me of orchestrating his death. They'll say some really awful, terrible things about me."

His brows furrowed.

She took a step toward him, then another, until the tips of her shoes pressed against the tips of his boots. "But I promise you, I didn't plan any of this. I would never have placed you in the position that you were in today if I could have prevented it. I'm so sorry that you got involved."

He slowly raised his hand toward her, giving her every chance to step away.

She didn't.

He feathered his fingers across her cheek, pushing back some of the hair that had fallen across her face. But, instead of dropping his hand, he cupped her cheek, as he stared down into her eyes. She felt the warmth of his touch all the way to her toes.

"Who else are you afraid of?" he whispered.

She wanted to trust him, to ask for his help. But this wasn't his fight. She couldn't involve him any more than she already had.

She gently pulled his hand down, squeezed it, then let it go.

"Good night, Chris."

He hesitated, then nodded. "Good night, Julie."

The door closed behind him. She sat down on the bed, listening to the sounds of the house settling around her, to the sound of him going upstairs, probably to get sheets and pillows for the couch. Water ran in the bathroom down the hall a few minutes later. And not long after that, the light under the door went dark.

She continued to sit on the bed, thinking about what had happened, about what would happen tomorrow, about what she needed to do. She twisted her hands in her lap, watching the minutes tick by on the clock. When the clock struck two, she stood and grabbed her purse.

Chapter 9

Chris used the tongs to put the last piece of bacon onto the paper-towel-lined plate with the others and turned off the stove. He shoved the hot pan of grease into the oven to be cleaned later once it cooled, then stepped back to make sure he hadn't forgotten anything.

Other than throwing the occasional steak or ribs on a grill when he had friends over and Max wasn't there as the master chef, cooking wasn't his thing. He tended to live on cereal, sandwiches and an occasional hot meal of catfish and grits at Mama Jo's Kitchen back in town. But since he'd practically kidnapped Julie last night, he figured paying her back with a stick-to-the-ribs breakfast was the least he could do.

Dillon's wife, Ashley, was one of the best cooks he'd ever met. Her kitchen was stocked with everything he could possibly need to prepare a feast—or, in this case, scrambled eggs with cheese, fried bacon and toast. He'd looked for canned biscuits to cook, but premade dough was probably an affront to someone like Ashley. She probably made them from scratch, which was beyond his capabilities. He'd had to settle for whole-wheat toast.

Now, all he had to do was go wake Julie. He checked his watch. Seven-thirty. On a normal day he'd have been at the office for a good hour by now. Maybe Julie wasn't an early riser like him. They had been up awfully late last night. And goodness knew she'd been through a terrible ordeal. He'd assumed the smell of bacon and freshly brewed coffee would bring her into the kitchen. But if she was too exhausted for those delicious smells to lure her out of bed, maybe he should give her just a little bit longer to sleep. Everything could be reheated. And he did have some calls to make.

He covered the food with paper towels to keep it from getting cold and plopped down at the table. The first call he made was to Dillon. After getting an update on Ashley and the baby, he explained to Dillon about what was going on with the case and why he'd crashed at Harmony Haven for the night. As expected, Dillon didn't mind one bit and had already seen the security camera text to let him know that Chris was there.

The second call didn't go nearly so well.

"What the hell were you thinking?" his boss yelled.

Chris winced and held the phone several inches from his ear. He waited until the yelling stopped before risking holding the phone closer. After suffering through a chastisement that had him feeling like a five-year-old, he explained his reasons to his boss and agreed that he'd go ahead and bring Julie to the police station after breakfast.

Nelson had left for Nashville late last night after the chief had essentially lied to smooth things over. He'd made it sound like it had been his idea all along for Chris to take Julie to some safe house for the night and that they'd escort her to Nashville today once she'd had a good night's rest. The chief said Nelson had seemed more than happy to believe him as she had a heavy caseload back in town.

Of course, Chris and the others had no intention of taking Julie to Nashville. Not until they'd gotten to the bottom of their investigation. But Nelson didn't need to know that.

He hung up and checked his watch again. The chief, of course, wanted them at the station ASAP. But with the ADA out of the picture, at least temporarily, there wasn't as much of a rush in Chris's opinion. He'd let Julie get a little more sleep, give her a hot breakfast, then they'd head back to town. Until he knew for sure just how "innocent" she was in what had happened at her house, he was going to try to give her the benefit of the doubt and treat her as a victim and a witness rather than like someone with more skin in the game. But he wasn't going to let those soft, doe eyes of hers make him let down his guard, either. Maybe he could ask her the questions he was dying to ask on the way to the station, too. This administrative leave thing was going to make it next to impossible to get answers once he turned her over to his boss.

He shoved his phone back into the holder on his belt as a knock sounded at the back kitchen door. Recognizing the silhouette of Dillon's main farmhand behind the filmy white curtain covering the glass, Chris waved in greeting. He hurried to the door and reached up to key the security code into the electronic keypad by the door. But the light wasn't red. It was green.

The alarm was already disarmed.

He yanked his backup gun out of his ankle holster, since the chief had made him turn over his primary gun, and held it down by his thigh. He had two more pistols locked in the pickup. He'd have to remember to strap one of those on his belt when he left. On duty or off, he didn't want to get caught without enough firepower if the need arose. Especially if someone was still after Julie Webb—which seemed possible based on the fear he'd still seen in her eyes last night.

He threw the door open. "Griffin, you seen anyone skulking around here?"

The answering smile on Griffin's sun-browned face was replaced with concern as he glanced around. "Just the workers, feeding the horses, mucking stalls. I saw your truck and thought you might have an update on Miss Ashley."

"Stay here."

Without waiting for the older man to reply, Chris hurried from the kitchen, through the great room to the still-closed door of the front guest room. He didn't stop to knock. He threw the door open, sweeping his pistol out in front of him, fully expecting to see an intruder standing over Julie's bed or perhaps already holding her hostage.

There wasn't anyone there. The bed didn't even look like it had been slept in.

"Chris?" Griffin had obviously ignored his order to stay put and was behind him in the doorway.

Chris ignored him and cleared the closet, then the

attached bath, before turning around. He strode across the room, the gun still at his side.

"What's going on?" Griffin asked, quickly backing up to let him through the doorway. "Should I call 911?"

"Not yet." He headed to his right, beside the staircase to the back hallway and the room at the back right corner of the downstairs. He headed inside and pulled up a chair in front of the main security camera console.

"Is Miss Ashley okay? Did something happen?"

The worry in Griffin's voice as he ran into the room finally sank in and Chris turned to face him. Last year Ashley had nearly been killed by some very bad people who were after her. Griffin had probably seen Chris's gun and thought the worst.

"She's fine. She and the baby are both fine. Dillon's with them at the hospital. They were able to stop the contractions, but they're keeping her for observation for a few days."

"*Gracias a Dios*. Thank God," Griffin whispered, making the sign of the cross on his chest. "I thought the bad men were back again to hurt Miss Ashley."

A pang of guilt shot through Chris for not taking a few extra seconds at the back door to reassure the old man. From what Dillon had told him, Griffin still had nightmares about the siege that had happened here when the men had caught up to Ashley last year.

Chris flipped on the computer monitors and entered the password into the menu to access the security footage. "Like I said, Ashley and the baby are fine. I'm here for another reason entirely." He keyed in some commands and accessed the recording from the cameras on the front and kitchen doors, with both displays side by side on the monitor in front of him. It didn't take long to find what he was looking for.

He cursed and pressed a key to pause the footage. Then he shoved his gun into his holster.

"Detective Downing? What's going on?"

Chris forced a smile. Griffin was always polite, but for him to call Chris "Detective" meant he was getting really worried.

"It's okay, Griffin. Everything's okay. When I went to open the kitchen door to let you in, I realized the security alarm was off. I thought something might have happened, so I had to check things out. But everything is fine."

The look of relief that swept over the older man's face was palpable. "Good, that is very good. Dillon will tease you about forgetting to set the alarm then." He grinned.

Chris smiled back. "Yeah, he'll get a kick out of that. Was there anything that you needed?"

"No, no. Just saw your truck, wanted to check on you and see about Miss Ashley. If you don't need me, I'll get back to work."

"Thanks, Griffin. Good to see you again."

"You, too."

As soon as Griffin left the room, Chris turned back to the monitor. It showed a picture of the front door opening a crack. From the inside. He pushed Play and the image expanded to show Julie Webb sneaking out the front door. Which meant she must have watched him key in the security code yesterday and she'd shut off the alarm.

He watched the video until she disappeared from the camera shot. He punched up several other videos, examining angles from other cameras. Then he turned off the monitors and pulled out his cell phone.

"You on your way?" Chief Thornton asked, recognizing Chris's cell phone number.

"Actually, no. There's something I need to take care of. It'll be a couple more hours before I can bring Julie to the station."

Chris drove his pickup across the field toward the weathered gray barn on the right side of Cooper's farm. The older man's white pickup was sitting beside the barn where he must have left it before going into the hospital. After last night, Chris had planned on calling someone else to clear the land he'd promised Cooper he'd clear. But after seeing the security video, and seeing Julie climb into the back of his pickup and hide under a tarp early this morning, he'd changed his mind.

He was going to make her tell him what she was hiding and why she'd snuck out of the house. To do that, he needed some time alone with her. His boss would think to check Harmony Haven if he got impatient waiting on him to bring Julie in. But he'd never think to look here. The only question now was how long Julie would let this little farce play out before she came out of hiding. She was about to find out that Chris could be a very patient man.

He parked next to the white pickup and killed his engine. He waited, checked the rearview mirror, waited some more. When the tarp didn't move, he let out an exasperated breath and hopped out of the truck, shoving the keys into his jeans pocket.

Two blood-bay mares and a palomino gelding idled lazily in the corral attached to the barn. Cooper's small farm was several miles from the nearest neighbor, but all of them were pitching in until he was back on his feet. One of them must have come by this morning already and fed and turned out the horses. That was the sum total of livestock on the farm. Cooper kept the horses for his grandkids when they came visiting. Otherwise, he rotated tobacco and hay in his fields, to augment his pension and keep himself from being bored.

Thousand-pound round bales of freshly cut orchard grass dotted the field behind the barn and the little one-story farmhouse a few hundred yards away. The grass was already drying to a golden brown that would become hay. In a few more days, another neighbor would bring equipment to gather up the bales. By the time Cooper was home, all he'd have to do was tend the summer garden he wanted for his own personal use. Which was why Chris was here.

Unless Julie quit being stubborn and made herself known, he'd be just as stubborn and go ahead and clear the acre of brush close to the house to make it easier for the owner to tend without having to walk so far. Cooper was getting a hip replacement, which meant exercise was good for him. But there was a limit to just how far he should have to walk and Chris aimed to help him out in that regard.

After another glance at his truck, he headed into the barn that housed Cooper's tractor and other farming equipment. He was just about to hook up the Bush Hog mower attachment to the back of the tractor when his phone vibrated. When he took it out of the holder and saw who was calling, a mixture of worry and dread shot through him.

"Dillon, did something happen? Are Ashley and the baby okay?"

A tired sigh sounded through the phone. "They're no worse than when you and I spoke earlier this morning. We're still fighting to keep the baby in the oven. Ashley's going stir-crazy, wanting to get out of bed. But the doctors won't let her move and they've been pumping her with meds to stop her contractions."

"Sorry, man. Is there anything I can do? Do you want me to bring something to the hospital?"

"You already have."

"What?"

"That ADA, Nelson? She sent two henchmen to the hospital an hour ago to ask me if I knew where you'd taken the witness. This is the first chance I've had to call and tell you."

Chris tightened his hands around the phone. "Henchmen? Are you talking about Henson and Bolton, her admin assistants? They should have gone back to Nashville with her."

"Well they didn't. I don't suppose you noticed they're both over six feet tall and built like bodyguards? You don't really think they're Nelson's gofers, do you?"

"Honestly, I'm embarrassed to say that I didn't pay them much attention at all last night. Other than noting they both had dark brown hair and wore matching gray suits, I probably couldn't pick them out of a lineup. I'm sorry they bothered you."

"Oh, I didn't let them bother me. When they knocked on Ashley's door and introduced themselves, I introduced them to hospital security and had them escorted outside. I didn't like the vibe I got from either of them. You might want to run a background check and see who they really are and why they're hanging with an assistant district attorney."

Chris leaned against the tractor. "You have a working theory?"

Dillon paused before continuing. "Not based on any facts. It's more of a feeling. I didn't trust them. Which makes me not trust Nelson, either. I think your next-door neighbor has landed you in the middle of something really bad. And since you're going to be my daughter's godfather, I just wanted to tell you to be careful."

Chris couldn't help grinning. "So, you're having a girl."

A chuckle sounded through the phone. "We'd planned on being surprised during the delivery, but they've been doing so many ultrasounds and checkups that we really couldn't avoid finding out the gender. So, yeah. We're having a girl."

"That's great. Any ideas on names yet?"

"We don't want to jinx anything, so we're waiting on that. Taking it one hour at a time. The doctor wants the baby to cook at least a couple more weeks, if possible. Until delivery, Ashley's on complete bed rest."

"She's going to go nuts lying around that long."

"Tell me about it. Hey, Chris. Back to this Julie Webb person and the goons who showed up this morning. I watched them from the hospital room window when they left. They were in two separate cars, which seems odd enough since they're both allegedly from out of town on a business trip together. What was even odder was that both cars were muscle cars. What's that sound like to you?"

"Like you said earlier, bodyguards. But the ADA wasn't with them?"

"No sign of her," Dillon said.

"Which means they aren't guards. We're back to the henchman theory."

"Pretty much. Be careful, all right? I mean it. Watch your six."

He glanced at the barn's huge double doors, made large enough to accommodate the tractor, and thought about his truck outside—and what was *in* the truck—or rather, who. His little game of outwaiting Julie was no longer viable, not if there were two thugs looking for her. He pushed away from the tractor and headed toward the doors to get her out of her hiding place. The bush hogging would have to wait.

"Thanks, Dillon. I'll check back later."

He ended the call and pushed through the double doors, just in time to see Cooper's white pickup truck bumping across the field toward the road.

With Julie Webb in the driver's seat.

Chris swore and ran toward his truck. He skidded to a halt at the driver's-side door, his boots sliding in the dirt. The front left tire—which had cost a cool five hundred dollars because it was so big—was completely flat. He whirled around in time to see the white pickup reach the road and turn north toward town. A moment later, Julie had rounded a curve and thick stands of pine trees hid her from sight.

A whinny had Chris turning around. The palomino brushed against the corral fence, its head extended over the railing as it tore chunks of sweet clover out of the ground.

Chris ran into the barn. Less than a minute later, he

had a harness and reins on the palomino. No time for a saddle. He led the gelding out of the corral, grabbed a fistful of mane and vaulted onto its back.

"Yah!" he yelled, squeezing his thighs against the horse. The gelding squealed and took off at a bone-jarring gallop across the field. Right before the horse reached the road, Chris yanked the reins, sending them both crashing into the woods.

Chapter 10

Gravel seemed to roll beneath the wheels like a wave as Julie fought to keep the truck on the road. She eased her foot off the gas and the pickup straightened out. Too fast. She was going way too fast for these bumpy country roads. If she didn't slow down she'd end up in a ditch.

Easing off the accelerator even more, she glanced in her rearview mirror. She'd caught a glimpse of Chris running out of the barn when she'd stolen his friend's truck. Thank goodness she'd let the air out of one of his tires. Facing him when he looked that angry wasn't something she hoped to do anytime soon.

Guilt swept through her as she sped up again on a straightaway. From the moment she'd met her sexy neighbor, he'd been nothing but nice. He'd done everything he could to protect her. And how did she repay him? She'd snuck out of the house before dawn, using the security code that she'd seen him enter into the key-pad when they'd gotten there. And then, when she'd re-alized she was in the middle of nowhere with no hope of escaping on her own, she'd hunkered down in the back of his four-by-four, hoping he wouldn't notice.

Her plan had worked. Except for the part where he didn't take her into town and, instead, drove to a farm even farther out in the boonies than the horse-rescue place had been.

It didn't matter. Now that she had transportation, she'd head to Destiny and leave the truck parked some-where obvious so the owner would find it. And leave a wad of cash hidden inside as an apology for taking it.

The trees seemed to encroach on the narrow road as she slowed for another one of the hairpin turns. At this rate, she might get there faster by walking.

She came out of the curve and onto another straight-away. A dark blur suddenly burst from the trees on the right and leaped onto the road fifty yards ahead of her truck. A horse! She slammed the brakes and desperately turned the wheel. The pickup began to slide sideways like a jackknifed semi.

Oh, God, oh, God, oh, God. She was going to hit the horse.

The animal gave a high-pitched whinny and bolted toward the trees on the other side of the road just as the pickup slid to a stop.

Julie's heart hammered in her chest, her breaths com-ing in great gasps as she stared through the windshield. Her hands gripped the steering wheel so tightly she could feel her pulse thumping in her fingers.

What in the world had just happened?

She blinked, drew a ragged breath and scanned the road, looking for the horse. There, thirty feet away on the left, it stood with its head down, calmly munching on the tall green grass beside the road. Reins hung down from its harness. But it wasn't wearing a saddle. She frowned. Had someone been on the horse when it dashed in front of her? Everything had happened so fast. But she was almost positive she'd seen something, someone, bent low over the horse's neck.

Her door flew open. She jerked around and let out a squeal of alarm.

In the opening stood a very angry looking Chris Downing.

His dark eyes seemed almost black as he glared at her. "Get. Out."

Chris stalked across the road toward the gelding, leaving Julie standing beside the truck, minus the keys this time, which Cooper had been foolish enough— or trusting enough—to leave in the cab. Then again, around these parts, people didn't make a habit of stealing their neighbors' vehicles. Unlocked doors were the norm. The only reason that Chris and Dillon were so security conscious was because in their role as police officers they saw more than the average citizen of the dangers that lurked out there.

Like from out of towners passing through, such as Julie Webb.

He cursed beneath his breath and forced himself to act as calmly as possible so he wouldn't spook the horse. He spoke to it in low, soothing tones as he took off the harness and scratched its velvety nose. Then he steered the horse around to the other side of the road and slapped its withers, sending it off at a trot back into the woods.

Julie's eyes widened as he strode toward her. She glanced at the harness in his hand, then the horse as it disappeared into the trees. He wasn't going to tell her that the horse would find its way back home just like a cat would. Let her wonder, and maybe worry just a bit about the havoc she'd caused.

He tossed the harness and reins in the bed of the truck and popped open the driver's door.

"Get in."

She glanced longingly toward the trees where the horse had gone, then at the road that led toward town.

"You just told me to get out."

He grabbed her around the waist and lifted her into the cab of the truck. Not giving her a chance to hop back out or argue with him, he climbed in after her, forcing her to slide over.

She glared at him and kept sliding, then grabbed the passenger-door handle.

Chris yanked her toward him and anchored her against his side with his arm around her shoulders.

"Let me go." Her eyes flashed with anger.

He leaned down until his face was just inches from hers, intentionally using his much larger size to get his point across.

"I'll let you go if you give me your word that you won't try to hop out of the truck."

A shiver went through her as she stared up at him, uncertainty replacing the anger in her eyes.

And just like that, Chris's own anger began to fade. Intimidating a young woman who'd been through what

Julie had been through didn't make him exactly feel proud of himself. He swore yet again and released her.

"All you had to do was ask me to take you back to town and I would have." He shoved the keys in the ignition and started the engine. "Slashing a five-hundred-dollar tire and stealing my friend's truck was completely unnecessary."

She was silent as he did a three-point turn in the middle of the road and headed toward Cooper's farm.

"I didn't slash your tire."

He glanced at her.

"I just let the air out," she clarified. "I don't have a knife." She held out her hands in a placating gesture. "Not that I would have cut the tire if I'd had a knife. I just needed a head start. I didn't want to hurt anyone, or their property. I would have left this truck parked in town for the owner."

"The owner is in the hospital recovering from surgery. He doesn't need the stress of being told by someone that his one and only truck has been stolen and then found downtown. Why did you do it? Why did you sneak out of Dillon's house and then hide in the back of my truck, only to steal Cooper's truck and make a run for it? It's not like you were under arrest. And you have a phone, don't you? If you'd wanted a cab, you could have called for one."

She snorted and gave a little laugh. "I would have called a cab, but I forgot the name of your friend's farm. And the GPS on my phone couldn't figure out where I was. Apparently, that horse place doesn't exist in whatever maps my not-so-smart phone has."

He steered around another curve. "It's called Harmony Haven." He glanced at her. "Are you afraid of me?"

"What? Afraid of you? Why would you think that?"

He shook his head in exasperation. "You snuck away, stole a truck to avoid me. Call it a hunch."

This time it was her turn to roll her eyes. "Okay, okay. I may not completely trust you, but I trust you more than I've trusted anyone else for a long time. It's just that the longer I sat in that guest room thinking about the questions you'd be asking me in the morning, the more I realized I didn't want to involve you further. This is my battle. Not yours."

He turned onto the long dirt driveway up to Cooper's farmhouse. When he reached the house, he threw the truck into Park but left the engine running to keep the cab cool. The summer heat was already uncomfortable even this early in the morning.

Turning to face her, he put his right arm across the back of the bench seat.

"Let me see if I have this all straight in my mind. Your husband tried to kill you—twice. I'm the police officer who had to kill him to save you. I think I'm already involved almost as deep as I can be."

Her face flushed a light pink. "Well, when you put it that way, it does sound like too little, too late. But at least I can protect you from here on out by not involving you anymore."

"What part of *I'm a police officer* did you not hear? Julie, I'm a detective and part-time SWAT officer. It's my job to protect you, and to find out what's going on, administrative leave or not. And if you're still in any danger, it's my job to figure out why and who is after you."

Her eyes widened.

He shook his head and let out a deep sigh. "I've been

a cop since I got out of college thirteen years ago. I can read body language. And right now yours is screaming that you think there's more to your husband's attempts on your life than typical domestic violence, if there is such a thing as typical in these cases."

When she didn't say anything, he shut the engine off and shoved his door open. "Come on. At least let me take you inside while we talk this out. And, once we do, if you still want to go into town, I'll take you myself. In *my* truck."

She didn't agree with his plan, but she didn't try to run either. He supposed that was progress.

They were heading toward the front porch when the sound of galloping hooves reached them. He immediately shoved her behind his back and drew his gun. The palomino gelding appeared around the corner, tossing its mane and blowing out a snort as it stopped a few feet from him.

Chris holstered the gun and opened the front door.

"Go on in," he said. When she didn't move, he added, "Please?"

She hesitated, then stepped inside.

Chris started to pull the door shut but she stopped him with a hand on his.

"What are you doing?" she asked.

"I'm going to put the horse back in the corral. I'll be right back."

Chapter 11

A few minutes later, Julie sat at the kitchen table in Cooper's house, watching a shirtless Chris sit down across from her. His shirt had been soaked with sweat from his ride on the horse, so he'd washed it out in the sink and hung it on a chair to dry. He'd also rinsed his hair under the faucet. Julie had freshened up in the bathroom as much as possible without taking a real shower. And now she was desperately trying to pretend he wasn't completely distracting her.

His thick hair was beginning to dry in waves of cinnamon brown that made her fingers itch to touch it. But far more enticing was his golden-skinned, impressively muscled chest.

Chris Downing had a mouthwatering body to go along with his handsome face. And she was in no way immune to his appeal. The only thing keeping her from blatantly staring at the dips and valleys of his muscular chest and abs was the fact that he was grilling her with questions—questions that were going a long way toward dampening her enthusiasm for the incredible male specimen sitting across from her.

He'd asked her to give him more details about her husband attacking her five months ago. She told him about that night and that right after he'd paid bail, he'd disappeared, gone off grid, only communicating through his lawyer. Which had left Julie looking over her shoulder all the time, worried he'd try to come back and finish what he'd started.

"The first month after he disappeared, things were okay. But then his family filed a civil suit, alleging I was lying about the attack. And little things started happening, like someone slashing my tires. I was convinced that either Alan, or his family, was harassing me. The ADA's office didn't have the budget to offer 24/7 protection, which I needed if I was going to stay in Nashville. Since most of my accounts have been frozen as a result of the civil case, I can't afford that kind of security, either. So I'd moved here until the criminal case against my husband was settled, or until I had to go back to fight the civil case. I was trying to keep a low profile."

"That worked out really well," Chris said, his tone dry. "Why do you think your husband's family is suing you? Sounds to me like there's plenty of evidence against your husband."

"Kathy said it's a device to try to undermine the criminal case against him."

Chris nodded. "The threshold for proof in a civil case is much lower than in a criminal case. A civil judgment could sway the media in their favor, maybe turn a juror, even though they're supposed to ignore things like that.

He tapped a hand on the table. "So the reason you called the ADA after the shooting is because of the criminal case? To keep Nelson in the loop?"

She nodded. "That and I really didn't know anyone else to call. It's not like I have a lawyer on retainer. I wanted her advice, and she immediately said she was on her way."

"Awfully nice of her."

"I guess."

He studied her for a moment. "What were you and your husband arguing about when he found you in Destiny?"

"Arguing?"

"I heard you scream, twice, heard voices raised in argument before I confronted your husband. The screams, I get. He threatened you, cut you with the knife. But what was it that you were fighting about?"

"I remember he was angry that I'd shot him in Nashville, and that I ran away, as he called it. He threatened me, grabbed my arm, shook me. I probably cried out when he did that. Mostly I just kept telling him to go away and leave me alone."

He stared at her as if he didn't believe her. She tried to remember what she and Alan were saying when Chris had barged into the house. But she'd been so scared. The angry words they'd exchanged were all jumbled up in her mind.

"The last time he confronted you, you shot him. Was he worried about a gun this time?" Chris asked.

"I don't have a gun. I had to surrender it as evidence when the police arrived at my home that night."

"Did your husband know that?"

"Probably. We never talked about… I can't be sure. Actually, I seem to remember him asking if I had my gun. So, yeah, I guess he was concerned about it."

Some of the suspicion seemed to leave his face, as if he'd been testing her and she'd passed. What would happen if she hadn't passed?

"Did he have the knife with him when he came inside? Did he take it from the kitchen? Or did he take it from you?"

So much for him not being suspicious anymore. "What are you talking about?"

"Are you the one who had the knife first? Did your husband wrestle it away from you?"

"I never had the knife."

"Then we won't find your fingerprints on it?"

She held her hands out to her sides. "I don't know."

"You don't know?" He sounded incredulous.

"When I came out of my bedroom, Alan was standing there, holding the knife. I don't know if he brought it with him or grabbed it from my kitchen."

"You have to know what knives you brought with you when you rented the house. Judging by all the boxes I saw, you didn't have time to unpack before your husband got there."

"True, I didn't get to unpack everything. But I did unpack the boxes for the kitchen. I was looking forward to preparing my first decent meal since arriving in Destiny. I really don't know whether he'd grabbed one of my knives or brought his own."

"What were you arguing about?" he asked again, barely giving her a chance to catch her breath between questions.

"I told him to leave me alone. Why are you badgering me?"

"Because things aren't adding up. If your husband's goal was to kill you, he'd have snuck up on you, stabbed or shot you before you even knew he was there. Instead, he confronted you. So here's the real question. What do you have that your husband wanted so badly that he was willing to risk getting killed?"

Chapter 12

Chris checked his shirt hanging over the kitchen chair beside him. It was finally dry enough to wear, so he pulled it over his head and smoothed it into place.

"I think Alan might have been talking about the key to the safe," Julie said from her seat across from him.

"Safe? What safe?"

"When Alan and I separated, about nine months ago, I had all the locks changed while he was at work. He'd been angry, moody, aggressive—like, in your face aggressive but never actually hitting me. I'd never seen him like that before and it scared me. So I got a restraining order. And had the locks changed. That made him even angrier. Over the months that followed, he kept calling. He would say he needed different things from the house. Every time he'd mention something, I'd pack it up and ship it to his apartment. But he was never satisfied. It seemed like he was making excuses to try to get me to let him come over. That whole back and forth arguing went on for four months. Then he broke in one night and you know the rest."

"Was there a specific incident that made you separate from him nine months ago?"

She considered his question, then shrugged. "More like a series of them. In the first years of our marriage, he never mentioned my family. But this past year, he started bringing them up for seemingly no reason. He asked if I had anything to remember them by. I told him I had what mattered, memories. That seemed to make him really angry. Then I said all I had of them, physically, was a box of pictures and junk. He demanded that I show him what I had. If he hadn't acted so odd, I probably would have. But he'd been acting so strange, I refused. He went ballistic. The next day I changed the locks."

"You mentioned a safe. Is that where you put this box?"

"No. The pictures, costume jewelry, Naomi's hair clips, my dad's baseball cards—they're all in a safety deposit box that I haven't opened since their deaths. The safe I'm talking about is in our house in Nashville. When Alan broke into my house here in Destiny yesterday, after calling me vile names and ranting about the shooting and me leaving, at some point he demanded that I give him the key."

"What key?" Chris asked.

"I was about to ask him the same thing when you came in and things spiraled out of control. I got the impression he had a lot more he wanted to say. But he never got a chance. If he thought I had something in the safe that belonged to him, he was wrong. The thing is, I filed for divorce after Alan attacked me. And I gave him everything that was listed in the pending divorce decree, on top of what I'd already given him. So all I can figure is that he lost something, maybe some important papers that he didn't want anyone to know about. I'm not sure. But, like you said, it had to be important. It just occurred to me that he might have been talking about the floor safe in the house in Nashville. It was there when we bought the place and I remember him saying it would be a good place to keep our birth certificates and passports, things like that. But then I forgot about it. I never used that safe, but maybe he did. And maybe he thought I had the key."

"Do you?"

She shrugged. "I honestly don't know. Alan was practically a hoarder. I was all about keeping things neat and simple. Any time he left stuff lying around the house I'd put it up. It's very likely if he left a key somewhere that I might have thrown it in a junk drawer. But even if he thought I had the key, wouldn't it be easier for him to break into the house and try to, I don't know, pick the lock? Seems crazy that he'd track me down out here just for a key."

"It probably depends on what's in the safe, if indeed that's why he came here. Floor safes are generally extremely heavy and require special equipment to install. He couldn't have just broken into your house and taken the safe with him. And unless he's a master lock-picker, he'd need a locksmith to help him break into the thing. It would be hard for him to get a professional locksmith to pick the front door lock and a safe lock. They'd know something was up and would probably call the police."

She nodded. "When you put it that way, I suppose that coming here might be worth the risk—if we're even going down the right path. There could have been another reason entirely for him coming here. But that's the only key I can think of."

"Have you told Nelson about the safe?"

She shook her head. "Why would I? You asking me about what Alan said is the only reason I thought of it now."

"Don't."

She frowned. "Don't tell the ADA? Why?"

"How well do you know her?"

"Again, why?"

"Because she's the one who told you to leave town, to hide so your husband wouldn't find you. And yet, he did. Besides her, who knew you were here, in Destiny?"

She grew very still. "There isn't anyone else. Kathy is the only person I told. But she wouldn't tell Alan where I was. Kathy is the one who's been helping me fight him in court."

"Then how did your husband find you?"

"You're the detective. You tell me."

Her sarcasm and obvious frustration had him smiling. He was pushing her hard, probably harder than the chief would have if she were back at the station undergoing an official interview. But this was probably his only chance to ask her questions before turning her over to the team, and he intended to get as many answers as he could.

"Did you come directly to Destiny after leaving Nashville?" he asked.

"No. I wasn't sure where to hideout. I drove around the state, checking out several small towns before settling on this one. It took me about a week of exploring to decide that Destiny was where I wanted to land."

"The car you drove here, is it yours?"

"It's mine."

"How have you bought gas and food since leaving your home?"

"All cash. I've seen enough TV crime shows to know not to leave an electronic trail."

He nodded. "Good. How did you lease the house here in Destiny?"

"Cash again. I saw the place in an ad, called the number, met the landlord in person, paid cash and signed a fake name." Her face flushed a light red. "Probably not legal, exactly, but again I was worried about Alan being able to find me. I suppose if the landlord had pushed for ID I'd have been in trouble. But he didn't."

"Around here, people aren't as suspicious as they might be in a big city. You never answered my question about Nelson. How well do you know her?"

"We're casual friends, just barely. I met her and Alan a couple of months into my senior year in college." Some kind of emotion flashed in her eyes. Sorrow? Pain?

"You okay?" he asked.

She drew a bracing breath. "Yes, sorry. Just…thinking. Anyway, I…was…having a tough time in school and pretty much kept to myself. Kathy was in one of my classes. I knew her name but that was about it. I think she took pity on me. We started hanging out every once in a while. One day, I guess she could see how down I was and she insisted that I go to the school's football game that night. She had an extra ticket because a friend had canceled. When we got there, we sat by Alan. Neither of us knew him, but he introduced himself and we got to know each other a bit during the game. After that, we'd occasionally go to movies or other college events."

"So it's fair to say the three of you became friends?"

"More like acquaintances than friends. I clicked pretty well with Alan and Kathy, but they were like oil and water with each other. She tolerated him but didn't really like him. I tried to stay friends with both of them, but Alan and I got serious pretty fast. He… helped me through a really tough time. And, well, when you're guy-crazy you sometimes forget about your other friends. Kathy and I didn't ever get very close because I was usually with Alan. We got married right after graduation. Or, well, my graduation anyway. Alan had failed a few courses and never finished his degree. After I graduated, he stopped taking classes and decided to go into his family's business, Webb Enterprises." She waved her hand. "Not that any of that is relevant."

Chris didn't want to assume anything wasn't relevant at this point, but he did have other questions he wanted to ask right now. "Did Nelson attend your wedding?"

"No. We didn't invite her." Her cheeks flushed a light pink. "It's embarrassing now to say that. I mean, she was a friend, even if we weren't really close. But like I said, Alan didn't like her. So, no invitation. I guess you'd say I chose Alan over her."

"Maybe you only thought she and Alan didn't get along. Maybe she liked him and resented you. After all, you did both meet him at the same football game."

She shook her head. "She was never anything but kind to me, never expressed any resentment. And Alan never looked twice at her. She wasn't his type."

She held up her hands as if to stop him from arguing. "Before you say it, I know—she's tall and blonde, which most guys like, while I'm short and a brunette. But even if he and Kathy had been able to get along, he just wasn't attracted to women like her, with her kind of forceful personality. Everything about her set him off, irritated him. And he showed me pictures of some of his former girlfriends. Every one of them was like me—short, brunette."

Chris could certainly see Julie's appeal over the glossier, more made-up look that Kathy Nelson sported. Nelson was sophisticated but seemed fake, whereas Julie seemed the girl-next-door type, a beautiful girl next door but still down to earth, approachable. Still, that didn't mean Alan couldn't have been attracted to both of them.

"If neither of you kept up with Nelson, then why is she so invested in your case that she drove all the way out here from Nashville?"

"We didn't keep up with her at all. The first time I had seen her since college was the night that Alan was arrested. And the reason she's taking this case so personally is because Alan is…was…something of a celebrity in Nashville. He comes from money. His family is well-known in high-society circles and he was a respected philanthropist. Kathy is a career muckety-muck looking for a way into the governor's office. She made no secret to me that she felt if she could win against someone as high profile as Alan Webb, she'd prove she was in nobody's pocket and was tough on crime. She'd make a name for herself and be well on her way to establishing her political career."

That part didn't surprise Chris at all. Even in Destiny, people had heard of Kathy Nelson and her political aspirations. But there might have been another reason, too. If Julie was wrong—if Kathy did like Alan and felt he'd chosen Julie over her—maybe being in charge of the case against him was a way to get even for him passing her over in college. That seemed unlikely, though, to hold that kind of a grudge over three years later. Especially since Kathy was married.

Chris made a mental note to check with his team to see if they were looking into Kathy as a potential suspect. Just to cover the bases.

"Let's get back to the night your husband attacked you in Nashville. When was that?"

"About five months ago, on my twenty-fifth birthday."

A sick feeling twisted in Chris's gut. "Not that there's a good day to try to kill you, but on your birthday? Really?"

"Yes. Really." She was twisting her hands together again. "Like I said earlier, we'd been separated for about four months. Looking back now, the marriage was never what I'd hoped it would be. He'd doted on me in college. But as soon as that ring was on my finger, things cooled off, changed. At first, I thought it was because he'd quit school and took over the family business. He was under a lot of stress. And I figured he was frustrated that he never got to work in the field he loved."

"What field was that?"

"Botany. He absolutely loved working with plants. He could talk for hours about their medicinal properties and how to get more yield from organically grown crops. He'd planned on having his own career for a while before having to take the reins of the company. But it didn't work out that way. He's an only child, and his father's health was failing. He had to step in much sooner than he'd hoped. Once he started working at Webb Enterprises, that's when he started getting depressed and closing himself off from me. Then again, maybe I'm making up excuses for him. Maybe it was just me he didn't like."

The hurt was there again, in the tightening of her jaw, the way her lips thinned. She'd loved her husband once upon a time—that was obvious. And even now, she couldn't fathom why he'd turned on her.

Neither could Chris.

Why had Alan tried to kill her? Twice?

She waved her hands again, as if waving away her words. "Shortly before we separated, I remember him coming home one night in a sour mood after work and shutting himself up in his office for hours. Wouldn't even come out for dinner. And once he did emerge, it was almost as if...as if he were a different person. He was...serious, angry. He insisted that I call in the next day and take a week's vacation, said we needed to get away. I couldn't just drop everything like that. People count on me." She twisted her hands. "At least, they used to. I had to quit work once the media got hold of the story about Alan attacking me and me shooting him. I became a liability to my coworkers at that point."

"Where did you work?"

She hesitated, looked away. "I started a nonprofit foundation, figured it was a good use of my business management degree and I could help people. The office was in downtown Nashville. We fought to raise awareness and money to fight orphan diseases—illnesses that are so rare that it isn't profitable enough for a drug company to devote money researching possible cures or even treatments. But the diseases are devastating to the victims and their families."

He studied her. Her voice was a little too bright, like the emotion was forced. She was hiding something. He'd sensed it from the moment she'd begun talking about the tough time she'd been having right before she'd met Alan. There'd been a flash of pain in her eyes then, the same flash of pain in her eyes right now.

"Julie?"

"Hmm?" She was staring toward the front window, at the acres of green grass that would need mowing soon.

"What was the name of the nonprofit?"

She swallowed hard. "Naomi's Hope Foundation."

Again, she wouldn't look at him. And then he got it.

"Was Naomi a friend or a family member?"

Her startled gaze shot to his. She stared at him so long he thought she wasn't going to answer. But then she sighed heavily, looking defeated.

"She was my sister, a year older than me. My parents went broke taking her to hospitals, flying around the country to different specialists. They even went down to Mexico once, looking into alternative medicines. Nothing helped. She had a condition so rare it didn't even have a name. It baffled every doctor who tried to treat her. It struck her during her senior year in college, my junior year at the same school. She died four months later. At least she wasn't in pain anymore. She was free. But my parents…"

She shook her head. "They were immigrants, my mom and dad. Star-crossed lovers from London. Both sets of their parents, my grandparents, didn't approve of them dating. So as soon as they were of legal age, they married and moved to this country. They left their families, their history, everything familiar to them to have a fresh start, to build a legacy of their own. They were Romeo and Juliet, basically, coming here for the American dream.

"They didn't have any money, their families had disowned them and they had to fight for everything they had, which was never much. Their entire life savings was built around sending Naomi and me to college. But when Naomi…" She shook her head. "Naomi was a daddy's girl. When she died, my father couldn't handle it. He shot himself. The day after his funeral, my mother took an overdose of sleeping pills and alcohol."

Tears were running down her face now. Her bottom lip trembled.

"I always wondered what went through their minds when they did it. I know they were devastated. We all were. But, somewhere along the way, they forgot they had another daughter. They left me all alone. I had no one to turn to. But I couldn't let their sacrifices be for nothing. Naomi died in the summer after my junior year, my parents right after that. A month later I enrolled for the fall session of my senior year. I felt I owed it to my parents to get my degree. But I was miserable, couldn't concentrate on my studies. A couple of months later, I was about ready to give up. And that's when I met Alan. He turned my life around. He was there for me, encouraged me. And then he…then he…"

She covered her face with her hands, her shoulders shaking as her misery overtook her.

Chris stood and crossed to her. He couldn't bear doing nothing, so he took a chance and damned the consequences. He pulled her to standing and wrapped his arms around her.

"I'm so sorry, Julie," he whispered, resting his cheek against the top of her head. "I'm so very, very sorry."

She'd stiffened when he first touched her. But then she seemed to melt against him, putting her arms around his waist and clinging to him while tears tracked down her face, soaking his shirt.

They stood there a long time while he whispered soothing words against her hair. The storm finally subsided, her tears stopped and she was no longer shaking.

Finally, with one last sniffle, she pushed back and gave him a watery smile. "Thank you."

The pain in her beautiful blue eyes had him wanting to pull her back into his arms. But he fought the urge and instead allowed himself only to gently push her tousled hair out of her eyes, then wipe the last of her tears from her cheeks before dropping his hands to his sides.

"Anytime." He smiled and stepped back to put some much-needed space between them.

She drew a shaky breath. "I don't think my heart or your shirt can take much more of this. You might as well finish asking your questions right now."

"We don't have to—"

"Yes. We do," she said. "I want to know why Alan did what he did. And you need the investigation resolved. Both of us need this case closed in order to get on with our lives. So go on. Ask whatever else you want to know."

"All right. What about the movers?"

"Movers?" She frowned. "What about them?"

"Yesterday afternoon, they brought your furniture and belongings. I assume they drove down from Nashville. Did you pay them cash, too? Or did you use a credit card when you hired them?"

"I went to the bank the day I left and withdrew several thousand dollars from my checking account so I could live on cash for a while. I paid the movers in cash like I did everything else."

"Several thousand dollars—from checking, not savings?" he asked. "I'm not exactly living paycheck to paycheck, but I'd have to dip into savings to pull out several thousand in cash."

"Even with the civil suit freezing our joint accounts, I still have plenty of money in my personal accounts. As long as I'm not too extravagant, I'll be okay until the case is settled. Money has never been a problem for Alan and me. Like I said, he took over the family business, an import/export empire. Even without receiving his botany degree, he'd taken enough classes in his minor—business management—to do really well running the company. And he was smart, really smart. The company was struggling when the economy went south. But within weeks of Alan taking it over, the profits soared."

That didn't sound right to Chris. A young kid, freshly flunked out of college, was able to turn around the family business? A lot of things about Alan didn't sound right. The next time Chris called his boss he was going to see how the background check on Julie's former husband was going. He wanted a complete history on Alan Webb, from birth to the grave.

Julie shoved her chair up to the table and remained standing, wrapping her arms around her waist. "That's what allowed me to work at the nonprofit instead of getting a job that paid real money. I'd offered to work at his family's business, to help him manage it. But he didn't want me to worry about that, insisted that I chase my dream of getting the government to devote resources to research orphan diseases like my sister's. It truly was the most decent thing he ever did."

The bitterness in her voice told him there was a lot more water under the matrimonial bridge, but he decided to steer clear of that for now. Making her miserable wasn't his goal. He'd only delve into that earlier line of questioning again if it was absolutely necessary.

"All right. Back to the moving company then. I'm surprised they took cash. Most companies like that require a credit card."

"Yeah, well. You'd be surprised what a few hundred dollars under the table can do for you."

"You bribed them."

"I did what I had to do to stay under the radar. It's not like Alan was involved in some kind of nefarious criminal activity and the government was giving me a new identity to testify against him. He was just a husband who'd tried to murder his wife. I was on my own. I would have used a fake name if I could. But they required ID, wouldn't budge on that. So, as soon as I decided that I wanted to leave Nashville, I had them put the things I would need into storage and left everything else in the house to deal with at a later time. Like I said before, about a week later I knew where I wanted to settle. After renting the place in Destiny, I called them to arrange a date and time for them to deliver my things."

"There's a direct link from your house to the moving company to here if someone wanted to follow it. That could be how Alan tracked you. But it's not like he could have watched the storage unit 24/7. He had to sleep sometime. If the movers had loaded up the unit while Alan was asleep, he'd have missed that link to you and wouldn't have been able to find you—assuming that he did find you through the movers. I'm betting he had a partner. He wasn't working alone in his quest to locate you." He studied her carefully. "And you're not surprised by that. Why not?"

She shrugged. "When your husband tries to kill you, trying to figure out why he wants you dead pretty much consumes your thoughts. The fact that he found me so fast this second time shocked me. And it made me think he had to be working with someone else. He had to have help. And I couldn't see him hiring a private investigator, not with the criminal case hanging over his head. That could look bad in court. Like he was stalking me. I figure it has to be someone bad, a criminal, someone likely as dangerous as Alan became. So, no, it doesn't surprise me. I figured he had a partner. The only question is who, and of course, whether they still want me dead now that Alan's gone."

Listening to the pain in her voice, the confusion and anger pretty much obliterated his earlier concerns that she might have intentionally used him as a tool to kill her husband. She was consistent in her answers. She didn't hesitate like she would if she was making up lies as she went along. And her body language struck him as honest, too. He'd bet all of his years of experience at interviewing witnesses that everything she was telling him now was true.

Or at least what she thought was true. But there was still one more thing bugging him.

"Have you told me everything?" he asked.

"Yes, of course."

"Then why are you still running? Why stow away in the back of my truck, and steal Cooper's truck, to get away from me if you've done nothing wrong and have nothing to hide? You said you think your husband has a partner who might be after you. So why wouldn't you trust the policeman who risked his own life to save you yesterday? It doesn't make sense, unless the real reason you want to be on your own is because you want to get even."

She blinked. "Excuse me?"

"You don't want some cop hanging around when you figure out who was working with Alan against you. Because you want revenge."

"That's ridiculous. I want to be safe, that's what I want."

"Then why run from me? I can protect you."

"I've known you for all of two seconds," she said, her voice shaking with anger. "I knew Alan for three and a half years, was married to him for three of those years. You tell me. Why should I trust you when I couldn't trust him?"

And that was the last piece of the puzzle he'd been looking for. It had been in front of him all along. He'd quit thinking of her as a conspirator and was thinking of her solely as a victim. But he still hadn't understood why she'd run. It all came down to trust. She'd been hurt, horribly hurt, and here he was berating her for not being willing to put her faith and her life in his hands when, as she'd said, she'd known him for all of "two seconds."

He'd been a complete ass and hadn't even realized it.

"Julie."

When she didn't reply, he moved a step closer and took her hand in his. She tried to tug it away, but he held fast.

"Julie, maybe you don't trust me completely yet. I get that. I understand it after everything you've been through. But look at this objectively. We both want the same thing. We want answers. The answer to why Alan tried to kill you—twice—will enable you to go back and live your life without having to look over your shoulder and worry that someone else is out there trying to hurt you. That same answer will help me resolve this case so I can go back to my life, to being a cop. We both want the same thing, to end this. So how about we work together, as a team, and end this once and for all."

He could see the indecision on her face, in the way she chewed her bottom lip as if debating her options. For a moment, he thought she'd turn and walk away. But then, very slowly, she put her hand in his.

He couldn't help but notice how soft her skin was and how good it felt to thread his fingers with hers. And from the way her blue eyes widened at the contact, he had a feeling she was thinking much the same thing— that it was nice holding his hand, too.

A tiny red circle of light appeared on her forehead.

He shouted a warning and yanked her toward him just as the front window exploded in a hail of rifle fire.

Chapter 13

"Stay down." Chris yanked his gun out of his holster.

Julie couldn't have gotten up if she wanted to, not with two-hundred pounds of protective male squashing her against the hardwood floor.

He rolled off her and jumped up in a half crouch, sprinting toward the window with his gun out in front of him.

Bam! Bam! Bam!

He fired through the gaping hole that used to be the front window, then dove toward the floor. Whoever was shooting at them outside let loose with another round of shots.

Julie covered her ears and squeezed her eyes shut. Bits of plaster and wood rained down where the bullets strafed the walls above her. When the chaos of noise and dust had settled, Chris was once again crouching over her, his gun pointed up at the ceiling. In his other hand was his phone.

"You okay?" he asked her.

She felt as if she'd inhaled a lungful of plaster dust, but nodded to let him know she was at least alive. As for "okay," she'd reserve judgment on that.

"It's Chris," he said into the phone. "I'm over at Cooper's farm, holed up in the house with Julie Webb. We're taking rifle fire."

Julie looked toward the shattered front window while Chris talked police codes that made no sense to her. This low to the floor, she couldn't see the road or even the acres of grass outside. All she could see was the wall of trees at the edge of the cleared portion of the property. Where was the shooter? Was he making his way toward the house even now? Ready to lean in through the opening and gun them down?

She should have been terrified, melting into a puddle of tears and nerves. And maybe if this was the first time someone had tried to kill her, she would have been. But after everything she'd been through, and everything she'd lost, the only emotion flowing through her veins right now was rage.

She was absolutely livid.

If the shooter did lean in through that window, she'd try to tear him apart, limb by limb, with her bare hands. Assuming he didn't shoot her first, of course. She was so sick of people trying to hurt her. And what about Chris? Once again his life was in danger because someone had decided to go after her, or at least that was what she had to assume. It made sense that between the two of them, she was the target. And here Chris was in the wrong place at the wrong time, again.

"Give me your backup gun," she snapped, as he ended his call.

"My backup gun?"

If their situation wasn't so dire, she'd have laughed at the stunned look on his face.

"You do have one, right? All the cops in movies and on TV have them. It's probably strapped to your ankle. I may not be an expert marksman, but I do know how to shoot. I've been to gun ranges. I want to help."

He said something under his breath and she was pretty sure she didn't want to know what it was from the exasperated expression on his face.

"Unless you have law enforcement or military experience that I don't know about, I'll keep my alleged backup gun where it belongs. Come on. You can help us by getting out of the line of fire so I don't have to worry about you. Our friend out there is going to get braver anytime now and I don't want you catching a bullet when he does."

"Or she."

He nodded. "Or she. Come on."

He crouched over her, shielding her body with his as he duck walked with her out of the main room and down a short hallway. No more gunshots sounded from outside, which had her even more nervous. Judging by his worried look, it made him nervous, too.

"In here." He pushed her through a doorway into a bathroom.

An old-fashioned claw-foot tub sat against the far wall, beneath a small, high window.

"Get in."

He didn't wait for her to figure out what he meant before he was lifting her and settling her inside the tub.

"This is cast iron. It's the best protection from stray bullets that I can give you."

The idea of bullets ripping through the walls hadn't even occurred to her. The anger that had helped her stay calm earlier began to fade, leaving her shaking so hard her teeth chattered.

"Wh-what a-bout you?" she asked between chatters. "Sh-shouldn't you g-get in, too?"

He'd been half-standing, peeking through the bottom of the window. But when she spoke he ducked down, an amused, half smile curving his lips.

"As much as I'd love to join you in the tub," he teased, "the timing isn't right." He added an outrageous wink and even managed a chuckle.

She couldn't believe he was flirting with her at a time like this—or that she found him utterly charming. She was about to tell him to knock it off and get into the tub with her before he got shot, when the sound of gunfire echoed through the house.

Chris dove to the floor.

A loud pinging noise had Julie throwing her hands over her ears and squeezing her eyes shut. The shots seemed to go on forever. When they finally stopped, she lay there, her breaths coming in great gasps, her hands still covering her ears.

Forcing her eyes open, she pulled herself up to sitting. Sunlight slanted through small round holes riddling the outside wall. Paint chips lay scattered on the floor—the same color as the tub. That pinging sound she'd heard must have been a bullet hitting the tub. And she'd been safe, just as Chris had promised.

But where was he?

She looked through the open door into the hallway,

but it didn't have any windows and was too dark for her to see anything.

"Chris," she whispered, not wanting the shooter to hear her if he was close by. "Chris? Where are you?"

No one answered. No footsteps sounded on the hardwood floor from the other rooms. Had he left her? Alone?

She swallowed, hard, trying to tamp down the rising panic that had her pulse hammering in her ears. It was too quiet outside. Had Chris gone out there to confront the shooter? Had he been forced to dive into the hallway to avoid getting shot, only to catch a stray bullet? If he was lying past the open doorway, injured, he could be bleeding out right now. She couldn't sit here and do nothing. She had to check on him, and if he was hurt, somehow she had to help him.

Her whole body shook as she started to pull herself up on her knees in the tub. Something shifted against her leg and she let out a squeal of surprise before she could stop herself. She looked down. Chris hadn't left her alone, after all.

He'd left her his backup gun.

Chris edged his way around the back of the house, pistol sweeping out in front of him. He kept to the grass to make as little noise as possible. Leaving Julie alone inside had nearly killed him. But as soon as the bullets started coming through the wall, he knew it was only a matter of time before the shooter breached the house. Julie had a much better chance of survival if Chris could intercept the shooter outside.

She'd have an even better chance if his SWAT team would get here.

He checked his watch. It had only been ten minutes since he'd called them. Donna, Colby and Randy had probably been at church, which was a good half hour away. Max usually went to the evening service like Chris. But Max lived even farther out than the First Baptist Church. Hopefully, his team was speeding toward him like a moonshiner running from a revenue officer. Still, best case, the first of them might arrive in another ten minutes.

He and Julie didn't have ten minutes—not against someone with a rifle and a laser scope.

He ducked down and peered around the corner of the house. The side yard was empty and he couldn't see anyone out front. But thick trees to his right marched all the way down to the gravel road. There were a million places for someone with a rifle to hide. If Chris couldn't reach cover, and get up close and personal with the shooter, his 9mm was just about useless. What he needed was a way to draw the gunman out and keep him away from the house, and Julie.

He eased back behind the wall, glancing toward the barn, his truck, the corral with the horses. They were nervous, agitated, running back and forth because of the gunfire. Too dangerous to try capturing one, let alone riding it to create some kind of diversion—assuming he could even make it that far without being picked off by the rifle. No, he needed something else to get the gunman's attention.

His gaze slid to the large silver propane tank set about fifty yards back from the house. It was slightly toward the right side of the property, close to one of the round hay bales drying in the sun. Acres and acres of wide-open field with more hay bales opened off to the right. And, past that, the barn and the horses—far enough away that they would be safe from harm, but close enough that the animals would be terrified and make their own racket. Dillon and Ashley would kill him for even considering what he was about to do. But he figured three traumatized horses in exchange for saving Julie's life was a bargain he was willing to make.

To his left, a deadly sprint from the house, the line of thick pine trees and oaks beckoned as cover—*if* he could reach them. Then he could circle around, locate the shooter and end this dangerous stand-off.

He raised his pistol and aimed it at the propane tank. *Bam! Bam!*

Chris jerked around at the sound of gunfire to his right. Julie was crouching in the back doorway, shooting toward the closest round hay bale. The long end of a rifle appeared at the left side, pointed right at her.

"Get back!" Chris squeezed off several shots toward the rifleman to give Julie cover to head inside.

But, instead of running into the house, she ran toward him, her eyes wide, face pale.

Wood siding exploded close to her head. Chris fired toward the hay bale again and ran toward Julie. The rifle jerked back. Chris grabbed Julie around the waist and shoved her down against the foundation of the house while he kept his gun aimed toward the hay.

"You need to get back into the house," he hissed, without turning around. "Get into the cast-iron tub until I take this jerk down!"

"Can't." She sounded out of breath. "I was worried you were hurt or needed help and was coming to look for you when the front door creaked open. Someone else is inside."

The rifle shoved through the hay. Chris and Julie both started shooting. Julie's gun clicked empty.

As soon as the rifle jerked back, Chris reloaded.

"I need more bullets." Julie ejected the spent magazine like a pro and held out her hand.

"The extra ammo for that gun is in my truck."

She gave him an aggravated look that would have made him laugh at any other time. Most people he knew in this situation would be cowering in fear. Not Julie. She was full of surprises.

A hollow echo sounded from inside the house. Whoever was in there was probably searching for Julie. If they came out back, the two of them were done for. They had to get to cover—now.

He grabbed her around the waist, jerking her up to standing and pointing her toward the trees.

She instinctively tried to crouch back down against the house. Chris pulled her up again.

"Run," he ordered. "I'll cover you. Get to the trees. Go!"

She took off running.

The rifle shoved through the hay. Chris fired off several shots, drawing the rifle bore toward him. Bullets pinged against the house right beside him. He swore and dove to the side. The sound of running feet sounded from inside the house, coming toward the back door. In desperation, Chris swept his pistol toward the propane tank and squeezed the trigger.

An explosion of heat and sound engulfed him, knocking him backward. His skull cracked against the wood siding, making his vision blur. He shook his head, trying to focus. A wall of thick black smoke and flames blasted toward him, offering him much-needed cover. Pushing away from the house, he took off in a wobbly run toward the trees.

Chapter 14

Julie peered around the same tree as Chris, looking toward the house and the burning remnants of the propane tank.

"I think the explosion took out the rifleman," Chris said. "The hay bale where he was hiding is obliterated. The question is, where's the second intruder?"

A shiver ran up Julie's spine. "I suppose it's too much to hope that the first gunman just got knocked out."

Chris looked at her over his shoulder, his brows raised. "You're worried about a man who tried to kill you?"

She shrugged, feeling silly. "I just don't like the idea of being responsible for someone's death."

A shuttered look came over his face. "Seems like I remember you thanking God yesterday after your husband was killed."

She jerked back, feeling his censure like a physical blow. "I never wanted Alan to die. I was thanking God that Alan couldn't hurt me again. But I didn't mean I was glad he'd been killed."

Chris's face softened. "It's not my place to pass judgment either way. I shouldn't have said anything." He turned back to the house, intently watching for signs of any gunmen.

Julie felt sick inside that he'd thought she was grateful for Alan's death. That was an awful thing to think about someone. Yet, here he was again, protecting her.

"Why?" she blurted out before she could stop herself.

"Why what?" Again, he didn't turn around, just kept his gun trained toward the house.

"Why are you helping me if you think I'm the kind of person who would rejoice over my husband being killed?"

He sighed heavily and reached toward her. "Take my hand, Julie."

She hesitated.

"Please."

His tone was gentle, imploring. She shoved her useless empty gun into the waistband of her khaki pants and put her right hand in his left one.

He tugged her up beside him, still not taking his gaze from the dying fire and the building.

"I'm a cop," he said. "A detective. It's my nature to doubt everything, to assume the worst. It's how I stay alive. Yes, I thought you were happy that your husband was dead." He glanced at her. "I also thought you might have planned the whole thing, moving in next to a cop and arranging that confrontation when you knew I'd be home."

She gasped and tried to tug her hand out of his grasp, but he tightened his hold.

"I don't think that anymore. Okay? I saw the truth in your eyes, heard it in your voice back in the house when you answered my questions."

His thumb lightly brushed the underside of her wrist, doing crazy things to her pulse and her breathing.

"You're a victim—"

"No. I am *not* a victim."

He squeezed her hand. "You're right. You're not. You're a witness, and a strong woman. Most people I know, most men I know, would have stayed in that bathtub. They wouldn't have gotten out because they were worried the police officer protecting them might need help. And the moment they heard someone else in the house, they would have frozen or run screaming. Instead, you covered me. You kept that rifleman busy when I was focused on shooting the propane tank. I might have saved you yesterday. But you saved me today. You're one of the bravest women I know. And, trust me, my respect for you has grown exponentially this morning."

"Thank you," she whispered, her throat tight. "And I do trust you."

He smiled and faced the house. Then he stiffened and pulled his hand from hers. "The second gunman's making a run for it. He's heading for the barn."

Julie leaned sideways, trying to see what he saw.

"Wait here!" Chris sprinted past her, arms and legs pumping as he ran toward the house. He stopped at the far corner, sweeping his gun out in front of him.

The horses let out shrill whinnies and bolted to the other side of the corral, as far from the barn as they could get. A dark figure seemed to materialize from out of nowhere, running around Chris's pickup toward the barn.

Chris dropped to his knees, aiming his pistol with both hands.

The sound of a distant siren filled the air, coming up the road.

"Yes, hurry. Please," Julie whispered, praying that help arrived soon. It was killing her watching Chris risk his life like this.

He fired off several shots. A metallic ping sounded from the truck where a bullet buried itself in the driver's-side door, narrowly missing the gunman.

The man returned fire. Chris let loose with a volley of shots. The gunman clutched his shoulder and spun around, dropping to the ground.

Chris took off, legs pumping like a champion sprinter as he ran toward the truck. Julie clutched the tree as she watched, bark cutting into her fingertips. The siren was much closer now.

The gunman rolled beneath the pickup, firing a couple of quick shots of his own. Chris dove toward the questionable cover of the fence, bringing up his pistol again. But the gunman had rolled out the other side.

Another pickup suddenly barreled into view, gravel and dirt spitting out in a dark cloud from beneath its wheels as it raced toward the corral. Lights flashed in the grill and its shrill siren filled the air. Julie recognized the driver as one of the SWAT officers she'd met after her husband was shot—Randy Carter.

Chris jumped up, motioning in the direction where the gunman had disappeared.

Another cloud of dust billowed up as a black Dodge

Charger raced from the other side of the barn where it must have been parked. It took off across the open field, bumping and weaving like a drunk between the enormous hay bales.

Julie heard Chris's shout as he waved for Randy to pursue the Charger. More sirens sounded from somewhere out front. Chris watched the truck chasing the Charger across the field. Julie could no longer see them because of the trees. When she looked back at Chris, he was jogging toward the ruins of the exploded propane tank and what was left of the rifleman's last hiding place.

Her fingers curled against the tree trunk again as she waited like he'd asked.

Two vehicles—an old black Camry and a white Ford Escape—pulled up on each side of the house, parking sideways at the far corner where the side yard and backyard met.

The drivers, a man and a woman, hopped out in full SWAT gear, both of them crouching down behind the engine blocks of their respective vehicles. They kept their long guns pointed up toward the sky in deference to Chris, but obviously they were there to support him in any way he might need.

He slowly straightened from crouching over something on the ground and motioned for both officers to join him. They rushed forward in unison, their motions well-rehearsed and sure, as if they'd practiced this type of situation hundreds of times.

After a brief consultation with Chris, the officers took off their helmets. Julie recognized them as having been at her rental home and later at the police station. She couldn't remember the man's name, but the woman, the one who'd arrived in the Escape, was Donna Waters. She'd sat beside Julie after the shooting.

And heard Julie praying her thanks.

She winced as Donna started toward her, apparently at Chris's request. Officer Waters probably thought Julie was a horrible person, as Chris had.

Straightening her shoulders, Julie pushed away from the tree to meet her halfway.

Donna was probably only a few years older than Julie, maybe twenty-eight or twenty-nine. Her blond hair was cut in a short, wavy style that flattered her heart-shaped face. They met in the side yard. Contrary to the chilly reception that Julie had expected— given the misunderstanding over her prayer after Alan's death—Donna gave her a sympathetic smile and hugged her.

"Bless your heart," the officer said when she pulled back. Genuine sympathy stared back from her blue eyes. "Not the best reception Destiny has ever given a newcomer. I'm so sorry, sweetie. How ya holding up?"

"Um, fine, I guess. Thank you."

Donna squeezed her shoulder. "I really hate to ask this. But Chris wants you to ID the body."

Julie took an instinctive step back. "The body?"

"You don't have to. It's totally okay, and understandable. But we think you might know the guy who tried to shoot you two. He was apparently facing away from the blast when Chris shot the tank. So…"

"His face wasn't burned up."

Donna nodded. "It'll just take a second. Only if you're okay with it. Chris told me to make sure you know you don't have to do this."

She swallowed the bile rising in her throat. "But he

thinks, you all think, that I know the man who…the rifleman?"

"We do."

"Why?"

"It's something you'd have to see to understand." She waited, then nodded again, smiling. "It was a lot to ask, after everything you've been through. Just wait here and I'll tell them you can't—"

"I'll do it." Julie hurried past her, walking at a brisk pace. For some unfathomable reason, Chris wanted her to look at a dead man. So that's what she was going to do. And if she didn't do it fast, before she had time to think, she knew she couldn't go through with it.

Donna rushed to catch up to her. Together they approached the two men. Julie kept her gaze trained on Chris. He was watching her like a hawk, looking as if he would grab her and pull her away if she showed any signs of faltering.

She stopped a few feet in front of him, sensing more than seeing the body on the ground at her feet.

"You don't have to do this," he said.

"I know. But you want me to?"

He slowly nodded. "I do."

She drew a shaky breath. "Okay. Then I will."

The man standing beside him—Max maybe?—gave them both a surprised look. She could see him in her peripheral vision, as if he was puzzled by their exchange. Was it unusual for a witness to trust a cop the way she did Chris? Maybe, probably. But she'd been through more trials and tribulations in the past twenty-four hours with him than she'd ever been with most of the people in her life. And every single time she needed him, he was there. She did trust him, completely. And that had her so scared she was shaking inside.

She closed her eyes, gathered her courage, then did what he'd asked.

She looked down at the body.

And then she knew why he'd asked her to come over here, hoping she could identify the man who'd most recently tried to kill her. Sadly, no, she didn't recognize him. Had, in fact, never seen him before in her life. Because if she had, she'd never have forgotten him.

He could have been her twin.

Chapter 15

Chris thanked the restaurant manager and closed the door to the private dining room. Several tables had been pulled together in the center of the room to accommodate Julie, the chief and the entire SWAT team minus Dillon—who was staying at the hospital with his wife.

Surprisingly, the chief was treating Chris just as if he was on active duty and had yet to gripe at him over spiriting Julie away from the station. Maybe the chief was giving him a break for surviving another close call. Or maybe he was rewarding Chris for getting Julie to really talk to them. Then again, it could just be that without Dillon the department was stretched too thin. Regardless of the reason, Chris was glad to be part of the team again.

A banquet of fried chicken, mashed potatoes, corn, lima beans and corn bread was laid out in front of them—the perfect Sunday lunch spread after a long morning at church. Or, in Chris and Julie's case, a morning spent dodging bullets and blowing up propane tanks.

He sat beside Julie, who seemed a bit stunned at the volume of food in front of them.

"Go on," Chris urged. "You haven't had anything to eat today."

She nodded and accepted a bowl of mashed potatoes from Donna, who was sitting on her other side.

Everyone was quiet as they ate, without the usual conversation or gossip they usually shared when all of them ended up at the same table—an event that was rare and usually enjoyed. But not today. Today food was just that—food, energy to get through whatever else was going to happen during this investigation.

Since Cooper's farm was a crime scene, it had been cordoned off and a dozen CSU techs and police officers were processing it for clues. Only five of those officers were Destiny police. The rest had been "borrowed" from the state police and neighboring counties, as often happened whenever there was a major crime scene.

Julie set a chicken leg on her plate and offered the platter to Chris. He murmured his thanks and put a breast and a thigh on his own plate before handing the platter across the table to the chief.

"So, the guy in the Charger got away?" Julie asked.

Randy winced beside the chief. "He got off a lucky shot and took out my left front tire. I overcorrected the resulting skid and slammed into a tree."

"I'm so sorry," Julie said. "You're okay?"

He nodded, looking pleased that she'd ask. "I'm fine.

My truck needed a new paint job. Now I get it for free, courtesy of the Destiny Police Department."

Thornton frowned his displeasure at his officer, but didn't deny that the department would pick up the tab.

Chris noted that Julie played with her food more than she ate. Not that he could blame her. His own usually healthy appetite—especially when it came to fried chicken—was nearly nonexistent. There were too many questions rolling around in his head. Plus the worry that something could happen to Julie. There was zero doubt now that more than one person was after her, trying to kill her. Whatever was going on was bigger than a soon to be ex-husband wanting to settle the score.

Several minutes later, Chief Thornton pushed back his plate and wiped his hands on his napkin. That seemed to be the signal that everyone had been waiting for. They all put their forks down.

"Before anyone asks," Julie said, "I've been racking my brain about the rifleman, like you all told me to do before we left Cooper's farm. I still don't know who he is…was."

"He sure had an uncanny resemblance to you," Chris said. "Just how sure are you that he wasn't a long-lost brother?"

She rolled her eyes. "If I had a brother, I'd know about it."

"Doppelganger," Randy said, with the solemnity of a sage oracle, as if he'd just figured out the secret to life.

Julie frowned. "Doppelganger?"

"Don't," Chris warned.

"Don't what?"

"Encourage him. He's got all kinds of crazy theories. We try not to get him started."

Randy pressed a hand against his shirt, feigning hurt even as he winked at Julie. "A doppelganger is an evil twin. They say everyone has one somewhere in the world. Today you met yours."

"Evil twin?" Julie asked.

Donna shook her head. "That's not what a doppelganger is. A doppelganger is a ghost, an apparition who's the spitting image of you. Obviously, if you'd met your doppelganger it would be a woman."

Randy crossed his arms over his chest. "Then how do you explain the gunman? He looked just like Mrs. Webb. But she insists she doesn't have any long-lost brothers. So what other explanation is there?"

Chris tossed his napkin on top of his plate. "Obviously, Julie is related to the gunman somehow. The CSU guys submitted his prints. Hopefully, we'll get a hit, and get it soon. In the meantime, we need to shake the Webb family tree and see who falls out. Julie, you can help by giving us some background on your family."

"I already told you about my sister, and what happened to my parents."

The pain in her voice had him hating himself for having to ask her even more questions. But worse would be standing at her graveside while they lowered her casket. To help, he briefed everyone on what she'd already told him.

Donna took a small notebook and pen from her purse. Like the others, she was still dressed in her Sunday best. But her dark blue dress was horribly wrinkled because of the body armor she'd worn earlier. She didn't seem to mind.

She made some notes and smiled at Julie. "Can you tell me your parents' names?"

Julie looked at Chris. "This is supposed to help you figure out the gunman's identity?"

"It's a starting place, victimology," Chris said. "In order to find out why your husband tried to kill you, and who else is after you, we need to know as much as we can about your history. That includes your family, your friends, your work—everything."

She let out a long-suffering sigh. "Okay. Fine. My mom was Beatrix. My father was Giles Linwood. They were both born and raised in London, England. But their parents didn't approve of them dating. Well, mostly my mom's parents didn't approve. Mom said they had some money and thought my dad was a gold digger. After my grandfather died, my grandmother—Elizabeth—took an even harder stance against my mom and dad dating. They ended up getting married anyway. Grandmother disowned my mom and she and my dad moved to America to start a new life.

"Disowned," Donna said. "Sounds old-fashioned."

Julie shrugged. "I don't know much about my grandmother, but old-fashioned covers it. She was big on loyalty and felt my mom had turned her back on the family by marrying my father."

"Did you ever meet her?" Chris asked.

"No. I've never heard from her or any of my parents' relatives. But my mother had a necklace that was given to her by my grandmother when Mom turned eighteen. She passed it on to my sister, Naomi, on her eighteenth birthday, saying it was a family tradition and that she must promise to always keep the necklace safe. When Naomi…when Naomi died, my mom told me to take the necklace, that it was mine now."

She shook her head. "That's all I have of my English

heritage, just a stupid necklace. Once my parents died, I had an estate sale, got rid of the furniture, clothes, things I figured someone else might need. I've never been much of a packrat. But I couldn't bear to let go of some things—pictures mostly, my mom's costume jewelry that she loved so much, Dad's baseball card collection. And the few things I had of Naomi's, including that necklace and her hairclips."

The earlier tortured look in her eyes faded as she smiled at the memory of her sister. "She had a fetish for the darn clips, snatched them up at flea markets and estate sales, the gaudier the better. If you pasted rhinestones or fake gems onto something to put in your hair, Naomi would drool over it. I'd forgotten about that. I put the box away for safe-keeping, but haven't looked at it even once since then. I think…looking at their things would make it too real that I'll never see my family again."

Chris was about to ask her more about her sister when the chief's phone rang. The chief apologized and stepped away from the table to take the call.

A few seconds later, Max's phone rang, too. Conversation stopped while both men took their calls. When they were done, Chris glanced back and forth between them.

"Well?" he asked. "Something about the investigation?"

The chief nodded. "Mine was. Kathy Nelson said she needs Mrs. Webb to return to Nashville in order to wrap up the loose ends of the criminal case that was pending against Mr. Webb. She's demanding that we escort her there right away." He arched a brow at Julie.

"I don't see why I need to be there. She already has

my statements about Alan breaking into our home in Nashville. What happened here doesn't change the case."

"I agree," the chief said. "Which is why I told her not to hold her breath, that you'd leave if and when you were ready."

Julie blinked, looking half-horrified that he'd talk to an ADA that way, and half-amused. "Um, thanks. I think."

Detective Max Remington leaned forward, resting his arms on the table at his seat on the end. "My call was about the case, too. The license plate check on the black Dodge Charger came through. The car is owned by a rental company. You'll never guess where it's based."

"Nashville," Chris said. "Do I get to guess who rented it?"

"You could, but I'd rather tell you. The car was rented by assistant district attorney Kathy Nelson."

Julie let out a gasp of surprise.

"She wasn't driving," the chief said. "The call I just took was from a landline in Nashville. I know because it was the ADA's receptionist who put the call through. And she told me Nelson was in court all morning, with another ADA, and they'd both just gotten back into the office. No way could she have done that and been driving through hay fields a few hours ago."

"Agreed," Chris said, still watching Max. "But I don't think the car was rented for her use. The Charger was rented for one of her assistants, wasn't it, Max?"

"Yep. The winning answer is Brian Henson. A second car, also black, this one a Chevy Camaro, was rented by Nelson for her other assistant, Jonathan Bolton."

"I don't remember seeing a Charger or a Camaro parked in the police when they were at the station," Chris said. "All I saw was Nelson's silver Mercedes. Why would she rent cars for her assistants—separate cars—but all three of them arrive together at the station?"

The chief stood and pulled out his phone again. "You don't have to say it. I'm calling Nelson back right now to ask about her assistants and her rental-car habits. This is getting really weird is all I have to say." He headed to the other side of the dining room.

"I don't understand," Julie said. "We're saying that Kathy's employee, Henson, tried to kill us this morning? And that because Kathy drove both of her administrative assistants to the police station for my interview, that she was—what—planning the attack and didn't want us to know what cars her men drove? That doesn't make any sense. She's an assistant district attorney. An old college friend. What would she have to gain by having me killed?"

"I'm not sure we're ready to make all of those leaps in logic, yet," Chris said. "We're just gathering facts. But if we do assume that Nelson is behind the attempt on your life this morning, then it makes sense to also assume that she could have been working with Alan and that together they may have orchestrated both times that he attacked you."

She pressed her hand against her throat. "I don't… I don't see how that's possible. She and Alan couldn't stand each other."

Chris leaned forward. "You sure about that? For all you know, Kathy and Alan may have been far more than friends in college and hid it from you. Maybe they already knew each other when you and her supposedly first met him."

Julie shook her head. "No. No, that can't be. I'm telling you, they really didn't get along in college. Besides, even if I were wrong—which I'm not—if they were interested in each other, all they had to do was date and leave me as the third wheel. We're the same age. We were all struggling college students, with nothing to gain or lose by becoming friends or hiding any attractions. What would be the point? If Kathy liked Alan, and vice versa, they'd have become an item instead of Alan and me." She spread her hands out in front of her. "On top of that, if Kathy liked Alan, it would have been in her best interest to let him know back then, not hide it and encourage me in my relationship with him, which is what she did."

"She encouraged you to date him?" Chris asked.

"Basically. I mean it wasn't like she pushed me toward him. But she seemed happy for me and made sure that I knew she didn't mind when I did essentially choose my boyfriend over spending time with her."

"You said it would have been in her best interest to date Alan," Chris continued. "Why?"

"Money, of course. He wasn't exactly flush in college, but he wasn't hurting either. Everyone knew he was the heir to Webb Enterprises, his father's import-export business, and that he was expected to take the reins of the company one day. Whoever ended up marrying Alan would have come into a lot of money. If this is about Kathy and Alan being some kind of partners, they would have become partners in college and gotten married. I had nothing to offer anyone. There was no financial benefit for Alan marrying me."

"I'm not so sure that's true," Max said from the end of the table, just as the chief resumed his seat.

The chief waved toward him. "I got some silly run-around answer from Nelson about her men wanting to explore the countryside, thus the rental of two cars. And she'd driven them to the station because they were all at the hotel together and it made sense to share a ride to Mrs. Webb's witness interview." He rolled his eyes.

"I'm still not buying it," the chief continued. "Especially since they didn't end up staying overnight at the hotel. Naturally, her response to my question about that was that they changed their minds after Julie left the interview. But unless the city of Nashville has money to burn in their budget, I don't see them reimbursing an ADA for renting her admin assistants cars." He waved at Max again. "Go on. You were about to say something else you found out?"

Max nodded. "Mrs. Webb, you mentioned your mother's family had some money. Any idea how much?"

Julie shook her head. "My mom didn't talk about her family very often. I got the impression they lived comfortably, but not anything crazy. It's not like they were millionaires, or however many pounds sterling it takes to make someone rich." She smiled, but Max remained stoic.

"You didn't mention your mother's maiden name earlier," Max said.

"Abbott, why?"

He nodded, as if that was what he'd expected. "Your grandmother was Elizabeth Victoria Abbott, correct?" Max asked.

Julie frowned. "Yes, that's right. Is there a point here somewhere?"

"Your grandmother's late husband was Edward. They were from old money and built that inheritance into an extremely lucrative corporation they simply named Victoria and Edward. Your grandfather died many years ago. But your grandmother is still alive and thriving. She's the CEO. And you're right that she's not worth millions. Her net worth is in the billions. About two-point-six billion, to be exact."

The room went silent.

Julie's mouth dropped open.

"There's one other piece of information I got from that call," Max said, shifting his glance to Chris and then the chief. "The fingerprint search on our dead rifleman got a match based on a passport-database search." He looked back at Julie. "His name was Harry Abbott."

Chapter 16

Julie yanked the comb through her wet hair, wincing when it caught on a tangle. She freed the comb and tossed it into the duffel bag that Donna had gotten for her from the rental house. The chief had been nice enough to let Julie take a shower in the bathroom attached to his office here at the police station. This luxury had surprised her and elicited a few snickers from the SWAT team.

Julie braced her hands on the countertop and stared into the mirror above the sink, thinking about what she'd learned during lunch. Her mom had painted Julie's grandmother as being ancient, in poor health. Julie had always assumed the woman had passed away by now. But now she knew her grandmother was alive and well, and at the helm of a multibillion-pound enterprise.

Not that it made any difference. Julie would have

loved to have a grandmother, regardless of her grandmother's financial situation. She longed for someone to help fill the holes in her heart left by the loss of her family. But obviously that sentiment wasn't returned. If Elizabeth Abbott had really loved her only daughter, she'd have done something over the years to reach out to her. And she'd have discovered she had two granddaughters to love, as well. But she never had. Which told Julie that her mother was right all along, and that she'd made the right choice in fleeing across the pond when she was just a girl herself.

Julie shoved her hair back from her eyes, straightened the bathroom, then grabbed the duffel and headed into the chief's office. She stopped short when she saw Chris writing on a whiteboard hanging on the wall opposite the desk.

He turned and smiled a greeting. Then his smile died as he looked at her. "Julie? What's wrong?"

She glanced at the closed door, relieved that no one else was in the office right now. She sat in one of the guest chairs in front of the chief's desk.

"I'm not normally a whiner. But I'm beginning to seriously dislike my grandmother even though I've never met her. I can't get past the fact that she's as rich as Midas but could never forgive her daughter and provide the help that Naomi needed, the help my parents could never afford. If she had, maybe Naomi would still be alive."

Chris crossed the room and crouched in front of her chair, taking her hands in his. "Are you saying your grandmother contacted your mother? That she knew she had granddaughters, and didn't do anything to intercede when your sister got sick?"

She clung to his hands, to the strength and support he offered, grateful to have one person she felt comfortable with, one person she could lean on right now.

"No. But I just can't see my loving, wonderful mother not reaching out to *her* mother to save her dying child. If there was anything humanly possible that could be done to save Naomi, my mom would have done it. So I have to believe that she did contact my grandmother, told her the situation and asked for her help."

Julie shook her head, tears tracking down her cheeks. "No help came. My grandmother chose her feud over trying to save the life of her eldest granddaughter. How can I ever forgive that?"

He pulled her into his arms and held her tight. Embarrassed to be crying on him again, she tried to think of something else—anything else—to stop her tears. But blanking all her troubles from her mind left far too much room to think about how good his arms felt around her.

The last time she and her husband had held each other like this had been too long ago to remember. That had to be why she felt so drawn to this man. She was lonely, starved for affection, desperate for someone who seemed to care what happened to her. But, really, who wouldn't be drawn to him?

His strong arms felt wonderful around her. His chest was the perfect pillow for her cheek. And he smelled so darn good. But of course there was so much more to him than the physical. He was brave, protective, loyal— the qualities that meant the most to Julie, probably because those were the qualities of a tight-knit family. And family meant everything to her. Which was why losing hers had been so devastating.

For just a moment, she allowed herself the fantasy of pretending that Chris was her family, that he was hers to hold and to keep and treasure. It was a delightful fantasy, and one that would be over far too soon. Because even if he felt the same draw, the same attraction—heart, soul and mind—to her that she felt to him, what kind of a future could there ever be for a relationship between so very different people?

She'd seen how close he was to his SWAT team, how they acted like their own little family. He could never give up something like that, give up the friends he was loyal to and cared about. And she wouldn't want him to. But she couldn't see herself in a small town like this for the rest of her life. Her work meant far too much to her, and it relied on charity, the kinds of donations she could only get by working in a large city with affluent pools of people to draw upon—a city like Nashville. Moving here, to Destiny, permanently, would mean giving up on finding cures that would help so many families like hers. That was something she just couldn't do.

Inhaling deeply, she selfishly enjoyed another tantalizing breath warmed by Chris's skin, perfumed by his masculine scent. Then she pushed herself back to sitting, forcing him to drop his arms.

He studied her intently, his dark eyes boring into hers. "You do know that I'm going to protect you, right? You seem…scared, or maybe worried."

Unable to stop herself, she caressed his face. Her heart nearly stopped when he rubbed his cheek against her hand. Oh, how she wished her life were different, that she had met this man in another place, another time.

He smiled, a warm, gentle smile she felt all the way to her toes.

"Everything's going to be okay, Julie," he said. "We'll figure this out. Together."

"Thank you," she whispered. Her gaze dropped to his lips, and she automatically leaned toward him. Her hands went to his shirt, smoothing the fabric.

A shudder went through him and she looked up. The open hunger on his face made her breath catch. And then he was leaning toward her, slowly, giving her every chance to stop him, to pull away, to say no.

She didn't want to say no.

She wanted his lips on hers, his arms around her, wanted to feel her breasts crushing against the hard planes of his chest. She wanted this. She wanted him, needed him.

His breath warmed her as he kissed first one cheek, then the other, before lowering his lips to hers.

Heaven. She'd died and gone to heaven, and it was far better than she'd ever thought it could be. His mouth moved against hers, softly, gently, a warm caress that made her feel cherished, wanted, needed, the way that she needed him. The kiss was so beautiful it made her want to cry all over again, this time with joy. And then the kiss changed.

Gone was the gentle lover. The hunger she'd seen on his face, in his eyes, she now felt in his touch, in the way his arms crushed her against him, the way his lips slanted across hers. His tongue swept inside her mouth, a hot, wild mating, urgent and demanding. Her pulse rushed in her ears, her heart beating against her ribs as she slid her arms up around his neck.

He groaned deep in his throat and lifted her out of the chair, turning with her in his arms and never taking his lips from hers. He pressed her back against the whiteboard. She lifted her legs, wrapping them around his waist. The kiss was hot, ravenous, full of need and longing for more, so much more.

She pulled her arms down to his shirt and began working the top button, then the next. When she reached the third, she slid her hands inside his shirt, reveling in the feel of his hot skin against hers. And just like that, they both broke the kiss, staring in shock at each other.

"Oh, my," she breathed. "I think I was about to tear your clothes off."

"I was about to help." He chuckled and pressed his forehead against hers. He drew a ragged breath before pulling back and smiling down at her. "Where did that come from?"

She shook her head. "I have no idea. But it probably happens to you all the time."

His eyes widened. "Why would you say that?"

She slid her arms up behind his neck, then realized what she was doing and forced them down. He eased back and helped her stand, keeping his hands on her shoulders as if she needed steadying—which she definitely did.

"Why did you say it happens all the time to me?" he repeated.

She rolled her eyes and waved toward the three undone buttons on his shirt. "Because of…that. You're gorgeous. And charming. And smart. And a dozen other things. Women probably throw themselves at you so much you have to fight them off."

Her cheeks grew hot under his incredulous stare. "What?" she demanded, feeling extremely self-conscious.

"Have you seen yourself in a mirror lately, Julie? You

can't tell me that you didn't notice how Max and the others kept looking at you during lunch. You're beautiful."

It was her turn to stare at him with an incredulous expression. "Now that I think about it, I remember seeing you bump your head after the propane tank exploded. Isn't that right? Now it all makes sense."

He laughed and buttoned up his shirt, much to her sorrow. And then she laughed, too, because this was the lightest she'd felt in months. Which made no sense at all considering that someone was trying to kill her.

That thought helped sober her up and, unfortunately, killed the good mood Chris had managed to put her in. Her gaze fell to the duffel bag, forgotten on the floor, and just like that all of the horrible things that had been happening since that night that Alan had broken into their Nashville home flooded back.

A gentle touch beneath her chin had her looking up into Chris's eyes. He gave her a sad smile. "You're back to worrying again, I see. I wish there was something that I could do to convince you it's all going to work out."

"Me, too." She pointed at the whiteboard. "What is all of that?"

He picked up a pen and piece of paper from on top of the desk and held them out to her. "I'll tell you in a minute. First, though. I'd like your written permission to search your home in Nashville and to open the safe. The chief will notarize the document. We'll need the house keys. And we'll use your written permission to get a locksmith to open the safe."

She took the paper, skimmed the two paragraphs of legalize. "How did you know the address?" She set the paper on the desk to sign it, then grabbed her purse from another corner of the desk.

"The night the chief interviewed you, the paperwork you filled out gave your basic info, including addresses. You don't remember?"

She worked the required key off her key ring as she shook her head. "Not really. Everything that night is kind of a blur at this point. And I'd prefer to keep it that way."

She set the house key on top of the form she'd signed and tossed the rest of her keys into her purse. "Do I need to sign anything else?"

"Not at the moment. I'll get one of our guys working on this right away." He picked up the key and paper and strode out of the office.

Julie crossed to the whiteboard, trying to make sense of what Chris had written on it. There were several columns, in varying colors, with bullets beneath each column.

"I'm a list maker," he announced as he came back into the office and shut the door. "If I can make a list out of something, it organizes my thoughts, helps me form a big picture and then put all the pieces together."

She smiled. "I'm a list maker, too. What does all of this mean?"

He walked her through it, and she noted how he'd used different colored markers for different categories. Suspects were written in green.

Kathy Nelson.
Brian Henson.
Jonathan Bolton.

Alan Webb—Deceased.
Harry Abbott—Deceased.

She rubbed her hands up and down her arms. "I thought Kathy had an alibi for when we were at Cooper's farm?"

"She does. But if she put out the hit, she's just as guilty. Even without evidence, that seems like the simplest explanation for everything. And usually the most straightforward explanation is the right one. I also don't believe in coincidences. When looking at this as a whole, Kathy and Alan working together against you is the basic premise that makes the most sense. But we have to figure out what they were after, which leads me to my next column."

He wrote on the board—Motive. And beneath that he created another list.

Love.
Money.
Revenge.
Hatred.
Hide something.

He turned around. "Every case I've ever worked fell into one of these categories, often more than one. At the heart of every murder, one of these overrides all else and drives the killer. Looking at Alan first, we know that he wanted to kill you. But it seems like he was also after something else—perhaps this key that you mentioned. So which of the motivations seems to make sense as to why he did what he did?"

She cocked her head, studying the list, thinking

about how her relationship with Alan had started, how it had been so warm and loving in college, and then how it had changed shortly after they got married. She grew still, trying to figure out what, if anything, that might mean.

"What is it?" Chris asked. "You've thought of something."

"You said you don't believe in coincidences. And yet Alan just happened to appear the moment when I needed him the most. Just a few months after I lost my family, and my support system, when I was at rock bottom, he was there. Strong, understanding, helping me work through my grief. Given everything else, that just feels…wrong."

Chris slowly lowered the dry-erase marker that he was holding. "Tell me how your family died again. Don't leave anything out."

She frowned. "I don't see how that—"

"Humor me."

She shrugged. "Okay. Naomi got sick—"

"And the doctors couldn't figure out what was wrong with her."

"Right."

"Why not?"

"Excuse me?"

He set the marker onto the ledge. "Doctors used to have to rely on their memories, or look up symptoms in some thick medical tome to try to figure out what illness or disease matched them. Nowadays, they can plug symptoms into any number of online tools and get a list of possible causes. Doesn't it seem strange that they couldn't do that in your sister's case?"

She shook her head, uncomfortable with where the

conversation seemed to be heading. "It's not strange. That's the thing about orphan diseases. They don't come up in internet searches if they're so rare that no one has input any information about them into a computer. The doctors said she must have had an orphan disease."

"But they couldn't give it a name?"

"No, they couldn't."

"Again, why not?"

She spread her hands in a helpless gesture. "I suppose because her symptoms kept changing. And each symptom came on so suddenly. Really, by the time my parents realized how seriously ill she was, and that she wasn't getting better, she only had a few weeks left. She died four months after the first day she got sick. But my parents had only started hounding the doctors about six or eight weeks before that. I think that's why it hit them so hard. They felt guilty for not seeking help sooner."

"I can totally see that, a parent thinking their child had a cold or virus, expecting it to go away on its own. It would be particularly difficult to realize how bad it was if the symptoms changed."

"Exactly. That's why my dad spiraled into a deep depression after her death. He felt he should have done more." She twisted her hands together in her lap. "We all felt we should have done more."

She braced herself for his sympathy, not wanting him to feel sorry for her. But, as if sensing how she felt, he gave her one quick empathetic look before grabbing a dry-erase pen and moving to the right side of the board. He wrote "Naomi" and "Symptoms" on top of a new column.

"Tell me her symptoms, in the exact order in which they appeared, and tell me how long they lasted."

"I don't understand. Why do you want me to relive that pain again?"

His jaw tightened. "I don't want to hurt you, Julie. But more importantly, I want to save your life. If that means I have to cause you a little pain to do it, then I will."

Had she really thought of this man as her fantasy-hero a few minutes ago? Her perfect man? Because right now, she just wanted to walk out of this office and turn her back on the wounds he was opening inside her.

"Julie, you told me that you trust me. Was that a lie?"

His gentle, soothing voice wrapped around her heart like velvet. "No," she finally said. "That wasn't a lie. I do trust you."

"Then work with me on this. Tell me Naomi's symptoms. What was the first thing you or your parents noticed?"

She worked with him for over half an hour on the list. Each time she thought they were done, he'd ask another question, force her to delve deeper into her memory, try to associate each appearance or disappearance of a symptom with some event in her life to help her make sure she had it right.

Finally, he stepped back from the board, taking it all in. He seemed deep in thought. And when he turned around, Julie could have sworn she saw a flash of anger in his eyes. But the emotion was quickly masked with one of his kind, gentle smiles. He took her hands in his and led her to the door.

He pulled it open, and she looked up at him in confusion. "You want me to leave?"

He waved at Donna, who was sitting at one of the

desks, typing on her computer. She hurried over, raising a brow in question.

"Donna, can you show Julie the kitchenette and get her something to drink? I need to make a phone call."

Donna smiled and put an arm around Julie's shoulders. "No problem. Come on, sweetie. Calories don't count during murder investigations. And thanks to Ashley, Dillon's wife, we've always got all kinds of goodies over here. I'll pull a batch of her banana nut muffins out of the freezer and heat them up. They're amazing."

She led Julie to what Chris had called a kitchenette but that was really just a long counter against the wall to the right of the chief's office door and to the left of the main door into the station. It was loaded with cookies and all kinds of other baked goods, with a coffeemaker on one end and both a small refrigerator and a freezer underneath the counter on the other.

"Soda, coffee or water?" Donna asked. "Pick your poison."

"Um, soda, I guess. Something with a lot of caffeine. Thanks."

"You got it." Donna opened the refrigerator.

Julie looked toward the chief's office, but Chris had already closed the door.

"Sorry to bug you again, Dillon. But this is really important," Chris said into the phone as he stared at the white board. Just thinking about what he now believed to be true had him wanting to go to the morgue and kill Alan Webb all over again

"Not a problem," Dillon whispered. "Give me a second."

Chris heard the sound of muted footsteps, as if Dillon was trying not to make any noise. A moment later, a click. "Okay. I'm out of Ashley's room. This is the first real sleep she's had since we got here and I didn't want to disturb her."

"Does that mean what I think it means?"

"We think this scary episode is over now, yes. She hasn't had any contractions in quite a while. Go ahead. Tell me what you've got."

"I'm asking you to go way back to your college days, to all those fancy medical classes you took when you wanted to be a large-animal vet."

"I'll pay you back for calling me old the next time I see you, especially since we're the same age. What classes specifically are you talking about?"

"Did you take any botany classes?"

"Of course. I needed to know what kinds of plants were poisonous and recognize the symptoms in case of accidental ingestion by an animal. Why?"

"That's what I figured. I've got a list of symptoms for you, and then I want you to tell me what comes to mind."

There was a long pause before Dillon spoke. "Shouldn't you be calling an actual botanist or doctor about this?"

"I will, or I'll have one of the guys follow up. But I figured this would be faster and you could at least tell me if what I'm thinking is crazy."

"All right. I've got my pen and notebook out. Go."

It didn't take long. The anger that had been building inside Chris was now ready to explode.

"What was this Alan Webb guy's major in college?" Dillon asked.

"Botany."

"You know what you need to do."

"Yeah. I need to exhume Naomi's body."

Chapter 17

Julie was backed into a corner, literally—the one in the chief's office between the window and the door to the bathroom. It was the farthest away she could get from everyone else in the office, because they'd all lost their ever-loving minds.

She shook her head, raking the chief, Max and Chris with her glare. She'd have glared at the very nice Donna, too, and even Randy or Colby, except that they were in the squad room handling other cases that had come in.

"I won't do it," she repeated. "Naomi's gone. Digging up her body won't change that." She looked at Chris. "I can't believe you would ask me to do this."

"Did you understand what I explained about the plants? How someone can extract solanine, glycoalkaloids, arsenic—"

"Oh, I understand just fine. What you're saying is

your police buddy Dillon studied plants in vet school, even though he never became a vet. And based on a short phone call and a list of symptoms I may very well remember wrong you two have come up with a crazy theory that my botany-major husband poisoned my sister. You think he switched up the plants he used so he could confuse the doctors. One set of symptoms would go away, a new set would begin, all so he could make it look like a natural death when there wasn't anything natural about it at all. Did I get that right, Chris? Did I explain your theory correctly?"

Tears, again the blasted tears, were running down her face. But this time they weren't tears of grief or fear. They were tears of anger.

"Did I get it right?" she demanded.

Chris slowly nodded. "Except for the part about this all being a crazy theory. I had Max confirm everything by calling a real botanist. We're not wrong about any of this, Julie. The botanist told us exactly how he could reproduce the same symptoms with plants that are easily available."

"Good for you. You get a gold star. Now, if you're through trying to rip my heart out, I'm leaving." She shoved away from the wall and strode toward the door.

Chris glanced at his boss, then moved in front of Julie, blocking her way.

"Move," she said.

"Not until you hear us out."

"I've heard all I want to hear and then some. I don't want to hear any more." She swiped at the tears. Dang it. Why couldn't she stop crying?

"Julie, please. We need to talk through this. I believe Alan poisoned your sister. If we can exhume—"

"No. I told you, no. I'm not changing my mind. And what you're saying doesn't make sense anyway. Alan never even met my sister. I didn't meet him until two months after my parents died, three months after Naomi died."

"I know." His voice was ridiculously calm. He motioned to Max. "Do you have that printout handy?"

Max pulled a sheet of paper out of his suit jacket pocket and handed it to Chris.

Julie tried to grab the doorknob, but Chris planted a foot to his left, again blocking her. He opened the paper and started to read what amounted to a short bio about Alan.

Julie shook her head, her hands fisted at her sides. "Some investigators you people are. You've got his birthdate wrong. He wasn't two years older than me. He and I were the same age."

"Max," Chris said in that infuriatingly calm, soothing voice. "Where did you get Alan's birthdate?"

A look of sympathy crossed Max's face as he answered. "Mrs. Webb, I know your husband told you he was your age. But it was a ruse so he could enroll in the same classes as you without raising red flags. Even more damning, the classes he took at your college were all audited, meaning they weren't graded and didn't apply toward a degree. That's because he'd already graduated. He already had his degree from another school. That's the real reason he told you he was dropping out. He couldn't pretend to be getting a degree when you graduated. Dropping out was how he covered up that he was never a degree-seeking student at your school."

She shook her head. "No." But her voice was barely above a whisper. Panic was closing her throat.

"In addition to his school records, which had his correct birthdate, I pulled his birth certificate and cross-referenced his information in the social-security database. And if that's still not enough proof, I had a librarian pull a copy of his high-school yearbook. He graduated high school two years before you did."

He pulled another piece of paper from his jacket and handed it to Chris. "Even more importantly, I tracked down one of your sister's friends from college. That's her written statement in response to my questions. I texted her a picture of Alan off the internet from when he attended a ribbon-cutting ceremony at one of the offices for his father's company."

Chris held the paper up for Julie to see. She refused to look at it.

"The friend remembered Alan, said he went to a lot of the same bars that she and Naomi went to during Naomi's senior year, just two months before she got sick. Naomi couldn't stand Alan. He kept hitting on her and wouldn't take no for an answer. A month after she first met him, she filed a complaint against him with the local police."

"But she never…she never told me about him," Julie whispered.

He shrugged. "Maybe she didn't want to worry her family and figured filing the police report would end the problem."

With that, Max pulled another piece of paper out and handed it to Chris.

"It's the arrest report," Chris said.

The room went silent as they all waited. She stared at

Max and slowly took the paper from Chris. The paper rattled because her hands were shaking so much. It was a brief report, printed on the police department's letterhead, with details like the date and the name of the officer who'd taken the statement, a statement signed by Naomi Linwood, their father's last name, Julie's maiden name.

There, at the end of the report, highlighted in yellow, was the name of the man who'd been essentially stalking Julie's sister—Alan Blackwood Webb. Exactly one month after the complaint was issued, Naomi called their mother to tell her she couldn't come home for a planned family dinner because she had an upset stomach and had thrown up three times. Four months later, Naomi was dead. And when Julie met Alan Blackwood Webb three months after that, he'd told her how sorry he was that he'd never had the pleasure of meeting her sister or her parents.

Julie lowered the piece of paper. A low buzz started in her ears.

"My father," she said, her throat so tight she could hardly talk, "killed himself, shot himself, shortly after Naomi…died. The funny thing is, he was always so vocal against guns. He didn't even own one. But no one questioned that. We were all too grief stricken. The police assumed he'd bought it off the street. There really wasn't much of an investigation."

"Julie." Chris reached for her, but she shoved his hand away.

"Now, my mother," she continued, "was devastated when my daddy died. She'd handled Naomi's death like a soldier. But Daddy—my mom just couldn't take losing him. Couldn't sleep. Got a prescription for sleep-

ing pills. They say she drank down the whole bottle of
pills with a glass of wine."

She choked on the last word, had to cough to clear
her throat. "Most people would assume the woman in
a household is the wine drinker, and that the beer in
the refrigerator is for the man of the house. But my
mama…" Julie shook her head. "My mama was the beer
drinker. I always thought it was odd that she chose to
end her life drinking something she didn't even like."

She looked up at Chris through a wall of tears she
could no longer stop. "He killed them. All of them. And
I never even asked any questions. I accepted their deaths
like everyone else. And then I married their killer."

The room began to spin around her. The buzzing got
louder and louder until it was all she could hear.

Until she couldn't.

Chris swore and caught Julie's crumpled form in
his arms.

"She's passed out. Get Dr. Brookes," the chief ordered, waving at Max.

"No," Chris said, settling her higher against his
chest. "She doesn't need a doctor poking at her. She
needs rest, and peace and quiet. Everything about her
life has come into question and she needs time to process it. Max, shove her purse into that duffel and take
it out to my truck, will you?"

"You got it." Max hurried to do what he'd asked,
leaving the office door open behind him.

Chris followed him out.

"Hold it," the chief ordered behind him. "You can't
just walk out of here with the witness. Again."

Chris ignored the surprised look on everyone's face

as he strode through the squad room. Max waited at the door, holding it open.

The chief stubbornly followed Chris into the parking lot and rushed to get in front of him when Chris stopped at his truck.

"Detective Downing, I'm ordering you to stand down. Take Mrs. Webb back into the station."

"Max, mind getting the door, please?" Chris asked.

Max seemed to be struggling to hide his grin as he held the passenger door open.

Chris settled Julie inside and fastened her seat belt before shutting the door.

"Detective," the chief barked, his face turning red.

Chris stepped around him and climbed into the driver's seat.

The chief stood in the open doorway. "If you do this, you're as good as resigning."

Chris hesitated and glanced at Julie's tear-streaked face. Somehow, in a ridiculously short amount of time, he'd gone from suspecting her of being a murderess to respecting and admiring her more than any woman he'd ever met. He'd seen her fight when others would have given up. And now, without meaning to, he'd finally ground her down to the point that she'd shut down just to survive. Taking her to a doctor or leaving her at the station to be confronted with the facts and interviewed yet again wasn't the way to heal her, to make her better. She needed to get away from the trauma she faced at every turn. And he was going to make sure she got exactly what she needed and deserved.

He turned back toward the chief. "Move."

The chief's face turned so red it looked as if he might have a stroke. Instead of moving out of the way, he called Chris every curse word that Chris had ever heard. And then he reached for his gun.

Max rushed forward. "Hey, hey, chief. Let's not get carried away."

"Shut up, Officer Remington." The chief glared at Max before looking back at Chris. "Here, take it. Yours is still locked up in evidence." He reached in his back pocket and took out a magazine, then slapped that in Chris's palm, along with the gun.

"Chief?" Chris wasn't sure what to say. And he didn't bother telling his boss he had other guns in the truck. He had a feeling that wouldn't go over well in the chief's current mood.

"That's all the ammo I got with me," the chief continued. "It's enough to keep the rattlers and bears away if you're heading up into the mountains, which is what I'd do in your situation. But if you run into any other kind of trouble, you call me. Hell, you call anyway. I want regular reports until we get all of this sorted out. You hear me, son?"

Chris was so surprised by the chief's gesture that he didn't have the heart to tell him that in addition to the weapons in his truck, he'd had Donna and Max both load up the duffel with plenty of ammo along with the clothing they'd gotten from Julie's and Chris's houses. At the time he'd assumed they'd end up in a hotel, perhaps one town over. But, as hot as this case was getting, the mountains sounded like a far better plan.

"Yes, sir," he finally said. "Thank you, Chief."

"For what? When the ADA calls asking where Mrs. Webb is, I don't know nothing. You can't thank me if I didn't do anything. You got me?"

"Yes, sir. I got you." He glanced at Max. "Keep working those angles we talked about. I'll call you later."

Max grinned. "You and Dillon always were the favorites. I'd be out on my ass if I pulled a stunt like this."

"You may still be if you don't get back in that station and follow up on those leads." The chief glared at both of them before whirling around and stalking back toward the front doors.

"Stay off the main roads as much as possible when you head out of here," Max warned. "I heard Alan Webb's family is hot over his death and might pay us a visit soon."

"When did you hear that?"

"A few minutes ago. One of my contacts warned me."

"You sure have a lot of contacts. Maybe we need to share some of them sometime."

"Nope. They're all mine." He gave Chris a jaunty salute and closed the door.

Chris checked Julie once more, then backed out of the space and took off down the road toward one of the lower peaks in the Smoky mountain range. There was a hunting cabin he and Dillon used up there during deer season. It was the perfect spot to let Julie process everything. And it also had a satellite dish, which meant that Chris could continue helping with the investigation, plus keep a tab on the efforts to locate the driver of that Charger, Brian Henson.

Chapter 18

Julie rolled over in the soft bed, sighing at the fresh, clean smell of the sheets. The bed was ridiculously comfortable. The pillows fluffy, down filled. Wait, her down-filled pillows were still in boxes. Weren't they?

She gasped and bolted upright in bed. Clutching the covers to her chest, she scanned the room. A lamp was on beside the bed, casting a soft yellow glow. The walls were polished, a honey gold, and the floor beside the bed was knotty pine. Other than the lamp, the night-stand it sat on and the bed, there was nothing else. Not even a chest or dresser. None of it looked familiar. So where was she? And how had she gotten here?

"Don't panic. You're safe."

She let out a squeak of surprise, then flushed at the embarrassing sound when she recognized Chris standing in the doorway.

"Are we back at Harmony Haven?" she asked. "I don't recognize the bedroom."

"I wanted you to have some rest, some peace and quiet. So I drove us to a cabin in the mountains."

He waved his hand to encompass the room. "The rest of the place is a bit more modern, not quite this rustic. But this is the only bedroom on the first floor and I wanted you close by so I'd hear you if you woke up in a panic. You were pretty much out of it. I wasn't sure how much you'd remember of the drive up here."

She didn't remember any of it.

She blew out a long breath and shoved her hair back. A quick look down confirmed that she was still dressed in the white blouse and khaki pants that she'd been in after her shower in Chief Thornton's office. Chris must have taken her here after leaving the police station. So why couldn't she remember any of that?

All of the memories of the last confrontation in the chief's office suddenly flooded back. She squeezed her eyes shut, fighting down the panic she'd felt earlier.

He killed them.

Alan, her husband, had killed her family.

And then he'd built a life—with her.

"It gets better."

Her eyes flew open. He'd stepped beside the bed, still dressed in the jeans and casual shirt he'd changed into after his shower. The words he'd just said sat like stones in her stomach.

"What do you mean, it gets better? Your wife murdered your family, too?"

He winced, making her regret her sarcasm. She drew a deep breath, trying to calm down.

"Not exactly," he said. "I've never been married. I

do know what it's like to lose someone you love. But what you're going through right now is way worse than anything I've been through. I shouldn't have said that. Sorry, I really am."

He turned as if to leave.

"No, wait. Please."

He gave her a questioning look.

She shifted in the bed, making room beside her. "Tell me about whoever you loved, and lost. Maybe…maybe it will help. Both of us."

He slowly sat down, facing her. "I've never talked about it with anyone else."

"Never?"

"No. I couldn't. I was too busy trying to be there for my best friend, to help him face his own grief. Announcing that the love of my life had just been killed in a car accident—when I'd never even told him about her—wouldn't have helped him. So I kept it inside. As the years went by, it got easier to just never talk about it."

"Your best friend? Isn't Dillon your best friend?"

"Yes."

"Then his grief—it was for the woman he named his farm after, his sister?"

"One and the same."

"That's the woman you loved and lost?"

He chuckled. "I loved Harmony, but not romantically. She was still a kid when she died, six years younger than Dillon and me." His smile faded. "But, yes, Harmony died back home, in Destiny, when Dillon and I were both away at college—separate colleges. The woman I loved, Sherry, was killed a week before Harmony. I stayed for Sherry's funeral, and to pull myself together enough to come home and tell my family and friends about her. Only, once I got here, I found out about Harmony. And Dillon was already home, and devastated."

He shook his head. "If I'd told him my own sorry tale he'd have tried to be there for me. It wouldn't have been right. I'd only been in love with Sherry for a few months. Dillon had lost his baby sister, a whole lifetime of memories. It wasn't the same."

Her heart ached for the loss Chris had suffered and for how he'd lived with it all of these years, keeping it inside. She reached for his hand and clasped it in both of hers.

"I'm so sorry, Chris. You shouldn't have had to bear that pain alone."

Slowly, ever so slowly, he leaned in toward her and placed the softest, sweetest kiss against her lips before pulling back.

"And you shouldn't have to bear your pain alone. That's why I brought you here, Julie. You've lost so much. Suffered an enormous amount of trauma, found out devastating secrets, all in a very short amount of time. I want you to know that you're safe here and I won't badger you with any more questions. We'll stay on the mountain until you're ready to come down. And in the meantime, my teammates will figure the rest of it out. We…they…will find out who's after you. And they'll stop him. I can't take away the pain you feel about what we believe happened to your family. But I can take away some of the stress, or at least try. Do you need anything? Are you hungry?"

"What I need right now is to feel normal. I don't want to talk about the case or my past or any of this. Just…

talk to me, for a few minutes. About something, any-thing, other than the investigation."

He cocked his head, a half smile playing around his lips. "Where did you grow up? Nashville?"

She nodded.

"Ever been to the Smoky Mountains before?"

"Hasn't everybody? I've ridden on the three-story go-kart tracks in Pigeon Forge, seen Dolly Parton per-form in Dollywood, gone to the stores in downtown Gatlinburg."

He grinned. "Typical tourist. You think you've seen everything, when you haven't seen anything." He stood. "Come on."

She flipped the covers back and took his hand.

He tugged her through an archway that she had as-sumed led to a closet. Then he unlocked and opened a door at the end. She could see blue sky and the dark green leaves of towering trees beyond.

"Wait, my shoes—"

"You don't need them."

"Easy for you to say when you're wearing shoes."

He pulled her through the doorway onto a balcony. She barely noticed the door closing behind them. Her mouth dropped open as she stared at the incredible beauty that stretched as far as she could see. Tall green pine and oak trees framed the vista to the left and the right, but directly below them the mountain steeply dropped away. A deep green valley stretched out below, and beyond that, going on for miles and miles were the blue-gray silhouettes of the Great Smoky Mountains. Little puffs of white mist rose in dozens of places, as if someone was making smoke signals. All of it combined to create a soft, beautiful haze of color and "smoke."

It was as if an artist had painted the mountains, then softened everything with a light color wash.

"It's beautiful," she said. "I can't believe I've never come up into the mountains before, not like this."

"The best places in the Smokies are the ones the tourists don't know about, the little turnoffs that lead deep into the forest. There are hundreds of waterfalls all through the mountains, pristine, looking as if no one has touched them or even seen them for thousands of years. It's all unspoiled beauty. Paradise."

He leaned past her, pointing down toward the valley below. "Look," he whispered, "to the right, just coming out of the tree line."

She watched in awe as a group of three deer emerged from the forest, a doe with two fawns. The mother sniffed the air, her large ears flicking back and forth as she scanned for signs of danger. Her young pranced around her on wobbly legs, oblivious to how hard their mother worked to keep them safe. A yellow butterfly rose and dipped around them, much to the delight of the fawns, who scampered after it.

"They're so…innocent…and happy. They're gorgeous," she said, keeping her voice low, not sure if it would carry down to the deer and scare them away.

He gave her a nod of approval. They stood beside each other until the deer disappeared, until the sun began to sink behind the mountains. Tiny little lights blinked on and off down in the valley, close to the tree line.

She laughed with delight. "Fireflies. I haven't seen those since I was a little girl."

A half smile played around his mouth. "They've always been here. You just have to know where to look."

"You grew up here?" She waved her hand to encompass the incredible vista surrounding them. "With all of this?"

He nodded. "Tennessee, the real Tennessee, the one the tourists never stop long enough to appreciate, is heaven on earth. I can't imagine any place more beautiful. I left for a few years to go to college, see a bit of the world. But my heart was always here. No matter where I go, I'll always come back to Destiny."

"You haven't mentioned a family." As soon as she said it, she worried that she might have stumbled into bad territory, that he might have memories in his past he'd like to forget, like she did. But the smile on his face told her otherwise. Family wasn't a bad memory for him. The love shining out of his eyes told her that, even without the smile.

"I reckon I'm related to half the people on this mountain," he teased. "I can't go anywhere without running into a second or third cousin, twice removed. And that's on top of my parents and three brothers. At church the Downings take up three pews. And we usually get together a couple of times a month at someone's house—potluck, everyone brings a dish. We roast marshmallows over an outdoor fire pit, tell ghost stories, swap lies about who caught the biggest fish last."

His smile faded as he looked at her. "I'm sorry. I shouldn't have gushed like that."

She shook her head. "Don't apologize. I asked. And I love hearing about your family, about your life out here. It sounds…wonderful. Tell me more."

The moon was high in the sky and the stars burning bright by the time they retreated inside, driven in by the no-see-ums, gnats and other flying bugs that descended onto the balcony, attracted by their presence.

Chris stopped beside her bed and gave her a soft kiss on her forehead. "You have to be starving by now. Are you a carnivore or one of those vegan people?" He shuddered, as if not eating meat was a fate worse than death.

"I can eat a steak with the best of them," she reassured him. "But I'm not hungry just yet. I think I'll just lie down a little bit longer, if that's okay."

"Of course. I'll be in the next room, just a knock on the wall away."

He started to turn away, but she tugged his hand, keeping him there. His brows raised in question.

She stood on her tiptoes and reached up and cupped his handsome face in her hands. The aching need she'd felt for him back in the chief's office, when they'd shared that soul-shattering kiss, was nothing compared to the way her heart yearned for him now.

There was something so adorable about this man, something that called out to her in every way. He was so kind, took such joy in the world around him. Her bruised and battered soul, even with everything still going on, seemed to feel better, to heal just a little bit more, every time she was around him. She couldn't just let him leave without knowing what he meant to her at this moment. Or how amazing it was to meet a man who put everyone else first, no matter what. That kind of selflessness was rare, a true gift, to be treasured, cherished.

She angled her lips up toward him, waiting, hoping. He was too tall for her to reach unless he wanted this, too. His eyelids dropped to half-mast, need and hunger reflected in his eyes as he leaned down and pressed his lips against hers.

But this was her kiss. She wanted to lead, and he let her. She kissed him, softly, gently, as he'd kissed her back at the station. She poured all the sweetness into her kiss, the raw, new emotions she felt for him but couldn't yet define. She tried to show him that she cared, that he mattered to her, so much that it confused her. All she knew was that he'd saved her life, but he was also saving her soul.

When he would have deepened the kiss, it nearly killed her to pull away. But she wasn't ready for more, not yet. She needed to think and rest and try to make sense of things.

The question was there in his eyes. She fanned her fingers over his cheeks, smiling up at him.

"I wasn't ready for you," she whispered. "You're a surprise. My heart..." She shook her head and smoothed her fingers across his shirt. "Thank you."

The poor man looked just as confused as she felt.

"Thank you for saving me, several times," she said. "Thank you for being there for me no matter what, for sharing the joy of your childhood, your family, your love for this mountain. But most of all, thank you for sharing your pain. I'm so sorry that you lost someone you loved. But it means more than you can possibly know that you shared that with me. It gives me hope that I can work through my own losses, move on and be...happy...one day. So, thank you."

She kissed him again, then dropped her hands and got into bed. She pulled the covers up to her chin. "I really am tired. I think everything that's happened has exhausted me. I'll just lie here awhile longer, okay?"

He looked like he wanted to say something, then sighed and changed his mind about whatever it was.

"I'll be in the next room if you need anything." He waved toward a closed door beside the nightstand. "That's the bathroom. The bag that Donna packed for you is in there."

After he left and pulled the door closed, she shut her eyes. All of his talk about family and happy times had lifted her up, but it also had her thinking about her own family, and feeling like a traitor for laughing and smiling after what had happened to them.

She tried to remember her family the way they'd been before her mother's alleged overdose, before her father supposedly shot himself, before Naomi's mysterious illness. And, mostly, she just tried to remember her family before Alan Webb injected himself into their lives and destroyed them all.

Chris had been standing over the cabin's kitchen table for about an hour now, moving papers back and forth, like pieces of a puzzle, but so far, he wasn't able to see the big picture.

The background information was pouring in, thanks to the emails and phone calls from his team. But, no matter how he looked at everything or how he classified it into various lists, he wasn't seeing the connections that he needed to make.

He straightened and rubbed the back of his neck. It looked like the only thing to come out of tonight's research session was an aching back and a crick in his neck.

The sound of feet padding across the carpet had him turning around to see Julie coming toward him. She'd changed into a tank top and shorts, revealing a mouth-watering amount of smooth, pale skin. Normally he was all about eyes, lips and curves. But Julie's legs were incredible and had him picturing how they'd feel wrapped around his waist while he—

"Turn around," she said. "And sit. I can help you with that stiff neck you were rubbing."

Since he didn't think he could speak right now without his tongue lolling out, he decided to do what she said. He sat. The moment he did, she slid her hands onto his shoulders and began rubbing and kneading them in slow circles, working out the tension that had coiled in his muscles without him even realizing it.

When she moved her hands to his neck and began massaging him again, his head dropped toward his chest and he let out a groan of pure ecstasy.

She laughed and continued her ministrations.

"You're really good at this." He closed his eyes, hoping she'd never stop.

"I'm good at a lot of things."

Her sexy whisper near his ear had his eyes flying open. Did she realize how her words sounded? The double meaning his suddenly lust-fogged mind had latched on to? He waited, barely breathing. When she didn't say anything else or lead him toward the bedroom, he silently berated himself for even thinking of her that way. He desperately wanted to make love to her, but that would be completely inappropriate.

The few kisses they'd shared were just as inappropriate, but he blamed them on the fact that they were both tired and not thinking straight. He couldn't use that excuse now. It was nearly ten o'clock at night, which meant she'd taken a three hour nap. And he'd slept for at least two hours on the couch before coming into the kitchen to work on the case.

Julie was a witness, and she needed time to work through the topsy-turvy changes in her life. Chris had no business thinking of her except as a woman he was duty-bound to protect.

Too bad his traitorous body wasn't listening.

His phone buzzed on the table. With Julie's hands still massaging his neck, he carefully leaned forward and picked up the phone. And just like that, the lust-induced fog evaporated. He reached up and took one of her hands in his, pulling her away from him.

"Thanks. Really," he told her. "But I've got to answer this."

The disappointment in her eyes had him wondering if maybe he *hadn't* imagined the sexy double entendre of her earlier words. And that made taking this call feel like torture.

He cleared his throat, gave Julie a pained smile as he held the phone against his ear. "Hi, Mom."

Julie's eyes widened. Then she started to laugh.

He frowned at her, which only made her laugh harder.

"No, Mom. No, I'm, ah, working." He listened to her next question and shook his head. "No, that's not Donna that you just heard. You don't know this woman." He shook his head again as his mother continued to badger him with questions. "No, it's not Nancy the 911 operator either. Nancy works from home, Mom. Yes, you can route 911 calls remotely these days." He rolled his eyes.

Julie grinned and blew him a kiss before retreating into the bedroom.

Chris groaned.

His mother demanded to know if he was hurt or something.

"What? Oh, no, sorry, Ma. I'm fine, promise. Are you okay? It's awful late. What? You can't sleep? Okay. Me? Just working a case—you know, same old, same old. Church? Oh, sorry. I forgot." He closed his eyes. Shoot. He had completely forgotten to call her and tell her he wouldn't make it to church.

While he listened to his mother go on and on about how important it was to go to church, he settled back and rested his head against the wood slats of the chair. Missing church was a cardinal sin in his mother's book. She would probably be up all night praying for his eternal soul. And if she had her way, he'd be up, too, listening while she prayed.

He sighed and shoved back from the table. The cool night air this high up on the mountain had put a definite chill inside the family room. He knelt down by the fireplace, saying the occasional "Yes, ma'am" into the phone whenever his mother paused for breath. Once he had a roaring fire going, he settled onto the massive sectional couch and rested his head on one of the throw pillows.

This was going to be a long night.

Chapter 19

The deep, husky sound of Chris's voice had faded long ago. He must have finally finished his phone call. But, unfortunately, he hadn't taken Julie's hint and joined her in the bedroom. Or maybe he had taken the hint, and the answer was no.

Sighing, she stared at the ceiling above her bed, the moonlight flooding in through the high-set windows giving her plenty of light to see by. The idea of making love to Chris Downing, once it had settled in her mind, wouldn't go away. She didn't need to know him for years to know he was a good man and that she was wildly attracted to him. In a matter of days she knew he was a far better person than she could ever hope to be, and had her thinking all kinds of what-ifs.

She looked toward the doorway. The kitchen light had been turned off long ago, replaced with the flickering of firelight. While her bedroom was warm with the heavy comforter surrounding her, the appeal of that fire beckoned, if only because Chris was out there, too.

Thumping the bed impatiently, she debated her options. Lie here all night, unable to sleep, wishing she was with Chris. Or go see whether he wanted her as much as his kisses implied. The worst he could do was say no. She'd be mortified, but she'd never heard of anyone really dying from embarrassment. And at least she wouldn't be lying here for the rest of the night wondering whether she'd blown her chance.

Decision made, she tossed back the covers before she chickened out and changed her mind. She opened the nightstand drawer, knowing what she would find. She'd looked in it earlier while hoping that Chris would follow her. After grabbing one of the foil packets, she padded across the carpet and into the family room.

The gorgeous fireplace was like a beacon, the flames dancing across real wood logs, heat flooding into the room. It was beautiful and made the gas-burning fireplace in her Nashville home seem like a pathetic pretender in comparison. But when she rounded the end of the brown leather sectional that faced the fireplace, she froze in awe.

There were so-called masterpieces hanging in her home, but none of them came close to framing the incredible male beauty before her. Chris must have gotten overheated from the fire. He'd shed his clothes, all except his boxers. With one arm crooked over his head, the muscles of his chest were displayed to advantage, golden light flickering across his skin.

A light matting of dark hair furred his chest and marched down the center of his abs to disappear beneath the waistband of his underwear. One of his legs was drawn up, his other hand draped over his knee. Thickly muscled thighs tapered to his calves. Even his feet were sexy. Everything about him was enticing and, yet, so perfect, so beautiful, she could have stood there forever just drinking him in.

No, no, what she was doing was wrong. Watching him without him knowing it was like being a voyeur, a Peeping Tom. She should either wake him up and risk his rejection, or go back to her room. Option number three, standing here all night marveling at him as he slept, while incredibly appealing, was not an option at all. She needed to do something. Soon. Now.

Good grief, the man was gorgeous.

She sighed and bit her lip in indecision.

An intake of breath had her gaze shooting to his face. His eyes were open and he was watching her. He made no move to cover up or sit up. Instead, he simply waited, his jaw tight, his pupils dilated. Like a hungry panther, languidly watching its mate. Any thought of being rejected died in the face of such raw need. He wanted her, needed her, as much as she wanted and needed him.

Slowly, she crossed the room, devouring him with her eyes, her fingers clenching at her sides. The foil crinkled in her grip. His gaze went to her hand, and when he saw what she was holding, his nostrils flared.

When she stopped in front of the couch, he held out his hands to her, an invitation she was helpless to resist. And then she was beneath him, the delicious weight of his body pressing her down, his lips greedily moving across hers in an openmouthed kiss that had her moaning and panting even before his tongue swept inside.

A draft of cold air across her shoulders told her that

he'd taken off her top. The man was an expert at undressing a woman. That both delighted and dismayed her. She didn't want to think about anyone who'd come before her—or the woman he'd professed to love back in his college days. She wanted this man completely to herself.

Before long they were both naked, heated skin sliding against heated skin. His hands were everywhere, caressing, molding, stroking, making her shiver with delight. She wanted to touch him as much as he wanted to touch her. They twisted and strained against each other, kissing and being kissed, touching and being touched.

Then he was pressing her down again, claiming her mouth with his. She vaguely registered the sound of the foil packet being torn. He must have taken it from her at some point. She didn't remember. He lifted off her, rolling the condom into place while he continued to make love to her mouth with his. And then, just when she thought she would die if he didn't take her, he moved between her thighs, pressing against her.

She eagerly lifted her legs, cradling him against her body. When he didn't press into her, she opened her eyes to see why.

He was staring at her, his face inches from hers. He smiled, gently kissed her, then framed her face in his hands.

"You're so beautiful, and strong, and brave," he whispered. "Are you sure about this? We haven't known each other that long. I'm supposed to be protecting you, not…doing this."

She slid her fingers across his ribs, making him shudder against her. "I'm more sure about this than anything in my whole life. Don't stop, Chris. Love me. Please. Just love me."

He shuddered again and swooped down to kiss her, his tongue thrusting between her lips as he thrust inside her body. The pleasure, the pressure of him filling her so completely while he did amazing things with his mouth and his hands had her arching off the couch, whimpering against him.

He tore his mouth from hers, his eyes squeezed shut, his jaw tight as he pumped into her, over and over, drawing her body into a tight bow of pleasure. She kissed the column of his throat, scored her nails down the muscles of his back, encouraging him with the words of lovers passed down through the generations.

Higher and higher he drew her up on waves of pleasure so exquisite she didn't think she could possibly go any higher. And then, with one clever stroke of his fingers, a deep thrust of his body inside hers, he took her to a new level.

He let out a savage growl and captured her mouth with his before sliding both hands beneath her bottom and angling her up. He withdrew once more, then plunged into her so deeply she exploded, shouting his name as she clung to him, her body shuddering with the strength of her climax. He thrust into her again, riding her through the waves of pleasure until he tightened inside her and came apart in her arms, his breath rushing out of him in a groan of ecstasy and making her climax all over again.

Like embers from a wildfire, they both slowly floated back to earth, wrapped in each other's arms, skin slicked with sweat. She could feel his heart hammering in his chest, feel the rush of her own pulse slamming in her veins.

He shuddered again, then slowly withdrew, turning her in his arms, spooning her with a thigh draped over hers as he turned them toward the fireplace. Her eyes fluttered closed. Her body felt boneless, cradled against his. He curled an arm over her belly, his fingers idly caressing the undersides of her breasts. She fell asleep with him whispering erotic love words in her ear and telling her how beautiful she was.

Chapter 20

Chris fanned the papers out on the kitchen table, trying again to refocus on the case and look at all of the clues in light of the latest reports he'd gotten just after the sun came up.

He glanced toward the ground floor bedroom. Julie was still getting ready to face the day, putting on makeup that he'd assured her she didn't need. For some reason, that had only made her more determined to fix her makeup and do something with her hair. He shook his head and looked down at the papers.

After making love twice more during the night, they'd both been exhausted and famished. They'd cooked omelets at four in the morning, taking turns feeding each other, laughing like a couple of newly-weds, before hopping into the shower together. If he wasn't careful, he could easily fall in love with the amazing woman.

The thought of his first love, Sherry, shot through his mind. Losing her had been devastating. Losing Julie? He couldn't even go there. It would destroy him. Maybe it was already too late to guard himself from caring too much. But it wasn't too late to protect her. He had to figure out who her late husband had been working with and why. If he didn't do that, he could never guarantee her safety.

He studied the newest list he was making, the same one that he'd started in the chief's office but never finished. This time he had more information.

Love.
Money.
Revenge.
Hatred.
Hide something.

Those were the possible motives he was working with.

Love. He hesitated. Did Julie love someone else? Was she involved with someone in Nashville? As soon as those thoughts went through his head, he discarded them. She was so honest with her feelings. There was no way that she could have made love with him last night, giving herself to him so completely, if she loved someone else. Her ex hadn't tried to kill her because of some love triangle. He crossed that one off the list.

Next possible motivation—*money.* Yesterday, he'd have been inclined to cross this one off the list, too. But that was before he'd received the in-depth financial study on Alan Webb and his family's import-export business. Everything was coming together now. And money seemed to be at the root of the whole damn thing.

"You look like you've got the weight of the whole world on your shoulders."

He looked up to see Julie crossing the kitchen toward him. Today she was wearing a blue blouse tucked into blue dress slacks, showing off all her curves. Her shoulder-length hair hung in glossy waves, with a simple side part. She didn't seem to be wearing much makeup, but what she did have on emphasized her eyes and her dark lashes, making him want to sit for hours just staring at her.

"Have I told you how beautiful you are?"

Her face flushed a delightful pink. "About a dozen times. Thanks." She cleared her throat. "What are you working on?"

He forced his gaze to the paper in front of him. "Finances. Specifically, you and your husband's. Did you know that his family's business was teetering on the brink of bankruptcy before you married him?"

She frowned. "That can't be right. Alan always had money in college. I think that's how he got a lot of people to like him—free drinks all around whenever he was in a bar. He never once said anything about running short on cash, or mentioned concerns about his father's company."

Chris shoved the financial report on Webb Enterprises across the table as she sat across from him.

"The company got a huge influx of cash from another corporation a few weeks after you got married."

Her brows furrowed as she skimmed the pages of the report. "What was the payment for?"

"It was listed as cash flow from an investment. But the state cops working on the financial side of the investigation can't find where any companies have invested in Webb Enterprises to produce revenue anywhere close to that amount. And the payments have continued, once a month, for years. Until recently, when they suddenly stopped."

She glanced up. "They stopped? When?"

"On your twenty-fifth birthday."

Her eyes widened. "My birthday? That's…a coincidence. Odd, but what other explanation could there be? What was this other corporation?"

"Victoria and Edward."

She blinked, her face going pale. "My grandmother's business?"

He nodded.

"Let me get this straight. My estranged grandmother, Elizabeth Victoria Abbott, the one who disowned my mother and never made any attempt to have anything to do with us, has been making cash payments to my husband ever since I got married? Is that what you're saying?"

"That's exactly what I'm saying."

"But…I never heard anything about it. Wait, wait." She held up a hand as if to stop him, a panicked look entering her eyes. "You said Webb Enterprises was going broke. But then my…grandmother…began making those payments. Then, all this time, Alan wasn't the wealthy one. It wasn't his business that was buying our fancy house and fancy cars. It was my distant relative in London?"

He nodded. "That's what it looks like."

She fisted her hands on the table. "Money. You said

one of the motives for murder is money. And you said that you don't believe in coincidences."

"Right." He watched her work through what he'd been working through all morning. He didn't have all the answers, but this was the biggest piece so far. It had to be the key. He waited to give her time to process everything, and to be there for her once she did.

Several minutes went by. When she looked at him again, the tears that he'd expected to see weren't there. Instead, she looked almost...relieved.

"So that's the answer then," she said. "That's why our marriage was so rocky, right from the start. Alan didn't marry me for love. He married me for money. Which is incredibly ironic considering his parents always acted like they thought I'd married him for his money." She shook her head. "This is crazy. Alan had to have been insane, a psychopath. He somehow knew about the link between my family and this corporation of my grandmother's and...what? Tried to figure out how to get the money? Oh, God above. It all makes sense now."

She pressed a hand to her stomach.

"What you said yesterday," she continued, "everything on the board—it's all true, and it all makes a horrible, macabre sense. Alan needed money. He found out about my grandmother, somehow. Then he hit on my sister. But she didn't like him. He must have realized he couldn't manipulate her so, instead, he killed her, and then my parents, leaving me as the one link to my grandmother. Let me guess. She regrets disowning my mother and set up a trust or something, right? You said she's still alive, so it can't be a simple inheritance. But it must still be set up to pay the heir—which, with the rest of my family dead—is me. Did I get it right, Chris?

Alan knew he could manipulate me, so he killed everyone else? That's it, isn't it?"

Her voice broke and she closed her eyes, drawing in deep breaths.

Chris hurried to her, crouching in front of her. He wanted to draw her into his arms, hold her. But her stiff posture and the expression on her face told him she wouldn't welcome his touch right now. She needed time to work it through. He would wait all day if he had to. And when she needed him, he would be here.

She sat there, her back ramrod straight, for several minutes, before finally opening her eyes. She blinked at him, her eyes dry, her look determined.

"I need to hear you say it," she said. "Tell me I'm right, or tell me I'm wrong. Just say it."

"I'm sorry, Julie. But I think you're absolutely right. The finance guys are trying to contact your grandmother and representatives at Victoria and Edward Corporation to get more details. But it might take a while to get that information. On this side of the pond, they've confirmed the amounts of the payments, when they began, when they stopped, the financial troubles at Webb Enterprises, which is again having trouble, by the way. They haven't been able to make payroll this past month. The company is again in jeopardy of going bankrupt."

Her lips curled with disdain. "Because, for some reason, the payments Alan was getting stopped on my birthday. Now his company, his parents' company, doesn't have that cash cushion every month so they're failing again."

"Seems like it, yes. The question of course is why the payments were made in the first place. What triggered them to start if your grandmother had disowned your mother? Somehow she or her lawyers must have found out about you and Naomi and she decided to send you money. Maybe the payments were contingent on college graduation, or getting married." He shrugged. "If the payments were meant for you, why did someone set them up to go to Alan? And, more importantly, why did they stop on your birthday? If we can answers to those questions, we'll understand why Alan tried to kill you after you turned twenty-five."

"And why someone is still trying to kill me," she finished. "Alan's not the only partner in this endeavor. You've been saying all along that he had to be working with someone else. That would explain why those men tried to kill us at Cooper's farm. They have to finish what Alan started. And if it's been about the money all this time, I have to think their goal is to get the payments going again."

"I doubt that's their goal."

She crossed her arms, resting them on the table in front of her. "I thought we agreed this is all about money."

"Oh, absolutely. It's definitely about money, even if some other motivations are coming into play. But if you've been—pardon my analogy—a cash cow all this time, why kill you if it's about the monthly payments? They've stopped already, and yet your life is still in danger. That has to mean some kind of cash payout. Maybe the monthly payments were part of a trust, and you're to get the full lump sum at age twenty-five."

She nodded. "Okay, okay. That could make sense. If there's a trust and I'm the sole heir, when I turn twenty-five I have to...do something? To get the lump-sum payout? But since I don't know, or didn't know, about the trust, Alan had to do something else." Her eyes widened. "He would be *my* heir. If I died, he would get the lump sum. Isn't that how these things work?"

Again, Chris shook his head. "In general, yes. But I don't see that as the explanation here. If it were as simple as killing you and making Alan the heir, he—"

"Would have killed me right after we got married," she finished.

He nodded. "Yes. I think he would have."

She got up and began pacing back and forth. "Alan needed me alive to get the original payments. That implies proof of life to the trustees. How would he do that without me knowing about it?"

"I think we're back to the partner theory again. Someone, perhaps working with the trust, had to be working with Alan. Maybe he provided proof to that person and they claimed to have seen you in person. Here, take a look at this."

He shuffled through a stack of papers and pulled one of them out. "I printed this from an email this morning. Randy drove to Nashville last night and worked with the local PD there to search your house. He brought a locksmith, too, who opened the safe. And this paper shows the contents."

She read the paper. "Birth certificates, for my parents, my sister, me." She pressed a hand against her throat. "Death certificates for my family. My marriage license?"

"I imagine these are what he used to get the payments started. But he wouldn't need them after that. So I doubt this is what he wanted when he came to Destiny looking for you."

"No, probably not," she agreed. She swallowed hard. "I'm not an expert on trusts. But I'm thinking they can be written up any way the maker of the trust wants. If my grandmother was holding wealth for my mother's heir, these birth and death certificates prove that I'm the heir. And the marriage license proves that Alan was my husband. Since my grandmother never made any attempt to see me or my family in person, she was probably perfectly willing to accept that I would feel the same way. Her trustees, or perhaps the partner we keep theorizing about, were fine accepting Alan as their surrogate. Pay Alan, they were paying me. The requirements of the trust are satisfied without any messy family reunions."

The bitterness in her voice had Chris pulling her into his arms without thinking. Instead of stopping him, she sank against him, holding on to him as he rocked her and stroked her hair. They sat that way for a long time, until she let out a shuddering breath and pulled back.

She kissed him, a sweet, soft kiss that rocked him to his soul.

"Thank you," she said. "I don't think I could get through this without you. It's a heavy burden, a lot to take in. If it weren't for you, I probably would have curled up in a fetal position long ago and given up."

He shook his head and squeezed her shoulders. "No. You wouldn't have done that. You're far too strong. Alan used you, he destroyed your family. Now he's dead. And I'm not going to apologize for saying that I'm glad he's dead."

She smiled. "I think I'm kind of glad he's dead, too, even though that sounds terrible." Her smile faded. "Where do we go from here? I still don't understand why someone else is after me or how Alan got this started without someone verifying it with me."

"That's definitely a piece we need to figure out. Plus we need to find out what's required by the trust once you attained age twenty-five to get the lump sum payout, which is the only thing that makes sense to me. Alan wanted you alive to get payments, but once you reached twenty-five, something changed and the payments stopped. At that point, he was still trying to get something from you. So that implies you have something he needed in order to get the lump sum."

She nodded. "But now that he's dead, his partner needs me dead. Why?"

"To cover their tracks I'm guessing. Since they're trying to kill you, not talk to you like Alan tried, then they've either found another way to get the money or they've given up on that and just want to ensure you can't lead anyone to them. Did your husband have your power of attorney? That could help explain how he got the trust to give him the payments in the first place."

"I never gave him a power of attorney. He never even asked."

Chris nodded. "It probably would have raised red flags to you if he'd asked right after you got married. I'm guessing he already had that part covered. Maybe he had a forger produce one for him. As much diabolical planning as he did in regards to your family, a simple power of attorney couldn't have been more than a blip on his radar."

She sighed. "True."

"When our finance guys cut through the red tape and get a copy of the trust document, that should clear up a lot of our questions and hopefully will point us in the right direction to figure out who was Alan's partner."

"One of the main things bugging me," Julie said, "is Harry Abbott. It can't be a coincidence that he shares my last name. Have you found anything else about him?"

"He appears to be your distant cousin, on your mother's side obviously, hence his last name. The team is still working on how that might figure on the case. Brian Henson, the one driving the black Charger, has to be another hit man your husband hired. Which means this still all seems to tie into the ADA somehow since Henson was her assistant. The team will need to look into Bolton, too, the other admin assistant, just in case he's part of this. If Nelson was Alan's partner, she may be tying up loose ends to make sure none of this comes back to bite her, especially given her political aspirations. Maybe she's the one who hired the hit men instead of your husband. Maybe she's protecting herself."

He gently lifted her off his lap and set her on her feet. "I'm going to talk all this through with Max. He's managed to cull some amazing contacts by networking at seminars and conferences. Maybe one of those contacts can put some pressure on your grandmother or the attorney's running the trust to get the information that we need. Maybe she can answer questions about Harry Abbott, too. Plus, we need to look into Kathy Nelson, see if we can tie her to any of this."

She nodded and moved to stand by one of the windows, looking out onto the mountains.

Chris called Max and brought him up to speed.

"Hold on," Max said through the phone. "The chief wants to tell me something."

Chris shoved back from the table and meandered around the furniture to Julie's side. He put his arm around her shoulders and pulled her against him as they looked at the achingly beautiful day, how the sun shone down onto the trees and mountains.

He was glad that he'd brought her here. He'd never intended to talk shop in the cabin, but they'd made a lot of progress. They could sit back now, enjoy the seclusion, enjoy each other and let her continue the healing process while his team caught up to Henson and looked into Nelson's dealings. A few days in the mountains without any other cabins for miles around could be exactly what Julie needed. Chris too. Because he was finding out that she was exactly what he needed.

As soon as Max came back on the phone and told him what the chief had said, Chris swore and grabbed Julie's hand.

"We're leaving—now," he told Julie and Max at the same time. He pulled Julie toward the bedroom while he worked out the planned route with Max. "That's right, we'll head down now and meet you in—Max? Max? You still there?"

He pulled the phone away from his ear. The signal still showed strong, but the phone had only static. He swore again, shoved the phone into the holder on his belt and grabbed the duffel from beside the bed.

"What's going on?"

The fear in Julie's voice made him hesitate. "A state cop was killed a few minutes ago after pulling over a speeder at the bottom of this mountain. Another cop saw the patrol car on the side of the road and found the dead trooper. When he viewed the dash cam he saw that the cop had pulled over a black Camaro. As he was walking up to the driver's window, a black Charger raced past and the driver shot the officer. The Camaro pulled out behind the Charger and they both took off down the road. It was Henson and Bolton. And the road they were on is the only one up this mountain."

"Oh, my God."

"Put your shoes on. We're leaving." After double-checking the guns and ammo in the duffel bag, he zipped it up and slung it over his shoulders like a backpack. He tightened the straps so it was snug and secure.

Julie had just put on her second shoe when the throaty roar of a powerful engine sounded from outside, then abruptly shut off.

Chris raced to the window.

The Charger was in the driveway. The Camaro was parked a little farther down the road.

Both cars were empty.

Chapter 21

Julie was shaking so hard she could barely keep her balance on the balcony stairs. Chris was right behind her, pistol in his right hand, left hand gripping the waistband on the back of her pants like a lifeline in case she lost her footing.

The front door to the cabin had burst open right after Chris had looked out the bedroom window. He'd fired several shots through the bedroom doorway and thought he might have nicked Henson on the shoulder. Chris had slammed the door shut and shoved the nightstand against it. Then he was urging Julie through the back hallway to the balcony.

It was bad enough knowing two hit men were looking for them and could suddenly appear from out of nowhere. Worse was trying not to panic at what waited for them down below. Julie tried to keep her eyes on the stairs, not the stilts under the house to her left that kept it from plunging down the side of the mountain. And certainly not on the fact that the stairs appeared to end several feet above the ground—ground that was steep and littered with razor-sharp-looking rocks. One wrong move and both of them would be killed.

"Stop," Chris ordered, jerking her back toward him.

She froze, her foot suspended in the air above the last step. He eased down to the stair beside her, then slammed his shoe against the step she'd been about to use. It exploded in a rain of sawdust and splintered wood.

"Dry rot," he whispered.

She shivered, wondering what would have happened if she'd been standing on that step when it collapsed. Since the pieces of wood from it were still bouncing down the side of the mountain, she really didn't have to wonder all that much. She swallowed, hard.

"Why do they even have these stairs if they don't reach all the way to the ground anyway?" She knew she sounded like a petulant child, but she was so tired of running and being shot at and having the constant threat of death hanging over her head. Surely she was allowed to complain every once in a while.

"There were probably another half-dozen stairs at one time. It's to provide access for examining the structure beneath the house and the foundation, to make sure it's secure."

He looked up behind them. Julie didn't see any signs of a gunman, but Chris's jaw tightened and he looked around, back toward the stilts, as if time was running out. One last glance down the mountain, then back to the stilts.

"Hold on to the railing," he whispered. "Don't move." He lifted his leg and grabbed a gun from his ankle holster, then shoved it into her front left pants pocket. "Just in case."

She made a choking sound in her throat. "In case of what?"

He looked back at the stilts again.

"Wait," she called out. "That's a six-foot leap, at least. And if you miss the tiny strip of land below us, you'll plunge off the side of the mountain. Please tell me you aren't going to try to—"

He jumped from the stairs, pushing off so hard the entire staircase wobbled.

Julie sucked in a breath and clung to the railing, staring in horror as Chris clung to the bottom stilt, trying to pull himself up on a crossbar. Dots swam in her vision and she realized she was still holding her breath. She forced herself to draw in some air while she sent up an anxious prayer for his safety.

He managed to get his fingertips around the crossbar, then pulled himself up to standing. He was about a foot above her now, but still a good six feet away. It might as well have been the Grand Canyon.

"Keep an eye out," he warned as he began unfastening his belt.

She looked at the balcony above them. "I don't see anyone."

"Good. Slide over to this side of the stairs. Hurry." He yanked out his belt and threaded the end through the buckle, then looped the other end of the belt around his wrist and back on itself, grasping the end in his palm.

She did as he'd asked and looked down. "The ground isn't too far away. Maybe I can jump."

"No. It's too rocky, too steep. Your momentum will throw you right off the cliff."

"Cliff?" She leaned over, then jerked back. "Oh. Yeah. The cliff. This is why I love Nashville and don't live in the country. I remember now."

He grinned. "You might have a point. It's not really a cliff. More like a really steep hill with lots of rocks. Still, taking a ride down there wouldn't be my first choice."

"Or mine."

After another quick glance up, he looked over his shoulder toward the house where the stilts were cut into the side of the mountain, essentially bolting the house in place. What was Chris's plan, for them to both cling to the stilts until help arrived? That might be great for him, but she'd never make it. Her legs were too short.

"You can make it," he said, as if hearing her thoughts. "I'm going to swing my belt toward you. Catch it and slide your hand in the loop. Then tighten it back until it hurts. I'm serious. Make it as tight as you can. I don't want your hand falling through."

"Maybe I could just go up the stairs and take my chances inside. They might not expect me to have a gun."

"They're hit men, Julie. They kill people for a living. They're probably better shots than I am. You really want to take that chance?"

She clutched the railing and looked down again. "Not really. But I don't want to become a human pancake, either."

He laughed. "You're adorable, you know that?"

"I'll bet you say that to all the women you drop down the sides of mountains."

"Counting you? You're right." He shrugged, then winked. "Come on. The only reason Henson hasn't come out that door with guns blazing already is he's giving me more credit than I deserve. He probably thinks I'm waiting on the balcony with a plan to ambush him."

"That might work."

"If it was just me, that's what I'd do. But there's no cover. You'd end up shot in the cross fire. Come on, Julie. Grab the belt."

Before she could think of another argument, he dropped down, hanging from the crossbar by his knees and swung the belt toward her. She grabbed it on the first try and quickly shoved her arm through the loop like he'd told her.

The belt was taut between them, pulling them toward each other, her left wrist looped in one end, his left looped in the other.

"Is your hand tight?" he called out. "So tight it feels like it's cutting off the circulation?"

"As a matter of fact, yes. I probably should loosen—"

The belt jerked and she was falling through the air. She would have screamed, but she slammed against Chris so hard the breath was knocked out of her. He grabbed her with both arms and shoved her up toward the beam, grunting at the effort as he hung upside down.

She gasped and scrambled onto the wood, grabbing another piece perpendicular to the one she was on and clinging to it for dear life. The belt slackened on her wrist. Chris had pulled his hand out of the other end.

Then he swung himself up beside her and grinned like a little boy at Christmas after getting a new bat and ball.

"That was cool, wasn't it?"

"Cool?" she muttered. "We could have died. That was the scariest thing I've ever done in my life."

His eyes widened as he looked past her.

She whirled around to see a man bent over the top of the balcony, holding the biggest, scariest-looking gun she'd ever seen. And he was pointing it at her and Chris.

"Hang on," she heard Chris yell as automatic gun-fire exploded all around them.

She grabbed for the crossbar.

And missed.

Suddenly she was free-falling into open air.

Chris leaped after Julie, twisting in midair, firing his pistol toward the gunman on the balcony. The rocky side of the mountain rushed up to meet them. He twisted again, jerking the end of the belt as hard as he could. She screamed and fell against his chest. He grabbed her just as his back slammed against the rocky side of the mountain.

Red-hot fire scraped across his back in the places unprotected by the duffel bag as they half skidded, half fell down the steep face. He used every ounce of his strength to try to keep Julie on top of him to protect her from the rocks, while scrabbling with his boots to try to slow them down.

"Chris!"

Julie's choked-out scream of warning had him twisting again to see a tree rushing up to meet them. He jerked sideways, rolling to avoid the deadly obstacle.

A garbled yell told him she'd been scraped hard. Again and again, he twisted, jerked, shuffled his arms and feet, fighting against physics and the forces of nature to try to protect his precious burden.

Finally the rolling and twisting slowed. Their shoes slammed against the earth, pulling them both up short. They flopped end over end, like rag dolls, into the tree line. The sudden cessation of sound and movement did nothing to stop the world from spinning. Chris squeezed his eyes shut, willing the dizziness to go away.

A pained moan had him opening his eyes. He was flat on his back and what was left of the duffel. Julie was clutched in his arms, her hair a tangled mess of leaves and twigs. She moaned again, and he forced himself to roll over, hissing in a breath at the throbbing fire his back and side had become.

He laid her down on the grass and smoothed her hair. A tiny line of blood trickled from the corner of her mouth. Her eyes were closed.

"Julie, can you hear me, sweetheart? Julie?"

Crack!

The ground kicked up beside him in a puff of green and brown.

He jerked back, looking up toward the house, high upon the mountainside above them. A lone gunman stood on the balcony, leaning over the railing, calmly aiming a rifle.

Chris swore and scooped Julie into his arms. He dove behind a tree as more rifle fire cracked around them. On hands and knees, he shuffled deeper into cover until he was certain they were protected. Then he carefully laid her down once again.

He tried to wake her up, but she didn't respond other than to moan in pain if he moved her.

Please, God. Don't let her die. Please.

He pressed his hand against her chest, judging her breathing. It was steady, strong. A check of her pulse reassured him it, too, was strong. Then why wasn't she awake? He ran his fingers through her horribly tangled hair, feeling for bumps. When he touched behind her right ear, she gasped and arched away from him.

He almost cried in relief.

That little arch of her back told him at least she wasn't paralyzed.

Thank you, God.

His hand came away bloody. He leaned down, clamping his jaw shut to keep from crying out himself. His back was on fire, mostly on his left side. But he'd worry about that later.

Bending over her, he pulled her hair away from her neck. The cut on her scalp wasn't deep, but it was ragged and bleeding heavily, as head wounds usually did. He worked the duffel bag off his back and dropped it beside them on the ground. When he saw the first-aid kit in the bottom, he couldn't help smiling. He owed Max big-time for packing the duffel, and doing it right.

A few minutes later, he had Julie's head wound packed and bandaged. The bleeding already appeared to be slowing down from the pressure of the wrap. He continued searching for other injuries. Her side had been badly scraped, probably from when he'd had to roll to avoid the tree. Nothing much he could do about that except to spray it with antibiotics for now. Like a burn, if he tried to cover it up, it would just lead to infection.

A sharp intake of breath had his gaze shooting to Julie's face. Her eyes were open.

He let out a shaky laugh as he leaned over her.

"What's your name?" he asked.

"Chris."

"That's my name. What's your name?" he asked again.

She shook her head, then pointed. "Chris, my God. Your side."

He frowned and looked down.

A piece of tree branch the diameter of a quarter had impaled him, from back to front, and was sticking out of his left side.

"Guess that explains why my back's on fire." He tried to laugh, but of course as soon as he saw the wound, it started throbbing and burning far worse than it had before.

"Tell me your name," he insisted yet again. He held up three fingers. "How many fingers do you see?"

"Julie and three. I'm fine. You're the one who's hurt." She started to get up, then groaned and lay back down. "The whole world is spinning."

"Concussion. We need to get you to a doctor."

She kept her eyes closed and sat up, then slowly opened them again. "It's better. What in the world happened? We fell over the cliff?"

"More like you fell and I dove." He'd probably aged thirty years watching Julie fall off that crossbar and fly down the mountain. If he'd jumped even a half second later he doubted he'd have reached her in time to cushion her fall when she hit the highest swell of ground.

If the mountain had been any steeper, neither of them would have survived.

"Can you stand?" he asked.

"I think so."

Together they pushed and pulled until they were both on their feet.

Julie started laughing. "If I look half as bad as you do we won't have to worry about the wildlife out here. They'll run away as soon as they see us."

He grabbed the duffel, and half the contents fell out. The material had been shredded. Since he'd lost his pistol in the fall, he was relieved to see one in what remained of the bag. Unfortunately, the extra magazines were scattered somewhere on the mountain.

He holstered his gun and checked Julie's pocket where he'd put his backup gun. Amazingly, the gun was still there. It would have been perfect if there was a knife in the duffel, but the two knives he'd seen in it earlier had escaped somewhere during their wild ride.

Looking at the sun, he tried to get his bearings. "We'll head that way." He pointed to his left. "That's east. It should lead to the nearest road. But we'll have to be as quiet as possible and keep a lookout the whole way."

"Why? It's not like the gunmen are going to leap off the balcony and try to free-fall down the mountain like we did. There's no way they'll catch up to us."

"There was only one gunman on the balcony—Henson. Bolton is still out there somewhere. And if I were him, I'd be heading down the mountain road right now to cut us off."

"Then shouldn't we go west or north or something, anywhere but east?"

"If you didn't have a concussion, I didn't have a tree in my back, and we had supplies to last a week or two, absolutely. East is our only option. It's just a few miles. Let's go."

Chapter 22

She was worried about him.

The injury in Chris's side looked excruciating. How was he even walking, let alone stepping over the downed trees in their path and keeping his balance on the uneven ground?

After a terse argument about not having time to tend to his wound, Chris had finally given in and let her do what she could in sixty seconds, no more. She'd sprayed it with the antibiotic he'd used on her earlier, then stuffed some gauze around the piece of branch where it protruded both in back and front.

He'd stood stiffly, barely moving through her ministrations, and then he'd gone about three shades paler. His eyes had been glazed with pain by the time she'd stopped. Even with the packing, he was bleeding steadily.

"We should stop. You're losing too much blood."

He shook his head and plodded on, occasionally looking up when the sky could be seen through the thick canopy overhead. The man was incredibly stubborn and amazing and wonderful. And it was tearing her heart into pieces watching him, knowing he would die before he'd give up, all because he wanted her to be safe.

Tears clouded her vision, but she briskly wiped them away. He'd told her she was strong and brave. She was neither of those things, but for him, she was damn well going to pretend. He didn't need one more thing to worry about, like trying to console her. Somehow she had to hold everything inside and protect him.

The weight of his backup gun, now strapped on her ankle courtesy of Chris's ankle holster, wasn't very reassuring. How was she supposed to protect Chris in a gunfight, against a man who killed for a living? Somehow, she'd have to figure it out though. Because Chris was getting weaker and weaker. No way was he going to be able to protect himself if the gunman caught up to them.

He wobbled, falling against a tree. She reached for him, but he shook her off, straightened and started forward again. How long could he keep this up? How long could he survive? And where the heck was their backup?

Chris's phone hadn't survived the fall down the mountain. But he'd spoken to Max right before Henson and Bolton had arrived. She and Chris were heading toward the same road that Chris had told Max they'd go to, albeit on foot instead of by car. Still, if the SWAT team cared about their friend and fellow officer, they should bring the cavalry up the mountain to find him. So where were they?

A small cracking noise sounded from somewhere up ahead.

Chris froze, reaching out his right hand to stop her. But she'd already stopped. They both stood as still as possible, breathing through their mouths to make as little noise as they could, waiting, watching, listening.

There. Another crack, slightly to the right, like someone's shoe crunching a dead, dry leaf or a twig.

He looked down, then to their left, motioning for her to follow. She walked where he walked, careful not to stray from the path. The woods, this mountain, was his domain. But she was learning fast, emulating him, doing whatever it took to survive.

They stopped behind two thick trees, peering through the crack between them toward the sounds they'd heard. Chris slowly raised his pistol, leveling it in the opening, sighting his target.

A deer stepped out from the bushes.

Julie laughed and relaxed against the tree.

Chris frowned but kept his pistol trained, not moving.

Julie turned back toward the deer.

A dark shadow moved behind the bushes.

Bam! Bam! Bam! Chris fired six or seven times before he stopped.

Julie held her hand over her mouth, frozen in place. A man staggered out onto the path, both hands red with blood as he held his stomach.

It was Henson.

"Help me." His plea was barely above a whisper. Then he dropped like a rock to the ground.

Chris grabbed Julie when she would have run to the other man.

"Don't. There's nothing you can do for him. And there's still one more gunman out there. Henson was on the balcony. He's the one who fired at us. If he found us, then the other guy has to be out here somewhere, too. And he's stalking us right now." He looked up at the sky. "Five, ten more minutes and we'll be at the road. If my team isn't already looking for us, we'll flag someone down. We're going to make it, Julie. Trust me."

He looked so haggard, so drawn, his complexion ashen. She wanted to weep. Instead, she smiled.

"I do. You'll take care of me. You always do." She looped her arm through his as if in comradery, when, really, she was just trying to hold him up.

His pistol was in his hand. She hop-skipped a few steps so she could grab hers from her ankle holster without stopping. Together, they headed deeper into the woods, side by side.

Rat-a-tat-tat-tat-tat!

Chris shoved her to the ground and dove on top of her. Bark and leaves exploded around them. Deafening automatic gunfire chewed into the trees near where they'd been standing.

Julie tried to bring her gun up, but his weight was pressing her wrist hard against the ground and she could barely move.

He fired toward the trees where the gunfire was coming from until his gun clicked. Out of bullets. He threw the gun to the ground. Then he was on his knees, lifting her, half-dragging her behind a tree.

Bullets sprayed the forest floor and the bark on the tree where he'd pulled her.

Then, suddenly, they stopped. Everything went quiet.

Chris was on his knees in front of her, his chest heaving with each breath he took. Blood coursed down his side, coating his arms, his hands. Julie was backed against the tree, holding the little ankle gun in her hands.

Crunching noises sounded to their left, their right. Was there more than one shooter now? And then the noise sounded directly behind Chris.

He stiffened.

Julie's breath froze in her lungs as Bolton stepped out from between the trees. The gun he held looked heavy, lethal, horrifying. It was a machine gun or something like that. All she knew for sure was that it was aimed at Chris's back.

"What do I do?" she whispered.

He gave her a half smile. "Live," he whispered. "Just live." He grabbed her gun and twisted around, using his body to shield her as he fired at Bolton.

Bam! Bam!

Boom!

The gunman blinked in shock, blood pouring from a hole at the base of his throat. Then he slowly crumpled to the ground.

Suddenly the woods filled with people: Randy, dressed in his SWAT gear, bending down to check the Bolton's pulse, shaking his head. Donna, also in SWAT gear, directing several state police, pointing back toward the path where the other gunman had gone down. Colby, staring in shock at Chris's side. And, finally, Max, dropping onto his knees beside Chris, who wasn't moving as Julie clutched him against her.

"Mrs. Webb, Julie, you have to let him go now."

Max's voice was kind, gentle, like Chris's. "Let him go, so we can help him."

She looked at the precious man in her arms. His eyes were closed. Blood covered his back and made her arms sticky where she held him.

"Medic," Max yelled, as if they were in the middle of a combat zone.

Maybe they were.

Two EMTs rushed through the trees with a gurney.

"Julie. Let them help him," Max said. "You have to let him go."

His words seemed to reach her through a fog of pain and grief.

"Julie? Julie, are you okay?"

Max's voice had changed. He swore and again yelled, "Medic."

Julie surrendered to the darkness around her.

Chapter 23

Julie couldn't believe that a month had passed since the shooting. And she also couldn't believe that she was once again sitting in the interview room at the Destiny Police Department, alone, waiting for others to join her.

She rubbed her left shoulder, trying to ease the ache where Bolton's bullet had passed through Chris's torso and buried itself in her upper arm. Both Chris and Max had shot Bolton. And since both of their bullets caused fatal injuries, they argued all the time over who should get the credit.

She smiled, glad to be alive, glad that Chris was alive. They were both still stiff and sore but would heal completely with time. She'd been released from the hospital a few days after admittance. But she'd still stayed, sleeping on a cot in Chris's room. Not that the two of them had any privacy.

Chief Thornton had assigned Detective Colby Vale to shadow her every move. He was essentially her bodyguard until they figured out who was trying to kill her. Thankfully, Colby was outside in the squad room right now, instead of in the interrogation room with her.

Chris had been released from the hospital yesterday. The skin on his back had been flayed away during their terrifying tumble down the mountain. He'd undergone several skin grafts. But at least he was up and walking, and finally allowed to leave the hospital.

She loved him. She'd realized that weeks ago during one of their many whispered talks in his hospital room, talks about everything from where they'd gone to kindergarten to their hopes and dreams. They hadn't talked about love yet, and she wasn't sure what the future held for them or if he felt about her the way she felt about him. The last month had focused more on recovery, and on wrapping up the case.

Which was why she was here. Chris had asked her to meet him at the station to discuss some new findings. She just wanted the case to be over and hoped this discussion meant that it finally was.

The door opened, and Chris stepped in, smiling as he crossed to the chair beside her.

"Hey, you," he said.

"Hey, yourself."

"Thanks for coming in," he said. "The chief will be here in just a minute."

"I can't believe you're already back at work. You aren't fully recovered yet. You should be home resting."

He shifted in his chair, the tension lines in his face telling her she was right, that he was in pain, and had no business being here.

"I'm going to tell the chief to send you home. This is ridiculous. You need more time to heal." She started to push her chair back, but he stopped her with a hand on her arm.

"Julie, I'm not back at work, not full-time. I've only been working over the phone with the chief and the others trying to tie up the loose ends on your case. And we just got some crucial information that I believe is going to help us wrap this up once and for all."

She slowly settled back against her chair. "You know who's behind everything? Who sent the hitmen after me?"

"Not exactly."

She was about to ask him to explain what he meant when the chief stepped into the room and closed the door behind him.

He nodded in greeting. "Mrs. Webb. Thanks for coming in." He sat at the end of the small table.

"Okay," she said. "The suspense is killing me. And, although I really appreciate that you've got Colby playing bodyguard, I'd love to be able to walk down the street without having a policeman shadowing my every move. Is it Kathy? You've found evidence to prove she's behind everything?"

Chris took one of her hands in his. "We don't have definitive proof yet. But I've got an idea of how to get it. And it's based on information the team has pulled together over the past few weeks, plus some surveillance photos they've taken of Kathy Nelson. It all starts with your cousin, Harry Abbott."

Julie frowned. "I don't understand. It starts with him?"

"He's the key to this whole thing and how your hus-

band was able to begin receiving payments from the
trust without you ever knowing about it. Harry Abbott
was a small-time lawyer. He worked for the law firm
that your grandmother hired to handle the trust. Apparently your grandmother was very ill shortly before
Naomi got sick. I don't know if that made your grandmother more aware of her mortality, or what. But that's
when she sent Harry Abbott to try to locate her daughter and find out if there were any grandchildren. By the
time she got information back, your family was gone.
So she created the trust for you. It was supposed to start
payments upon either college graduation or marriage."

"Seriously?" Julie said. "So if I didn't get enough
education, or decided my life was perfectly fine without a man in it, she wouldn't have deemed me worthy
of receiving any money?"

He shrugged. "She's old-fashioned. What can I say?"

"She sure is. Go on."

"Your grandmother said she hired that particular law
firm to handle the trust because of your cousin. He
was family and she preferred to keep things like that
in the family."

"You've actually spoken to her?"

He nodded. "On the phone, yes. Once we got through
the layers of assistants and bureaucracy to get to her, she
was quite forthcoming. Like I said, Harry was assigned
the task of tracking down your grandmother's American relatives on behalf of the trust. But the temptation
of all that money was too much. He resented that his
side of the family wasn't in the direct line to inherit, and
he planned on getting his hands on that money, probably felt he deserved it. Once he located your family,
he looked around for someone as diabolical as he was,

and found Alan. They made a pact—that if Alan could marry into the family and help Harry provide proof to the trust regarding the heir, then they could share the monthly proceeds."

"How do you know all of this? Harry's dead."

The chief tapped the table to get her attention. "Extensive research and interviews with people who'd interacted with Harry when he was in the States. I don't like unsolved puzzles, and I'm not about to let some ADA abuse the trust of her constituents and give police a bad name without paying her debt to society. I threw half my police force at this. And we got results."

"Thank you," she said. "I sincerely appreciate it. But I'm even more confused than ever. I thought we were talking about my cousin. Now we're back to Kathy?"

Chris looked to the chief, who nodded, as if giving him permission to take up the story again.

"I'll try to get to the point," Chris said. "Harry colluded with Alan. But Alan wasn't having much luck with your family. Naomi didn't like him, so he decided you were his best chance. After eliminating your family, he apparently tried flirting with you but you were too distraught to notice. You did, however, have a friend you associated with—Kathy."

"So they did know each other before I met Alan," Julie said.

"Yes. The meeting at the football game was a setup. Alan and Harry were getting desperate so they brought her in as a way for Alan to get your attention. We believe, and it's backed up by financial records of Harry's accounts, that the monthly payments were split into thirds."

"Harry's accounts? Not Kathy's?"

"She's too clever for that. We think she's hiding her money offshore. She's slick. Hard to pin anything on her. But she's the only person who makes sense as a surviving partner who has something to lose if her role is exposed, thus the hitmen. Plus, now that we know the full requirements of the trust—including a clause about your twenty-fifth birthday that your grandmother amended four months before your birthday—we have a theory about what Kathy is trying to do to get that final lump sum."

"Four months before my birthday? Wait, that's when things in my marriage took a nosedive, got really bad."

He nodded. "I know. I think that's when Harry broke the news to Alan."

She looked back and forth, from the chief to Chris. "What news?"

"That the payments would stop on your birthday unless you personally traveled to England to visit your grandmother, and that you bring the Abbott necklace with you—the one your mother gave to Naomi that used to belong to your grandmother. I'm pretty sure that's what Alan was looking for when he attacked you. He wanted the key to the safe so he could destroy the documents he had at your house. But he also wanted you to tell him where you had Naomi's things so he could get that necklace."

She held her hands up. "Wait. So not only did I have to finish college or get married in order to inherit, I also had to hold on to a necklace? What if I'd sold it, or lost it? I'd be out of luck?"

"Looks that way. Your grandmother is…a bit strict, uptight I guess. She really seems to value family and loyalty. I guess that's why it hurt her so much when your mother ran off with your father. It felt like a betrayal to her. And putting that stipulation about the necklace in the trust was her way of rewarding her heir only if they valued the history and legacy that necklace represented."

"You almost sound like you admire her," Julie accused.

"She's from a different generation, a different country, with a unique upbringing I could never understand. Let's just say that I'm trying to keep an open mind and see it from her perspective. Regardless, you can imagine Alan's reaction when he found out those details from Harry."

"He was probably furious. He couldn't take me to England, not without revealing what he'd been doing all this time. And, the necklace? No wonder he kept badgering me about my family's things. He needed to get the necklace without making me suspicious by specifically asking for it. Wait. It wouldn't do him any good without me though." She shook her head. "Did he think he could force me to lie to my grandmother? To not admit that Alan had been receiving the payments all along?"

Chris shot another look at the chief, then took both her hands in his this time. The concern on his face put her on edge.

"You're scaring me, Chris."

"I don't mean to. But the questions you're asking are exactly what I asked. And I don't believe for one minute that you would have meekly gone along with Alan's plan if that's what he wanted you to do. That's why Alan and his co-conspirators came up with a new plan. Alan was supposed to get the necklace from you. I think he was trying to get you to tell him where you kept your family's things without making you suspicious enough to kick him out or anything. Then, when you never revealed that information and you turned twenty-five—"

"He got desperate. Planned to kidnap me to force me to tell him."

"Right," Chris said. "But you foiled the first attack. I foiled the second. He never got a chance to get the necklace."

"Where does that leave us?" she asked.

The chief pulled a photograph from his suit jacket pocket. Chris let Julie's hands go and took the picture, placing it face down on the table in front of her.

"Hypothetically, if Alan could have gotten the necklace, then there was only one more thing he'd need after that—to take you to England with him. But he knew that wasn't an option, that you wouldn't go. So he and his co-conspirators had to make plans months ago in anticipation of your twenty-fifth birthday, for another way to fool your grandmother. Remember I said that the chief had someone performing surveillance on Kathy?"

She nodded, a sick feeling settling in her stomach. "Yes."

"She rented a house out in the country about three and a half months shy of your twenty-fifth birthday, two weeks after your grandmother changed the conditions of the trust. Apparently Kathy rented it for another woman, someone whom neighbors said was recovering from some kind of trauma, based on the bandages and the fact that nurses used to stop by every few days. She's fully recovered now. And this is what she looks like."

He flipped the picture over.

Julie pressed her hands against her mouth.

The woman in the picture looked exactly like Julie.

A week later, Julie opened the front door of her Nashville home to admit her visitor. "Thank you for meeting me here. So many things have happened in the past few months and I've only been back in Nashville for a couple of days. It's good to see a familiar face." Julie stepped back, pulling the front door open for Kathy Nelson.

"Of course, of course." Kathy stepped inside. "I'm just so relieved that everything is settled. No more looking over your shoulder and wondering if someone is out to hurt you. I still can't believe Alan was after your money all along, and willing to kill you for it. I'm so very sorry that the men Alan recommended to me as assistants ended up being such horrible people, hitmen of all things. Of course I had no idea."

Julie forced a smile. "Yes. How could you have known? The whole thing is so hard to believe. I didn't even realize you and Alan had kept in touch over the years."

Kathy's eyes narrowed a moment, then she seemed to realize what she was doing and her face smoothed out, her eyes widening innocently. "We didn't, not really. But he is, was, an important businessman in town. When he saw that the ADA's office was looking for help, he reached out to offer a suggestion. I don't know who was more surprised when he found out I was the ADA and when I found out that he was the one calling."

Nodding, as if she bought the rather thin story, Julie absently played with the gold chain around her neck, partially lifting it from beneath her shirt so some of the distinctive jewels showed.

Kathy went still, her gaze riveted on the jewelry. She cleared her throat and smiled stiffly. "My, what a lovely necklace you're wearing. I don't think I've ever seen anything quite like it."

Julie pulled it the rest of the way out from under her shirt. "It was passed down through my mother's side of the family. I kept it in a safe-deposit box for years along with other family mementos. But after everything that's happened, well, I just want to feel closer to her." She undid the chain and pulled off the necklace. "Then again, I'm told the gems are real. I probably should put it back in the bank to keep it safe."

She crossed to the desk in the front hallway and placed the necklace in the top drawer. "I'll do it tomorrow." She turned around. "Where are my manners? I asked you here for lunch. I doubt a busy attorney like you has a lot of time on her hands. I've got soup and salad waiting in the dining room. Let's enjoy a nice meal and catch up, shall we?"

Kathy took both of Julie's hands in hers. "It really is good to see you again. I'm so glad you're back. And you're right, I'm starving, and don't have a lot of time. Let's eat."

Julie tugged her hands free, forcing another smile as she led Kathy to the dining room.

Less than an hour later, she stood on the front stoop, waving as Kathy drove away. Then she stepped inside, and into Chris's arms.

"You're shivering." He pulled her close.

"You have no idea how hard it was to sit across from

that woman making small talk, knowing all along that she conspired with my husband and my cousin against me. Either way, she had her tracks covered. If Alan had been able to get the necklace, she'd have used that poor woman she'd bribed to have plastic surgery to look like me. Then what? Kill her? Probably. And then kill me of course. Imagine how elated she must feel now, patting herself on the back for keeping my look-a-like alive just in case she could figure out how to use her to get the money, even without the necklace. It must feel like Christmas to her now, seeing me wear that piece of jewelry."

He pulled her back and smiled down at her. "You've baited the trap," he said. "Now, all we have to do is wait."

"There's still so much that could go wrong. That poor woman trusts Kathy. She doesn't know that Kathy will probably kill her as soon as she gets the lump-sum payment."

"We're not going to let that happen. You have to trust me."

She slid her arms up behind his neck. "I do. I trust you. I always have."

He grinned. "Always? Really?"

"Well, okay, maybe not always. It took a few hours."

She kissed him, but all too soon the kiss was over.

"Speaking of a few hours, we don't know how long it will take Kathy to make her move. Go upstairs like we agreed. We'll take it from here."

"Okay. Be careful, Chris. Promise?"

"Promise."

She headed up the winding staircase.

* * *

The break-in, when it came, was done so swiftly and professionally that the alarm didn't even go off. But Chris and his men were waiting, and watching. And when the burglar handed Julie's necklace through the open limousine window, they followed at a discreet distance.

Assistant district attorney Kathy Nelson was apprehended at the airport, along with a woman who bore an uncanny resemblance to Julie Webb. Chris was astonished at just how alike the two appeared. But the imposter's eyes gave her away. They were dull, a window to a dead soul inside, a woman who'd seen the worst of what life had to offer and had been broken down many years ago and expected nothing better for herself.

After talking to Julie, the woman agreed to take a plea deal and testify against Kathy. In return, she would go under the knife again to get her old face back. That was something that Julie insisted upon. In addition, she'd get the therapy that she needed. And Julie would help her get an apartment and a job, plus provide her a small nest egg to help her start a new life.

The chief thought Julie was crazy to do all of that for a woman who, because she was going to pretend to be Julie, had given Alan, Kathy and her cousin the ability to complete their master plan and then kill Julie to cover their tracks. But Chris understood. Julie was too kindhearted not to help someone who'd been willing to give up her own identity out of desperation for a new life. It was the girl's background that had convinced Julie that she wasn't the hardened criminal the chief thought her to be. The girl was a runaway, had sold herself on the streets just to survive. Julie felt the imposter deserved another chance.

Chris loved that about Julie, that she saw the good in people. That she put others' happiness above her own. She was the kindest woman he'd ever met, and he was deeply in love with her. And that's what made this so damn hard.

He was about to let her go.

As she entered the coffee shop a block from her Nashville home, she looked around for him. She thought he was here to say a temporary goodbye now that the court case was over and he didn't have to testify again. They hadn't talked about long-term plans yet, even though she'd tried to bring it up several times. He'd kept dodging the conversation, knowing she would agree in a heartbeat to move back to Destiny with him. After all, her grandmother was funding Naomi's Hope Foundation now and there was nothing else keeping her here in Nashville.

That had been another surprise to some, that Julie would want to continue the Foundation even though the eventual exhumation had proved that Naomi didn't have an orphan disease. But it didn't surprise Chris. Finding cures for orphan diseases was a cause Julie believed in and she couldn't turn her back on those in need. Apparently, her grandmother agreed. She'd been more than willing to fund the charity.

But she'd decided not to go through with the trust's lump sum payment.

Not without some stipulations, at least. Stipulations that she'd told Chris, but hadn't yet told her grand-daughter. Julie was going to find out the terms for herself very soon. And there were about a billion reasons for Julie not to go back to Destiny. Or to Chris.

She just didn't know them yet.

When she saw him, her face lit up and she smiled, as she always did. He watched with a heavy heart as she approached his table. She gave him a quick kiss as he held out her chair for her, a kiss that nearly killed him.

He sat across from her while a waitress took her order. As soon as the waitress moved away from the table, he pulled the envelope out of his pocket and handed it to her.

"What's this?" she asked.

He pushed his chair back and stood. "It's a letter from your grandmother. I wanted to deliver it in person, make sure that you got it. My cab's waiting out front. I've got to go now. The chief is anxious for me to start a new case."

She frowned. "You're leaving Nashville? Right this minute?"

"Right this minute." Unable to stop himself, he leaned down and kissed her. "Goodbye, Julie."

And then he walked out of the coffee shop, and out of Julie's life forever.

Chapter 24

Steaks sizzled on the double-decker grill on Chris's back deck. Once again, Max presided over the cooking. And once again, another young intern from the Destiny Police Department helped him load potatoes and foil-wrapped corncobs onto another section of the grill.

"One week." Dillon grabbed a beer from the cooler at Chris's feet.

Since Dillon was watching Ashley show off her and Dillon's new baby girl, Letha Mae, to half the police force crowding the deck, he wasn't sure what his friend meant.

"One week until what?"

Dillon used his bottle to indicate the intern. "I give this new intern and Max one week. I said two weeks last time and lost the bet."

Chris shrugged and snagged himself a beer. "Looks

like we need more ice. I'll get some from the freezer in the garage."

Dillon stopped him with a hand on his shoulder. "Why don't you just get a ticket and fly to London and sweep Julie off her feet? We're all tired of you moping around like a lovesick calf. It's depressing."

Chris shoved his hand off his shoulder. "A billion dollars, Dillon. Julie's grandmother offered her a billion dollars if she'd agree to live in London with her. And the cherry on top is the old woman wants to pick Julie's next husband. If Julie refuses, she loses all that money. Now you tell me. What woman would give up a billion dollars to marry some redneck cop in Nowhere, Tennessee?"

"This woman would."

Chris froze, then slowly turned. Julie stood at the bottom of the deck stairs, staring up at him. She looked so…damn…good. He hadn't seen her in well over a month, and he couldn't quit drinking her in. God, how he loved her. But, wait, what had she said?

He took a step toward her, then stopped. "What are you doing here?"

She rolled her eyes and marched to the top of the deck. "If that's a proposal, I've heard better. And considering my first husband, that's saying something." She crossed her arms and tapped her shoe.

He took another step toward her, then another, until he was standing right in front of her.

"I didn't think I'd ever see you again."

"Why not?" she asked. "Because you thought I loved money more than I loved you? Seriously? I would think you knew me better than that after everything we've been through. And you should also know that I thought it was wonderfully romantic that my mother and father gave up everything for a future together, and didn't let my grandmother choose who they should love. So why would I, for even one minute, consider letting her choose who I should love?"

By the end of her speech, the deck had fallen silent and she was jabbing him in the chest with her pointer finger.

Chris winced and pulled her hand down. But instead of letting go, he entwined his fingers with hers.

"Can you say that again, please?"

She frowned. "My entire speech? I didn't memorize the darn thing."

"No, just the part where you said you loved me."

Her frown faded, and a smile slowly grew in its place. Then she frowned again. "Wait, that came out all wrong. You're supposed to tell me you love me first. Forget I said that. What I meant to say is that you're too stubborn for your own good and you shouldn't have walked away in that coffee shop. You should have known that, of course, I'd go visit my grandmother, because she is family, after all, and old, and deserved to know about what kind of person Naomi was and—"

"I love you."

She sputtered to a stop in the middle of her sentence. "What did you say?"

"I love you." He framed her face in his hands. "I'm stubborn, stupid and shouldn't have doubted you. I'm sorry. And I love you. And I want to marry you."

He dropped to one knee.

Her mouth fell open and she pressed her hands against her chest.

"No, wait." He stood up. "Wait right here."

He turned around and ran into the house.

Julie blinked and looked around the deck. What had just happened? Everyone was staring at her, looking just as shocked as she felt. She'd flown from half the world away to get here, fully expecting Chris to beg her forgiveness and ask her to marry him. A little groveling might have been nice, too. Instead, he'd dropped to his knee, then ran away.

Her cheeks flushed hot with embarrassment.

She was about to turn around and slink back to her car when Chris ran out of the house. He stumbled to a halt in front of her and once again dropped to one knee. His face was red and he seemed out of breath, as if he'd run up and down the stairs a few times.

"Julie," he said, between deep breaths, "I need your left hand for this."

She crossed her arms. "I'm not sure I trust you now."

He gave her that irresistible half smile. "Yes, you do. You've always trusted me."

"Well, almost always," she said.

He pulled a black velvet box out from behind his back and opened the lid. A solitaire diamond ring sat in the middle of the plush velvet, sparkling in the sunlight.

She gasped and covered her mouth with her hands.

"It's not very big," he apologized. "But it's the best I could do for now on a cop's salary."

She cleared her throat and lowered her hands. "When…when did you buy that?"

"The day I got out of the hospital. But I wanted all of the loose ends tied up so nothing would stand in our way when I proposed. Then your grandma sent that letter and I thought—"

"You thought wrong."

"I know, I know. I'm trying to fix that now. Julie Elizabeth Webb—"

"Linwood. Julie Elizabeth Linwood. I changed it back to my maiden name."

"Julie Elizabeth Linwood, I love you. Will you do me the honor of becoming my wife?"

In answer, she held out her left hand and smiled so hard her face hurt.

Chris slid the ring onto her finger and stood. "I love you."

"I love you, too."

He swooped down and kissed her.

The deck erupted in applause and laughter as everyone rushed forward to congratulate them.

It was impossible to kiss Chris the way she really wanted to with everyone slapping their backs and telling them how happy they were for them. She broke the kiss, laughing and beaming up at him.

He framed her face in his hands, staring at her in wonder. "I can't believe you gave up all that money to be with me."

"I didn't have a choice," she teased.

"You didn't?"

She shook her head. "It all came down to destiny."

His answering smile filled her heart and soul with happiness. And then he kissed her again, the way a man kisses a woman when he loves her more than life itself, the way a man kisses a woman…when he's found his destiny.

* * * * *

Paula Graves, an Alabama native, wrote her first book at the age of six. A voracious reader, Paula loves books that pair tantalizing mystery with compelling romance. When she's not reading or writing, she works as a creative director for a Birmingham advertising agency and spends time with her family and friends. Paula invites readers to visit her website, paulagraves.com.

Books by Paula Graves

Harlequin Intrigue

Campbell Cove Academy

Kentucky Confidential
The Girl Who Cried Murder
Fugitive Bride
Operation Nanny
The Smoky Mountain Mist

The Gates: Most Wanted

Smoky Mountain Setup
Blue Ridge Ricochet
Stranger in Cold Creek

The Gates

Dead Man's Curve
Crybaby Falls
Boneyard Ridge
Deception Lake
Killshadow Road
Two Souls Hollow

Visit the Author Profile page
at Harlequin.com for more titles.

THE SMOKY MOUNTAIN MIST

Paula Graves

For the old Lakewood gang,
those still with us and those gone,
who made trips to the Smokies so much fun.

Chapter 1

Rachel Davenport knew she was being watched, and she hated it, though the gazes directed her way that cool October morning appeared kind and full of sympathy. Only a few of her fellow mourners knew the full truth about why she'd disappeared for almost a year after her mother's sudden death fifteen years ago, but that didn't change the self-consciousness descending over her like a pall.

She locked her spine and lifted her head, refusing to give anyone reason to doubt her strength. She'd survived so far and didn't intend to fall apart now. She wasn't going to give anyone a show.

"It's a lovely gathering, isn't it?" Diane, her father's wife of the past eight years, dabbed her eyes with a delicate lace-rimmed handkerchief. "So many people."

"Yes," Rachel agreed, feeling a stab of shame. She

wasn't the only person who'd lost someone she loved. Diane might be flighty and benignly self-absorbed, but she'd made George Davenport's last days happy ones. He'd loved Diane dearly and indulged her happily, and she'd been nothing but a caring, cheerful and devoted wife in his dying days. Even if Rachel had resented the other woman in her father's life—and she hadn't—she would have loved Diane for giving her father joy for the past eight years.

"I sometimes forget that he touched so many lives. With me he was just Georgie. Not the businessman, you know? Just a sweet, sweet man who liked to garden and sing to me at night." Fresh tears trickled from Diane's eyes. She blotted them away with the handkerchief, saved from a streaky face by good waterproof mascara. She lifted her red-rimmed eyes to Rachel. "I'm going to miss the hell out of that man."

Rachel gave her a swift, fierce hug. "So am I."

The preacher took his place at the side of the casket and spoke the scripture verses her father had chosen, hopeful words from the book of Ephesians, her father's favorite. Rachel wanted to find comfort in them, but a shroud of loss seemed to smother her whole.

She couldn't remember ever feeling quite so alone. Her father had been her rock for as long as she could remember, and now he was gone. There was her uncle Rafe, of course, but he lived two hours away and spent much of his time on the road looking for new acts for his music hall.

And as much as she liked and appreciated Diane, they had too little in common to be true friends, much less family. Nor did she really consider her stepbrother, Diane's son, Paul, anything more than a casual friend, though they'd become closer since she'd quit her job with the Maryville Public Library to take over as office manager for her father's trucking company.

She sometimes wondered why her father hadn't ceded control of the business to Paul instead of her. He'd worked at Davenport Trucking for over a decade. Her father had met Diane through her son, not the other way around. He had been assistant operations manager for several years now and knew the business about as well as anyone else.

Far better than she did, even though she'd learned a lot in the past year.

She watched her stepbrother edge closer to the casket. As his lips began moving, as if he was speaking to the man encased in shiny oak and satin, a dark-clad figure a few yards behind him snagged Rachel's attention. He was lean and composed, dressed in a suit that fit him well enough but seemed completely at odds with his slightly spiky dark hair and feral looks. A pair of dark sunglasses obscured his eyes but not the belligerently square jaw and high cheekbones.

It was Seth Hammond, one of the mechanics from the trucking company. Other Davenport Trucking employees had attended the funeral, of course, so she wasn't sure why she was surprised to see Seth here. Except he'd never been close to her father, or to anyone else at the company for that matter. She'd always figured him for a loner.

As her gaze started to slide away from him, he lifted the glasses up on his head, and his eyes snapped up to meet hers.

A zapping sensation jolted through her chest, stopping her cold. His gaze locked with hers, daring her to look away. The air in her lungs froze, then burned until she forced it out in a deep, shaky sigh.

He looked away, and she felt as if someone had cut all the strings holding her upright. Her knees wobbled, and she gripped Diane's arm.

"What is it?" Diane asked softly.

Rachel closed her eyes for a moment to regain her sense of equilibrium, then looked up at the man again.

But he was gone.

"I don't know. She looks okay, I guess." From his parking spot near the edge of the cemetery, Seth Hammond kept an eye on Rachel Davenport. The cemetery workers had lowered the oak casket into the gaping grave nearly twenty minutes ago, and most of the gathered mourners had dispersed, leaving the immediate family to say their final private goodbyes to George Davenport.

"It's not a coincidence that everyone around her is gone." The deep voice rumbling through the cell phone receiver like an annoying fly in Seth's ear belonged to Adam Brand, FBI special agent in charge. Seth had no idea why the D.C.-based federal agent was so interested in a trucking company heiress from the Smoky Mountains of Tennessee, but Brand paid well, and Seth wasn't in a position to say no to an honest job.

The only alternative was a dishonest job, and while he'd once been damned good at dishonesty, he'd found little satisfaction in those endeavors. It was a curse, he supposed, when the thing you could do the best was something that sucked the soul right out of you.

"I agree. It's not a coincidence." Seth's viewpoint from the car several yards away wasn't ideal, but the last thing a man with his reputation needed was to be spotted watching a woman through binoculars. So he had to make do with body language rather than facial expressions to get a sense of what Rachel Davenport was thinking and feeling. Grief, obviously. It covered her like morning fog in the Smokies, deceptively ephemeral. She stood straight, her chin high, her movements composed and measured. But he had a strong feeling that the slightest nudge would send her crumbling into ruins.

Everyone was gone now. Her mother by her own hand fifteen years ago, her father by cancer three days ago. No brothers or sisters, save for her stepbrother, Paul, and it wasn't like they'd grown up together as real siblings the way Seth and his sister had.

"Have you seen Delilah recently?" Brand asked with his usual uncanny way of knowing the paths Seth's mind was traveling at any given moment.

"Ran into her at Ledbetter's Café over the weekend," Seth answered. He left it at that. He wasn't going to gossip about his sister.

Brand had never said, and Seth had never asked, why he didn't just call up Delilah himself if he wanted to know how she was doing. Seth assumed things had gone sideways between them at some point. Probably why Dee had left the FBI years ago and eventually gone to work for Cooper Security. At the time, Seth had felt relieved by his sister's choice, well aware of the risk that, sooner or later, his sister's job and his own less savory choice of occupations might collide.

Of course, now that he'd found his way onto the straight and narrow, she was having trouble believing in the new, improved Seth Hammond.

"I got some good snaps of the funeral-goers, I think. I'll check them out when I get a chance." A hard thud on the passenger window made him jerk. He looked up to find Delilah's sharp brown eyes burning holes into the glass window separating them. "Gotta go," he said to Brand and hung up, shoving the cell phone into his pocket. He slanted a quick look at the backseat to make sure he'd concealed the surveillance glasses he'd been using to take images of the funeral. They were safely hidden in his gym bag on the floorboard.

With a silent sigh, he lowered the passenger window. "Hey, Dee."

"What are you doin' here?" His sister had been back in Tennessee for two weeks and already she'd shed her citified accent for the hard Appalachian twang of her childhood. "Up to somethin'?"

Her suspicious tone poked at his defensive side. "I was attending my boss's funeral."

"Funeral's over, and yet here you are." Delilah looked over the top of the car toward the Davenport family. "You thinking of conning a poor, grieving heiress out of her daddy's money?"

"Funny."

"I'm serious as a heart attack." Her voice rose slightly, making him wince.

He glanced at the Davenport family, wondering if they had heard. "You're making a scene, Dee."

"Hammonds are good at making scenes, Seth. You know that." Delilah reached into the open window, unlatched the car door and pulled it open, sliding into the passenger seat. "Better?"

"You ran into Mama, did you?" he asked drily, not missing the bleak expression in her dark eyes.

"The Bitterwood P.D. called me to come pick her up or they were throwing her in the drunk tank." Delilah grimaced. "Who the hell told them I was back in town, anyway?"

"Sugar, there ain't no lyin' low in Bitterwood. Too damned small and too damned nosy." Unlike his sister, he'd never really left the hills, though he'd kept clear of Bitterwood for a few years to let the dust settle. If not for Cleve Calhoun's stroke five years ago, he might never have come back. But Cleve had needed him, and Seth had found a bittersweet sort of satisfaction in trying to live clean in the place where he'd first learned the taste of iniquity.

He sneaked a glance at George Davenport's grave. The family had dispersed, Paul Bailey and his mother, Diane, walking arm in arm toward Paul's car, while Rachel headed slowly across the cemetery toward another grave nearby. Marjorie Kenner's, if he remembered correctly. Mark Bramlett's last victim.

"I know vulnerable marks are your catnip," Delilah drawled, "but can't you let the girl have a few days of unmolested grief before you bilk her out of her millions?"

"You have such a high opinion of me," he murmured, dragging his gaze away from Rachel's stiffened spine.

"Well-earned, darlin'," she answered, just as quietly.

"I don't suppose it would do any good to tell you I don't do that sort of thing anymore?"

"Yeah, and Mama swore she'd drunk her last, too, as I was puttin' her ginned-up backside to bed." Bitter resignation edged her voice.

Oh, Dee, he thought. *People keep lettin' you down, don't they?*

"Tell me you're not up to something."

"I'm done with that life, Dee. I've been done with it a few years now."

Her wary but hopeful look made his heart hurt. "I left the truck over on the other side of the cemetery. Why don't you drive me over there?"

He spared one more glance at Rachel Davenport, wondering how much longer she'd be able to remain upright. Someone had been working overtime the past few weeks, making sure she'd come tumbling down sooner or later.

The question was, why?

"I didn't get to talk to you at the service."

Rachel's nervous system jolted at the sound of a familiar voice a few feet away. She turned from Marjorie's grave to look into a pair of concerned brown eyes.

Davis Rogers hadn't changed a bit since their breakup five years ago. With his clean-cut good looks and effortless poise, he'd always come across as a confident, successful lawyer, even when he was still in law school at the University of Virginia.

She'd been sucked in by that easy self-composure, such a contrast to her own lack of confidence. It had been so easy to bask in his reflected successes.

For a while at least.

Then she'd found her own feet and realized his all-encompassing influence over her life had become less a shelter and more a shackle.

Easy lesson to forget on a day like today, she thought, battered by the familiar urge to enclose herself in his arms and let him make the rest of the world go away.

She straightened her spine and resisted the temptation. "I didn't realize you'd even heard about my father."

"It made the papers in Raleigh. I wanted to pay my respects and see how you were holding up." He brushed a piece of hair away from her face. "How *are* you holding up?"

"I'm fine." His touch left her feeling little more than mild comfort. "I'm sad," she added at his skeptical look. "And I'll be sad for a while. But I'm okay."

It wasn't a lie. She *was* going to be okay. Despite her crushing sense of grief, she felt confident she wasn't in danger of losing herself.

"Maybe what you need is to get out and get your mind off things." Davis cupped her elbow with his large hand. "The clerk at the bed-and-breakfast where I'm staying suggested a great bar near the university in Knoxville where we can listen to college bands and relive our misspent youth. What do you say, Rach? It'll be like Charlottesville all over again."

She grimaced. "I never really liked those bars, you know. I just went because you liked them."

His expression of surprise was almost comical. "You didn't?"

"I'm a Tennessee girl. I liked country music and bluegrass," she said with a smile.

He looked mildly horrified, but he managed to smile. "I'm sure we can find a honky-tonk in Knoxville."

"There's a little place here in Bitterwood we could go. They have a house bluegrass band and really good loaded potato skins." After the past few months of watching her father dying one painful inch at a time, maybe what she needed was to indulge herself. Get her mind off her losses, if only for a little while.

And why not go with Davis? She wasn't still in love with him, but she'd always liked and trusted him. It was safer than going alone. The man who'd killed four of her friends might be dead and gone, but the world was still full of danger. A woman alone had to be careful.

And she *was* alone, she knew, bleakness seeping into her momentary optimism.

So very alone.

For the first time in years, Seth Hammond had a place to himself. It wasn't much to talk about, a ramshackle bungalow halfway up Smoky Ridge, but for the next few weeks, he wouldn't have to share it with anyone else. The house's owner, Cleve Calhoun, was in Knoxville for therapy to help him regain some of the faculties he'd lost to a stroke five years ago.

By seven o'clock, Seth had decided that alone time wasn't all it was cracked up to be. Even if the satellite reception wasn't terrible, there wasn't much on TV worth watching these days. The Vols game wasn't until Saturday, and with the Braves out of play-off contention, there wasn't much point in watching baseball, either.

He'd already gone through the photos from the funeral he'd taken with his high-tech camera glasses, but as far as he could tell, there was nobody stalking Rachel Davenport at the funeral except himself. He supposed he could go through the photos one more time, but he'd seen enough of Rachel's grief for one day. He'd uploaded the images to the FTP site Adam Brand had given him. Maybe the FBI agent would have better luck than he had. Brand, after all, at least knew what it was he was looking for.

He certainly hadn't bothered to let Seth in on the secret.

You have turned into a dull old coot, Seth told himself, eyeing the frozen dinner he'd just pulled from Cleve's freezer with a look of dismay. *There was a time when you could've walked into any bar in Maryville and gone home with a beautiful woman. What the hell happened to you?*

The straight and narrow, he thought. He'd given up more than just the con game, it appeared.

"To hell with that." He shoved the frozen dinner back into the frost-lined freezer compartment. He was thirty-two years old, not sixty. Playing nursemaid to a crippled old man had, ironically, kept him lean and strong, since he'd had to haul Cleve Calhoun around like a baby. And while he wasn't going to win any beauty pageants, he'd never had trouble catching a woman's eye.

An image of Rachel Davenport's cool blue eyes meeting his that morning at the funeral punched him in the gut. He couldn't remember if she'd ever looked him in the eye before that moment.

Probably not. At the trucking company, he was more a part of the scenery than a person. A chair or a desk or one of the trucks he repaired, maybe. He'd become good at blending in. It had been his best asset as a con artist, enabling him to learn a mark's vulnerabilities without drawing attention to himself. Cleve had nicknamed him Chameleon because of his skill at becoming part of the background.

That same skill had served him well as a paid FBI informant, though there had been a few times, most recently in a dangerous backwoods enclave of meth dealers, when he'd come close to breaking cover.

But looking into Rachel Davenport's eyes that morning, he'd felt the full weight of being invisible. For a second, she'd seen him. Her blue eyes had widened and her soft pink lips had parted in surprise, as if she'd felt the same electric zing that had shot through his body when their gazes connected.

Maybe that was the longing driving him now, propelling him out of the shack and into Cleve's old red Charger in search of another connection. It was a night to stand out from the crowd, not blend in, and he knew just the honky-tonk to do it in.

The road into Bitterwood proper from the mountains was a winding series of switchbacks and straightaways called Old Purgatory Road. Back in the day, when they were just kids, Delilah, a couple of years older and eons wiser, had told Seth that it was named so because hell was located in a deep, dark cavern in the heart of Smoky Ridge, their mountain home, and the only way to get in or out was Purgatory Road.

Of course, later he'd learned that Purgatory was actually a town about ten miles to the northeast, and the road had once been the only road between there and Bitterwood, but Delilah's story had stuck with him anyway. Even now, there were times when he thought she'd been right all along. Hell *did* reside in the black heart of Smoky Ridge, and it was all too easy for a person to find himself on a fast track there.

Purgatory Road flattened out as it crossed Vesper Road and wound gently through the valley, where Bitterwood's small, four-block downtown lay. There was little there of note—the two-story brick building that housed the town administrative offices, including the Bitterwood Police Department, a tiny postage stamp of a post office and a few old shops and boutiques that stubbornly resisted the destructive sands of time.

Bitterwood closed shop at five in the evening. Everything was dark and shuttered as Seth drove through. All the nighttime action happened in the outskirts. Bitterwood had years ago voted to allow liquor sales by the drink as well as package sales, hoping to keep up with the nearby tourist traps. While the tourist boom had bypassed the little mountain town despite the effort, the gin-guzzling horse was out of the barn, and the occasional attempts by civic-minded folks to rescind the liquor ordinances never garnered enough votes to pass.

Seth had never been much of a drinker himself. Cleve had taught him that lesson. A man who lived by his instincts couldn't afford to let anything impair them. Plus, he'd grown up dodging the blows of his mean, drug-addled father. And all liquor had done for his mother was dull the pain of her husband's abuse and leave her a shell of a woman long after the old bastard had blown himself up in a meth lab accident.

He'd never have gone to Smoky Joe's Saloon for the drinks anyway. They watered down the stuff too much, as much to limit the drunken brawls as to make an extra buck. But they had a great house band that played old-style Tennessee bluegrass, and some of the prettiest girls in the county went there for the music.

He saw the neon lights of Smoky Joe's ahead across Purgatory Bridge, the steel-and-concrete truss bridge spanning Bitterwood Creek, which meandered through a narrow gorge thirty feet below. The lights distracted him for only a second, but that was almost all it took. He slammed on the brakes as the darkened form of a car loomed in his headlights, dead ahead.

The Charger's brakes squealed but held, and the muscle car shuddered to a stop with inches to spare.

"Son of a bitch!" he growled as he found his breath again. Who the hell had parked a car in the middle of the bridge without even turning on emergency signals?

With a start, he recognized the vehicle, a silver Honda Accord. He'd seen Rachel Davenport drive that car in and out of the employee parking lot at Davenport Trucking every day for the past year.

His chest tightening with alarm, he put on his own emergency flashers and got out of the car, approaching the Honda with caution.

Out of the corner of his eye, he detected movement in the darkness. He whipped his gaze in that direction.

She stood atop the narrow steel railing, her small hands curled in the decorative lacework of the old truss bridge. She swayed a little, like a tree limb buffeted by the light breeze blowing through the girders. The air ruffled her skirt and fluttered her long hair.

"Ms. Davenport?" Seth's heart squeezed as one of her feet slid along the thin metal support and she sagged toward the thirty-foot drop below.

"Ms. Davenport is dead," she said in a faint, mournful tone. "Killed herself, you know."

Seth edged toward her, careful not to move too quickly for fear of spooking her. "Rachel, that girder's not real steady. Don't you want to come down here to the nice, solid ground?"

She laughed softly. "Solid. Solid." She said the word with comical gusto. "'She's solid.' What does that mean? It makes you sound stiff and heavy, doesn't it? Solid."

Okay, not suicidal, he decided as he took a couple more steps toward her. *Drunk?*

"Do you think I'm cursed?" There was none of her earlier amusement in that question.

"I don't think so, no." He was almost close enough to touch her. But he had to be careful. If he grabbed at her and missed, she could go over the side in a heartbeat.

"I think I am," she said. Her voice had taken on a definite slurring cadence. But he decided she didn't sound drunk so much as drugged. Had someone given her a sedative after the funeral? Maybe she'd had a bad reaction to it.

"I don't think you're cursed," Seth disagreed, easing his hand toward her in the dark. "I think you're tired and sad. And, you know, that's okay. It means you're human."

Her eyes glittered in the reflected light of the Charger's flashers. "I wish I were a bird," she said plaintively. "Then I could fly away over the mountains and never have to land again." She took a sudden turn outward, teetering atop the rail as if preparing to take flight. "She said I should fly."

Then, in heart-stopping slow motion, she began to fall forward, off the bridge.

Chapter 2

He wasn't going to reach her in time.

A nightmare played out in his head as he threw himself toward her. His hands clawing at the air where she'd been a split second earlier. His body slamming into the rail that stopped him just short of throwing himself after her over the side of the bridge. He could see her plummeting, her slender body dancing like a feather in the cold October breeze until it shattered on the rocks below.

Then his fingers met flesh; his arms snaked around her hips, anchoring her to him. Though she was tall and thin, she was heavy enough to fill the next few seconds of Seth's life with sheer terror as he struggled to keep her from tumbling into the gorge and taking him with her.

He finally brought her down to the ground and

crushed her close, his heart pounding a thunderous rhythm in his ears. She pressed closer to him, her nose nuzzling against the side of his neck.

"This is nice," she said, her fingers playing over the muscles of his chest. "You smell nice."

His body's reaction was quick and fierce. He struggled to regain control, but she wasn't helping him a bit. Her exploring hands slid downward to rest against his hips. His heart gave a jolt as her mouth brushed over the tendon at the side of his neck, the tip of her tongue flicking against the flesh.

"Taste good, too."

He dragged her away, holding her at arm's length in a gentle but firm grip. "I need to get you home."

She smiled at him, but he could see in the dim light that her eyes were glassy. Clearly she had no idea where she was or maybe even who she was. Whatever chemical had driven her up on the girder was still in control.

"Rachel, do you have the key to your car?" He didn't want to leave her car there to be a hazard to other drivers trying to cross the bridge.

She shook her head drunkenly.

Keeping a grip on one of her arms, he crossed and checked the vehicle. The key was in the ignition. At least she hadn't locked the door, so he could move it off the bridge. But did he dare let Rachel go long enough to do so?

"Rachel, let's take a ride, okay?"

"'Kay." She got into the passenger seat willingly enough when he directed her there, and she was fumbling with the radio dials when he slid in behind the steering wheel. "Where's the music?"

"Just a minute, sugar." He started the car. A second later, hard-edged bluegrass poured through the CD speakers—Kasey Chambers and Shane Nicholson. He had that album in his own car.

She started singing along with no-holds gusto, her voice a raspy alto, and complained when he parked the car off the road and cut the engine.

"Just a minute and we'll make the music come back," he promised, keeping an eye on the road. There had been no traffic so far, but his luck wouldn't hold much longer. He needed to get her out of there before anyone else saw the condition she was in.

He almost laughed at himself as he realized what he was thinking. He'd been a cover-up artist from way back, trying to hide the ugly face of his home life from the people around them. He'd gotten good at telling lies.

Then he'd gotten good at running cons.

Still, he thought it was smart to protect Rachel Davenport from prying eyes until she was in some sort of condition to defend herself. He didn't know what had happened to her tonight, or how big a part she'd played in her own troubles, but he didn't care. Everybody made mistakes, and she'd been under a hell of a lot more pressure than most folks these past few weeks.

She could sort things out with her conscience when she was sober. He wasn't going to add to her problems by parading her in front of other people.

He buckled her safely into the passenger seat of the Charger and slid behind the wheel, pulling the bluegrass CD from a holder attached to his sun visor. He put the CD in the player and punched the skip button until the song she'd been singing earlier came on. She picked up the tune happily, and he let her serenade him while he thought through what to do next.

Delivering her to her family was the most obvious answer, but Seth didn't like that idea. Someone had gone to deadly lengths in the past few weeks to rip away her emotional underpinnings, and Seth didn't know enough about her relationship with her stepmother and stepbrother to risk taking her home in this condition. She seemed friendly enough with them, but they didn't appear particularly close. In fact, there was some speculation at work whether Paul Bailey was annoyed at being bypassed as acting CEO. He might not have Rachel's best interests at heart.

The particulars of George Davenport's will had become an open secret around the office ever since he'd changed it shortly after his terminal liver cancer diagnosis a year ago. Everybody at the trucking company knew he'd specified that his daughter, Rachel, should be the company's CEO. It had been a bit of a scandal, since until that point in her life, Rachel Davenport had been happy working as a librarian in Maryville. What did she know about running a business?

She'd done okay, taking over more and more of her father's duties until his death, but would Paul Bailey have seen it that way?

The song ended, and the next cut on the album began, a plaintive ballad that Rachel didn't seem to know. She hummed along, swaying gently against the constraints of the seat belt. She was beginning to wind down, he noticed with a glance her way. Her eyes were starting to droop closed.

Maybe he should have taken her straight to the hospital in Maryville to get checked out, he realized. What if she'd overdosed on whatever she'd taken? What if she needed treatment?

He bypassed the turnoff that would take him to the Edgewood area, where Bitterwood's small but influential moneyed class lived, and headed instead to Vesper Road. Delilah was housesitting there for Ivy Hawkins, a girl they'd grown up with on Smoky Ridge.

A detective with the Bitterwood Police Department, Ivy was on administrative leave following a shooting that had left a hired killer dead and a whole lot of questions unanswered. Ivy had taken advantage of the enforced time off to visit with her mother, who'd recently moved to Birmingham, and had offered Delilah a place to stay while she was in town.

"Rachel, you still with me?" he asked with alarm as he noticed her head lolling to one side.

She didn't answer.

He drove faster than he should down twisty Vesper Road, hoping the deer, coyotes and black bears stayed in the woods where they belonged instead of straying into the path of his speeding car. He almost missed his turn and ended up whipping down Ivy Hawkins's driveway with an impressive clatter of gravel that brought Delilah out to confront him before he even had a chance to cut the engine.

"What the hell?" she asked as she circled around to the passenger door.

"You did some medic training at that fancy place you work, right?"

Delilah's eyebrows lifted at the sight of Rachel Davenport in the passenger seat. "What's wrong with her?"

"That's what I'd like to know." He gave Rachel's shoulder a light shake. She didn't respond.

"What are you doing with her?"

"It's a long story. I'll tell you about it inside." He nodded toward the door she'd left wide-open.

Inside the house, he laid Rachel on the sofa and pressed his fingers against her slender wrist. Her pulse was slow but steady. She seemed to be breathing steadily.

She was asleep.

He stood up and turned to look at his sister. She stared back at him, her hands on her hips and a look of suspicion, liberally tinged with fear, creasing her pretty face.

"What the hell happened? Did you do something to her?"

Anger churned in his gut, tempered only by the bitter knowledge that Delilah had every reason to suspect him of doing something wrong. God knew she'd dug him out of a whole lot of holes of his own digging over the years until she'd finally tired of saving him from himself.

"I found her in this condition," he explained as he pulled a crocheted throw from the back of the sofa and covered Rachel with it. "On Purgatory Bridge."

"On the bridge?"

"*On* the bridge," he answered. "Up on the girders, about to practice her high-dive routine."

"My God. She was trying to kill herself?"

"No. She's on something. I thought maybe you could take a look, see if you could tell from her condition—"

"Not without a tox screen." Delilah crossed to the sofa and crouched beside Rachel. "How was she behaving when you found her?"

"Drunk, but I didn't really smell any liquor on her." The memory of her body, warm and soft against his, roared back with a vengeance. She'd smelled good, he remembered. Clean and sweet, as if she'd just stepped out of a bath. "She was out of it, though. I'm not sure she even knew who *she* was, much less who I was."

"Was she hallucinating?" Delilah checked Rachel's eyes.

"Not hallucinating exactly," Seth answered, leaning over his sister's shoulder.

She shot him a "back off" look, and he stepped away. "What, then, exactly?"

"She seemed really happy. As if she were having the time of her life."

"Standing on a girder over a thirty-foot drop?"

"Technically, she was swaying on a girder over a thirty-foot drop." Even the memory gave him a chill. "Scared the hell outta me."

"You should've taken her to a hospital."

Worry ate at his gut. "Should we call nine-one-one?"

Delilah sat back on her heels, her brow furrowed. "Her vitals look pretty good. I could call a doctor friend of mine back in Alabama and get his take on her condition."

"You have a theory," Seth said, reading his sister's body language.

"It could be gamma hydroxybutyrate—GHB."

Seth's chest tightened with dread. "The date rape drug?"

"Well, it's also a club drug—lower doses create a sense of euphoria. You said you found her near Smoky Joe's, right? She might have taken the GHB to get high."

He shook his head swiftly. "No. She wouldn't do that."

Delilah turned her head to look at him, her eyes narrowed. "And you would know this how?"

"We work in the same place. If she had any kind of track record with drugs, I'd have heard about it."

Delilah cocked her head. "Really. You think you know all there is to know about Rachel Davenport?"

He could tell from his sister's tone that he'd tweaked her suspicious side again. What would she think if he told her he was working for her old boss, Adam Brand?

As tempted as he was to know the answer, he looked back at Rachel. "If it's GHB, would it have made her climb up on a bridge and try to fly?"

"It might, if she's the fanciful sort. GHB loosens inhibitions."

Which might explain her drunken attempt at seduction in the middle of Purgatory Bridge, he thought. "How can we be sure?"

"A urine test might tell us," Delilah answered, rising to her feet and pulling her cell phone out of the pocket of her jeans. "But it's expensive to test for it, and it's almost impossible to detect after twenty-four hours." She shot her brother a pointed look. "Do you really want it on record that she's got an illegal drug in her system?"

Delilah might look soft and pretty, but she was sharper than a briar patch. "No, I don't," he conceded.

"We can't assume someone did this to her," she said, punching in a phone number. "After all, she just buried her father. That might make some folks want to forget the world for a while."

As she started speaking to the person on the other end of the call, Seth turned back to the sofa and crouched next to Rachel. She looked as if she was sleeping peacefully, her lips slightly parted and her features soft and relaxed. The calm expression on her face struck him hard as he realized he had never seen her that way, her features unlined with worry. The past year had been hell for her, watching her father slowly die in front of her while she struggled to learn the ropes of running his business.

He smoothed the hair away from her forehead. Most of the time when he'd seen her at the office, she had looked like a pillar of steel, stiff-spined and regal as she went about the trucking business. But every once in a while, when she didn't know anyone else was looking, she had shed the tough facade and revealed her vulnerability. At those times, she'd looked breakable, as if the slightest push would send her crumbling to pieces.

Had her father's death been the blow to finally shatter her?

Behind him, Delilah hung up the phone. "Eric says we just have to keep an eye on her vitals, make sure she's not going into shock or organ failure," she said tonelessly.

"Piece of cake," he murmured drily.

"We could take shifts," she suggested.

He shook his head. "Go on to bed. I'll watch after her." He certainly wouldn't be getting any sleep until she was awake and back to her normal self again.

There was a long pause before Delilah spoke. "What's your angle here, Seth? Why do you give a damn what happens to her?"

"She's my boss," he said, his tone flippant.

"Tell me you're not planning to scam her in some way."

He slanted a look at his sister. "I'm not."

Once again, he saw contradictory emotions cross his

sister's expressive face. Part hope, part fear. He tamped down frustration. He'd spent years losing the trust of the people who loved him. He couldn't expect them to trust him again just like that.

However much he might want it to be so.

Blackness melted into featureless gray. Gray into misty blobs of shape and muted colors and, finally, as her eyes began to focus, the shapes firmed into solid forms. Windows with green muslin curtains blocking all but a few fragments of watery light. A tall, narrow chest of drawers standing against a nearby wall, a bowl-shaped torchiere lamp in the corner, currently dark. And across from her, sprawling loose-limbed in a low-slung armchair, sat Seth Hammond, his green eyes watching her.

She'd seen him at her father's funeral, she remembered, fresh grief hitting her with a sharp blow. She'd looked up and seen him watching her, felt an electric pulse of awareness that had caught her by surprise.

And then what? Why couldn't she remember what had happened next?

Her head felt thick and heavy as she tried to lift it. In her chest, her heart beat a frantic cadence of panic.

Where was this place? How had she gotten here? Why couldn't she remember anything beyond her father's graveside funeral service?

She knew time must have passed. The light seeping into the small room was faint and rosy-hued, suggesting either sunrise or sunset. The funeral had taken place late in the morning.

How had she gotten here?

Why was *he* here?

"What is this?" she asked. Her voice sounded shaky, frightening her further. Why couldn't she muster the energy to move?

She needed to get out of here. She needed to go home, find something familiar and grounding, to purge herself of the panic rising like floodwaters in her brain.

"Shh." Seth spoke softly. "It's okay, Ms. Davenport. You're okay."

She pushed past her strange lethargy and sat up, her head swimming. "What did you do to me?"

His expression shifted, as if a hardened mask covered his features. "What can you remember?"

She shoved at the crocheted throw tangled around her legs. "That's not for me to answer!" she growled at him, flailing a little as the throw twisted itself further around her limbs, trapping her in place.

Seth unfolded himself slowly from the chair, rising to his full height. He wasn't the tallest man she'd ever met, but he was tall enough and imposing without much effort. It was those eyes, she thought. Sharp and focused, as if nothing could ever slip past him without notice. Full of mystery, as well, as if he knew things no one else did or possibly could.

Her fear shifted into something just as dangerous. Fascination.

Snake and bird, she thought as he walked closer, his pace unhurried and deceptively unthreatening.

"What's the last thing you remember?" He plucked at the crocheted blanket until it slithered harmlessly away from her body. He never touched her once, but somehow she felt his hands on her anyway, strong and warm. A flush washed over her, heating her from deep inside until she thought she was going to spontaneously combust.

What the hell was wrong with her?

He asked you a question, the rational part of her brain reminded her. *Answer the question. Maybe he knows something you need to know.*

Instead, she tried to make a run for the door she spotted just beyond his broad shoulders. She made it a few steps before her wobbling legs gave out on her. She plunged forward, landing heavily against the man's body.

His arms whipped around her, holding her upright and pinning her against his hard, lean body. The faint scent of aftershave filled her brain with a fragment of a memory—strong arms, a gentle masculine murmur in her ear, the salty-sweet taste of flesh beneath her tongue—

She tore herself out of his grasp and stumbled sideways until she came up hard against the wall. Her hair spilled into her face, blinding her. She shook it away. "What did you do to me?"

She had meant the question to be strong. Confrontational. But to her ears, it sounded weak and plaintive, like a brokenhearted child coming face-to-face with a world gone mad.

Or maybe it's not the world that's gone mad, a mean little voice in the back of her head taunted.

Maybe it's you.

Chapter 3

Seth met Rachel Davenport's terrified gaze and felt sick. It didn't help that he knew he'd done nothing wrong. She clearly believed he had. And he would find few defenders if she made her accusation public.

Cleve Calhoun had always told him it never paid to help people. "They hate you for it."

What if Cleve was right?

"You're awake." The sound of Delilah's voice behind him, calm and emotionless, sent a jolt down his nervous system.

Rachel's attention shifted toward Delilah in confusion. "Who are you?"

"Delilah Hammond," Delilah answered. She took the crocheted throw Seth was still holding and started folding it as she walked past him toward the sofa. "How are you feeling?"

"I don't know," Rachel admitted. Her wary gaze shifted back and forth from Delilah to Seth. "I don't remember what happened."

Delilah slanted a quick look at Seth. "That's one of the symptoms."

"Symptoms of what?" Rachel asked, looking more and more panicky.

"GHB use," Delilah answered. "Apparently you did a little partying last night."

"What?" Rachel's panic elided straight into indignation. "What are you suggesting, that I did drugs or something?"

"Considering my brother found you about to do a double gainer off Purgatory Bridge—"

"I don't think you planned to jump off," Seth said quickly, shooting his sister a hard look. "But you were not entirely in control of yourself."

Delilah's eyebrows arched delicately. Rachel just looked at him as if he'd grown a second head.

"I was not on Purgatory Bridge last night," she said flatly. "I would never, ever…" She looked nauseated by the idea.

"You were on the bridge," he said quietly. "Apparently whatever you took last night has affected your memory."

"I don't…take drugs." Her anger faded again, and the fear returned, shining coldly in her blue eyes.

"Maybe someone gave something to you without your knowledge."

Seth's suggestion only made her look more afraid. "I don't remember going anywhere last night. I don't—" She stopped short, pressing her fingertips against her lips. "I don't remember anything."

"If you took GHB—"

Seth shot his sister a warning look.

She made a slight face at him and rephrased. "If someone slipped you GHB or something like it, it's not uncommon for you to experience amnesia about the hours before and after the dosage."

"What's the last thing you remember?" Seth asked.

Rachel stared at him. "I want to go home."

"Okay," he said. "I can take you home."

She shook her head quickly. "Her. She can take me."

Damn, that hurt more than he expected. "Okay. But what do you plan to tell your family?"

Her eyes narrowed. "Why?"

"I didn't know if you'd want people to ask uncomfortable questions."

Her expression shifted again, and her gaze rose to Seth's face. "My father would know what to do."

He nodded. "I'm sorry he's not here for you."

Her eyes darkened with pain. "Did you know my father asked if I thought he should hire you?" she said slowly. "He told me your record. Admitted it would be a risk. I don't know why he asked me. At the time, I didn't have much to do with the company. I guess now I know why."

"He trusted your instincts," Seth said.

She looked down at her hands. "Maybe he shouldn't have."

"What did you tell him?" Delilah asked, her tone curious. "About Seth?"

Rachel's gaze snapped up to meet Seth's. "I told him to give the man a second chance."

"Thank you," Seth said.

"I've been known to be wrong."

Ouch again.

Her eyes narrowed for a moment before she looked away, her profile cool and distant. To Delilah, she said, "I would appreciate a ride home. Do you think I should go to a doctor? To get tested for—" She stopped short, agony in her expression.

"Probably," Delilah said. "I could drive you to Knox-ville if you don't want to see anyone local."

She shot Delilah a look of gratitude, the first posi-tive expression Seth had seen from her since she'd awo-ken. "Yes. Please."

As Delilah directed her out to the truck, she looked over her shoulder at her brother. "I'll take care of her." She followed Rachel out into the misty morning driz-zle falling outside.

He nodded his gratitude and watched them from the open doorway until the truck disappeared around the bend, swallowed by the swirling fog. Then he grabbed his keys and headed out to the Charger, ignoring the urge to go back inside and catch some sleep.

He had to talk to a man about a girl.

No sign of recent sexual activity. The doctor's words continued ringing in her ears long after he'd left her to dress for departure. He'd said other things as well—preliminary tox screen was negative, but if she'd con-sumed GHB or another similar drug, it might not be easily detectible on a standard test. And depending on how long it had been since the drug was administered, it might not show up on a more specific analysis. He'd seemed indifferent to her decision not to test for it.

She supposed he had patients who needed him more than she did.

"How are you doing?" Delilah Hammond looked around the closed curtain, her expression neutral. There was an uncanny stillness about the other woman, an ability to remain calm and focused despite having a drug-addled woman dumped in her lap to take care of. She had a vague memory that there had been a Hammond girl from the Bitterwood area who'd become an FBI agent.

"I'm fine," Rachel lied. "Are you an FBI agent?"

Delilah's dark eyebrows lifted. "Um, not anymore. I left the FBI years ago. I work for a private security company now."

"Oh."

"What did the doctor tell you?" she asked gently.

"No sign of sexual activity, but they also couldn't find a toxicological explanation for my memory loss. Something about the tests not being good at spotting GHB or drugs like it."

"You don't have any memory of where you might have gone last night?" Delilah picked up Rachel's discarded clothes from the chair next to the exam table and handed them to her.

"None. The last thing I remember is being at the cemetery."

Delilah left the exam area without being asked, giving Rachel a chance to change back into her own clothes in private. When Rachel called her name once she'd finished dressing, Delilah came back around the curtain.

"Look, I'm going to be straight with you," Delilah said. "Because I'd want someone to be straight with me. I know about Mark Bramlett and the murders. I know that they all seemed to be connected to Davenport Trucking in some way. Or, more accurately, connected to you."

Rachel put her fingertips against her throbbing temples. "Why do I feel as if everybody knows more about what's going on in my life than I do?"

"If someone's targeting you, up to this point it's been pretty oblique. But drugging you up and leaving you to fend for yourself outside on a cold October night while you're high as a kite?" Delilah shook her head. "That's awfully direct, if you ask me. You really need to figure out why someone would want you out of the way."

"You think I should go to the police."

The other woman's brow furrowed. "Normally, I'd say yes."

"But?"

"But is there any reason why it might not be in your best interest for the police to be involved?"

Rachel's head was pounding. "I don't know. I can't think."

"Okay, okay." Delilah laid her hands on Rachel's shoulders, her touch soothing. "You don't have to make that decision right now. Let's get you home and settled in. Is there someone there who can keep an eye on you until you're feeling more like yourself?"

"No," Rachel said, remembering that her stepmother had made plans to leave for Wilmington after the funeral. Diane's sister had invited Diane to visit for a few days. Paul had his own place, and while she and her stepbrother were friendly enough, she wouldn't feel comfortable asking him to play nursemaid. She already suspected he thought she was in over her head at the trucking company. He might even be right.

She didn't want to give him more reasons to doubt her.

"I'd offer to watch after you myself, but I have to drive to Alabama as soon as I can get away. I have a meeting with my boss, and it's a long drive. But you're welcome to stay at the house while I'm gone."

She wondered if Seth was staying there, too. She didn't let herself ask. "I'm okay. I'll be fine at home by myself."

"Are you sure?"

Rachel nodded, even though she wasn't sure about anything anymore.

"Smoky Joe" Breslin wasn't exactly thrilled when Seth roused him from bed on a rainy morning to answer a few questions, and his responses were laced liberally with profanities and lubricated by a few shots of good Tennessee whiskey. Seth had never been much of a drinker, so he nursed a single shot while Breslin knocked back three without blinking.

"Yeah, she was in here last night. Looked like a hothouse flower in a weed patch, but she seemed to be enjoying the music. And there were a few fellows who enjoyed lookin' at her, so who was I to judge?"

"Was she alone?" Seth asked.

"No, came in with some frat boy type. He tried a little something with her and she gave him a whack in the face, and some of the boys escorted him out. Not long after that, she headed out of here."

"What kind of condition was she in?"

"I don't know. I wasn't really watchin' when she left. I know she wasn't fallin'-down drunk or nothin'."

"You didn't check to make sure she wasn't driving?"

"Hell, you know how it can get around here on a busy night! I can't babysit everybody who comes here for the show. I do know she didn't have much to drink, so I didn't worry too much about it."

Which meant that unless she'd gone somewhere else to drink, it hadn't been alcohol alone that had put her up on that bridge.

"What can you tell me about the frat boy?" he asked Joe.

The older man grimaced. "Just some slicked-down city fellow. You know the type, comes in here with his nose in the air givin' everyone the stink-eye like he was better than them. I was glad to see the girl give him what for, if you want my opinion." Joe poured another glass of whiskey and motioned to top off Seth's.

Seth waved him off. "Did he pay for the drinks?"

"Yeah."

"Cash or credit?"

"Credit. One of them gold-type cards for big spenders. Flashed it like it was a Rolex watch or something."

"Would you have the receipt?"

Joe cut his eyes at Seth. "You pullin' another scam? I don't put up with that around here. You know that."

"No, no scam." He took no offense. "The woman he hit on is a friend of mine, see. I'd like to talk to the man about his behavior toward her."

"I see." Joe shot him an approving look. "Well, tell you the truth, she seemed to handle him pretty good all by her lonesome. But I'll see what I can dig up for you. Just promise me you're not gonna beat him up or shoot

him or anything like that. I don't want the cops trackin'
you back here and giving me any trouble."

"Just want to talk," Seth assured him, although if he
found out that Frat Boy had anything to do with drugging Rachel Davenport, he couldn't promise he'd keep
his fists to himself. She'd come way too close to going
off the bridge the night before. She wouldn't have been
likely to survive that fall.

Maybe the guy had slipped her something hoping it
would make it easy to get lucky with her rather than to
make her go off the deep end and hurt herself, but that
distinction sure as hell didn't make drugging her any
less heinous a crime.

And there was still the matter of the murders. Over
the past two months, four women connected to Rachel Davenport had been murdered in what had ini-
tially seemed like random killings. Until investigators
found the perpetrator and learned he'd been hired to
kill those women and make the deaths look random.
With his dying words, he'd admitted that it was "all
about the girl."

All about Rachel Davenport.

Joe came back from the cluttered office just off the
bar bearing a slip of paper. "Guy signed his name 'Davis
Rogers.'"

The name wasn't familiar. Could have been someone Rachel knew from Maryville or even an old friend
in town for her father's funeral. He'd ask her about him
when she got back from the hospital.

The thought of her trip to Knoxville made his chest
tighten as he left Smoky Joe's Saloon and headed toward
the road to Maryville. He'd taken the past two days off
work, but he was scheduled to work the next four. He

had some vacation time coming to him, and he figured this might be the right time to take it.

He was surprised to find Paul Bailey in the office when he asked to see whoever was in charge while Rachel was out. Bailey had the account books open and looked up reluctantly when Seth stepped inside.

"Mr. Bailey, I've had a family situation come up. I know it's short notice, but I have a couple of weeks of vacation built up, and I'd like to take them now if possible."

Bailey's gaze was a little unfocused, as if his mind was still on whatever he'd been doing before Seth interrupted. "Yeah, sure. Nobody else has any days off scheduled, and they'll be happy to have the extra hours this time of year, with the holidays coming up. Just let Sharon at the front desk know what days you're taking, and she'll put it on the schedule."

"Thank you." Seth started to turn away, then paused. "I'm real sorry about Mr. Davenport."

"Thank you," Bailey answered with a regretful half smile.

On impulse, Seth added, "By the way, do you know a Davis Rogers?"

Bailey's gaze focused completely. "Why do you ask?"

"I just ran into a guy with that name last night at a bar," Seth lied. "He mentioned he knew the family. We drank a toast to Mr. Davenport."

"Last night?"

Seth kept his expression neutral. "Yeah. He mentioned he was thinking about selling his car, and I know someone in the market. I should've gotten his phone number, but I didn't think about it until afterward."

"He's not from here," Bailey said with a dismissive wave. "Probably couldn't work out a sale anyway before he heads back to Virginia."

Seth had a vague memory that Rachel had gone to college somewhere in Virginia. So, maybe an old college friend.

Maybe even an old boyfriend.

A sliver of dismay cut a path through the center of his chest. He tried to ignore it. "Thanks anyway." He left the office before Paul Bailey started to wonder why one of his fleet mechanics was suddenly asking a lot of nosy questions.

He stopped in the fleet garage, where he and the other mechanics shared a small break room. The three mechanics working in the garage today were out in the main room, so he had the place to himself.

Grabbing the phone book they kept in a desk drawer, he searched the hotel listings, bypassing the cheaper places. Joe Breslin had described Davis Rogers as a slicked-back frat boy, which suggested he'd stay at a nice hotel.

Was that Rachel's type? Preppy college boys with their trust funds and their country club golf games?

Drop it, Hammond. Not your concern.

She wasn't exactly what he considered his type, either. She was attractive, clearly, but quiet and reserved. And maybe if he hadn't begun to put clues together that suggested the recent Bitterwood murders were connected to Davenport Trucking, he might never have allowed himself to think about Rachel Davenport as a person and not just a company figurehead.

But ever since he'd given up the con game for the straight and narrow, he'd shown an alarming tendency to take other people's troubles to heart. And Rachel Davenport's life was eaten up with trouble these days.

An old twelve-step guy he knew had told him over-compensation was a common trait among people who felt the need to make amends for what they'd done. They tended to go overboard, wanting to save the whole damned world instead of fix the one or two things they could actually fix.

And here he was, proving the guy right.

Using his cell phone, he called Maryville hotels with no luck. He was about to start calling Knoxville hotels when he remembered there was a bed-and-breakfast in Bitterwood that offered the sort of services a guy like Davis Rogers would probably expect from his lodgings. The odds were better that he was staying in Knoxville, but Sequoyah House was a local call, so what would it hurt?

The proprietor at Sequoyah House put him right through to Davis Rogers's room when he asked. Nobody answered the phone, even after several rings, but Seth had the information he needed.

He had a few tough questions for Davis Rogers, and now he knew where to find him.

Chapter 4

On the ride back to Bitterwood, Rachel realized she had no idea where her car was parked. Seth had said he'd found her on Purgatory Bridge, so it made sense that she'd left her car somewhere in the area. Delilah agreed to detour to the bridge to take a look.

Sure enough, as soon as they neared the bridge, Delilah had spotted the Honda Accord parked off the road near the bridge entrance, just as Seth had said.

"Do you have your keys?" Delilah asked as she pulled the truck up next to Rachel's car.

"Yeah. I found them in my pocket." God, she wished she could erase the last twenty-four hours and start fresh. But then, she'd have to face her father's funeral all over again. Feel the pain of saying goodbye all over again. The stress of staying strong and not breaking. Not letting anyone see her crumble.

What would those mourners at the funeral have thought, she wondered, if they'd seen her acrobatics on the steel girders of Purgatory Bridge last night?

She shuddered at the thought, not just the idea of making a spectacle of herself in front of those people, but also the idea of Purgatory Bridge itself. Crossing the delicate-looking truss bridge in a car was nerve-racking enough. Standing on the railings with land a terrifying thirty feet below?

Unimaginable.

The morning rain had gone from a soft drizzle to sporadic showers. Currently it wasn't raining, but fog swirled around them like lowering clouds. As Rachel crunched her way across the wet gravel on the shoulder of the road, Delilah rolled down the passenger window. "You sure you feel up to driving?"

"I'm fine," she said automatically.

"Take care of yourself, okay?" Delilah smiled gently as she rolled the window back up, shutting out the damp coolness of the day. Rachel watched until the truck disappeared around the bend before she slid behind the wheel of the Honda.

The car's interior seemed oppressively silent, her sudden sense of isolation exacerbated by the tendrils of fog wrapping around the car. Outside, the world looked increasingly gray and alien, so she turned her attention to the car itself, hoping something would jog her missing memory.

What had she done the last time she was in her car? Why couldn't she remember anything between standing at her father's gravesite and waking up in a strange room with Seth Hammond watching her with those intense green eyes?

A trilling sound split the air, making her jump. She found the offending noisemaker—her cell phone, which lay on the passenger floorboard. Grinning sheepishly, she grabbed it and checked the display. She didn't recognize the number.

"Hello?"

"Rach! Thank God, I've been trying to reach you for hours."

"Davis?" The voice on the other end of the line belonged to her grad school boyfriend, Davis Rogers. She hadn't heard from him in years.

"I thought maybe you regretted giving me your number and were screening my calls. Did you get home okay?" Before she could answer, he continued, "Of course you did, or you wouldn't be answering the phone. Look, about last night—"

Suddenly, there was a thud on the other end of the line, and the connection went dead.

Rachel pulled the phone away from her face, startled. She looked at the display again. The number had a Virginia area code, but Davis had spoken as if he was here in Tennessee.

She tried calling the number on the display, but it went to voice mail.

He'd said he'd been trying to call her. She checked her own voice mail and discovered three messages, all from Davis. The first informed her where he was staying—the Sequoyah House, a bed-and-breakfast inn out near Cutter Horse Farm. She entered the information in her phone's notepad and checked the other messages.

In the last message, Davis sounded upset. "Rachel, it's Davis again. Look, I'm sorry about last night, but he seemed to think you might be receptive. I've really missed you. I didn't like leaving you in that place. Please call me back so I can apologize."

She stared at the phone. What place? Surely not Smoky Joe's. Why was her ex in town in the first place—for her father's funeral? Had she seen him yesterday?

And why had his call cut off?

Sequoyah House was a sprawling two-story farmhouse nestled in a clearing at the base of Copperhead Ridge. Behind the house, the mountain loomed like a guardian over the rain-washed valley below. It was the kind of place that lent itself more to romantic getaways than lodgings for a man alone.

But maybe Davis Rogers hadn't planned to be alone for long.

Most of the lobby furnishings looked to be rustic antiques, the bounty of a rich and varied Smoky Mountain tradition of craftsmanship. But despite its hominess, Sequoyah House couldn't hide a definite air of money, and plenty of it.

The woman behind the large mahogany front desk smiled at him politely, her cool gray eyes taking in his cotton golf shirt, timeworn jeans and barbershop haircut. No doubt wondering if he could afford the hotel's rates.

"May I help you?" she asked in a neutral tone.

"I'm here to see one of your guests, Davis Rogers."

"Mr. Rogers is not in his room. May I give him a message?"

"Yes. Would you tell him Seth Hammond stopped by to see him about a matter concerning Rachel Davenport?"

He could tell by the flicker in her eyes that she recognized his name. His reputation preceded him.

"Where can he reach you?"

Seth pulled one of the business cards sitting in a silver holder on the desk. "May I?" At her nod of assent, he flipped the card over and wrote his cell phone number on the back.

The woman took the card. "I'll give him the message."

He walked slowly down the front porch steps and headed back to where he'd parked in a section of the clearing leveled off and covered with interlocked pavers to form a parking lot. Among the other cars parked there he spotted a shiny blue Mercedes with Virginia license plates.

Seth looked through the driver's window. The car's interior looked spotless, with nothing to identify the owner. If Ivy Hawkins weren't on administrative leave for another week, Seth might have risked calling her to see if she could run down the plate number. She'd investigated the murders that had started this whole mess, after all. She'd damned near fallen victim to the killer herself. She might be persuaded.

But her partner, Antoine Parsons, had no reason to listen to anything Seth had to say. And what would it matter, really? Seth already knew Davis was staying at Sequoyah House. Though if the car with the Virginia plates was his, it did raise the question—if he wasn't in his room, and he wasn't in his car, where exactly was he?

As he headed back toward the Charger through the cold rain, a ringing sound stopped him midstep. It seemed faint, as if it was coming from a small distance away, but he didn't see anyone around.

He followed the sound to a patch of dense oak leaf hydrangea bushes growing wild at the edge of the tree line. The cream-colored blossoms had started to fade with the onset of colder weather, but the leaves were thick enough to force Seth to crouch to locate the phone by the fourth ring. It lay faceup on the ground.

Seth picked up the phone and pressed the answer button. "Hello?" he said, expecting the voice on the other end to belong to the phone's owner, calling to locate his missing phone.

The last thing he expected was to hear Rachel Davenport's voice. "Davis?"

Seth's gaze slid across the parking lot to the car with the Virginia plates. His chest tightened.

"Davis?" Rachel repeated.

"It's not Davis," he answered slowly. "It's Seth Hammond."

She was silent for a moment. "This is the number Davis Rogers left on my cell phone. Where is he? What's going on?"

"I don't know. I heard the phone ringing and answered, figuring the owner might be looking for his phone."

"Where are you?"

"Outside Sequoyah House." He pushed to his feet and started moving slowly down the line of bushes, looking through the thick foliage for something he desperately hoped he wouldn't find.

"What are you doing there?" She couldn't keep the suspicion from her tone, and he couldn't exactly blame her.

"I went and talked to Joe Breslin at Smoky Joe's Saloon. He remembered seeing you there with a man last night. So he looked up the man's credit card receipt and got a name for me."

"I was at Smoky Joe's with Davis?" She sounded skeptical. "That is definitely not his kind of place."

"Maybe it's yours," he suggested, remembering her sing-along with the bluegrass CD.

"Did you talk to Davis?"

"The clerk said he wasn't in his room, so I left him a message to call me." He paused as he caught sight of something dark behind one of the bushes. "I used your name. Hope you don't mind." He hunkered down next to the bush and carefully pushed aside the leaves to see what lay behind.

His heart sank to his toes.

Curled up in the fetal position, covered in blood and bruises, lay a man. Seth couldn't tell if he was breathing. "Rachel, I have to go. I'll call you back as soon as I can."

He disconnected the call and put the cell phone in his jacket pocket. The tightly packed underbrush forced him to crawl through the narrow spaces between the bushes to get back to where the man lay with his back against the trunk of a birch tree. He'd been beaten, and badly. His face was misshapen with broken bones, his eyes purple and swollen shut. Blood drenched the front of his shirt, making it hard to tell what color it had been originally. One of his legs lay at an unnatural angle, suggesting a break or a dislocation.

Seth touched the man's throat and found a faint pulse. He didn't know what Davis Rogers looked like, but the proximity of the battered man and the discarded cell phone suggested a connection. He backed out of the bushes, reaching into his pocket for his own cell phone to dial 911.

But before his fingers cleared his pocket, something hit him hard against the back of the neck, slamming him forward into the bushes. His forehead cracked against the trunk of the birch tree, the blow filling his vision with dozens of exploding, colorful spots.

A second blow caught him near the small of his back, over his left kidney, shooting fire through his side. That was a kick, he realized with the last vestige of sense remaining in his aching head.

Then a hard knock to the back of his head turned out the lights.

After ten minutes had passed without a call back from Seth, Rachel's worry level hit the stratosphere. There had been something in his tone when he'd rung off that had kept her stomach in knots ever since.

He'd sounded…grim. As if he'd just made a gruesome discovery.

Given the fact that he'd answered Davis's phone a few seconds earlier, Rachel wasn't sure she wanted to hear what he'd found.

What if something bad had happened to Davis? He'd been her first real boyfriend, the first man she'd ever slept with. The first man she'd ever loved, even if it had ultimately been a doomed sort of love.

She might not be in love with him anymore, but she still cared. And if Seth's tone of voice meant anything—

Forget waiting. She was tired of waiting. Seth had said he was at Sequoyah House. The bed-and-breakfast was five minutes away.

She grabbed her car keys and headed for the door.

If she wanted to know what was going on, she could damned well find out for herself.

Everything on Seth's body seemed to hurt, but not enough to suggest he was on the verge of dying. He opened his eyes carefully and found himself gazing up into a rain-dark sky. He was drenched and cold, and his head felt as if he'd spent the past few hours banging it against a wall.

He lifted his legs one at a time and decided they were still in decent working order, though he felt a mild shooting pain in his side when he moved. Both arms appeared intact, though there was fresh blood on one arm. No sign of a cut beneath the red drops, so he guessed the blood had come from another part of his body.

He couldn't breathe through his nose. When he lifted his hand to his face, he learned why. Blood stained his fingers, and his nose felt sore to the touch. He forced himself to sit up, groaning softly at the effort, and looked around him.

He was in the woods, though there was a break in the trees to his right, revealing the corner of a large clapboard house. Sequoyah House, he thought, the memory accompanied by no small amount of pain.

Some of his memories seemed to be missing. He knew who he was. He knew what day it was, unless he'd been out longer than he thought. He knew what he'd been doing earlier that day—he'd been hoping to talk to Rachel Davenport's old friend Davis Rogers. But Rogers hadn't been in his room, so Seth had given the desk clerk a message for Rachel's friend and left the bed-and-breakfast.

He remembered walking back to the parking area where he'd left the Charger.

What then?

His cell phone rang, barely audible. He pulled it out from the back pocket of his sodden jeans and saw Adam Brand's name on the display. Perfect. Just perfect.

Then an image flashed through his aching head. A cell phone—but not this cell phone. Another one. He'd heard it ringing and come here into the woods to find it.

But where was the cell phone now?

He answered his phone to stop the noise. "Yeah?" The greeting came out surly. Seth didn't give a damn—surly was exactly how he felt.

"You were supposed to check in this morning," Brand said.

"Yeah, well, I was detained." He winced as he tried to push to his feet. "And the case has gone to hell in a handbasket, thanks for asking."

"What's happened?"

"Too much to tell you over the phone. I'll type you up a report. Okay?"

"Is something wrong? You sound like hell."

Seth spotted a rusty patch in the leaves nearby. His brow furrowed, sending a fresh ache through his brain. "I'll put that in the report, too." He hung up and crossed to the dark spot in the leaves.

The rain had washed away all but a few remnants of red. Seth picked up one of the stained leaves and took a closer look.

Blood. There was blood here on the ground. Was this where he'd been attacked?

No. Not him. There had been someone else. An

image flitted through his pain-addled mind, moving so fast he almost didn't catch it.

But he saw enough. He saw the body of a man, curled into a ball, as if he'd passed out trying to protect his body from the blows. And passed out he had, because Seth had a sudden, distinct memory of checking the man's pulse and finding it barely there.

So where was the man now? Had whoever left this throbbing bump on the back of Seth's head taken the body away from here and dumped it elsewhere?

If so, they'd apparently taken the discarded cell phone, as well, because it was no longer in the pocket of his jacket.

He trudged through the rainy woods, heading for the clearing ahead. His vision kept shifting on him, making him stagger a little, and it was a relief to reach the Charger after what seemed like the longest fifty-yard walk of his life. He sagged against the side of the car, pressing his cheek against the cold metal frame of the chassis for a moment. It seemed to ease the pain in his skull, so he stood there awhile longer.

Only the sound of a vehicle approaching spurred him to move. He pushed away from the car and started to unlock to door when he realized the Charger was listing drastically to one side. Looking down, he saw why—both of the driver's-side tires were flat.

He groaned with dismay.

The vehicle turned off the road and into the parking lot. Seth forced his drooping gaze upward and was surprised to see Rachel Davenport staring back at him through the swishing windshield wipers of her car. She parked behind him and got out, her expression horrified.

"My God, what happened to you?"

He caught a glimpse of his reflection in the Charger's front window and winced at the sight. His nose was bloody and starting to bruise. An oozing scrape marred the skin over his left eye, as well.

"Should've seen the other guy," he said with a cocky grin, hoping to wipe that look of concern off her face. The last thing he could deal with in his weakened condition was a Rachel Davenport who felt sorry for him. He needed her angry and spitting fire so she'd go away and leave him to safely lick his wounds in private.

But she seemed unfazed by his show of bravado, moving forward with her hand outstretched.

Don't touch me, he willed, trying to duck away.

But she finally caught his chin in her hand and forced him to look at her. Her blue eyes searched his, and he found himself utterly incapable of shaking her off.

Her touch burned. Branded. He found himself struggling just to take another breath as her gaze swept over him, surveying his wounds with surprising calm for a woman who'd been swinging from the girders of Purgatory Bridge just the night before.

"Did you lose consciousness?" she asked.

"A few seconds." Maybe minutes. He couldn't be sure.

She looked skeptical. "Do you remember what happened?"

"I remember coming here to talk to your friend. He wasn't in his room."

"Right, but you found his cell phone."

He felt relieved to know his memory was real and not some injury-induced confabulation. "Right."

"But you cut me off. Said you had to go."

He caught her hand, pulling it gently from his chin

and closing it between his own fingers. "Rachel, it's fuzzy, and I may be remembering things incorrectly—"

"Just say it," she pleaded.

He tightened his grip on her hand. "I think your friend Davis may have been murdered."

Chapter 5

The cold numbness that had settled in the center of Rachel's chest from the time she'd gotten Davis Rogers's call began spreading to her limbs at Seth's words. "Why do you think that?"

He told her.

She tugged her hand away from his and started walking toward the edge of the mist-shrouded woods. Seth followed, his gait unsteady.

"I can't prove any of it," he warned. "If you call the Bitterwood P.D., they won't believe a word of it. I'm not high on their list of reliable witnesses."

"I need to know for myself. Where was the blood?" Her feet slipped on wet leaves as she entered the woods.

Seth's hand closed around her elbow, helping her stay upright, despite the fact that he was swaying on his feet. "Over here." He nudged her over until they came to a stop near a large stand of wild hydrangea bushes. A fading patch of rusting red was trickling away in the rain, but it definitely looked like blood.

Rachel picked up one of the red-stained leaves and lifted it to her nose. A faint metallic odor rose from the stain. "It's definitely blood."

"I don't know what happened to him. I swear."

She turned to look at him. He really did look terrible, blood still seeping from a scrape on the right side of his forehead and his nose crusted with more of the same. "You don't remember who did this to you?"

"No. Everything's a blur." He looked pale beneath his normally olive-toned skin. As he swayed toward her, she put out her hands to keep him from crashing into her.

"You're in no condition to drive."

He shot her a lopsided grin. "Neither is my car."

When they got back to the parking lot, she saw what he meant. Both of the driver's side tires were flat. She couldn't tell if they'd been punctured or if the air had just been let out of them. Didn't really matter, she supposed.

"Get in my car," she said, ignoring the wobble in her own legs. She didn't have time to fall apart. There was too much that needed to be done. She'd think about Davis later.

"Bossy. I like it." Seth shot her a look that was as hot as a southern summer. An answering quiver rippled through her belly, but she ignored it. He sounded woozy—probably didn't know what he was saying. And even if he did, neither of them was in any position to do much about it.

"I'm going to call the police and report Davis missing," she told him as she slid behind the wheel. "I'm going to have to include you in my statement."

He shook his head, then went stock-still, wincing. "Ow."

She turned to face him. He tried to do the same, but she could tell the movement was painful for him. Just how badly had he been beaten? "Seth, I can't leave you out of it, because you've left a trail that leads to you. You gave your name to the clerk. Your car is sitting here in the parking lot with flat tires, and if we call a wrecker to come get it, that's just another trail that leads to you."

His expression darkened. "You don't know what it's like to be everyone's number one suspect."

"You're right. I don't. But I can tell the police what I do know. I was talking to Davis when the line went dead. Then when I called Davis's phone, you answered—" She stopped short, realizing how that would sound to the police.

Seth's eyes met hers. "Exactly."

"If Davis is dead, I can't just do nothing."

"Just don't tell them I answered the phone."

He wanted her to lie to the police? "I can't leave something like that out of my statement."

He looked as if he wanted to argue, but finally he slumped against the seat. "Do what you have to."

She leaned back against her own seat, frustrated. What was she supposed to do now? Ignore his fears? Tell him he was overreacting?

She couldn't do that. Because she didn't plan on telling the police everything, did she? She certainly wasn't going to tell them she'd spent most of the previous evening apparently so drugged out of her head that she'd thought a balance beam routine on the girders of Purgatory Bridge was a good idea.

"I know what it's like to have people judging your every move," she said quietly.

He slanted a curious look her way.

"I don't want the police to know what happened to me last night. And you haven't pushed me at all to tell anyone the truth."

"I figured if you wanted it known, you'd tell it yourself."

She nodded. "I won't tell them you answered Davis's phone."

He released a long, slow breath. "Rachel, you know I didn't do anything to him. Right?"

She wondered if she was crazy to believe him. What did she know about him, really? He kept to himself at work, making few friends. She'd heard stories about his years as a con man, though she and her father had decided to judge him on his current work, not his checkered past. And he'd been a good worker, hadn't he? Showed up on time or early, did what he was asked, never caused any trouble.

But was that reason enough to trust what he said?

"I guess not." He reached for the door handle.

She caught his arm. He turned back to her, his gaze first settling where her fingers circled his rain-slick forearm, then rising to meet hers. In the low light, his eyes were as deep and mysterious as the rainy woods outside the car.

"You saved my life last night, and you've asked for nothing in return. You didn't even try to use it against me just now, when you could have. Any con man worth his salt would have."

He grimaced. "I'm no saint."

"I'm not saying you are. I'm just saying I believe you."

The interior of the car seemed to contract, the space between their bodies suddenly infinitesimal. She could feel heat radiating from his body, answered by her own. Despite his battered condition, despite the million and one reasons she shouldn't feel this aching magnetism toward him, she couldn't pretend she didn't find him attractive.

He wasn't movie-star handsome, especially now with his nose bloody and purple shadows starting to darken the skin beneath his eyes, but he was all man, raw masculinity in every angle of his body, every sinewy muscle and broad expanse.

He had big, strong hands, and even with a dozen conflicting and distracting thoughts flitting through her head at the moment, she could imagine the feel of them moving over her body in a slow, thorough seduction. The sensation was fierce and primal, intensely sexual, and she had never felt anything quite like it before.

"What now?" he asked, breaking the tense silence.

Her body's response came, quick and eager.

Take me home with you.

Aloud, she said, "I guess I call the police so they can start looking for Davis." She pulled out her phone and made the call to 911.

"I need to clean up," Seth murmured.

"Here." She reached across to the glove compartment, removed a package of wet wipes and handed them to him. "Best I can do."

He looked at the wet wipes and back at her, one eyebrow notching upward.

"Habit. I was a librarian," she said with a smile. "I dealt with a lot of sticky hands all day."

He pulled a wipe from the package and started cleaning off the blood, using the mirror on the sun visor to check his progress. When he finally snapped the wet wipe package closed, he looked almost normal. His nose wasn't as swollen as it had appeared with all the blood crusted on it, and the scrape on his forehead, once cleaned up, wasn't nearly as large as it had looked. Only the slight darkening of the skin around his eyes gave away his battered condition, and the rusty splotches where the blood from his face had dripped onto the front of his dark blue shirt.

"Better?" he asked.

She nodded. "You're going to have to answer questions regardless."

"I know." He slanted another wry grin in her direction, making her belly squirm. "I'd just like to look my best when I talk to the cops."

Uniformed officers arrived first to take their statements, but within half an hour, a detective arrived, a tall, slim black man with sharp brown eyes and a friendly demeanor. He'd come around the trucking company asking questions last month after a couple of their employees had been murdered, Rachel remembered. Antoine Parsons. Nice guy.

He didn't look particularly nice as his gaze swept the scene and locked, inevitably, on Seth's battered face. "Seth Hammond. You do have a funny way of showing up at all my crime scenes lately."

Seth's smile was close to a smirk. Rachel felt the urge to punch him in the shoulder and tell him to stop making things worse. But apparently he just couldn't help it. "Antoine, Antoine, Antoine. Still sucking up to the Man, I see. How's that working out for you?"

Antoine barely stopped an eye roll. "We have a missing person?"

Rachel stepped in front of Seth to address the detective. "His name is Davis Rogers. I was talking to him on the phone when I heard a thud and the phone went dead."

"You came here to look for him?"

"He'd left an earlier message on my voice mail, telling me where he was staying. It seemed the obvious place to look. I got here and found his car parked in the lot. But he's not in his room. And I found a patch of blood in the leaves nearby." She waved toward the woods.

Antoine's gaze slid back to Seth's face. "Who gave you a pounding, Hammond?"

"Not sure," he answered.

"What are you doing here? You with Ms. Davenport?"

"I came looking for Rogers. He wasn't in his room, so I was about to leave when I thought I saw something in the woods."

"Just happened to see something in the woods?" Antoine was clearly skeptical. Rachel was beginning to understand why Seth hadn't wanted her to include him in this police investigation at all. Maybe he'd earned the distrust, but clearly nobody in the Bitterwood Police Department was going to give him any benefit of the doubt.

"I heard something, actually." Seth slanted a look her way. She saw fear in his eyes but also rock-hard determination in the set of his jaw. "I heard a cell phone

ringing. I found it on the ground beneath those bushes."
He pointed toward the hydrangeas.

He was telling the truth about the phone, she realized with a thrill of surprise.

"It was Ms. Davenport, calling Rogers."

Antoine's brows lifted. "You said you were looking for Rogers. Why?"

She saw the hesitation in Seth's face. The truth, she realized, could be a scary thing. And not just for Seth. For her, too.

But it was better than the alternative.

She took a deep breath and answered the detective's question for Seth. "He was trying to find out what happened to me last night."

It took almost two hours to work through all the questions Antoine had for both of them. His attitude toward Seth had settled into guarded belief, though Seth knew it would last only as long as it took to get in trouble again.

At least Antoine had asked good, probing questions. Unfortunately, neither Seth nor Rachel had any good answers. She still couldn't remember most of what had happened the night before, and Seth's memory of the attack that had left him bruised and half-conscious was similarly spotty.

He'd refused a trip to the hospital, though the paramedics thought he'd sustained a concussion. His mind was clearing nicely, and most of the aches and pains in his body had faded to bearable. He probably did have a mild concussion, but he didn't think it was any worse than that. He'd go spend the night at Delilah's and let her play nursemaid.

Except apparently Delilah was out of town for the night. "She said she was driving down to Alabama for a business meeting," Rachel told Seth after he'd assured the paramedics he'd have his sister keep an eye on him.

Well, hell. He'd just have to keep an eye on himself.

"You could stay with me tonight." Rachel's blue eyes locked with his, but her expression was impossible to read.

"That's kind of you—"

"I'm not sure it's kind," she said, the left corner of her mouth quirking upward. "I could use another set of eyes and ears in the house. I'm not inclined to stay there alone after all of this."

So when Antoine finally agreed to let them leave, Seth called a wrecker service to take the Charger to the local garage and got into the passenger seat of Rachel's car.

"You don't have to do this," he told her as she buckled herself in behind the steering wheel. "I'll be okay."

"I was serious. I don't want to be alone. I'm not sure I'm safe alone with everything that's going on."

She probably wasn't, he realized. "I'm sorry about Davis. I hope I'm wrong about what happened to him."

Her lips tightened. "I wish I believed you were."

"Do you know why he was here?"

"He must have come to the funeral." She looked close to collapse, he realized, so he didn't ask anything else until they reached the sprawling two-story farmhouse on the eastern edge of Bitterwood, a few miles south of Copperhead Ridge and light years away from the hardscrabble life Seth had lived growing up on Smoky Ridge.

Until her father's cancer diagnosis, Rachel had kept

her own apartment in Maryville, living off her earnings as a public librarian. But everything had changed when a series of doctors confirmed the initial diagnosis—inoperable, terminal liver cancer. Too late for a transplant to help. They'd given him four months to live. Chemo, radiation and a series of holistic treatments had prolonged his life by a few more months, but shortly before his death, George had said, "No more," and spent the remainder of his time on earth preparing his daughter to run the trucking company he'd built.

Seth knew all these intimate details about Rachel's life because Davenport Trucking was like any business that maintained a family atmosphere—everybody knew everybody else's business. Few secrets lasted long in such a place.

But he didn't know what Rachel thought about the drastic change in her life. Did she regret leaving the library behind? From what he knew of her work at Davenport, she had a deft hand with personnel management and seemed to have a natural affinity for the finance end of the business. People who'd grumbled about her selection as her father's successor had stopped complaining when it became clear that the company wouldn't suffer under her guidance.

But nobody seemed to know what Rachel herself thought about the job. Did the benefit of fulfilling her father's dying wish outweigh the loss of a career she'd chosen for herself?

"This house is too big for just one person," Rachel commented as she unlocked the front door and let them inside. "I don't think Diane plans to come back here. Too much of my mother here for her tastes."

The front door opened into a narrow hallway that

stretched all the way to a door in the back. Off the hallway, either archways or doors led into rooms on either side. To the immediate right, a set of stairs rose to the second floor, flanked by an oak banister polished smooth from years of wear. "Did you ever slide down that banister?" he asked Rachel.

"Maybe." A whisper of a smile touched her lips. "Think you can make it up the stairs? The bedrooms are on the second floor."

He dragged himself up the steps behind her, glad he was feeling less light-headed than he had back at the bed-and-breakfast. Rachel showed him into a simple, homey room on the left nearest the stairs. "I'll make up the bed for you. Why don't you go take a shower? The bathroom's the next door down on the right. There's a robe in the closet that should fit you. I'll see if Paul's left any clothes around you can borrow for the night."

When he emerged from the shower fifteen minutes later, he returned to the bedroom to find the bedcovers folded back and a pair of sweatpants and a mismatched T-shirt draped across the bed. A slip of paper lay on top of them. "Sorry, couldn't find any underwear. Or anything that matched. After I shower, we'll find something to eat."

She had finished her shower first and was already downstairs in the cozy country kitchen at the back of the house. "Something to eat" turned out to be tomato soup and grilled cheese sandwiches.

Rachel had finally shed the dress she'd worn to Smoky Joe's the night before, replacing it with a pair of slim-fitting yoga pants and a long-sleeved T-shirt that revealed her long legs and slender arms. She was thinner than Seth normally liked in a woman, but he couldn't find a damned thing wrong with the flare of her hips or the curve of her small, firm breasts.

"Is tomato soup okay? I should have asked—"

"It's fine. I can grill the sandwiches if you want."

She turned to look at him, smiling a little as she took in his mismatched clothes. Her stepbrother, Paul, was a little slimmer than he was, so the clothes fit snugly on his legs and shoulders. "Are you sure you're feeling up to it?"

"The shower worked wonders," he assured her, bellying up to the kitchen counter beside the stove, where she'd already prepared the sandwiches and set out a stick of butter for the griddle pan heating up over the closest eye. He dipped to get a better look at the stove top, relieved that it was a flat-top electric with no open-flame burners.

She gave him a sidelong glance as he moved closer to where she stood stirring the soup. "I'm not used to cooking with company."

"Me, either." He dropped a pat of butter on the griddle pan. It sizzled and snapped, and they both had to jump back to avoid the splatter.

Rachel laughed. "I see why. You're dangerous."

"We could switch," he suggested. "Surely I can manage stirring soup."

Switching positions, they brushed intimately close. As Seth's body stirred to life, he realized the cut of the sweatpants wasn't quite loose enough to hide his reaction if he didn't get his libido under control, and soon.

Just stir the soup. Clockwise, clockwise, switch it up to counterclockwise—

"Why are you so interested in what happened to me last night?" Rachel broke the tense silence.

He glanced at her and found she was looking intently at the griddle, where she'd laid both of the sandwiches in a puddle of sizzling butter, her profile deceptively serene. Only the quick flutter of her pulse in her throat gave away her tension.

"What is it they say? Save a person's life and they're your slave forever after? Maybe I'm just waiting for you to pay up."

She cut her eyes at him as if to make sure he was teasing. "Yeah, that'll happen."

He grinned. "Maybe I'm sucking up to the new boss."

Wrong thing to say. Her slight smile faded immediately. "New boss. I haven't even let myself think about that yet."

"Is that going to be a problem? Me being an employee, I mean. And being here like this. Because I'm feeling a lot better, really. I don't have to stick around so you can watch out for my mental state."

"That's not what I meant," she said. "I was thinking about being the boss, period. All those people depending on what I do and say now."

He had stopped stirring while they were talking, and a thin skin was forming on top of the soup. He started stirring again, quickly whisking the film away. "Hasn't that been the case for a while now?"

She was quiet a moment. "I guess so. It just didn't feel real as long as my father was around to be my safety net."

To his dismay, he saw tears glisten in her eyes, threatening to spill. The urge to pull her into his arms and hold her close was almost more than he could resist. He settled for laying one hand on her shoulder and giving it a comforting squeeze.

She wiped her eyes with the heel of one hand and flipped the sandwiches over. "I had a long time to prepare for my father's death. And it was a relief by the end to see him finally out of pain. But now that I'm past that numb stage—"

"Your dad was a good man. Not many people would've taken a chance on someone like me. This world's a worse place with him gone."

His words had summoned tears again, but also a smile, which she turned on him like a ray of pure sunshine that brightened the room, even as the drizzle outside darkened the day.

He smiled back briefly, then forced his attention back to the soup before he got any deeper into trouble.

Chapter 6

After lunch, Rachel made a pot of coffee and they took their cups into the den on the eastern side of the house, where a large picture window offered a glimpse of Copperhead Ridge shrouded with mist. The rain had picked up again, casting the trees in hues of blue and gray. When she turned on the floor lamps that flanked the room, the scene outside faded into reflections of the warm, comfortably furnished den and the two slightly bedraggled people who occupied it.

Seth found his own reflection depressing, given how quickly his bruises were darkening, making him look like the loser of a cage match. He turned his attention instead to Rachel, whose honey-brown hair lay in damp waves around her face. Scrubbed clean and pink, she looked about a decade younger and prettier than she had any right to be.

"How's your head feeling?" she asked.

Light, he thought. But it didn't have much to do with his mild concussion. "Better. Not really hurting anymore."

Her brief smile faded quickly. "I don't know what to think about Davis."

"You mean whether or not he's still alive?"

She sank into an armchair across from the sofa, curling her legs under her. She waved for Seth to sit across from her on the sofa. "I mean if he's dead. How am I supposed to feel about it?"

"I don't know that you're *supposed* to feel any particular way," Seth offered. "You just feel what you feel."

"I did love him once. He was the first man—" She stopped short, a delicate blush rising in her cheeks. She slanted a quick look at Seth. "It didn't last. We wanted such different things out of life."

Whatever it had been that Davis Rogers had wanted out of life, it was surely closer to Rachel's desires than anything Seth had done or wanted to do in his own life. If she and Davis had been miles apart, she and Seth were separated by whole galaxies.

But it doesn't matter, does it? That's not why you're here.

"I haven't even seen him in years. We ran into each other a while back at a football game in Charlottesville. Said hi, promised to call but never did—" She closed her eyes. "Why did he come here?"

"Probably to attend your father's funeral and see how you were."

"And now he might be dead because of me."

Seth reached across the space between them, covering her hands with one of his. "If he's dead, it's because someone beat the hell out of him."

"Because of me."

He crouched in front of her, closing his fingers around her wrists. "Look at me."

Her troubled blue eyes met his.

"I know someone's been methodically removing people from your life to isolate you. I know whoever's pulling the strings hired Mark Bramlett to kill four women who were close to you. And now, maybe, he's killed your old boyfriend, who came to town to make sure you were okay. I think he may have been behind drugging you last night, too."

Rachel's eyes darkened with suspicion. "How do you know this?"

"I started to suspect something was going on when I realized three of the four Bitterwood murders involved women who'd worked at Davenport Trucking. That was strange enough. Then I asked around and found out that Marjorie Kenner had been your friend and mentor—another librarian, right?"

"Right." She looked stricken by his words, as if the mere reminders of all she'd lost had hit her all over again. He wished he'd found some way to soften his words, but he doubted anything he could have said would have made her feel the pain any less keenly.

"What I don't know," he added more gently, "is why. If someone wanted to get you out of his way—"

"His?"

"His, her—whichever. If someone wanted you out of the way, why not just kill you?"

She blanched. "I don't know."

"I think you do. You just can't say it out loud for some reason."

She slanted a troubled look at him. "How do you know so much about me?"

He ran his thumb lightly over her knuckles, gentling her with the movement. He saw her start to relax a little, soothed by the repetitive movement of his thumb. "I know because I observe. I used to be a con man, you know. That's what con men do. Observe, compile, formulate and exploit."

Her nostrils flared with a hint of distaste. "You're approaching my trouble like you would approach a potential mark?"

"Might as well use those skills for good."

Her eyes narrowed a little, but she gave a slight nod. "So what have you observed?"

"You're scared of something. Not everyone can see it, because you hide it really well. But I see it, because that used to be my job. Finding a person's vulnerable spots and figuring out how to use them."

"But you haven't found out what it is."

"Not yet."

Her lips twisted in a mirthless smile. "And I'm supposed to spill what it is to you, make it easier?"

"I'm not the one trying to hurt you."

"How do I know that?" She pulled her hands free of his grip and pushed him out of her way, rising and pacing the hardwood floor until she reached the picture window. She met his gaze in the window reflection. "I don't really know you. And what I do know scares me."

He couldn't blame her. What he knew about himself would scare anyone. "I don't want to see you get hurt, and whether you like my skill set or not, I can use it to help you out. So whatever you can tell me, whatever you're comfortable sharing—I'll listen. I'll keep your confidence, and I won't use it against you."

She turned around to look at him. "I'm taking a huge risk just letting you stay here, aren't I?"

She wasn't going to tell him what scared her so much, he realized. It was disappointing. Frustrating. But he didn't blame her.

"Okay." He nodded. "I can leave if you want me to."

She licked her lips and held his gaze, searching his expression as if trying to see what was going on inside his mind. "No. I know you're feeling better, but head injuries can be quirky. I'd rather you stay here where I can look in on you every few hours to make sure you haven't gone into a coma."

He grimaced. "What, you're planning to wake me up every couple of hours or something?" He added a touch of humor to his voice, hoping to lighten the mood.

It worked. Her lips quirked slightly, and there was a glitter of amusement in her blue eyes when she answered, "That's exactly what I'm planning to do."

Behind the humor, however, he heard a steely determination that caught him by surprise. She apparently took the job of keeping an eye on him seriously, and he suspected it was as much for her own sake as his. Maybe it gave her a welcome distraction from the strain and grief of her life these days.

He nodded toward the picture window. "Do you always leave these windows open like this?"

Her brow furrowed. "Most of the time. It's such a beautiful view."

"It is," he agreed. "But it gives people a pretty good view of you, too."

Her eyes darkened, and she wrapped her arms around herself as if she felt a sudden chill. "I never thought about that."

She wouldn't have. She wasn't used to being a target, and Seth wished like hell she could continue living her life without precautions. But there was too much danger out there, focused directly on her, for her to let her guard down that way anymore.

The windows were curtain-free, but he thought he saw levers on each double-paned window that suggested between-the-glass blinds. "Whenever it's dark enough outside to see your reflection in the windows, you should close the blinds."

She pressed her lips in a tight line, as if it annoyed her to have to make even that small accommodation to the dangerous world around her. A sign of a charmed life, he thought, remembering how early in his own life he'd learned to take precautions against the dangers always lurking, both outside and in.

Another way he and Rachel Davenport were worlds apart.

Starting at the opposite end of the room, he helped her close the blinds until they met in the middle. She paused at the last window, gazing out at the darkness barely visible beyond their reflections.

"You think I'm spoiled," she said quietly.

He didn't answer. He'd more or less been thinking exactly that, although not with any disapproval. He envied her, frankly.

"There's a lot about my life you don't know." She closed the blinds, shutting out the rainy afternoon, and turned to look at him, her expression softening. "You look terrible. I think you may have a broken nose."

It certainly hurt like hell, but he'd examined the bones himself while taking his shower, where he could throw out a stream of profanities without offending anyone. Cracked or not, the bones and cartilage were all in the right places. "It'll heal on its own."

"Said in the tone of a man who's had a broken bone or two."

"Or ten." He made a face. "I'm fine."

She looked skeptical but didn't press him on it. She crossed back to the armchair and curled up on its overstuffed cushions, pulling her knees up to her chest.

He didn't feel like sitting, so he wandered around the den, taking in the good furniture—some antiques, most not—and the eclectic collection of knickknacks dotting the flat surfaces around the large, airy room. Tiny animals sculpted from colored quartz formed a menagerie on a round side table near the sofa. On the fireplace mantel sat a small collection of Russian nesting dolls, painted in bright colors.

The fireplace itself was, thankfully, cold and unlit, though the extra heat might have helped to drive away the afternoon chill still shivering in his bones. He'd live without it, thank you very much.

He didn't care for fire.

The house he'd grown up in would have fit in this room, he thought, or close to it. He, Dee and his parents had lived there in grim strife for nearly fourteen years, until his father had blown the whole damned thing up, and himself with it.

He wondered what Rachel Davenport had been doing around the time of that explosion. Probably up to her eyeballs in homework from Brandywine Academy, the expensive private school she'd attended to keep her away from the Appalachian hillbillies who filled Bitterwood's public schools.

Envy is an unattractive trait. Cleve Calhoun's voice rumbled in his ear, full of wry humor. Hilarious advice coming from the man who'd used envy, greed, pride and vanity with great expertise against all his hapless marks. But however bad his motives for teaching Seth a few practical life lessons, Cleve had been right most of the time. Envy *was* an unattractive trait. And unfair to the envied, in Rachel's case.

It wasn't her fault she'd been loved and protected. Every child should be so blessed.

"Shouldn't you be resting?" Rachel asked.

He turned to look at her. "I'm not tired."

Her eyes narrowed slightly. "This isn't your first beating." It wasn't a question.

He didn't know whether to laugh or grimace. He managed something in between, his lips curving in a wry grin. "No, ma'am. It's not."

"Did you deserve them?"

That time, he did laugh. "Some of the time."

"Why did you choose the life you did?"

He wandered back over to the sofa, thinking about how to answer. When he'd been younger, he might have told her he didn't choose to become a con man. That life had chosen for him. He'd spent a lot of time blaming everyone in the world but himself for his troubles.

But everyone had choices, even people who didn't think they did. Delilah's childhood had been the same as his, but she'd chosen a different path, one that had made her a hero, not a criminal. He could have chosen such a path if he hadn't let hate and anger do him in.

That had been his choice. Nothing that happened before excused it.

"When I was young," he said finally, sitting on the sofa across from her, "I had a choice between two paths. One looked hard. The other looked easy. I chose easy."

A little furrow formed in her brow as she considered his words. "That simple?"

He nodded. "That simple. I was angry and tired of struggling. I was eaten up with envy and mad at the whole damned world. So when a man offered me a chance to get everything I wanted and stick it to people who stood in my way, I took it. I reckon you could even say I relished it. I was good at it, and in a twisted way, I think it gave me a sense of self-worth I'd never had before."

"So why aren't you still doing it?"

"Because nothing good, nothing real, gets built on lies."

Her solemn blue eyes held his gaze thoughtfully. "Or you could be lying to me now. Maybe this act of repentance is all for show."

"I guess that's for you to figure out."

She buried her face in her hands, rubbing her eyes with the heels of her hands. "I'm so tired."

He knew she wasn't just talking about physical tiredness. The past few months must have been hell on her emotionally, losing so many people who mattered to her, including her own father. "Why don't you go lie down? Take a nap."

"I'm supposed to be keeping an eye on you, remember?"

"I'm fine. Really. The ol' noggin's not even hurting anymore." *Well, not more than a slight ache,* he amended silently. And it was mostly at the site at the back of his head where he'd taken the knockout blow.

After a long, thoughtful pause, she rose to her feet with easy grace. He wondered idly if she'd taken ballet lessons as a child. She had the long limbs and elegant lines of a dancer.

Delilah had always wanted to take dance lessons, he remembered. He wondered if his sister had made up for lost time once she'd gotten away from Smoky Ridge. He'd have to remember to ask her.

"There's food in the fridge if you get hungry." She waved her arm toward the cases full of books that lined the walls of the den. "Lots to read, if your head's up to it. There's a television and a sound system in that cabinet if you'd rather watch TV or listen to music."

"In other words, make myself at home?"

Her lips quirked. "I'm not sure it's safe to give you that much rope."

He grinned back at her, unoffended. "Smart girl."

She headed for the stairs, but not before Seth saw her smile widen with pleasure.

Rachel hadn't planned to take a nap. She had felt tired but not particularly sleepy when she'd climbed the stairs to her room on the second floor, but the whisper of rain against the windows and the long and stressful day colluded to lull her to sleep within minutes of settling on the chaise lounge in the corner of her bedroom.

When she next opened her eyes, the gloom outside had gone from gray to inky black, and the room was cold enough to give her a chill. She rose from the chaise, stretching her stiffened muscles, and started toward the bathroom when she heard it.

Music.

Seth must have taken her at her word and turned on the stereo system, she thought, surprised by his choice of music. She hadn't figured him for a Chopin fan.

Then she recognized the tune. Nocturne Opus 9, Number 2. It had been her mother's favorite.

It had been playing the night she'd died.

Rachel walked slowly toward the bedroom door, her gut tightening with dread. There were no Chopin CDs in the house. What the police hadn't taken as evidence, her father had gotten rid of shortly after her mother's death.

How had Seth found anything to play?

Did he know about how her mother had died? He might know the mode of her death, of course—the suicide had made the papers—but the gory details had never showed up in the news or even in small-town gossip. The police and the coroner had been scrupulously discreet, from everything her father had told her of the aftermath of her mother's death.

So how could he know about the music?

She pushed open the door. And stopped suddenly in the center of the hall as she realized the music wasn't coming from the den below.

It was coming from the attic above.

Acid fear bubbled in her throat, forcing her to swallow convulsively. Was she imagining the slow, plaintive strains of piano music floating down from above?

Was she reliving the night of her mother's death, the way she had relived it in a thousand nightmares?

She had heard music that night as well, swelling through the otherwise silent house. It had awakened her from a dead sleep, loud enough to rip through the fabric of her tearstained dreams.

She'd felt nothing but anger at the sound. Anger at her mother's harsh words, at the stubborn refusal to see things her way. She'd been fifteen and pushing against the fences of her childhood. Her father had been the more reasonable of her parents, in her eyes at least. He'd recognized her need to unfurl her wings and fly now and then.

Her mother had just wanted her to stay in the safe nest she'd built for her only child.

A nest that was smothering her to death.

She'd hated the sound of that music, the piercing trills and the waltz cadence. She'd hated how loud it was, seeming to shake the walls and shatter her brain cells.

Or maybe that had just been how it had seemed afterward. After she'd climbed the ladder up to the attic and seen her mother swaying to the music, her gaze lifted toward the unseen heavens, one hand waving in rhythm and the other closed around the butt of George Davenport's Colt .45 pistol.

Terror stealing her breath, Rachel stared up at the ladder. The very thought of climbing into the attic was enough to make beads of sweat break out across her forehead and slither down her neck like liquid fear.

But she had to know. Not knowing was worse, somehow.

Biting her lip so hard she feared she'd made it bleed, Rachel reached up and pulled the cord that lowered the ladder to the attic. Music spilled out along with the ladder, louder than before. Not the rafter-rattling decibels of her memories but loud enough.

Swallowing hard, she started to climb the ladder,

clinging to the wooden rungs as if her life depended on it.

She'd had no warning of what she'd find that night. There were things she'd gotten used to about her mother—her obsession with cleanliness, her moodiness, her occasional outbursts of anger—but none of those things had seemed more than the normal foibles of life.

Maybe her father had sheltered her from the worst of it. Or maybe it wasn't as bad when her father was around. But he'd gone on a business trip, one that had eventually led to his securing the capital to start his own trucking business after working in truck fleet sales for most of his adult life. He was due back that night, but he'd been gone for almost a week.

Maybe a week had been all it had taken for her father's palliative influence to wear off.

Rachel tried to put the memories out of her head as she forced herself up the final few rungs and stepped into the attic. But the memories rose to slap her in the face.

A plastic drop cloth lay on the hard plank floor of the attic, just as it had that night. And across the drop cloth, blood splashed in crimson streaks and puddles.

Fresh blood.

Seth had found an old Dick Francis novel in one of the bookshelves and settled down to read, but his weariness and the rain's relentless cadence made it hard to stay awake. He'd closed his eyes for just a moment and suddenly he was back on the road to Smoky Joe's Saloon, the steel girders of Purgatory Bridge gleaming in his headlights.

He parked behind Rachel's Honda and got out, deeply

aware of the brisk, cool wind whipping his hair and his clothes. It was strong. Too strong. It would fling Rachel right off the bridge if he didn't get to her.

But no matter how far he walked, she was still a few steps farther away, dancing gracefully along the narrow girder as if she were walking a tightwire. Her arms were out, her face raised to the sky, and she was humming a tune, something slow and vaguely familiar, like one of the classical pieces his sister had learned in her music class at school and tried to pick out on the old, out-of-tune upright piano that had belonged to his grandmother.

Suddenly, Rachel turned to look straight at him, her eyes wide and glittering in the faint light coming from the honky-tonk down the road.

"You can't save us all," she said.

A gust of wind slammed into his back, knocking him off balance and catching Rachel's clothes up in its swirling wake, flapping them like a sail. She lost her balance slowly, almost gracefully, and even though he threw himself forward, he couldn't stop her fall.

He crashed into the girder rail in time to hear her scream. It seemed to grow louder and louder, even as she fell farther and farther away. The thirty-foot gorge became a bottomless chasm, and the scream went on and on....

He woke with a start, just in time to hear a scream cut off, followed by dreadful silence.

Chapter 7

Taking the stairs two at a time, Seth reached the second-floor landing in seconds. Down the hall, Rachel lay in a crumpled heap at the bottom of a ladder dropped down from an opening in the ceiling.

"Rachel!" Ignoring the aches and pains playing chase through his joints and muscles, he hurried to her side, nearly wilting with relief when she sat up immediately, staring at him with wide, scared eyes. "Are you okay? Are you hurt?"

"I don't know." She sounded winded. "I don't know if I'm okay."

She looked terrified, as if she'd been chased down the ladder by a monster. Tremors rolled through her slim body like a dozen small earthquakes going on inside her, making her teeth rattle. Her fingers dug into his arms.

He wrapped her in a bear hug, cocooning her against his body. She melted into him, clinging like a child.

What the hell had she seen?

"I need to go downstairs," she moaned. "Please, I can't be up here."

He helped her to her feet and led her down to the den, looking around desperately for a bar service. "Do you have any brandy?"

She shook her head as she sat on the sofa. "Dad had liver cancer. We all stopped drinking after the diagnosis."

Of course. "Okay, well, maybe some hot tea."

As he started to get up from where he crouched in front of her, she grabbed his hands and held him in place. "Don't go."

"Okay." He settled back into his crouch, stroking her cold fingers between his. "Can you at least tell me what happened?"

"I don't know."

But he could see she did know. She just didn't want to tell him.

A hank of hair had fallen into her face, hiding half her expression from him. He pushed it gently back behind her ear. "Maybe you had a bad dream?"

She shook her head.

"Not a dream?"

She looked less certain this time when she shook her head. "I don't think it was. I've never sleepwalked before."

"Then it probably wasn't a dream," he agreed. The concession didn't seem to give her much comfort. "Do you remember why you went up the ladder? Does it lead to the attic?"

She nodded. "I was dozing. And then I heard the music."

A snippet of memory flashed in his head. Rachel, gliding precariously along the girder rail, humming a song to herself.

"Was it this song?" he asked, humming a few notes.

Her head whipped up, her eyes locking with his. "How did you know?"

The anger in her tone caught him off guard, and he had to put one hand on the sofa to keep from toppling over. "I dreamed it. Just a minute ago."

Her eyes narrowed. "It's Chopin," she said tightly. "A nocturne. I heard it coming from the attic."

"So you went up to the attic to see where the music was coming from?"

Her lips trembled, and the bracing anger he'd seen in her blue eyes melted into dread. "I went up because I already knew where it was coming from."

He didn't know what she meant. "What did you find?"

"Everything but the body." Her gaze wandered, settling on some point far away.

He stared at her with alarm. "What body?"

Her gaze snapped back to his. "My mother's."

Letting her words sink in, he tried to remember what he knew about her mother's death. It had happened when she was young. He'd been a teenager himself, on the cusp of learning an exciting if larcenous new life at the feet of Cleve Calhoun. The death of some rich woman on the east side of town hadn't registered.

She'd killed herself, he knew. No other details had ever come out, so he'd figured she'd taken pills or slit her wrists or something.

If she'd killed herself in the attic, maybe she'd hung herself. "When you say everything was there but the body—"

"I mean everything," she said flatly. Her voice had gained strength, and her trembling had eased. "There was a plastic drop sheet, just like that night. She hated messes, so she was determined not to make one, even when—" Rachel stopped short, her throat bobbing as she swallowed hard. "The music playing was Chopin's nocturne. And afterward—the blood—"

Oh my God, he thought. *She saw it.*

"Did you find her?" he asked gently, hoping that was the extent of what she'd experienced that night, as bad as it must have been.

She looked up at him with haunted eyes. "I saw it happen."

He stared back at her a moment, finally understanding her reaction to whatever she'd witnessed up in the attic. "Oh, Rachel."

She looked away from him. "I saw it again. I know I saw it."

But she wasn't sure, he realized. She was doubting herself. Why?

"Do you want me to go take a look?" he offered.

Her gaze whipped back around to his. "You think I've lost my mind."

He didn't think that, although given her experience in the attic years ago and the stresses of the past few days, he had to wonder if she'd misinterpreted whatever it was she'd seen. "I just think I should take a look. Maybe there's an intruder in the house."

The idea of a third party in the house seemed not to have occurred to her, which made Seth wonder if she suspected him of trying to trick her. The wary looks she was sending his way weren't exactly reassuring. "I'll go with you."

He frowned. "Are you sure?"

She nodded quickly, her eyes narrowing.

It was a test, he realized. He'd been with her ever since she'd fallen out of the attic, so if he were the culprit, everything would be as she'd left it.

It was a chance he'd take. If someone was trying to gaslight her, he might still be in the house. They might still be in danger.

He climbed the ladder first. She waited until he'd stepped into the attic to start up after him, clutching the rungs with whitened knuckles. She moved slowly, with care, giving him a few seconds to view the room without any comment from her.

It was a small space, rectangular, with a steeply peaked ceiling of exposed rafters. The floor was hardwood planks, unpolished and mostly unfinished, though in the center of the room, large splotches and splashes of dark red wood stain marred the planks.

He looked doubtfully at the stain. In the dim light from the single bare overhead bulb, the splotches of red *did* look like blood. But what about the drop cloth? That was a pretty significant detail for her to have conjured up with her imagination.

Except she hadn't, had she? She'd told him the drop cloth had existed. In the past, on the night of her mother's suicide.

"No." Behind him, Rachel let out a low moan.

He turned to find her staring at the wood stain, her head shaking from side to side.

"I saw the drop cloth," she said. "I did. And there was blood. Wet blood."

Seth looked back at the stain. It was clearly dry. No one would ever mistake it for wet blood. So either Rachel had imagined everything—

Or someone had been here in the attic with her, hiding, and removed the evidence after she'd run away from the terrifying sight.

"You don't believe me," she accused, color rising in her cheeks. "You think I'm crazy."

"No, I don't," he said firmly, hiding his doubts. Until this moment, except when she was clearly under the influence of some sort of drug, Rachel had seemed completely sane and lucid. Plus, he'd worked for her company for over a year now and watched her tackle the tasks of learning her father's lifework with determination and tenacity.

She deserved the benefit of the doubt.

"Where was the drop cloth?" he asked.

She waved toward the stained area. "Right there. Over that stain. It was stretched out flat, covered with blood. Splotches and puddles. Still wet."

She walked slowly to the center of the floor, gazing down at the stain. Her troubled expression made his chest tighten. "I didn't imagine it. I know I didn't."

Okay, Hammond, think. If you were trying to con her into believing she'd lost her mind, how would you go about it?

"Who has access to the house?"

She relaxed a little at his pragmatic question. "I do, of course. My stepmother, but she's in North Carolina. Her sister lives in Wilmington, and Diane went to spend a couple of weeks with her. I think my stepbrother,

Paul, probably has a key. And my father used to keep a key in his office at the trucking company in case one of us locked ourselves out and there wasn't anyone else around."

"Do you know if it's still there?"

"I don't know. I was planning to go through my dad's office next week and see if there was anything else that needed to be handled." Grief darkened her eyes.

Impulsively, he pulled her into his arms.

She came willingly, pressing her face against the side of his throat. When she drew away from him, she seemed steadier on her feet. "You think someone set me up?"

"I've been asking myself what steps I'd take to try to convince you that you were losing your mind."

"You think that's what's going on?"

"Look at you just a few minutes ago. Shaking like a leaf and not sure you could trust your own eyes."

She looked stricken. Her reaction piqued his curiosity, but he kept his questions to himself. If it was something he needed to know, she'd tell him soon enough.

"Remember how I told you I thought those murders were part of trying to target you?"

She nodded, her expression guarded.

"What if the goal was to make you appear crazy?"

She didn't answer, but her eyes flickered with comprehension. It made sense to her, he realized. Maybe even seemed inevitable.

"Your mother was already dead, and your father was dying. If I were ruthless and wanted to make you doubt your sanity, I'd take steps to isolate you even further. I'd take away your support system. Amelia Sanderson had been your friend since you were both in college, right?" He had learned that much while nosing around town about the murders.

She nodded, a bleak look in her wintry eyes.

"April Billings was your first hire, and you saw a lot of yourself in her, didn't you?" He could tell by the shift in her expression that he'd gotten it right. He usually did, he thought with a hint of shame. It had been one of his most useful talents, his ability to read people, relationships and situations. "And you'd made Coral Vines your own personal rehabilitation project. You'd helped her find a grief counselor to deal with her pain about her husband's death. I bet you'd even given her information about a twelve-step program for her alcohol addiction."

"How do you know this?" she asked in a strangled voice.

"I used to do this for a living. Reading people. Finding out their secrets and figuring out their relationships so I could use the knowledge to my advantage."

She couldn't stop her lip from curling with distaste, though she schooled her expression quickly. It didn't matter. He felt enough disgust for his past for the both of them. "And Marjorie was like a mom to me," she added, filling in the next obvious blank. "My mentor."

"But you still didn't break, did you?" He touched her face before he realized he was going to. He dropped his hand quickly, bracing himself for her rebuke.

But all she did was smile a shaky smile. "No, I didn't break."

"I don't think it's a coincidence you were drugged the night of your father's funeral. You were as vulnerable as you'd ever been at that moment, I would guess. He couldn't let the opportunity pass."

"This doesn't make any sense. It never has. Your

sister said she thought these murders were about me, and you said it, too, but why? Why would you think it? Just because I knew them?" She shook her head, clearly not wanting to believe it. "I saw the stories in the papers—Mark Bramlett was connected to serial murders in Nashville, too. What makes you think he was anything more than a sick freak who got off on killing women? Why does everyone think someone hired him?"

She didn't know about Mark Bramlett's last words, he realized. The police hadn't told her.

"I was there when Mark Bramlett died," he said.

"What? Why?"

"I'd tracked down the truck Bramlett used for the murders to help Sutton Calhoun find Ivy Hawkins. You remember Sutton, right? The guy who was investigating April Billings's murder?"

She nodded. "Yeah, he and Ivy came to me for a list of the trucks we rented out. That's how they found Bramlett."

"I wanted to know why Bramlett killed those women. I knew them all, you know. Amelia was always kind to me, and she didn't have to be. April Billings was full of life and so much potential. I grew up with Coral Vines on Smoky Ridge. She was the sweetest kid there ever was, and after her husband died, I tried to help her out with things around her house she couldn't do herself."

"I didn't know."

"Marjorie Kenner tried to steer me right, back in school. I didn't listen, but I never forgot that she tried." He thought about the kindhearted high school librarian who'd fought for his soul and lost. "I wanted justice for them, too. I wanted to see Bramlett pay."

"Did you?"

He nodded slowly. "I watched him die. But before he went, he said something."

She closed her hand around his wrist, her fingers digging urgently into his flesh. "What?"

"I'd told Ivy Hawkins I thought you were his real target. And as he died, he told her I was right. He said, 'It's all about the girl.'"

Rachel looked horrified. "He said that? Why did no one tell me?"

"I don't know. But I can probably get in touch with Ivy Hawkins if you want confirmation."

Rachel turned away from him, her gaze moving over the attic, settling finally on a darkened corner. "I wonder—" She walked toward the corner, leaving Seth to catch up. "Do you have a light?"

He pulled his keys from his pocket and engaged the small flashlight he kept on the keychain. The narrow beam of light drove shadows out of the dark corner, revealing another trapdoor in the attic floor.

And wedged in the narrow seam of the door was a thin piece of torn plastic.

As Rachel reached out for it, Seth caught her hand. "Fingerprints."

She looked up at him, a gleam of relief in her eyes. "It's from the drop cloth. It was really here." She tried to tug the door open, but it didn't budge.

Seth reached into another pocket and pulled out his Swiss Army knife. Tucked into one compartment in the case was a small pair of tweezers. He used them to pluck the piece of plastic out of the trapdoor seam.

The flimsy plastic was shaped like a triangle, smooth on two sides and ragged on the third, where it had apparently ripped away from the bigger sheet of plastic. In one corner of the plastic, a drop of red liquid was almost dry. Seth caught a quick whiff of a sharp iron odor.

"Is that—"

He nodded. "Blood."

She put her hand over her mouth.

"Rachel, whoever did this could still be in the house."

Her eyes went wide. "Oh my God."

"Where does this trapdoor lead?"

"A mudroom off the kitchen, I think. I've never used this exit, but there's a trapdoor in the ceiling of that room."

"Are there any weapons in this house?"

She swallowed hard. "My dad had a Glock. He kept it in his bedroom drawer. I guess it's still there."

"Do you know how to use it?"

She looked sick. "Yes."

"Let's get you downstairs and locked in that room. Then I'll take a look around."

"Don't you need the gun, then?"

He shook his head. "With my record, a gun is more trouble than it's worth." He had the Swiss Army knife, and he was pretty good at fighting with whatever weapons he could find. Unless their intruder was carrying a gun himself—and Seth had a feeling he wasn't—Seth would be safe enough. He wasn't the target. Rachel was.

Rachel appeared unnerved until they reached the second-floor hallway, clear of the ladder. She seemed to calm down once she was on solid ground.

She unlocked her father's gun from its case and, with more or less steady hands, went about the task of loading ammunition into the magazine while Seth watched. She met his gaze with scared but determined eyes. "Done."

"I'll be right back." He closed the door behind him, waiting until he heard her engage the lock before he went in search of the intruder.

The stairs creaked as he descended to the first floor, making him wince. He paused at the bottom and listened carefully for any sound of movement. He heard rain battering the windows and siding. Electricity humming in the walls. His own quickened breathing.

But no other sounds.

He crossed the main hallway, checking room by room until he was satisfied they were empty. Reaching the kitchen, he stood in the center of the warm room, struck unexpectedly by the memory of his body brushing against Rachel's here earlier that afternoon, back when his worst worry was whether or not his body betrayed his unanticipated arousal.

He'd give anything to go back to that moment right about now.

The mudroom was off the kitchen, she'd said. He went to the small door on the other side of the refrigerator and listened through the wood for any sound on the other side. He heard nothing but silence.

Backtracking to the kitchen counter, he went to the knife block by the sink and selected a long fillet knife. He crossed back to the mudroom, gripped the knife tightly in his right hand and opened the door.

Nobody jumped him as he entered. The room was empty.

He looked for signs of recent occupation. At first glance, the room appeared undisturbed. No mud on the floor, no telltale drops of blood from the drop cloth the intruder must have taken with him.

But there wouldn't be, would there? That had been the point of the drop cloth, to keep the evidence contained for easy, complete removal. Rachel's tormenter wanted her to doubt her own mind, which meant he couldn't leave any clues behind.

Maybe he'd heard Seth's voice earlier, outside the attic when he'd first responded to Rachel's cries. That might have pushed him to make a hasty exit at the first opportunity, which had come when Seth had taken Rachel to the den to recover from the shock of what she'd seen.

The intruder had moved fast, rolling up the drop cloth and the evidence it contained, and made a quick escape through the mudroom hatch. But in his haste, he hadn't realized one corner of the drop cloth had snagged in the trapdoor seam.

Had he taken the time to fold the drop cloth into a more manageable square before he left the attic? Possibly not. Which meant he'd have been moving at a clip, trying to get out of the house before he was discovered. Maybe he'd left other evidence behind besides the torn piece of plastic sheeting.

The back door was locked when Seth tried the handle, but anyone with a key could have locked it behind him as he left. Using the hem of his borrowed T-shirt, Seth turned the dead bolt and opened the door to the backyard. Beyond the mudroom door, he found a flagstone patio, not the muddy ground as he'd hoped. Not that it would have mattered, he supposed. With the rain coming down in torrents, any footprints the intruder might have left would have been obliterated in seconds.

He closed the door against the driving rain and turned, looking at the mudroom from a different angle. The room was essentially bare of furnishings save for a low, built-in bench with storage space beneath. There was nothing in any of the storage bins, suggesting the room was rarely used.

He looked at the trapdoor in the mudroom ceiling. It was two floors down from the attic. What lay between the attic trap door and the one in the mudroom?

Only one way to find out.

He caught the latch and pulled the trapdoor open. A wooden ladder unfolded and dropped to the ground.

Tightening his grip on the knife, he stepped onto the ladder and started to climb.

Chapter 8

Seth had been gone forever, hadn't he? Rachel checked her watch and saw that only a few minutes had passed.

Time crawls when you're scared witless.

She had settled on the cedar chest at the foot of her father's bed, trying not to think about his final moments here, as he breathed his last, labored breaths and finally let go.

Someone had changed the sheets and neatened the room after the coroner's visit. She and Diane had both been far too shattered to have thought of such a thing, so it must have been Paul. He'd been a rock for them both, a steady hand here at home and at the trucking company, as well.

He hadn't always been a big fan of his mother's second marriage—he'd worried that their relationship would make things awkward between him and her father at work, for one thing—but for the past few months, as her father fought the cancer that had ultimately taken him, Paul had put in a lot of long hours at work, helping take up the slack.

She wasn't sure what she'd have done without him. So why hadn't she called him to help her this morning instead of depending on strangers? Why did she feel certain, even now, that a man as enigmatic and unpredictable as Seth Hammond was the best person to help her?

A noise coming from the other side of the room froze her midthought. She picked up the gun from where she'd set it on the cedar chest beside her and turned toward the sound.

There. It came again. It sounded like footsteps coming from just inside her father's closet.

Then came the rattle of the doorknob turning.

Her chest tightening, Rachel lifted the small pistol, trying to remember what she knew about a good shooting stance. She hadn't done enough shooting to internalize these rules, damn it! Why hadn't she practiced more? What was the point of learning to shoot if you couldn't remember the lessons when it counted?

Fighter's stance, her sluggish brain shouted. Weak foot forward, strong foot back and slightly out, lean into the shot.

The door opened slowly, and Rachel's heart skipped a beat.

Seth Hammond emerged from the darkened closet, spotted the barrel of the gun aimed squarely at his chest and immediately ducked and rolled.

He hissed a profanity from behind the bed. "I think I just lost ten years of my life!"

She laid the gun on the chest and hurried around to where he crouched, his head down and his chest heaving. "How did you get into that closet?"

"That's where the trapdoor in the mudroom leads," he told her, lifting his head to look at her. "There's a hatch in the top of the closet that leads up to the attic. It has a pin lock hasp—that's why you couldn't open it from the attic."

Of course, she thought. There was a whole level between the attic and the mudroom. Why hadn't she thought of that?

He pushed to his feet. "I didn't find any evidence downstairs in the mudroom, but I couldn't find a light in the closet for a look around."

"There's a light switch, but it's in a weird place." She opened the closet door and reached inside, feeling for the switch positioned inside one of the built-in shoe hutches. The overhead light came on, revealing the roomy walk-in closet her father and Diane had shared during their marriage.

Diane's belongings took up most of the room, with her father's clothes and shoes filling only a quarter of the space. The area was neat and organized, Rachel knew, because while Diane could be flighty about many things, she was dead serious about her clothes and accessories, and she kept her things where she could locate them with a quick glance.

Which made the shoe box jutting at an odd angle from one of the shelves seem all the more out of place.

Rachel crossed to the box and saw that the top was slightly displaced, as well. And on the corner of the bright yellow box, a dark crimson smear was still glistening, not quite dry.

"More blood," she murmured, feeling ill.

Seth came up behind her, a solid wall of reassuring heat. She squelched the urge to lean back against him, aware that she was already leaning on him more than was probably wise.

He seemed remarkably steady for a man who'd sustained a head injury just a few hours earlier, showing few signs of pain or disorientation since he'd come here with her. On the contrary, he'd been a rock just as she'd had her feet knocked out from beneath her.

What if that's not a coincidence?

She shook off the thought. Seth had earned a little trust from her, hadn't he? A little benefit of the doubt.

"There was a lot of blood on that drop cloth," she said aloud. "Too much."

"May not be human, though." Seth's voice was reassuring. "It wouldn't have to be. Easy enough to get animal blood to set this up, and you could do it without breaking any laws."

She turned to look at him. "He's worried about breaking the law?"

"Never break the law if you don't have to. First rule of the con game."

"I thought the first rule of the con game was that you couldn't con an honest man." She wasn't sure where she'd heard that, but she'd always considered it to be a reasonable assumption. Honest men didn't fall for deals that were too good to be true.

Seth shook his head. "Honest men can be conned. Everyone has a price, even if the price is honorable." He grimaced. "I guess never breaking the law if you don't have to isn't necessarily the first rule of the con game, but it was the first rule Cleve Calhoun taught me."

She didn't miss the hint of affection in his voice when he spoke of his old mentor. He may have walked away from the life Calhoun had taught him, but clearly he hadn't stopped caring about the old man.

"Whoever's behind this isn't used to skirting the law," he added.

"How can you say that? He's already hired someone to kill four women. He's drugged me and probably killed Davis Rogers—oh God." Her voice cracked. "Davis. I wonder if the police have found him yet."

"I think we'd have already heard from them if they had."

She closed her eyes, fighting off her growing despair. She needed to stay strong. Not let this mess destroy her.

Not again.

"What I meant about this guy not being used to breaking the law is he's hired other people to do it so far," Seth added quietly.

"What makes you think he didn't beat up Davis himself?"

"If he was a practiced killer, he'd have killed those women himself. But he didn't. He hired someone else to do it. He doesn't want his hands dirty if he can avoid it."

Rachel heard something in Seth's voice that pinged her radar, but he spoke again before she could pin it down.

"What do you want to do now?" he asked.

"I think we need to call the police."

He nodded, though he clearly found the idea unappealing. "Okay. But call Antoine Parsons directly, not nine-one-one."

That made sense—Antoine already knew the details of the case. He seemed fair and honest, too. "You don't have to be here for it," she offered, aware that he still looked uncomfortable.

He shot her a sheepish grin. "Yeah, I do. I'm a material witness."

She started toward the phone but stopped halfway, turning back to look at him. "Seth, do you have any idea who's doing this?"

"Who's doing it? No." He shook his head firmly. "But I have an idea *why* he's doing it."

To Antoine Parson's credit, he didn't automatically start grilling Seth about why he'd been there with Rachel when the craziness started. First, he caught them up on the search for Davis Rogers. "We've searched the woods behind the bed-and-breakfast, but there's a lot of wilderness to cover in that area, and if the point of knocking out Mr. Hammond was to keep him from calling the paramedics to help Rogers, it's unlikely they'd hide the body anywhere near those woods."

Rachel flinched at his use of the word *body*. Seth's chest ached in sympathy, and he barely kept himself from giving her a comforting hug.

"We've also contacted the police in Virginia to let them know we have a report that Rogers is missing," Antoine added. "If he contacts his family or any of his friends back home, they've been asked to let us know."

Antoine had brought along a uniformed police officer to help him with the interviews. The two of them separated Seth and Rachel to get their independent statements.

Antoine took Seth's, naturally. But to Seth's relief, he approached his questions in a straightforward way and seemed to believe Seth's answers. "Bold, just walking in here and setting something up that way," the detective remarked. "Especially with you both right here in the house."

"I'm not sure whoever did this knew I was here," Seth said. "My car's in the shop having the tires fixed. The only car here is Rachel's. He might have assumed she was alone."

Antoine gave a slow nod. "And you didn't see anything of what Ms. Davenport saw in the attic?"

"Just the piece of drop cloth plastic I gave you and a stain on a shoe box in the closet that might be blood. But I think I did hear the music that Rachel heard playing." He told Antoine about his dream, leaving out the part about Rachel on the bridge girder. "I know it was just a dream, but how did I dream that particular song at that particular time?"

"Would be a hell of a coincidence," Antoine agreed. "Do you think this is connected to the previous murders?"

"Of course."

"Of course." Antoine looked thoughtful. "What's in this for you, Hammond?"

Ah, Seth thought. *Now we get to the grilling part.* "I knew the murder victims. I liked them, and I like Rachel Davenport, too. Her father took a chance on me when he hired me at the trucking company when most people around here wouldn't spit on me if I was on fire."

Antoine smiled a little. "I wish I could feel sorry for you, but…"

"I'm not the bad guy here."

"No, I don't think you are," Antoine agreed.

The other policeman, Gavin McElroy, joined Antoine in a huddle near the doorway of the den, leaving Seth and Rachel alone across the room.

Seth crossed to where she stood near the windows, rubbing her arms as if she was cold. "You okay?"

"Yeah." She managed a smile. "I'm sure I sounded crazy to poor Officer McElroy."

He heard a faint undertone to her words that was beginning to make a bleak sort of sense to him. She was very concerned about appearing sane, understandably. After all, her mother had committed suicide.

"You're not crazy," he told her firmly. The look of gratitude she sent his way made his stomach hurt.

Did she fear her mother's instability was hereditary? She wasn't much younger than her mother had been when she'd died. It was probably something she worried about now and then.

Maybe more often than now and then.

Did the person now tormenting her know that she harbored such a fear? The two direct attacks on her so far seemed aimed less at hurting her than convincing her she was losing her mind—first the drugging incident, inducing a state of near psychosis, then the gaslighting attempt in the attic, designed to make her believe she was seeing things that didn't exist.

Going back even further, the murders of people who'd been important to her seemed ominously significant now, too. If he'd wanted to drive Rachel to mental instability, he could think of no better way to prepare the ground than to brutally eliminate all of her emotional underpinnings. Every one of those murders had been a powerful blow to Rachel Davenport. Could that effect have been their entire purpose?

"You said you thought you knew why someone is

targeting me," Rachel murmured, keeping her voice too low for Antoine and Gavin to hear. "Did you tell Detective Parsons?"

"Not yet. I wanted to run it by you first."

"You could have told me before they got here." She sounded a little annoyed. He'd kept his thoughts to himself while they'd waited because he needed to think through his suspicions before he committed to them. If he was wrong, he might be pushing the investigation in the wrong direction, putting Rachel in graver danger.

But after talking to Antoine, and realizing the police didn't have a clue what was driving the attacks surrounding Rachel, he was growing more certain he was right.

Someone wanted Rachel out of the way, and he was pretty sure it had everything to do with Davenport Trucking.

"If you were to resign as CEO of Davenport Trucking tomorrow, who becomes CEO?" he asked quietly.

She shot him a puzzled look. "There's a trustee board my father set up before he died. If something happened to me, they would make the decision, I think. I don't know. My father knew I was committed to running his company. I gave him my word."

"But accidents happen. People get high and fall off bridges, right?"

Her gaze snapped up again. "You think all of this is about getting me out of the way at Davenport?"

"What if you were deemed mentally unstable? Would that get you out of the way?"

She looked horrified. "Probably."

Antoine and Officer McElroy walked back to where they stood, ending the conversation for the moment.

"We'll get a lab crew here later as soon as we can to process the access points to the attic," Antoine told them. "Meanwhile, Officer McElroy is going to stay here to preserve the chain of evidence until they arrive."

"Do we have to stay here?" Rachel asked bluntly.

Antoine looked surprised. "No, I don't suppose so, but I'm not sure you should be out on the roads in this weather."

"I don't plan to go far." She gave Seth an imperious look that did more to relieve his worries about her mental state than anything he'd seen so far. She looked like a pissed-off warrior princess, one he had a feeling he'd follow to the end of the universe if that's what she desired.

He was in serious, serious trouble.

The cabin near the base of Copperhead Ridge had been in her father's family since her great-grandfather had built it with his own hands in the late twenties. Or so the story went. Rachel looked at the slightly shabby facade with a fond smile as she pulled the Honda into the gravel driveway near the front door.

"What is this place?" Seth had been quiet for most of the short drive, but once she killed the engine, his low drawl broke the silence.

"According to family lore, my great-grandfather built this place to cover a family moonshining operation during Prohibition." She slanted a look his way. "I'm not sure that's entirely true."

He met her look with a hint of a smile. "Good stories rarely are."

"I think it might have been embellished to give the Davenports a little hillbilly cred." She smiled. "We were damned Yankees, you see. My great-grandfather was the third son of a shipbuilding family in Maryland that had only enough money to support two sons. So he was left to find his own way in the cold, cruel world."

"And chose Bitterwood, Tennessee?" Seth gave her a skeptical look.

"There's beauty here, you know. It's not all harsh."

"Guess it depends on what part of Bitterwood you come from."

She conceded the point. "My grandfather told me his daddy knew from the moment he set eyes on Bitterwood that it was home."

Seth's expression softened. "I guess I can't argue with that. I always end up back here no matter how far I roam."

"I love this place." She nodded toward the cabin. "My grandmother was a Bitterwood native. Her roots go back to the first settlers. She and my grandfather would bring me here during summer vacations from school and we'd rough it." She laughed. "Well, I considered it roughing it."

In fact, for a primitive log cabin, the place was relatively luxurious. A removable window unit air conditioner cooled the place in the heat of summer, and a woodstove kept it cozy on all but the coldest of winter days. It had been wired with electricity a couple of decades ago, when the town borders extended close enough to the cabin to make it feasible. And with a nearby cell tower, she never had much trouble getting a phone signal.

Seth climbed the porch steps behind her, carrying their bags. She'd packed a few things before leaving her house, and they'd stopped by the bungalow on Smoky

Ridge where Seth lived in order to pick up clothes for him, as well.

The shabby old house belonged to Cleve Calhoun, the con man who'd brought Seth into that lifestyle, Seth had told her, his expression defensive. He'd moved in with Cleve again a few years back, after the older man had suffered a debilitating stroke. Now that Cleve was at a rehab center in Knoxville for the next few weeks, Seth was thinking about looking for a place of his own.

Rachel wondered what sort of place a man like Seth would like, watching with curiosity as his sharp green eyes took in the decor of the cabin. She'd decorated it herself several years ago, when her grandfather had left it to her in his will. She'd been twenty-two, fresh out of college and torn between sadness at one part of her life passing and a whole vista of opportunity spreading out before her.

As a permanent place of residence, the cabin posed too many problems to be practical, but she had always treated it as an escape when life started to become overwhelming.

Was that why she'd come here now?

"Nice digs," he said with a faint smile.

"I love this place," she admitted.

"I can see why." He looked at her. "Do you come here often?"

"When I need to."

He nodded as if he understood. "Why did you bring me here? You don't bring people here normally, do you?"

She looked at him through narrowed eyes, a little spooked by how easily he could read her. "No, I don't."

"Because it's a refuge."

"Yes." She felt naked.

Suddenly, he looked vulnerable, as well. "Thank you. For trusting me enough to bring me here."

His rapid change of demeanor caught her by surprise. She hadn't realized, until that moment, that she had any sort of power over him. He'd seemed so sure, so in charge, that she hadn't given any thought to being able to influence him in any way.

It was an unexpectedly heady feeling, one that made her feel reckless.

And alive.

He was beautiful, she thought, standing there in the middle of her haven. Beautiful and feral, constantly on the edge of flight. Despite the facade of civilization, despite his obvious attempts to fight his own wild instincts, he would never be fully tame. He would never be genteel or domesticated. He'd always be a wild card.

And she'd never wanted a man more than she wanted him, in spite of that unpredictability.

Or maybe because of it.

"I wanted you here with me," she said aloud, unsure that he would understand what she meant by it. Not sure she wanted him to.

But she should have known better. He had a wild thing's instinct for reading another creature's motives.

Fight or flight, she thought. Which would he choose? To run?

Or to engage?

When he moved, it was swift and fierce, the decisive action of a predator with a singular purpose. He came to an abrupt stop in front of her, his gaze so intense it set off tremors low in her belly. "Do you know what you're getting into?"

Probably not, but she had no intention of retreating. "Do you?"

His mouth curved in response. She imagined the feel of those lips on hers, and the tremors inside her spread in waves until she felt as if she were going to crumble apart.

Then he touched her, a light brush of fingertips against her jaw, sparking fire in her blood.

She rose, closing the space between them until her breasts flattened against his chest. His wiry arms ensnared her, crushing her even closer, until his breath heated her cheeks. "I'm dangerous," he whispered.

She met his gaze. "I know."

Threading her fingers through his crisp, dark hair, she kissed him.

Chapter 9

Her mouth was hot and sweet, the fierce thrust of her tongue against his pouring gasoline on the fire in his belly until he thought he'd explode. He wanted her more than anything he'd ever wanted his whole life, a realization that scared the hell out of him even as it drove him to walk her backward until they ran up against the cabin wall.

She made a low, explosive sound against his mouth as her back flattened against the polished logs. Her legs parted, making room for his hips to settle flush to hers, and any hope of hiding the effect she had on his body was gone as he thrust helplessly against her hips. Neither the borrowed sweatpants nor her thin cotton yoga pants offered much of a barrier between their bodies, making it all too easy to take what they both seemed desperately to want.

Stop, his mind begged him. *Think.*

There was a reason he was still alone, a reason why he hadn't coaxed one of the pretty Tennessee mountain girls to take a chance on a man like him. Even reformed, he wasn't much of a catch. He was rough around the edges and wild at heart. A girl willing to settle for less than perfect could still do better.

Rachel Davenport didn't have to settle. If all she wanted was a quick roll in the hay with a hard-bodied redneck, maybe he'd give it a go, but not when she was this vulnerable. Not the day after her father's funeral, the day she'd lost another man who was important to her.

Not the day she'd had a nerve-shattering scare and probably wanted nothing more than to feel something besides fear.

As he started to pull back, her hands moved with sureness over his body, sliding down his back to cup his buttocks, pulling him closer. For a second, everything resembling lucid thought rushed out of his head, driven away by raw male hunger for completion. He drove his hips against hers again, making her whimper. The sound was maddening, fueling his lust to the edge of control.

She tugged his shirt upward, baring his belly to the light caress of her fingertips. She dragged her mouth away from his and pressed a hot kiss against the center of his chest, her tongue dancing lightly over the curve of his pectoral muscle.

She looked up at him, her blue eyes drunk with desire. "Is that good?" she asked, her thumb tracing a circle around his left nipple. "Did you like that?"

"Yes," he breathed.

She bent her head and dropped a soft kiss along the ridge of his rib cage. "And that?"

He knew where she was headed. He knew if he let her keep going, he wouldn't be able to make any sort of coherent decision about right and wrong.

There had been a time, he realized, when the question of right and wrong wouldn't have occurred to him at all.

Did he really want to be that man again?

With a groan, he threaded his fingers through her hair and urged her to look up at him. She appeared confused but also wildly aroused, her cheeks flushed and dewy, her lips dark from his kisses.

He kissed her again, a long, slow kiss that had an oddly fortifying effect on his resolve. Rachel Davenport deserved to be wooed, with kisses that went somewhere besides straight to sex.

Even if he wasn't the man who could give her that.

When he let her go, she slumped back against the wall, staring at him through half-closed eyes. Her breath was swift and ragged, her hair a tangled curtain around her face. "Seth?"

"This isn't really what you want," he said, keeping a careful distance.

Her brow furrowed. "You don't get to make that decision."

"Okay. It isn't what *I* want."

Her gaze dropped pointedly to his sweatpants, where his body betrayed exactly what he wanted. When her blue eyes rose to meet his again, there was triumph in them. "Really."

"Rachel, please." He turned his back on her, pacing toward the front window, where night had fallen early due to the rain. His reflection stared back at him, the wild-eyed gaze of a man on the edge.

"If you think you're being noble—"

"I don't think I'm capable of being noble. I just want to be fair."

She let out an exasperated sigh. "You think I'm not in my right mind."

He shook his head, even though it was what he thought, in a way. "I think we both want to forget the past couple of days, however we can make that happen. And maybe that seems like a good idea right now, but it won't once we've crossed a line we can't uncross."

He waited for her to respond, but she remained silent. Finally, he dared a quick look at her. She still leaned against the wall, her gaze on him. Some of the heat in her eyes had died, however, as if his words had sunk in and extinguished the fire inside her.

"I don't do one-night stands," she admitted after another long, silent moment. "I don't think that's how I was looking at this."

He didn't know if her confession made him feel better or worse. Maybe a little of both, he decided, though her admission that she saw him as more than a body on which to slake her lust certainly complicated matters.

"I'm not good for you," he said simply.

"You're not bad for me."

He laughed a little. "There are hundreds of people out there who'd beg to differ."

"You've done bad things. But you're not bad. Bad people don't try to change. They don't see the need."

He felt enough in control to face her completely. He pressed his back against the hardwood frame around the panes, concentrating on the discomfort and giving his body a chance to cool down and regain control. "There's a difference between wanting to be good and being good."

"Only in degrees."

She was stubborn, he thought. And naive. "In a few days, once we figure all this out, you're going to look back at this moment and thank me for keeping my head."

Her eyes rolled upward. "You give me any more of that paternalistic hogwash and it won't take a few days."

Fair enough, he thought. "I don't want regrets, either."

The look she shot his way was utterly wicked, catching him by surprise. "You wouldn't have regretted it."

He laughed. "Maybe not."

She lifted her chin, her expression shifting back to cool neutral. "Okay. I get that this is a volatile situation with really rotten timing. And I know we're not what anyone would consider a suitable match. So, you win. We don't let this happen again, not while we're trying to figure out what's happening to me and why."

He felt a squirm of disappointment that she'd conceded so quickly, but he pushed that unhelpful thought aside. "I do think someone should be with you at all times, though. You've already had two strange incidents on top of whatever happened to your friend Davis, plus the previous murders. I don't think it's safe for you to be alone right now."

"Should I hire a bodyguard?" She sounded reluctant.

Seth thought about his orders from Adam Brand. Brand, for reasons Seth didn't quite understand, had hired Seth to keep an eye on Rachel. So far, he hadn't shared that fact with her, since Brand hadn't given him permission to approach her on an official level.

But maybe it was time to talk to Brand again. He was overdue to give the man an update. He'd try to make the FBI agent see that Rachel deserved to know everything that was going on.

"I can do it," he said in answer to her question. "I can protect you."

Her dark eyebrows notched up. "I thought we decided to keep our distance from each other."

"We agreed not to…get busy with each other," he said with a wry grin. "Not quite the same thing."

"One would certainly make the other harder to resist."

True, but letting Rachel Davenport out of his sight for long was not something he was willing to contemplate. He might not understand Brand's interest in Rachel, but he understood his own. He wasn't going to let her become a casualty in whatever game her tormenter was playing.

Especially now that he had a pretty good idea why she'd been targeted.

But before he told her his theory, he needed to talk to Brand. The FBI agent could pull some strings and see if the local cops were making any progress in finding Davis Rogers, for one thing. Antoine had claimed to be forthcoming, but Seth didn't kid himself. The cops would never trust him, not really, and nothing guaranteed Antoine would keep him in the loop.

Seth had a feeling what happened to Rogers might be more than just collateral damage aimed at weakening Rachel's hold on reality. Rogers had seen her the night before, at Smoky Joe's. What if he'd seen or heard something that could incriminate the person who was really behind these attacks on her?

"Rachel, this morning at Sequoyah House, you said you talked to Davis Rogers before you heard the thud and his phone cut off, right?"

She looked puzzled by the change of topic. "I didn't really understand what he meant by what he was saying, but I guess he must have met me last night at some point. He said something about being sorry about what he did."

Joe Breslin had said the man Rachel was with had made a pass at her. Could that have been why Davis Rogers had felt the need to apologize? "Can you remember what he said exactly?"

Her brow furrowed. "He said he'd been trying to reach me—I guess that makes sense. My phone was locked in my car. Then he said he needed to apologize about last night—oh!" She crossed to where she'd laid her fleece jacket on the back of the sofa and pulled her cell phone from the pocket. "I played this for the police but not for you."

She punched a couple of buttons and a male voice came out of the phone's tinny speaker. "Rachel, it's Davis again. Look, I'm sorry about last night, but he seemed to think you might be receptive. I've really missed you. I didn't like leaving you in that place. Please call me back so I can apologize."

"*He* thought you might be receptive," Seth repeated. That jibed with what Joe had told him, but who was the "he" Rogers had been talking about?

"I think maybe he tried to kiss me or something."

"And you didn't let him."

She shot Seth a look. "I broke up with Davis years

ago. I still care about him, and I desperately hope you're wrong about how bad his condition was and that we find him alive and okay. But I'm not in love with him anymore."

"Is he in love with you?"

"I don't think he ever was," she said flatly. "I'm not sure Davis loves anyone quite as much as he loves himself." She pressed her fingers against her lips. "God, that sounds terrible, especially since he could be dead because he came here to see me."

"Remember how I told you I went to talk to Smoky Joe this morning, and that's how I knew to look for Davis?"

She nodded.

"Joe said the man you were with made a pass at you, and you rebuffed him. I figure that man must have been Davis Rogers."

"Why didn't you tell me before?"

"I thought it was something you'd prefer to remember on your own."

Her expression took on a slightly haughty air, reminding him that no matter how tempting he might find her, and how receptive she might be, there was a whole lifetime of differences between them, in experiences, in education, in culture and in outlook. "You had no right to make that decision for me."

"Won't happen again," he snapped back.

She closed her eyes. "I'm sorry. I shouldn't have barked at you."

His anger ebbed as quickly as it had risen. He had no right to get up on his high horse considering he was still keeping the secret about Adam Brand. "No harm done."

"I wonder what he meant—that 'he' seemed to think

I might be receptive to Davis's advances," Rachel murmured thoughtfully. "Who's the 'he' Davis is talking about?"

"I was wondering that, too."

"I don't think Davis knows anyone here in Bitterwood besides me. I mean, he knew my dad, of course, but my father's dead. I guess he might have met Diane once—she and my dad married around the time Davis and I broke up—"

"What about your stepbrother?"

"Paul?" She frowned. "I don't think so. We've gotten fairly friendly over the past few months, dealing with the company and taking care of my father's last wishes, but—" She shook her head. "We were both adults when our parents met. We didn't form any kind of family bond, and I can't imagine him giving Davis advice about my love life."

Bailey didn't seem the matchmaker type, Seth conceded. Or the criminal type. He was an efficient, if perpetually distracted, office manager, helping George Davenport and his daughter keep the company going. But company scuttlebutt notwithstanding, Seth had never thought Paul seemed to want to run the company.

But someone did.

"How can we find out who's next in line for the CEO job if you can't step in?" he asked.

Rachel looked up at him. "The only thing I know for sure is that, until my father's will is executed and I'm declared in charge, the company is under the control of a trust. And even then, the trust managers can make a change within the first year if I were to die. In other words, I can't put the disposition of the CEO job in my own will until I've run the company for at least a year."

"What if you couldn't take the job from the outset?"

"I don't know. It hasn't been an issue, since I already agreed to take on the responsibility."

"Do you regret it?" he asked out of curiosity.

"Agreeing to run the company?" Her brow furrowed, and she gave the question the thought it deserved. "I don't regret keeping my father's company alive. I don't regret the time I spent with my dad learning the ropes, or the peace it gave him to know the company would be staying in the family."

"That's not entirely what I asked."

"I miss being a librarian," she admitted with a faint smile. "But I can volunteer on weekends. Or take time out to go read to the kids on story day."

"Is that enough?"

"It will be." Her voice was firm. "It has to be."

A shrill noise split the tense silence that fell briefly between them. They both reached for their cell phones.

It was Rachel's phone. "Hello?"

She listened for a moment, her expression so tight it made Seth's chest hurt. "Yes, I understand." Another brief pause and she added, "Yes. I can do that. Okay. Thank you."

She hung up the phone, her expression carefully still as she slowly lifted her gaze to meet Seth's. What her features lacked in expressiveness, her blue eyes made up for, blazing with pain and fear.

"What is it?" he asked carefully.

Her throat bobbed with a deep swallow. "That was Antoine Parsons. A motorist on the Great Smoky Mountains Parkway pulled over near Sevierville to take a picture of the mountains and spotted a man's body lying about twenty feet down an incline. The Sevier County police called the Bitterwood P.D. because of the APB they'd put out on Davis."

"Is it him?"

"He didn't have any identification on him, but he does have a few identifying marks. They want me to take a look at the body and see if it's him."

"No," he said flatly.

Her eyebrows lifted. "No?"

"They can't ask you to look at a body like that," he said firmly, remembering how the man in the bushes had looked. His recall of the event had been coming back to him slowly but surely, and what he remembered of the man's condition only strengthened his resolve. "The man I saw in the bushes was badly beaten. You might not even be able to recognize him—his face was a mess—"

"I don't think it's his face they want me to look at," she said quietly. "He has birthmarks and scars on his body that I'd be able to identify."

The sudden, entirely inappropriate flood of jealousy burning through his system only made him angrier— at himself, at the police for putting her in such a horrible position and, most of all, at the monster who was wreaking havoc all around her life for what seemed, to Seth, the most ridiculously petty reason he could think of—control of a moderately successful midsize trucking company.

How could the job of running Davenport Trucking be worth five murders and the wholesale destruction of Rachel's life? It made no sense, but it was the only logical motive Seth had been able to come up with after weeks of pondering the question.

What was he missing?

"If you go, I'm going with you," he said firmly.

She sent him a look of gratitude. "I'd appreciate that."

He looked down at his borrowed clothes. "I'd better change."

"Right." She waved toward a door to the right. "There's a bedroom behind that door. You can have it tonight."

He took his overnight bag into the bedroom and closed the door behind him. As he dressed, he took a moment to call Adam Brand for an update.

The FBI agent sounded harried when he answered. "Not the greatest time, Seth—"

"A lot's happened." He outlined the events of the day as economically as he could. "I'm about to go with Rachel to take a look at the body."

"This is bad." Brand didn't sound surprised, Seth noticed.

"But not unexpected?"

There was a brief pause on Brand's end of the line. "Not entirely."

"You're not going to tell me what you know, are you?"

"Not yet. Just keep an eye on Ms. Davenport and let me know everything that happens. I promise I'll tell you what I know as soon as I have all my ducks in a row on my end."

"I'm going to tell her I'm working for the FBI."

"No."

"I'm not comfortable lying to her."

"Seth, one of the reasons you've been so valuable to us is the fact that you're a damned good liar. Don't pretend you're suddenly a paragon of virtue. Just do what you do well and don't try to do my part of the job."

"I'm not going to keep lying to her," Seth insisted firmly. "I don't need your permission. I'm just giving you a little warning."

"You could screw things up badly if you tell her."

I could screw things up worse if I don't, he thought. "I'll tell her she has to be discreet. She'll understand. She can be trusted."

"If it gets around that the FBI is looking into some little stalker case in Bitterwood, Tennessee, it could screw up a very big, ongoing investigation."

"An investigation into what?"

"I can't tell you that." Brand had the decency to sound as if he regretted keeping Seth in the dark, at least. But Seth was losing patience with the skullduggery.

"Good night, Adam." He used Brand's first name deliberately. Adam Brand wasn't his boss, even if he paid the bills, and Seth would be damned if he'd kowtow to the man.

He hung up and tucked his phone in his back pocket. Out in the front room, he found Rachel at the window, her forehead pressed against the windowpane. At the sound of his footsteps, she turned to look at him. She'd been crying, though her eyes were mostly dry now.

Forgetting his promise to keep his distance, he crossed to where she stood, wrapping her up in a fierce hug. She stood stiff for a second before she relaxed in his arms, her cheek against his collarbone. Her arms curled around his waist, pulling him closer.

"Tell me I can do this," she said.

He wanted to tell her she didn't have to. But he'd seen the desperation in her eyes, the fierce need to be in control.

To be all right.

He released a slow, deep breath. "You can do this."

She nodded, her expression firming into iron-hard determination. "Let's go." She let go of him and walked slowly to the door, leaving him to follow.

Chapter 10

She'd seen death twice in her life. First at the age of fifteen, when her mother's madness had led her to suicide. Some details were fuzzy in her memory but not all. Rachel still remembered the stark moment when she'd realized her mother had gone and wasn't coming back.

More recently, she'd watched her father die, a peaceful drift from slumber to utter stillness, protected from the cruelties of his life's end by the drugs his doctor had given him to make it easier to let go. They'd dulled his pain and given him a peace in death that his disease had denied him in life.

But until the moment the Sevier County morgue attendant pulled back the sheet on the battered body of Davis Rogers, she'd never seen death resulting from murder.

His face was battered almost beyond recognition,

but the hourglass-shaped birthmark on his left biceps and the long white scar on his right knee filled in the blanks for her. It had been nearly seven years since she'd been in any kind of relationship with Davis, but he'd kept fit, the intervening years doing little to change the body she'd once known intimately.

Grief gouged a hole in her heart, and she turned away after nodding to the deputy sheriff who'd accompanied them into the morgue.

Seth stood just behind her, and it seemed as natural as breathing to walk into his arms when he reached out to her. He pulled her close for a moment before leading her out into the corridor, where the air seemed immediately lighter.

"I'm sorry," he murmured against her hair.

She wanted to cry, felt it burning its way into her chest, but she let it rise no further. She wasn't going to fall apart, especially not here in the midst of strangers like the deputy, who watched them both through narrowed eyes.

A few feet down the hallway, Antoine Parsons pushed away from the wall and crossed to where she, Seth and the deputy stood. "Is that the man you saw at Sequoyah House?" he asked Seth.

"Same clothes. Same condition." Seth moved his hand comfortingly up and down Rachel's back, but she felt tension gathering in him like a thunderstorm rising up a mountain. "I didn't think he had much of a chance of making it without help."

"We're still working on cause of death." The deputy, who'd introduced himself as John Mallory, seemed more interested in keeping his eye on Seth than meeting Antoine Parson's gaze. Seth himself seemed acutely aware of the deputy's scrutiny, though he tried not to show it.

He'd warned her, she thought. People looked at him differently because of who he was. What he'd been. And maybe if she'd never seen another side of him— the kind man, the brave protector—she'd be inclined to view him the same way.

She had viewed him with suspicion as recently as a few hours ago.

But that had been before he'd kissed her.

Was that all it took? Was that how easily she gave her trust?

She felt herself edging away from him, even as the thoughts roiled through her mind. He let go, let her move away, not looking at her as he did so. His gaze was fixed on John Mallory, his chin high and his mouth set with stubborn pride.

But even though he wasn't looking at her, she felt as if his defiant stance was meant for her as much as it was meant for the deputy. *This is who I am. This is what I deal with every day. If you can't handle it...*

"I'd like to request formal release of the body into the custody of the Bitterwood Police Department," Antoine said to Mallory. "Based on eyewitness testimony, we have reason to believe the assault leading to Davis Rogers's murder took place in the Bitterwood jurisdiction."

"Not so fast," Mallory said. "Until the C.O.D. is determined, the location of his death is still at issue."

"You really want this case?" Antoine argued. "You're about to have this man's family and their grief and questions crashing down on you. There's damned little evidence to go on, thanks to the rain and the removal of the body from the place where he was attacked. You're buying yourself a damned near unsolvable case, John."

"And you want it why, Antoine?"

"Because I think it may be connected to an open case in Bitterwood." Antoine flicked a quick look at Seth.

A slight twitch of Seth's eyes was his only response.

"I'll tell you what," Mallory said after a moment of consideration. "I'll talk to the sheriff, see if I can't get him to agree to a joint investigation, based on the testimony and pending the determination of the C.O.D. Then, if the cause of death suggests that the murder took place in the Bitterwood jurisdiction, we'll hand the whole thing over. Deal?"

Antoine didn't look happy, but he gave a nod. "I can live with that."

"Ms. Davenport gave us some information that should help us locate and inform Mr. Rogers's family of his death, so I'm going to go get the notifications started." Mallory shot Antoine a wry look. "Unless you'd like to handle that part of the investigation?"

Antoine smiled. "You found the body. You make the notifications."

Once Deputy Mallory was out of earshot, Antoine turned to Seth. "He really, really doesn't like you."

"I have that effect on a lot of people," Seth replied in a bone-dry tone. "I think in his case, it has more to do with Cleve Calhoun than with me. Cleve sucked Mallory's cousin into some land deal he's still holding a grudge about. Can't say I blame him. He lost a hell of a lot of money."

"If only he hadn't been so greedy, he could have avoided it?" Antoine asked. "Isn't that what you fellows say? Can't con an honest man?"

Seth slanted a look at Rachel, a hint of a smile curving his lips, though none of the amusement made it into his hard green eyes. "Something like that. I don't reckon that makes for much of an excuse, though."

"What happens now?" Rachel asked, finding the tense posturing between Seth and Antoine exhausting.

"Deputy Mallory will contact your friend's family. They'll make a formal identification for the record and, meanwhile, we'll get a warrant to search his room and his vehicle at Sequoyah House. I've already had it sealed off and posted a couple of officers at the bed-and-breakfast pending the warrant."

"Is there anything else we can do to help?"

Antoine looked at Seth. "If you could tell more about what you saw before you got hit on the head, we'd be better off. Maybe you saw the person who did it and you just don't remember."

Seth shook his head. "I doubt I'd be alive now if I'd seen who hit me." He glanced toward the door of the morgue. "Whoever did this doesn't seem interested in leaving witnesses behind."

"Witnesses to what?" Antoine asked.

Rachel wondered the same thing. What could Davis have seen that would warrant someone beating him to death? As far as she could tell, he'd come to town for her father's funeral. At most, he'd have been in Bitterwood for maybe a day before he was murdered.

The only thing he might have witnessed of any significance was what had happened to her at Smoky Joe's Saloon.

Which had to be the answer, Rachel realized.

"He was with me at Smoky Joe's Saloon last night," she said.

"I spoke to Joe Breslin earlier today," Seth explained as Antoine shot Rachel a curious look. "He told me he saw a man fitting Davis Rogers's description with Rachel last night at his bar. The man made a pass at Rachel, she rebuffed him and he left, according to Joe."

"Is that what his phone call was about?" Antoine asked. "The one you played for me?"

Seth looked at Rachel. "If he left before you did, what could he have possibly seen?"

"You think you were drugged." Antoine also looked at her. "Could Rogers have done it?"

She shook her head. "He wouldn't do that to me."

"It's been a few years since you were together," Seth pointed out. "Maybe someone flashed a little cash at him—"

"He's a plaintiff's lawyer in Richmond and has done very well for himself. You saw where he was staying. Sequoyah House isn't cheap."

"Maybe he still holds a grudge about your breakup," Antoine suggested.

"He broke up with me," she answered bluntly. "I mean, it was mutual—we had both realized by then that we just wanted different things in life. But he was the one who finally made the move to end it. He's never tried to hurt me. You heard his message."

Her gut tightened as she realized the final call, the one she'd heard cut off with a thud, truly had been his last. At some point after that call had ended so abruptly, he'd been beaten to death.

Tears rose in her eyes, stinging hot. She blinked them back, but they kept coming, rolling down her cheeks in a sudden, unstoppable flood.

Seth's hands closed over her shoulders, warm and

strong. It would be so easy to lean back against him, let herself melt in his solid heat.

But once she started depending on him, it might be difficult to stop. And he'd already made it clear that he wasn't in the market for any sort of entanglement.

"I'd like to borrow your phone again," Antoine said suddenly. "I'd like to record those last messages to you, if that's okay. Should have done it earlier. I could get a warrant, but this would be faster."

"Of course." She handed over her phone.

"I'll get it back to you as soon as I'm done. If you'd like to come to the station with me, I can record while you wait."

"Why don't we get something to eat?" Seth suggested. "Ledbetter's Café is just around the corner." He looked up at Antoine. "Want us to bring you something?"

Antoine looked surprised by the offer. "Yeah. Sure. A pulled pork sandwich and some of Maisey's sweet potato fries." He pulled his wallet from the inside pocket of his jacket and handed Seth a ten, his eyes glinting with amusement. "You really are good at getting people to hand over their hard-earned money, aren't you, Hammond?"

Seth grinned back. "At least this time, you'll get a sandwich and fries out of it."

After the trip to the morgue, Rachel didn't have any appetite, but she let Seth cajole her into an omelet on toast. She managed to eat most of it, even though it seemed to stick in her throat. She sat back finally and watched Seth work his way through a plateful of barbecue ribs and Maisey Ledbetter's homemade slaw.

He ate with gusto, she noticed, like a man who appreciated a good, hot meal when one came his way. Even now, there was a hungry look about Seth Hammond that made her wonder how many times he'd been uncertain where his next meal would come from.

Seth ordered Antoine's barbecue plate as they got ready to leave, adding a slice of lemon meringue pie with a few dollars of his own money. At Rachel's questioning look, he shot her a sheepish grin. "I stole his pie at lunch one day in high school. He never knew who did it, but since I'm in the making-amends business these days—"

"Nice of you."

"Nice would have been if I hadn't nicked his pie in the first place."

Antoine raised an eyebrow at the unexpected slice of pie but thanked them and traded Rachel's cell phone for the food. He also had some information from the crime scene unit at Rachel's house. "They went over the place pretty thoroughly, but other than the piece of plastic and the shoe box you found, they couldn't find anything else of interest."

"What about the blood?"

"Not human. Animal of some kind, which wouldn't be hard to come by in a farming community like this."

She felt a rush of relief. "Thanks for checking."

"You're free to go back to your house, but if I were you, I'd change the locks as soon as you can. And put an alarm system in place."

"I'll definitely do that."

"I wish we had the manpower to send patrols by your house regularly, but we're already stretched pretty thin with a detective on leave and another recently retiring—"

"I understand," she said quickly, aware she was luckier than most people in her position. She could afford to hire protection if she needed it. Most people couldn't.

"I'm not going to ignore what's happening to you." Antoine's voice softened with concern. "I know this is the fifth murder connected to whatever's going on with you, and I won't avert my eyes and pretend it's not happening. I'm going to do my damnedest to figure out who's behind it."

"We've had some thoughts about that," Seth told him. He glanced at Rachel as if seeking permission to say anything further.

She gave a nod.

"The best I can tell, everything started about nine weeks ago, right?" Seth looked around the bull pen, his expression wary. "Is there someplace a little less open where we can discuss this?"

Antoine seemed surprised by the question, but he led them down the hall to a small room equipped with a table, three chairs and a video camera mounted high in one corner. He showed them the button on the wall that controlled the camera. "It's off."

Seth looked at it closely, then took the lone chair on the far side of the table, leaving Rachel and Antoine to sit in the other two. "Sorry if I'm coming across paranoid, but I'm not sure who to trust these days."

Antoine shot him a wry look. "Tell me about it."

Rachel frowned. "What does that mean?"

"Are you suggesting there's someone on the police force involved with what's happening to Rachel?" Seth asked.

"I don't know. I don't have any particular reason to think so, but I have reservations about the way some things are done around here. I'm just saying I understand Hammond's caution."

"I'm wary of anyone with a badge," Seth said wryly. "Though a lot of that's my own damned fault."

"Too bad. We're having all kinds of trouble with fraud cases these days, the economy being what it is." Antoine sighed. "There are just too many ways to part good folks from their hard-earned money, and it wouldn't hurt to have an insider on our side."

"I'm wondering if money isn't the driving force behind what's going on at Davenport Trucking," Seth said.

Rachel looked at him, surprised. "We're pretty successful, I'll grant you, but I'm not sure we're five murders worth of successful."

"You'd be surprised how cheaply murder can be bought," Antoine muttered.

Seth twined his fingers on the table in front of him, the muscles and tendons flexing and unflexing, drawing Rachel's gaze. A couple of hours ago, those hands had been on her. Touching her. Branding her.

She swallowed with difficulty.

"You said you think it started nine weeks ago?" Antoine nudged.

Rachel realized Seth's gaze was on her, green eyes blazing with awareness, as if he'd been reading her thoughts. She flushed.

"With the first murder. April Billings. Summer intern at Davenport Trucking. She'd just had her going-away party at the office the day she was killed. Remember?"

Rachel nodded, pain darting through her chest. "She

was so excited to be going back to college. She had missed all her friends over the summer, and she had managed to get into a really popular class in her major that she was looking forward to attending." She blinked hard, fighting tears at the memory. "She made me want to go back to college all over again."

"You were close to her?" Antoine asked.

"Yeah. I guess she gravitated to me because I'm a librarian. I mean, I was. That was what she wanted to be, too. And she'd have been a good one." Rachel dashed away a tear that had slipped free of her control. "I really wanted that for her."

Seth's gaze softened. "She was a nice girl. She should've had that life she wanted."

"Who knew that you and April were friends?" Antoine asked Rachel.

"Anybody who worked there knew," Seth answered for her. "Rachel is big news around the company. Even the guys in the garage were speculating what it meant that Mr. Davenport had clearly brought her on to be his successor."

"You were?" Rachel hadn't realized.

"Well, sure. You'll be the boss. We aren't sure if you plan to keep running the place the way your daddy did or if you'll change things around." There were secrets in his green eyes but also amusement. Rachel realized there were things he could tell her—wanted to tell her— but not until they were alone.

That realization—that shock of intimacy—made her feel warm all over.

"Was anyone hostile to the idea?" Antoine asked.

Seth gave a quick shake of his head. "Worried, maybe. Jobs can be hard to come by these days. People feel lucky to be employed, and anything that threatens to change things—"

"But surely they knew the company was doing well, even with my father's illness," Rachel protested. "He worked hard to make everyone feel comfortable and secure with what was happening."

"It's easy to feel secure when you're not one paycheck away from ruin."

Even though she knew Seth didn't mean his words as a rebuke, they still stung a little. Because he was right. She'd never had to worry where her next meal would come from. Or whether or not she'd be able to make the next mortgage payment or pay the next utility bill.

"I still don't see how those worries constitute a motive for murder," she said more sharply than she'd intended.

"No," Seth agreed. "What's happening here is too personal."

"You mean this is all about hurting Ms. Davenport?" Antoine sounded skeptical, to Rachel's relief. Because the idea that someone hated her enough to kill people to torment her was utterly horrifying.

"Not that exactly," Seth said with a quick shake of his head. "But I do think that whoever's doing this knows enough about her life and her history to choose his actions to injure her in the worst possible way."

He knows, she realized, recognizing the hint of pity in Seth's eyes. *He knows about the missing year.*

But how? How could he know? Almost nobody outside of the clinic in North Carolina knew how she'd spent the year following her mother's death. Her father had told everyone that she'd gone to school abroad to get away from the aftermath of her mother's suicide, and nobody had questioned it because nobody but her father had seen the state she was in that night. He'd taken quick steps to protect her.

How could any of this be about what had happened fifteen years ago? How was that even possible?

"But what's the point?" Antoine asked. "What does hurting Ms. Davenport this way accomplish?"

"It could drive her out of the CEO position at Davenport Trucking," Seth suggested.

Rachel shook her head. "We don't pull in those kinds of profits. Sure, we do well. People get paid, and we make a comfortable profit. I'm not hurting for money. But no way are all these murders about taking over Davenport Trucking. There's no upside."

For the first time, Seth looked doubtful. "It's the only thing so far that's even close to answering all of the questions."

"Why not just kill me, then? Why torment me instead?"

"If you're killed now, what happens to the company?" Antoine asked. "Who gets your shares?"

"My mother's brother. Rafe. He owns about twenty percent of the company already because he put up seed money when the company started. But Uncle Rafe doesn't want to run the company. My father even offered the job to him before he brought me into the picture, and Uncle Rafe said no. He's a musician and a promoter."

"We need to find out what happens if you're still alive but unable to run the company," Seth said quietly. "It seems to be the point of trying to drive you crazy, and that appears to be what's going on here."

"I told you, I don't know. I've never asked that question." Maybe she should have, she realized, given her history.

"Who *would* know?" Antoine suddenly looked interested.

"My father's personal lawyer, of course. Maybe my stepmother, Diane—but she's out of town. It's possible he'd have told Garrett McKenzie—

"Former mayor Garrett McKenzie?" Antoine whistled softly.

"Old family friend." She had never felt self-conscious about her family connections before, but both Antoine and Seth were making her feel like a pampered princess with their reactions.

Was that fair? Was she supposed to feel ashamed of having a father who had worked hard and provided well for his family?

"Anybody else?" Seth asked.

"The lawyer for sure. I'm not positive about Diane or anyone else." She risked another quick look at Seth, trying to read his expression. But he was suddenly closed off, impossible to read.

Just when she most needed to know what he was thinking.

Chapter 11

The house was midnight quiet, even with all the lights blazing. Rachel had wanted to return to her father's house to spend the night rather than the cabin. There'd been a look of stubborn determination in her eyes when she'd told him her decision. They'd stopped to get their things at the cabin and arrived just as the grandfather clock in the den was chiming twelve.

Rachel watched him carry their bags inside with a look of apology in her weary eyes. "I know you think I'm crazy to come back here. But I won't be run out of my house. Not by the son of a bitch who's doing this."

He admired her determination, even if he'd prefer to stash her somewhere safer. "Understood."

"I must be taxing your patience."

"Oh, not for a few days yet."

The teasing reply earned him a tired smile. "You're a trouper."

"So are you."

Her response was another quick smile and a shake of her head as she dropped her car keys on the entry table and kicked off her shoes.

"You need sleep," he told her. "Go on up to bed. I'll lock up."

She caught his arm as he turned toward the door. "How do you know about the time I spent in Westminster?"

He considered pretending he didn't know what she was talking about. But she deserved better than to be treated like a child. "Is that where you were? Is it a hospital?"

She took a small step back, her hand falling from his arm. "You don't know?"

Great. Now she thought he'd tricked her. "I didn't know the details. I just guessed the situation."

Her lips pressed into a thin line. "I can see why you were so good at what you used to do. You're really kind of spooky."

"I guessed about Westminster because it was the only thing that would explain the elaborate ruse in the attic."

Her brow lifted. "Restaging the moment of my big meltdown?"

"You were really shaken by what you saw. I could tell you were beginning to doubt yourself when we didn't find the evidence you expected right away."

She closed her eyes, as if she could blot out the memory of those moments. "I used to relive that night. Over and over again. Trying to stop it. Trying to reach her before she pulled the trigger. I went almost three months with no more than an hour or two of undisturbed sleep each night. I came really close to dying because of it. I couldn't eat. I lost a lot of weight. Couldn't think straight. All I could do was remember something I couldn't change, no matter how hard I tried."

He brushed his fingers against her face, unable to stop himself. She leaned into his touch, her face lifting even as she kept her eyes tightly shut. He brushed his lips against her furrowed brow. "I'm sorry."

She rested her head against his chest. "She wanted me to die with her."

His heart contracted. "She tried to kill you?"

She shook her head quickly. "Remember that window in the attic, the one by the trapdoor? When I got up to the attic, that window was open. The wind was blowing outside, whipping the curtains around. She told me she'd opened it for me. Because she knew how much I wanted to fly."

Seth closed his eyes, remembering Rachel's drug-induced words on the bridge. *She said I should fly.*

"I was fifteen going on thirty. I wanted to be grown, to be my own woman. When she was lucid, that idea seemed to terrify her. But when she was drowning in madness, she told me to fly."

He hugged her close. "I'm sorry."

"For a long time I couldn't remember much of it at all. I was terrified people were hiding things from me about her death, that I'd done something to hurt her."

"My God."

"Most of the memories came back on their own. And I knew what I didn't want to remember." She looked up at him with hard, shiny eyes. "There was a moment, right after she pulled the trigger and was lying there, bleeding all over that drop cloth, that the thought of flight seemed so sweet, so tempting. I remember, I walked past her body to the open window and stared down at the patio below. Those flagstones looked hard. Unforgiving. But it would be over in a flash, and then the pain would be gone."

He pressed his lips to her forehead again, swallowing the horror swirling in his chest at her words.

"I'm terrified of heights now. Just climbing the ladder into the attic scared the hell out of me. I think it comes from the memory of standing at that window, staring down at my own death."

He stroked her hair, hating her mother for doing such a thing to her. "How many people know about West-minster?"

She looked up at him. "Almost nobody. My father came up with an elaborate story about my going to live with a great-aunt in England and going to school there. All my old friends didn't know what to say to a girl whose mother had killed herself, so it wasn't much trouble to discourage them from trying to reach me."

"I've never heard a word about it, and you know what a gossip mill this town can be."

"I've wondered whether my father was protecting himself as much as he was protecting me. From the stigma of having a mentally ill daughter as well as a wife who committed suicide." She looked shamed by the admission. "I shouldn't have said that. I know he was protecting me. And he didn't see me as mentally ill now or he wouldn't have left the business to me."

"And nobody else knew?"

"Well, my great-aunt in England knew, because she

had to be the alibi. Uncle Rafe and Aunt Janeane—they live in Bryson City, near Winchester. My doctors and nurses at the clinic. My father, of course." She crossed her arms over her body, rubbing her arms as if she was cold.

Seth pulled off his denim jacket and wrapped it around her. "Better?"

The smoldering gaze she lifted to meet his almost made his knees buckle. "Thank you."

Get your mind on the stalker. Think about the kind of payback you want against him.

The ideas for revenge flooding his head helped cool his ardor, along with a slight step backward to take him out of the immediate impact of her delicate scent and sad-eyed vulnerability. "What about the trustees of your father's business? Would any of them know?"

"I don't think so. Well, maybe my stepmother. She's always treated me as if I'm a little fragile." Her brow creased again. "A lot of people do when they know my mother committed suicide."

"It's a trauma most people can't imagine."

"I hope they never have reason to know what it feels like." She shivered. "You don't suspect Diane, do you?"

Thanks to Mark Bramlett's final words, they knew the person who'd hired him to commit the first four murders had been a man. But Diane Davenport could have hired someone to do all the dirty work for her, he supposed. Even the solicitation. "How much would she stand to gain if you were removed as CEO?"

"As far as I know, nothing more than she'd gain if I remained CEO. That's something I need to ask my father's lawyer in the morning."

Seth wondered if he'd be able to turn off his mind

tonight long enough to get some much-needed sleep. While logic told him it wasn't likely the intruder from earlier that day would repeat an invasion so soon after the police had scoured the place for evidence, instinct told him he needed to stay on full alert.

"Maybe I should sleep down here on the sofa," he suggested.

Her cheeks flushed pink as she smiled. "I'm way too tired to make any moves on you tonight. Your virtue is safe with me."

He smiled at her attempt to lighten the mood. "I appreciate that, but I was actually thinking about the best way to keep you safe."

Her smile faded. "From intruders?"

"I don't think it's likely anyone will try anything tonight, after all the police presence today, but my gut says better safe than sorry."

"You listen to your gut a lot?" The question was serious.

"I do."

She slowly walked toward him, closing the distance between them. He found himself unable to back away, frozen in place by the desire in her eyes. She laid her hand in the middle of his chest and let it slide slowly down to the flat of his stomach. "What does your gut tell you to do with me?"

He couldn't stop a dry laugh from spilling from his throat. "I don't think that's my gut talkin', sugar."

Her eyes widened slightly, then she laughed, the sound belly deep. It was a glorious sound, he thought. Rich and deep and utterly sane. If he'd harbored a doubt about her mental stability, that laugh crushed it to powder.

"I like you, Seth Hammond. I hope like hell you decide to stick around once this is all over." She rose to her tiptoes and pressed her mouth to his, the kiss light and undemanding.

It nearly unraveled him anyway. His whole body trembled as he watched her walk away, up the stairs and out of sight.

Seth didn't look as if he'd gotten much sleep when he greeted Rachel the next morning with a cup of hot coffee and a creditable omelet. "I think you should call the company lawyer as soon as his office opens. See if he can work us in this morning."

She took the omelet and cup of coffee to the small table in the kitchen nook, "Got our agenda all worked out for today, have you?"

"The sooner we figure this out, the better," he said firmly.

The sooner you get to leave, you mean, she thought with a hint of morning-after bleakness. All her confidence of the night before had faded into doubts by the time she'd drifted to sleep. At least her subconscious had been certain of his ability to keep her safe. If she'd dreamed at all last night, she couldn't remember it and it hadn't disturbed her sleep.

She called the lawyer as soon as his office opened and he agreed to see her right away if she could get there before nine. His office was in Maryville, about twenty minutes away, but fortunately she'd showered and dressed before making the call, so they reached Maryville with time to spare.

"Am I going to be forced to fire you for ditching

work?" she asked lightly as they passed the big Davenport Trucking sign on West Sperry Road.

"I took vacation days. Cleared it with your stepbrother before I went looking for Davis Rogers."

"Very conscientious."

"What about your stepbrother?" he asked with a sideways glance toward her. "If you were incapacitated, could he take over as the CEO?"

"I don't think he wants to be CEO. His passion is hospitality. He used to work at a big resort on the Mississippi Gulf Coast before things went bad down that way and a lot of people were laid off. I think he's still hoping to get back into that line of work someday. I think he's only stayed at Davenport Trucking this long because his mother married my father. I won't be surprised if he gives me his notice sooner rather than later."

"Okay." Seth fell silent until they reached Ed Blount's office in the Maryville downtown area. The lawyer's office was located in an old two-story white clapboard house converted to upstairs and downstairs offices. Blount's suite was on the lower floor, and he greeted Rachel with an affectionate kiss on the cheek and a look of puzzlement.

"I didn't expect to see you this soon," Ed told her. "If you're here about the will reading—"

"It's not that," she said quickly. "I do have a question about my father's business, though."

"Okay." Ed spotted Seth, his sandy eyebrows lifting.

"Ed, this is Seth Hammond. Seth, Ed Blount."

Seth's face was a mask. "We've met."

From the look on the lawyer's face, it must not have been a pleasant acquaintance. "What is he doing here?"

"I can go," Seth said.

"No." She caught his wrist, holding him in place. She turned back to Ed. "Let's just stipulate that Seth was no doubt a complete ass in the past, and you have every right to distrust him for whatever it was he did to you—"

"It wasn't to him," Seth said. "It was his daughter."

She shot him a look. He met her gaze, unflinching for a moment. Then his eyes dropped, and he turned his head away.

"She thought you loved her," Ed growled.

"I know."

"That's it? You know?"

Seth's gaze lifted slowly. "I could tell you that I regret it, but you're not going to believe me, and it won't make her feel a damned bit better."

"What about her college money? Can you give that back to her?"

Rachel's heart sank painfully at the look of shame on Seth's face. But he didn't look away from Ed. "I tried."

Ed stared at him. "When?"

"About a year ago. She shoved it back to me and told me she didn't want my dirty money."

"Where is it now?"

"I gave it to the soup kitchen in Knoxville. I know Lauren used to volunteer there."

"That's where she met you," Ed snarled. "You played on her soft heart and convinced her you were just down on your luck and looking for someone to believe in you."

Seth's expression grew stony. His voice, when he spoke, was dry and uninflected. "I did."

"You broke her heart."

"I know."

"I'm sick of hearing that!" he bellowed, charging toward Seth.

"Ed." Rachel grabbed the lawyer's arm and put herself between him and Seth, struggling to keep a sudden tremor in her knees from spreading to the rest of her limbs. "You had to work me in and I don't want to run out of time because of this."

"I'll wait outside." Seth exited abruptly, closing the door behind him, leaving Rachel alone with Ed.

The lawyer glared with loathing at the closed door, his breathing coming in short, harsh grunts. "What the hell are you doing with that man?"

"It's a long story. And it's not relevant to what I'm here to find out."

Ed stared at her in consternation, visibly trying to collect himself. Finally, in a calmer tone of voice, he asked, "What are you here to find out?"

She nudged him toward his office door, shooting an apologetic smile toward the pretty red-haired receptionist who had watched the whole debacle with her mouth in an O of surprise. "I need to know what would happen to Davenport Trucking if I were no longer able to act as CEO."

Well, that had gone well.

Seth sank onto the top porch step and stared across the tree-shaded street at the mostly full parking lot of a sprawling one-story medical clinic. Pediatrics, he realized as the cars came and went with their cargo of harried moms and coughing, sniffling children.

Maybe he should write Rachel a note, leave it on her windshield and walk back to Davenport Trucking. He could hang around until lunchtime and see if one of the guys in the fleet garage could drive him to the rental car place in Alcoa in exchange for lunch.

But before he talked himself to his feet, the door opened behind him and Rachel stepped out, stopping short as she spotted him on the porch step. "Oh. I was halfway expecting you to be gone."

He rose and turned to face her, his spine rigid with a combination of shame and stubborn pride. "I was halfway to talking myself into going."

"You warned me," she said quietly, nodding toward the car.

"I did." He fell into step with her as they walked to the Honda.

"Didn't you realize who we were going to see?"

"I didn't connect the names." He forced a grim smile. "Lots of Blounts in Blount County, Tennessee."

"Did you really try to pay her back?"

He slanted a look at her, trying not to be hurt by the question. "Yes."

"And when she refused, you gave the money to the soup kitchen?"

"Foundations of Hope. Downtown. Ask for Dave Pelletier."

She paused with her key halfway to the ignition. "You always sound as if you're telling the truth."

"And you can't trust that I am." It wasn't a question. He saw the doubt in her eyes.

"I want to."

"That's not enough. You have to be sure, and you can't afford to let time and experience prove my motives are sincere."

"I don't know who to trust at all." She looked so afraid, and he hated himself for adding to her distress.

"Sometimes you just have to trust your instincts," he said quietly. "What do your instincts tell you?"

She lifted her gaze to meet his. "That you want to keep me safe."

A strange sensation, part agony, part joy, burned a hole in the center of his chest. "You're crazy."

Even though tears shined in her eyes, she laughed. "That's not a nice thing to say to a woman with my mental health history."

He laughed, too, even though he felt like crying, as well. "I won't hurt you. Not if there's anything I can do to avoid it. And if you ever begin to doubt me, you say so and I'll be gone."

"Deal." She held out her hand.

He shook it, his fingers tingling where hers touched him. He resisted the powerful urge to pull her into his arms and let go, turning to buckle himself in. "What now? What did you learn?"

"A lot. But I'm not sure how it's going to help us."

Chapter 12

"So the trustees choose the CEO?" Seth asked a few minutes later, after Rachel had summarized what Ed Blount had told her. "Is that the gist of it?"

Rachel nodded as she threaded her way through traffic on Lamar Alexander Parkway, heading toward the mountains. "There are parameters, of course. My father apparently left a list of approved candidates that the trustees have to choose from first. If none of those candidates is willing to take the job, the trustees are tasked with a circumscribed candidate search. My father apparently left detailed instructions."

"Blount wouldn't give you the details, though?"

"Not before the reading of the will next Tuesday...."

"But?" he prodded, apparently reading her hesitation.

"He mentioned that my uncle helped my father come

up with the list. I think Uncle Rafe might be willing to tell me now if I ask him."

"So let's ask him."

She shot him a smile. "Where do you think we're heading?"

Her uncle lived across the state line in Bryson City, where he and his wife, Janeane, ran a music hall catering primarily to Smoky Mountains tourists. The drive from Maryville took over two hours, but Rachel couldn't complain much about the view as their route twisted through the Smokies, past bluffs cut into the earth and sweeping vistas of the mountains spreading north and east, their tips swallowed by lingering mists that even the sunny day had not completely dissipated.

They arrived at Song Valley Music Hall in time for lunch. The fall tourist season was just starting, which meant they didn't have their choice of tables when they walked into the dimly lit dining hall, but they didn't have to wait in line, either.

Uncle Rafe himself came out to greet them, menu in hand and a smile on his face. His eyes widened as he recognized her. "Rachel, my dolly! You should have called to let me know you were coming. I just gave away the last front-row table for the show!"

"That's okay—we'll enjoy it anyway." She gave her uncle a kiss and turned to Seth. He looked uncomfortable, which struck her as odd, considering his history as a con artist. Weren't con men chameleons? "Uncle Rafe, this is Seth Hammond, a friend of mine. Seth, this is my uncle Rafe Hunter."

Her uncle's blue eyes narrowed shrewdly. "Hammond."

Seth nodded. "Yes, sir."

"Any kin to Delbert Hammond?"

Seth's expression froze in place. "My father."

Uncle Rafe nodded slowly. "There's a resemblance."

Seth's mask slipped a bit, revealing dismay in his green eyes. "So I'm told."

Rafe cocked his head to one side. "You're the one got burned."

Rachel looked from her uncle to Seth. His left hand rose and settled against his right shoulder, kneading the skin through his shirt. "That's right. Long time ago."

"Heard you've been playing nursemaid to Cleve Calhoun for the last little while. That true?"

"Yes, sir." Seth's hand dropped away from his shoulder. "He's at a rehab place now, though. His son talked him into giving it a go."

"You couldn't get him to agree?"

"Don't reckon I tried, really. I've never had any luck talking Cleve into much of anything.

Uncle Rafe smiled a little at Seth's admission. "I'll buy that. You still in the life?"

"Uncle Rafe—"

"I am not," Seth answered.

"You sure?" Her uncle's gaze went from Seth's stony face to Rachel's.

"I've found there's no long-term job satisfaction in lying to people for a living."

Uncle Rafe's gaze swept back to meet Seth's. "I don't know, son. I'm a showman, and what is that but lying to people for a living? Putting on an act, sucking them into a narrative of my choosing?"

"The people at a show know what they're seeing isn't real," Seth answered slowly. "They're willing participants in their own deception."

Uncle Rafe's well-lined face creased with a smile. "Damn good answer, boy." He hooked his arm through Rachel's and led her to the second row of tables facing the large stage. "Gotta go start deceiving this room full of willing participants in their own deception," he said with a wink in Seth's direction. "You'll stick around after the show, of course?"

"Absolutely," Rachel agreed. "I need to ask you a few questions about the trucking company. Will you have time between lunch and dinner?"

"I'll make time, dolly girl." He gave her a quick kiss and headed for the back of the restaurant.

The food at her uncle's place was good, simple home cooking. Janeane ran the kitchen, while he booked the acts and kept the daily shows going, varying things up every few weeks to keep it fresh for returning customers, Rachel told Seth while they were waiting for their orders. "Probably sixty to seventy percent of their customers are tourists," she added. "But they get a lot of locals, too, who like to take in a show. He brings in a lot of young, upcoming bluegrass and country performers. He has a real talent for knowing who's going to be the next big thing."

"You're proud of him," Seth said with a smile.

"Yeah, I am."

His smile shifted slightly. "Nice to have someone to be proud of."

"You don't?"

"There's Dee. She's the real star of the family." Rachel could tell from the look in his eyes that he thought the world of his sister. "I knew when we were little she was going to be special. She never let anything that was going on around us faze her. She knew what she wanted, and she went after it. And she always did it the right way. No shortcuts. No stomping all over someone else to get ahead. I used to think my parents must have stolen her from some nice family, 'cause she wasn't a damned thing like the rest of us."

"Are you two close?"

The pain she occasionally glimpsed in his eyes was back. "No. My fault. I wore out my welcome with Delilah a long time ago."

"She helped you out with me."

He reached across the table, lightly tapping the back of her hand. "That was for you, sugar. Not for me."

"She doesn't believe you've changed?"

A mask of indifference came over his face. "Nobody does."

"I do," she said without thinking.

His gaze focused on hers, green eyes blazing. "You don't know me, Rachel. And most of what you've heard and seen should scare the hell out of you. Don't make up some fantasy about the misunderstood tough guy who just needs someone to care. I'm not misunderstood. People understand exactly who I was. I've earned their disgust."

"You're not pulling con jobs anymore—"

"So? I did. I did them willingly, with skill and determination."

"And then you stopped."

He shook his head. "Because I finally disgusted even myself! Do you understand what I did?"

She found herself floundering for an answer. "You lied to people and conned them out of money—"

"I hurt people," he said in a low, hard growl. "Not

with a gun or a knife but with my lies. Do you know Lauren Blount, Rachel?"

She shook her head. "Not really."

"When I met her, she was nineteen. Pretty as a postcard and as sweet as Carolina honey. I convinced her I wanted a life with her, but because of my meth-dealing daddy and how he blew up my whole family, I couldn't catch a break. Showed her my burn scars, told her how I got them saving my mama from the burning house after my daddy nearly killed us all."

"Is that really what happened? That's what Uncle Rafe was talking about earlier, right? About your getting burned."

He met her gaze. "So what if it was? That's what con men do, don't you get it? We take the truth and use it to sell our lies. I had burn scars from draggin' my mama out of that house 'cause she was too drunk to get out herself, and yeah, it makes a real pitiful story. Women see your scars, get all soft and gooey about how you're some hero, and they don't even see you're playing them like fiddles."

She looked away, feeling ill.

"I had Lauren eating out of my hand. I told her I had this idea for a business, see, and I needed some seed money, but no banks or businesspeople were going to take a chance on some old hillbilly like me. I made it sound like a sure thing. I made it sound like our future. And she ate it up. She saw the poor sad sack who just needed a good woman's love to make things okay for him, and she went for the bait in a heartbeat. Just like I knew she would."

"Then what did you do?"

"She gave me the money she'd saved up for her next two semesters of college. Cried a little as she did it, telling me that even if nobody else believed in me, she did."

Tears burned Rachel's eyes as she tried to picture herself in Lauren Blount's situation. Madly in love and wanting so much to help him out. Would she have given him the money?

She didn't think she liked the answer.

"I took the money and I left town. Left her a note telling her that she needs to be careful about who she trusts in the future." He smiled, but it was a horrible sight, full of anger and self-loathing. "She's taken that warning to heart. I don't think she trusts anyone anymore."

Silence fell between them. Finally, Rachel found the courage to speak. "Didn't she press charges against you?"

He shook his head. "She gave me the money willingly, and I was vague about what I planned to do with it. She would have had to try to prove her case in court, and she didn't want to face that kind of scrutiny." He grimace-smiled again. "Lucky me."

"My God."

His green eyes flashed at her again. "Now you're getting it."

She felt sick. "What made you quit the con game?"

"Cleve's stroke."

She narrowed her eyes. "Really."

"He was helpless for a long while. His own son didn't want to hear from him. He had no one in the world to take care of him but me. I realized I didn't want to give up even part of my life for the old bastard. What had he ever done for me but turn me into a criminal?"

"Why did you help him, then?"

"Because there was no one else. Someone had to."

"It could have been the state. Or he could have hired a caretaker. It didn't have to be you."

"It did." He looked down at the flatware bundle wrapped up in a slip of paper by his elbow. He pulled the flatware to him and began to play with the bundle, turning it slowly in a circle as if he needed time to organize his thoughts. After a minute, he pushed it aside and looked up at her. "It took a day or two, but I remembered that Cleve had taken me in when I had no one else. Everybody turned on my family, and especially me, because they all knew I was going to turn out like my daddy anyway. Why bother?"

"What about your mother? Couldn't she have helped you?"

"My mama is a drunk. Has been since I was a kid because it was the only way she could keep livin' with a man who beat her up for fun."

Rachel covered her mouth in dismay.

"Tawdry, ain't it?" He'd slipped easily back into the hard mountain twang of his raising. "That's the Hammonds of Smoky Ridge for you."

"What do you think would have happened if Cleve hadn't taken an interest in you?"

"I'd be in jail. Maybe even hooked on meth. Maybe dead."

"Cleve saved you from that."

"And introduced me to a life that seemed like a no-brainer at the time. I could lie with the best of them. I'd been lyin' all my life, coverin' up for what happened in that house." His lips curved slightly, but his gaze seemed focused somewhere far away. "It was so easy."

"Until it wasn't."

His gaze snapped back to hers. "You know what con men really do, Rachel? They kill your soul. You start out a normal person. Caring. Trusting. And then he strikes, and you're never the same. You trust no one. Nothing. You're afraid to be nice, because it makes you vulnerable. You're afraid to care because it makes you an easy mark. You meet a nice guy, a good guy, a guy who would treat you right, and you can't let yourself believe him because you know sweet words and a tender touch can hide a monster." He leaned toward her, his gaze so intense it made her stomach quiver. "That's what I did to Lauren Blount. It's what I did to God knows how many people along the way."

She didn't know what to say. She didn't even know what to feel.

"I did that." He sat back, looking away. "I don't know how a man can forgive himself for that. I don't know how he lives with it. He can try to pay back the money, he can promise he'll never do anything like that again, but he can't change the fact that he had that kind of evil inside him and he let it have free rein. How do I live with that?"

She had no answer. The things he'd told her, the things he'd described, sickened her. Yet, the obvious guilt and remorse he felt touched her heart, as well. He'd been young and desperate, and while he was right—those facts weren't excuses for the things he'd done—they were, at least, mitigating factors.

At thirty, was Seth Hammond the same man he'd

been at twenty? Obviously not. But was she crazy to take a chance on a man who'd lived the kind of life he had?

The food came, but she'd long since lost her appetite. Seth toyed with his food as well, eating little. He seemed determined not to look at her for the rest of the time, and it was a relief when the music started, giving them both somewhere to park their reluctant gazes for a while.

Uncle Rafe came back to their table after the music set was over and looked with dismay at their barely touched plates. "Didn't like the food?"

"My fault," Seth said quietly. "I brought up a stomach-turning topic just as the food arrived."

Uncle Rafe's eyes narrowed as he waved over a waitress and asked her to put the food in a couple of to-go boxes. "Take it with you. Maybe you'll be hungry later. Now. What was it that you needed to ask me about the trucking company?"

"This is going to sound like an odd question, but it's important. When Dad came to you to discuss his will, he asked you to help him make up a roster of preapproved candidates for the job of CEO if I were unable to fulfill my duties. I asked Ed Blount to give me the list, but he won't do it before the will reading next week. I need to see the list now."

"Goodness, girl, whatever for? You're the CEO, free and clear, so what does the list matter now?"

"Someone may be trying to change the situation," she said quietly.

Uncle Rafe leaned closer. "Change the situation how?"

Rachel glanced at Seth. He was looking at her, finally, his gaze intense. He gave a little nod, and she lifted her chin and met her uncle's troubled gaze. "I think someone's trying to drive me crazy."

Chapter 13

The Song Valley Music Hall's office was a small room in the back of the building, nestled between the large kitchen and the public restrooms. The decor was strictly old-fashioned country charm, but Seth was relieved to see that whatever his eccentricities, Rafe Hunter took his business seriously. A new computer with a flat screen monitor and an all-in-one printer/copier sat in one corner. Shiny steel file cabinets took up one wall, while a well-organized storage cubby occupied the other.

Rafe went straight to the computer and called up a document file. At a glance—all Seth got before Rafe sent the file to print and closed it up—there were six names on the list. "Do any of those people know Mr. Davenport was considering them as possible CEOs?" he asked.

"I believe George let them know. He wouldn't want to give the trustees a list of people unwilling to consider the job, after all."

The paper came out of the printer, and Rafe plucked it up and handed it to Rachel. "There's your list. I hope to God you're wrong about your suspicions, dolly. Maybe you should come stay here with Janeane and me for a while."

"It's not a bad idea." Seth tamped down the part of him that was begging her to tell her uncle no. It made sense for her to get out of Bitterwood for a while. She could let Seth look into that list of people while she stayed safely out of it.

Safely away from him, too.

"No," she said, and part of him nearly wilted with relief. "This is my life we're talking about. I'm tired of letting everyone else make decisions for me. I need to be part of ending this mess."

"Are you rethinking your decision to be the company CEO?" Rafe gave his niece a probing look.

"I don't know," she said finally. "I never thought I wanted to take over the company permanently, but I love the people there and I want the company to be a success. My dad believed I was the person who could do it, and the more time I've spent there over the past year, the more convinced I am that he's right. I can do this job. I can do it well and take care of our customers and our employees. And I really want to, at least for a while longer. I can always go back to being a librarian later."

Rafe cupped her cheek with one big hand. "Why don't you tell me what's been going on?"

As Rachel related the things that had happened around her for the past two months, Seth found himself watching Rafe carefully for his reaction. Could he have his own reasons for wanting control of the company? The music hall seemed to be successful, but appearances could be deceiving, as Seth well knew. Rafe could be neck-deep in debt. He might be a compulsive gambler or have a bad drug habit that sucked his profits dry.

It might have been too obvious to kill Rachel before her father's death, since Rafe would be the prime suspect. He was at the top of the list to get control of the company if she were dead. Which would also make him the prime suspect if her death was suspicious in any way.

But if she were unable to fulfill the requirements of the job due to mental health problems, Rafe would have a great deal of influence if he wanted it, and nobody would suspect he'd engineered the situation.

He'd helped create this list of people to take her place. Might he have taken an even greater role, as her closest living relative, if she were declared incompetent?

If he harbored such wicked thoughts, they certainly didn't show in his horrified expression as he listened to Rachel's story. "My God, you should have called your aunt Janeane and me for help."

"I wasn't sure what was going on," she admitted. "If Seth hadn't found me on that bridge, I don't even know if I'd be alive."

Rafe blanched, his hand shaking as he lifted it to her face again. "Who would do such a thing to you?"

"I don't know."

"We think it must have something to do with Davenport Trucking," Seth said. "That's why we need the list."

Rafe's gaze snapped up to meet his. "What is your part in all this?"

The easy answer, of course, was that FBI Special Agent in Charge Adam Brand had asked him to keep an eye on Rachel. But since he hadn't shared that information with her yet, he didn't think it was a good idea to spill the beans in front of her uncle.

"I work at Davenport Trucking," he answered. "The family's been good to me, and I know a little something about deception. I guess in some ways, I'm uniquely suited to unravel a plot against Rachel."

"Thank you kindly for your help, then. But I can take care of her now. Dolly, you need to pack up and come stay with Janeane and me."

"No." Rachel's response was quiet but firm. "I'm an adult, and I will take care of myself."

"Rachel—" Seth began.

She turned her cool blue gaze to him. "Yes?"

He didn't want to argue with her in front of her uncle, so he nodded toward the list. "Anything stand out?"

She took a look at the list, her brow furrowed. "Not really. Most of the people are Davenport Trucking employees—Stan Alvis, who's the chief financial officer, Drayton Lewis, our comptroller, your direct supervisor at the garage, Gary Adams—hmm." She frowned a little.

"What?" Seth asked.

"Paul is on this list." She looked up at her uncle. "If he was willing to be CEO, why didn't my dad give him the job outright?"

Rafe shrugged. "He wanted it to be you. In fact, I'm the one who suggested Paul. I figured Diane would be hurt if we didn't, and the boy has been a loyal employee for nearly a decade now."

Seth considered what he knew about Paul Bailey. The guy came across as a put-together, confident businessman, but even though he'd been with the company for years, he didn't haunt the doors of the place the way George Davenport had, or even some of the other people on the short list. Seth's own boss, Gary, worked long hours and was a stickler about getting the job done right. He was blue-collar and rednecked, but Gary was smart, too. What he lacked in formal education, he made up for with his inquisitive mind and strong work ethic.

If Seth were picking a new CEO, he'd definitely go for Gary Adams over Paul Bailey, despite the seeming disparity between the two men.

But he wasn't looking for a CEO.

He was looking for a killer. Which of the people on that list wanted the job badly enough to kill for it? And why?

Delilah Hammond had spent almost half her life away from Bitterwood and normally thought it a good thing. Her first eighteen years growing up on Smoky Ridge had been a long, exhausting exercise in avoidance. She'd dodged her father's blows and her mother's selfish neediness. She'd kept clear of Seth's self-destructive anger and the constant temptations of drugs, booze and sex, determined to get an education and get the hell out of the mountains with her future intact.

Good grades and hard work had earned her scholarships to college. More hard work had gotten her through the FBI Academy and onto a fast-paced domestic terrorism task force. Later, she'd left the bureau for the private sector and ended up where she was now, working for former marine Jesse Cooper and his family's security agency. She had a life. A purpose. Bitterwood, Tennessee, should have been in her rearview mirror, not her windshield.

But as she wound her way through the curves of Vesper Road toward Ivy Hawkins's house, closer and closer to the brushed-velvet peak of Smoky Ridge, she felt an odd, pulling sensation in the center of her chest.

Home, she thought, and bit her lip at the image. Just no getting away from it after all.

There was a black Jeep Wrangler parked in the driveway, she saw as she turned off Vesper Road. Ivy Hawkins was back.

As it turned out, so was Sutton Calhoun, Ivy's boyfriend and one of Delilah's oldest friends and a colleague at Cooper Security. He came out onto the porch before Delilah had opened the driver's door of his truck, the expression on his tanned face fiercely grim.

Delilah's stomach cramped at the sight of him. Had something happened on his trip to northern Iraq? Nobody at Cooper Security had mentioned any trouble when she'd been there for the meeting last night.

"You're back," she greeted him, not bothering with a smile. He clearly wasn't in the mood.

Ivy Hawkins came out and stood beside him on the porch, her dark eyes blazing with anger. "Have you seen your brother lately?"

Oh, no, she thought. "Not since yesterday morning," she answered, climbing the steps slowly. "Why?"

Sutton gestured with his head for her to follow him inside the house. He led her into the study, where Ivy kept her computer. The laptop was open, and a photo of Rachel Davenport filled the screen.

Delilah walked closer, studying the photo with a frown. The photo had been taken at the funeral, she realized. Mourners were gathered around her, but she was definitely the focus of the image.

"Where did that come from?" She braced herself for the answer.

Sutton reached behind the laptop and pulled out a pair of sunglasses attached to a neck cord. It took a second look to realize the neck cord had a small connector jack built in. When Sutton picked up a small, rectangular plastic device and plugged in the cord, she realized what it really was.

"A spy camera." She looked up at Sutton. "Where'd you find this?"

"At my father's house." He put the unit down. "It was lying out in the open, next to the computer."

"And you think it's Seth's."

"Don't you?"

Delilah looked at the photo of Rachel Davenport still up on the computer screen. She'd caught Seth at the funeral and called him on being there, accusing him of trying to run some kind of con on Rachel.

He'd said he was there just to say goodbye to his employer. Clearly, he hadn't told her everything.

She closed her eyes. "How many photos?"

"About a hundred, spanning the past two weeks. He's been keeping an eye on Rachel Davenport primarily, although there were also some photos of the trucking company personnel. I don't know what your brother is up to, but it can't be good. He's put a hell of a lot of sweat and coin into following that woman around."

She forced herself to ask the obvious question, even though it made her sick to think about. "You think he's connected to the murders?"

The look of pity Sutton sent her way felt like a gut punch. "I honestly don't know."

"Where is Seth now?" Ivy asked. She was clipping her badge to the waistband of her jeans, Delilah realized.

"You're back on the job?" she asked. Ivy had been on administrative leave since Mark Bramlett's death.

"As of today," she said with a lopsided smile. "Never realized how much I'd want back on the job until I was forced off."

"What about you, Sutton? Still planning to give your notice and move back here to Hillbilly Heaven?"

Sutton put his hands on Ivy's shoulders. "Already gave my notice. The Iraq mission was my last one. I'm back in Bitterwood to stay."

Funny, Delilah thought, how a place so full of bad memories still had a way of getting under the skin. She'd never figured Sutton would come back to Bitterwood any more than she would. "Are you planning to arrest Seth?"

"Not sure we have what it takes to get a warrant," Ivy admitted. "But I'm definitely going to ask him a few questions."

"You should have stayed with your uncle and aunt."

The first words Seth had spoken in almost two hours came out so soft she almost didn't hear them. She turned down the radio and met his brooding gaze. "I'm not going to hide in Bryson City. If someone's screwing around with my life, I have a right to know about it."

"That doesn't mean you have to be in the crosshairs."

"If this is your way of backing out of the investigation, just say so."

"I'm not saying that," he said quickly.

She turned onto the narrow, winding road that led to her family home, her stomach tensing as she thought about what might await her at the end of the road. She hadn't yet called the locksmith to change the locks nor gotten an estimate from an alarm company. Maybe she'd been depending on Seth Hammond too much. She needed to be able to meet Seth on equal footing, not as a victim. That's not the way she wanted him to think of her. Not by a long shot.

"If you want out, I'll understand. I don't want you to see me as an obligation.

His unnerving silence stretched out long enough for them to reach the end of her driveway. As she turned down the drive, his next words nearly ran her off onto the lawn. "I'm working for an FBI agent."

She righted the car, put on the brakes and looked at him. "What?"

"I've done some informant jobs for an FBI agent my sister once worked with. Mostly undercover kind of stuff, places I could easily go that the FBI couldn't. A few weeks ago, just after Mark Bramlett died, my FBI handler called me and asked me to keep an eye on you."

Rachel pulled up outside the garage doors and parked, turning to look at Seth. He gazed back at her, clear-eyed.

"Why?" she asked.

"He didn't say exactly."

"You didn't ask?"

"I asked. He didn't say. All he told me is that this one wasn't for the FBI. It was personal."

"Personal?" That answer made even less sense than the FBI being interested in her life. "What's his name?"

Seth looked reluctant, but he finally answered, "Adam Brand. He's a special agent in charge in the Washington D.C. field office."

"I've never heard of him."

"I don't think it's that kind of personal."

"There's more than one kind of personal?"

He gave a soft huff of laughter. "There's all kinds of personal, sugar. But what I mean is, I got the feeling he's talking about your situation being of interest to him for a personal reason."

"And you didn't press him on it?"

"We've always had a need-to-know kind of relationship," he explained with a half smile. "If I need to know, he'll tell me. If he doesn't tell me, I don't need to know."

"You're okay with that?"

"I'm not crazy about it," he admitted. "But I've helped the FBI stop some very bad people from doing terrible things." His grimace suggested some of those terrible things had come very close to happening to him. "Adam Brand is one of the good guys, and there aren't many of them willing to give me a break."

"So what did Agent Brand ask you do to, where I'm concerned?"

"Just keep an eye on you."

"Is that why you were on the spot to help me at Purgatory Bridge?"

He shook his head. "That was dumb luck. I was just heading to Smoky Joe's for a good time."

"And ended up plucking my sorry backside off a bridge." She gave him an apologetic look.

"I'm glad I was there." The warmth in his voice seemed to spread to her bone marrow.

"So am I."

Silence fell between them, sizzling with unspoken desires. He wanted her—it burned in his eyes, scorching her—but he made no move to take what he wanted. What they both wanted.

She made no move, either, tethered in place by caution. Desire was a chemical thing that didn't always take reality into consideration. Wanting him wasn't a good enough reason to throw caution to the wind.

Was it?

"We need to get inside and see if anyone's left you any new surprises." He dragged his gaze away and opened the passenger door.

She stifled a sigh. Even if she was willing to take a chance, clearly Seth had different ideas.

Maybe it was for the best.

A thorough room-by-room inspection of the house showed no sign of an intruder. Seth took a second look around while Rachel was making calls to the locksmith and the alarm company that handled the trucking company's security. He wandered back downstairs as she was jotting down the appointment time she'd set with the security company for the following day.

"Did Delilah say when she'd be back from Alabama?" he asked, dropping onto the sofa across from where she sat.

"No. Why?"

"I need to go see Cleve at the hospital in Knoxville.

I promised him I'd stop in at least once a week, and I'm running out of week."

"I think maybe you're running, period."

His gaze whipped up to meet hers. "Meaning?"

"Ignoring this thing between us doesn't make it go away."

His brow furrowed. "Rachel, we agreed—"

"What scares you about it?" she asked.

"It scares me that you're not scared," he answered flatly. "You're a smart woman. You've got to know that I'm a risky bet."

"Every relationship is a risk."

"You've lost a lot already. You're vulnerable and lonely—"

"So, I'm emotionally incapable of knowing what I want? Is that what you're suggesting?"

He closed his eyes a moment, frustration lining his sharp features. When he opened his eyes, they blazed with helpless need. "You're a beautiful woman. You seem so cool and composed on the outside, but then you give me this glimpse of the passion you got roiling around inside you and I just want to bathe myself in it." Raw desire edged his voice. "I've got no right to want you so damned much, but I do. And if you don't stop me, I don't know if I can stop myself."

She felt the last fragile thread of caution snap, plunging her into the scary, exhilarating ether of pure, blind faith. She rose from the sofa and walked over to where he sat.

"I don't want to stop you." She touched his face, sliding her fingers along the edge of his jaw. "Don't stop."

He turned his face toward her touch, his eyes drifting closed. "Rachel—"

Bending, she pressed her mouth to his, thrilling as his lips parted beneath hers, his tongue brushing over her lower lip and slipping between her teeth to tangle with her own tongue. He tasted like sweet tea and sin.

He wrapped his arms around her waist, pulling her down to him until her legs straddled his. She settled over his lap, acutely aware of the hard ridge of his erection against her own sex. A guttural sound rose in her chest as she pressed her body more firmly against his, molding herself around the hard muscles and flat planes of his body.

His hands slid down her back and curved over her bottom, his fingers digging into the flesh there, pulling her even closer. His breath exploded from his throat when she rocked against him, building delicious friction between their bodies.

"What am I going to do with you?" he groaned against her throat, his lips tracing a fiery path along the tendons of her neck.

She whispered her answer in his ear and eased off his lap, pushing to her feet. She held out her hand, locking gazes with him.

She saw questions there, but also a fierce, blazing desire to give her what she'd asked for. Slowly, his hand rose and clasped hers, and he let her tug him to his feet.

Their bodies collided, tangled, then melded. He wrapped one arm around her waist, pulling her against him, while his free hand threaded through her hair to tug her head back. He claimed her mouth in a slow, hot kiss, no frantic clash of teeth and tongues but a thorough seduction, full of purpose and promise.

"You look so prim and proper on the outside," he

whispered against her temple as he led her to the stairs.
"But you've got a danger monkey inside you."

She laughed at the term. "Danger monkey?"

He didn't answer until they'd reached the door of her
bedroom. He stopped there, turning to look at her. As
always, the intensity of his gaze made her legs wobble
a little, and she grabbed the front of his shirt to hold
herself upright.

"Being with me is a risk, Rachel. People will look at
you differently. They'll tell you you're crazy. Tell me
you know that."

She could barely catch her breath, but she managed
to find the words. "I know that. I don't care." Growing impatient, she tugged the hem of his T-shirt upward, baring the flat plane of his belly to her wandering
hands. She splayed her fingers over his stomach and ran
them upward, through the crisp dark hairs of his torso.
They tangled in the light thatch on his chest, drawing
a low groan from his throat.

Then her fingers ran across the rough flesh of his
burn scar, and he froze.

Her gaze lifted to meet his. "Is that where you were
burned?"

He nodded. "One of the places."

"Let me see."

He slid his shirt off, baring the scars on his chest
and shoulder. She examined them first with her gaze,
then with a featherlight touch of her fingers. "It must
have hurt like hell."

"It did. They told me at the hospital that I was lucky.
Most of my burns were second degree, which would

heal better. But one of the doctors said they also hurt worse."

"Your mother must have considered you her hero."

Her words seemed to wound him. "My mother stayed drunk for days after the fire. All she ever said to me was that I should have saved my father, too. I didn't have the heart to tell her there wasn't enough left of him after the explosion to save."

Rachel pressed her cheek against his scarred shoulder. "I'm sorry. That must have been so terrible for you."

He threaded his fingers through her hair and made her look at him. "Don't feel sorry for me. That's one thing I don't need from you."

Her pity melted in a scorching blaze of desire. "Okay. So what's one thing you *do* need from me?"

He dipped his head and kissed her again. She heard the rattle of the doorknob as he groped for it, felt the shift of their bodies as he backed into the bedroom, drawing her along with him.

The backs of her knees connected with the bed, and she tumbled backward onto the mattress, Seth's body falling with her. He settled into the cradle of her thighs, dragging his mouth away from hers.

"I've never wanted anything as much as I want you," he whispered.

A thrill of power coursed through her, making her heart pound and her head spin. She rolled him over until she was on top of him, her hands clasped with his, pinning him to the mattress. She lowered her head slowly, kissing her way from his clavicle to the sharp edge of his jaw. She stopped, finally, at the curve of his ear, nipping lightly at the lobe.

"Prove it," she answered.

With catlike grace, he flipped her onto her back again, feral desire blazing from his eyes.

Slowly, thoroughly, he did as she'd asked.

Chapter 14

"What did you want to be when you grew up?"

Rachel's sleepy voice pierced the hazy cloud of contentment on which Seth had been floating for the past few minutes. He roused himself enough to think about what she'd asked. "I think mostly I just wanted to grow up."

Her fingers walked lightly up his chest. "I guess there wasn't much room for dreams in that kind of life, huh?"

"I think the dreams were all unattainable on purpose," he answered after a moment of thought. "If you let yourself dream small, there was the possibility that it could come true. Which meant it hurt all the more when it didn't. But if you dreamed big, you knew from the start that it was impossible. So it couldn't really hurt you."

She was quiet for a long moment. "I used to want to be a writer."

"You did?" He supposed he could see it. She'd been a librarian, and her house was full of books. The temptation to create rather than simply consume was strong. He knew from his own experiences working as a mechanic the pleasure of being an active part of making something work. He'd always loved cars, even as a kid when having one of his own had seemed an impossibility. But he loved working on them even more, seeing what made them go, what could make them stop, how to make them work more efficiently.

"I did. But my father was always such a pragmatist. He liked to point out the odds against success in any endeavor. I don't think it occurred to me until much later on that he wasn't meaning to discourage me. He just wanted me to have the facts."

"And you let the facts deter you."

"I found an easier way to work with books."

"Easier isn't always better."

Rachel propped her head on her hand and looked down at him, her honey-brown hair falling in a curtain over his shoulder. "That's a very wise observation."

He laughed, shaking his head. "That's just bad experiences talking, sugar, not wisdom."

"Where you do think wisdom comes from?" She bent and kissed the scar on his chest, then touched it with her forefinger. "You checked the stove for a burner the other day."

He grimaced. "Fire and I don't mix well."

She slapped his chest lightly, making it sting in an oddly pleasurable way. "Like heights and me."

"You run from things that are bad for you." He gave her a pointed look. "Usually."

She rolled onto her back. "Stop it, Seth."

He turned onto his side to look at her, propping himself up on his elbow. She was only half-covered by the tangled sheets, her torso gloriously naked. In the golden late afternoon light slanting across the bed, she looked like a gilded goddess, all perfect curves and mysterious, shadowy clefts. She belonged in a better place than this, he thought. She deserved to be worshipped and adored by a worthy man.

What if he could never be that worthy, no matter how hard he tried?

"When I'm with you, I want to be perfect."

She met his gaze with smiling eyes. "Nobody's perfect."

"Wrong answer, gorgeous. You're supposed to say, 'But you are perfect, Seth. You're perfectly perfect. There's never been anyone more perfect in the history of the world.'"

She laughed. "Nobody sane would say that."

"Thanks a lot."

"I don't want perfect." She rose up on her elbow as well, facing him. "I want someone who makes the effort to do the right thing for the right reasons. When I look at you, when I watch you dealing with all the suspicion and temptations you have to deal with, that's what I see. I see a man who's made terrible mistakes that he still suffers for, but he tries. He tries so hard to be a better man."

Her words scared him. "What if I'm not that man?"

"You are," she insisted, pressing her hand flat on his chest. "You're just afraid to believe it."

He wanted to believe it. He had spent the first fifteen years of his life wishing away reality and he'd spent the last five years doing the same thing, though for different reasons.

Dreaming the impossible because it hurt less when it didn't come true.

But what if those dreams weren't really impossible? What if he could have a decent life, surrounded with good people who cared about him and wanted the best for him? Other people could live that life—what if he could, too? Was that really too impossible to believe?

A distant rapping sound filtered past his thoughts. After a few seconds of silence, the sound came again.

Rachel's head lifted toward the bedroom door. "Is that someone knocking on the door?"

The rapping downstairs had grown more insistent. With a low growl of impatience, Rachel swung her legs over the side of the bed and started gathering up her clothes, dressing as she went. Seth shrugged on his own clothes, joining her downstairs at the door.

"Wait." He put his arm in front of her as she started to open the door, holding her back. "Let me see who it is first."

He put one eye to the peephole and felt a ripple of surprise. Sutton Calhoun's face stared back at him through the fisheye lens.

"Who is it?" Rachel asked.

"An old friend." *Turned enemy,* he added silently. He unlocked the door and opened it.

The indistinct, distorted images that had flanked Sutton in the fisheye lens turned out to be Seth's sister, Delilah, and small, dark-eyed Detective Ivy Hawkins. Seth didn't know what he found more alarming, the grim looks on all three faces or the Bitterwood P.D. badge clipped to the front of Ivy's belt.

"Has something happened?" he asked.

"Seth Hammond, the Bitterwood Police Department would like to ask you some questions," Ivy said in a low, serious tone.

The sinking sensation in his chest intensified. "About what?"

Ivy's dark eyes flickered toward Rachel. "Your involvement in the harassment and stalking of Rachel Davenport."

"That's ridiculous," Rachel exclaimed, stepping forward. "Seth is not stalking me."

"We've found a disk of photos that would suggest otherwise," Sutton snapped, his gaze firmly fixed on Seth's face. Seth didn't miss the disgust, tinged with disappointment, in his old friend's eyes.

"You think I'm behind what's been happening to Rachel," he said.

"I saw the photos." Delilah sounded more hurt than angry. "I saw the sunglasses camera—that's expensive equipment. Where did you get the money?"

"Sunglasses camera?" For the first time, Rachel's voice held a hint of uncertainty.

"You were wearing them at the funeral," Delilah said, her gaze pleading with him to give her a reasonable excuse.

"He was snapping photos of you at your father's funeral," Sutton said.

Seth felt Rachel's gaze on him. He turned slowly to look at her.

Her blue eyes were dark with questions. "You were wearing sunglasses at the funeral. I remember that."

"I was," he agreed. "And they were camera glasses. Remember, I told you I was working for the FBI."

For a moment, some of the doubt cleared from Rachel's expression.

"Working for the FBI?" Delilah stared at him. "But how? You'd have had to pass background checks—" She stopped, shaking her head. "Seth, please—"

She wanted to believe him, he saw with some surprise. More than she doubted him. "Call Adam Brand," he said quietly. Urgently.

Delilah blanched at the mention of Brand's name, not for the first time. Seth had long suspected something bad had gone down between his sister and the FBI agent almost eight years earlier, when she was still working for the bureau.

Ivy pulled her phone from her pocket. "I'll call him."

As Delilah recited the D.C. office number from memory, Seth slanted a look at Rachel. She gazed back at him, trying to look supportive, but doubts circled in her blue eyes like crows in a winter sky.

"I'm not lying about this," he told her. But listening to his low, urgent tone, he could see why the doubt didn't immediately clear from her eyes. He sounded desperate and scared.

Because he was.

"He's not in his office," Ivy told them a moment later. "The person who answered said he'd taken a few days off and was out of pocket."

Seth frowned. Brand hadn't said anything to him about going on vacation. In fact, in all the time he'd been dealing with Brand, the man hadn't taken more than a day or two off at a time.

"He never goes on vacation," Delilah murmured, echoing his own thoughts.

"Why don't we go down to the station and sort through all of this?" Ivy suggested in a calm, commanding tone. Seth looked at her thoughtfully, remembering when she'd been a snot-nosed little brat who'd followed him and Sutton all over Smoky Ridge. She'd grown up, he realized, into a tough little bird.

He looked at Rachel again. Her eyes were on Delilah, her expression pensive. Seth followed her gaze and saw his sister staring at him with blazing hope rather than doubt.

She believed him, he realized with astonishment. "We'll keep calling," Delilah said quietly.

Sutton, however, was having none of it. "What's the point? You really think the FBI's going to hire a con man to keep tabs on a grieving heiress? That's like assigning an alligator to guard the pigpen."

Seth turned to look at Rachel. Her eyes had gone reflective. He couldn't tell what she was thinking, and that scared him to death. "Rachel—"

"Are you going to take him in?" She turned her cool gaze to Ivy.

Ivy nodded. "Yeah. I am."

Seth looked from Sutton's stony face to Ivy's. "You gonna cuff me?"

Ivy's left eyebrow peaked. "Is it going to be necessary?"

He was tempted to make it so. Go out in a blaze, since it's what everyone seemed to expect of him.

But he simply shook his head. "Let's get this over with."

He looked back as he walked out of the door, hoping to catch Rachel's eye and try one last time to make her see that he was telling the truth.

But she had turned away, her cell phone to her ear.

He trudged down the porch steps, feeling suddenly dead to the core.

Rachel stood beneath the hot shower spray, her mind racing. She'd never been a woman of impulse, heedless of warning signs. Even as a child, she'd been a rule follower, thanks to her father, who'd always explained the reasons behind his strictures in ways she could understand.

Logic told her she should be down there at the police station right now, demanding that Seth explain his lies and machinations. But she just couldn't believe any of the allegations against him.

She knew all the reasons she should, of course. Though nobody had showed her any pictures, she didn't doubt they existed. Ivy Hawkins was a cop with no reason to lie. And even Seth's own sister had said she'd seen the photos.

But that didn't mean Seth had been doing something to hurt her. He'd told her he was working for the FBI, and she'd believed him. If he was following her on the orders of the mysterious Adam Brand, it made sense he might use covert surveillance equipment to do so.

She'd called the trucking company as soon as Ivy Hawkins had made it clear she was taking Seth in for questioning, wondering if there was any sort of fund available from the company to help employees with legal problems. But their lawyer had been doubtful. "What you're describing doesn't sound as if it's connected to the employee's work at the company," Alice Barton had told her. "He wouldn't qualify."

She'd known the legal fund idea was a long shot, but she had a feeling Seth might have been more open to accepting her help if it came from the company instead of her own resources. No matter. She was going to figure out a way to help him whether he liked it or not.

Out of the shower, she dressed quickly, letting her hair air dry as she pondered what to do next. She needed to see the photos, she realized. See the so-called evidence against Seth. There might be something in those photos that could clue her in to who was really trying to destroy her life.

Before Delilah had dropped her off at her car the day after the Purgatory Bridge incident, she'd given Rachel her business card with her cell phone number. Where had she put it?

She was digging through the drawers of her writing desk, looking for the card, when there was another insistent knock on the door. Distracted, she almost opened the door without looking through the peephole. She stopped at the last moment and took a peek.

It was her stepbrother, Paul.

Relaxing, she opened the door. "Oh. Hi."

He pushed past her into the house. He looked around, as if he expected to find someone else there with her. "Are you okay?"

"What's wrong?" she asked, closing the door behind them.

"I just got a call from Jim Hallifax at the locksmith's place down the street from the office. He said you were changing the locks here because you'd had an incident with an intruder."

She stared at him, confused. "Why on earth would Jim Hallifax call you about that?"

Paul stared back at her a moment, looking a little sheepish. "I, uh, mentioned in passing that you were taking your father's death badly and that I was worried about you being here all alone. I guess he thought I'd want to know that you'd had some trouble."

She shook her head. "He had no business telling you that."

"Are you angry that I know?"

She took a deep breath and let it out slowly. "No. But I'm fine. Really." At least, she had been while Seth was there. Now that she was alone, however, she felt vulnerable again.

"You shouldn't stay here alone. I could move in for a little while, at least until the locks are changed."

"I'm getting an alarm put in, too," she assured him. "Dad resisted it forever, but I just don't think it's safe to live here without some form of protection."

The phone rang, interrupting whatever Paul was going to say in response. For a second, Rachel thought it might be Seth, but she realized he'd have called her cell phone. She let it ring, not in the mood to talk to anyone else at the moment. The machine would pick up the message.

"Call from Brantley's Garage," the mechanized voice drifted in from the hallway where the phone was located. Rachel frowned, trying to remember why Brantley's Garage would be calling. As the message beep sounded, she remembered. Seth's car with the flat tires. They'd given Brantley her phone number in case he couldn't be reached by his cell.

She didn't reach the phone before the caller started

leaving a message. "Mr. Hammond, this is Wally from Brantley's Garage. Your car is ready to pick up."

She grabbed the phone. "Wally, Mr. Hammond isn't here, but I'll be sure he gets the message. Thanks." Bracing herself, she hung up the phone and turned to look at her stepbrother.

He stared at her, his expression disbelieving. "Why would the garage call here to reach Seth Hammond?"

"Because he was staying here with me."

Paul stared at her as if she'd lost her mind. "Why?"

She sighed, realizing she was going to have to tell someone everything that had happened, sooner or later. There was no point in trying to hide from her choices any longer. She'd made them, and if they turned out to be mistakes, she'd have to live with them, because she had no intention of apologizing.

"It's a long story," she said. "And it started a couple of nights ago on Purgatory Bridge."

Chapter 15

"Are you charging me with something?" Seth blurted before Ivy Hawkins and Antoine Parsons asked the first question.

"Should we?" Ivy asked.

"Charge me or let me go," he said flatly.

"We can hold you for twenty-four hours without charging you for anything," Antoine said in a quiet tone. "I'd rather not do either, frankly. I'd like to believe you've gotten your act together, because I remember you as being an okay guy back in the day, before all that mess went down with your dad and you got sucked into Cleve Calhoun's world."

So, Seth thought, *Parsons gets to be the good cop.* He looked at Ivy, who was watching him with thoughtful eyes. "I've told you everything. Meanwhile, Rachel Davenport is home alone at a house that's been broken into at least once, after over a month of incidents targeting her and the people around her. Including five murders."

"Why did the FBI want you to keep an eye on Rachel Davenport?" Antoine asked.

"Adam Brand didn't say. All he told me was that it wasn't an official FBI inquiry."

"Was that unusual?"

"Never happened before," he admitted.

"And you didn't question the order?" Ivy interjected.

"Of course I did. But look—Adam Brand's an FBI agent, which means he's a secretive guy by default. He tells me only what he thinks I need to know in order to do the job he gives me. I didn't need to know why I was keeping an eye on Rachel."

"You weren't even curious?" Ivy sounded doubtful.

"Honestly? I didn't care. I was already keeping an eye on Rachel before he called." He gave her a pointed look. "But you already know that."

He saw Antoine slant a quick look at Ivy and realized the pretty little police detective apparently hadn't done much talking with her partner about Seth's part in bringing down serial killer Mark Bramlett. He supposed she might not have had time to tell him much before the police department put her on administrative leave.

"I certainly didn't know you were stalking her," Ivy denied.

"I'm not stalking her," he protested, though he supposed that an outside observer might think so. He'd been spending many of his off-work hours keeping an eye on Rachel Davenport and the people around her, ever since he'd started putting two and two together about the serial killer victims, all of whom had shared a connection with Rachel.

"You've been following her. Taking photos of her. Insinuating yourself in her life. Know what that sounds like to me?" she asked.

"Like a con man picking out a new mark," he answered.

She looked a little surprised to hear him say it out loud. "Then you see the issue I have with your story."

"And here's the issue I have with the way your department has handled this investigation," he snapped back. "It took four murders before you'd so much as admit in public you were looking for a serial killer. And it took you longer still to tie all four people to Rachel Davenport."

"You knew earlier?" Antoine asked with a slight rise of one dark brow.

"Y'all never step foot into any of the beer joints around these parts, do you?" He shook his head. "You like to sit here in your nice, clean police station and pretend there's not any crime in these parts, not like there is in the big city, even though these hills are full of desperate, poor people. That's why someone can offer twenty grand to kill someone and you'll never hear a word of it, because you're too scared to get down in the dirt where the bad guys wallow."

Antoine looked surprised. But not Ivy. Because she was sleeping with Sutton Calhoun, of course. They were talking marriage and babies and the whole sappy lot, from what Seth had heard. Of course, Sutton had told her what Seth had told him about the twenty-grand hit he'd heard about.

"Sutton told me about that," Ivy said quietly. She

gave Antoine an apologetic look. "I should have told you. I'm sorry. It was only hearsay, and Sutton didn't know who Seth had talked to."

"It would have helped with our investigation," he said. "You want to tell us who told you?"

"The guy's nowhere around these parts anymore. He got out of town not long after that happened. I don't even know his real name. Just the name he went by when we crossed paths now and then. Calls himself Luke, but he's fast to tell you it's short for Lucifer, because he's a fallen angel." Seth grimaced. "My theory, he's some poor preacher's black sheep son. His mama probably prays for him every night and cries about him every day."

"What did Luke tell you, exactly?" Antoine asked.

"That he had been offered a hit job."

"And you didn't think to mention this to us before now?"

"Luke didn't take the job, and if you snatched him up, he'd know I was the one who told. I might need information from him in the future."

Ivy's brow furrowed. "Information for what?"

"Anything. Everything." Seth leaned forward. "You don't know what it's like living outside proper society, do you? Sure, your mama's got a bit of a reputation for bringing home deadbeats, but people mostly understood that was just because she wanted someone to love her. They may not have approved, and I'm sure some of them thought she was stupid, but nobody ever thought she was a bad person."

Ivy gave a slight nod.

"Right now, I can't depend on society to see me as anything but trouble. And I'm not lookin' for sympathy when I say that—I know I brought on my own troubles. But it doesn't change my situation. There are times when I have to depend on people you wouldn't want to be seen with. Hell, I don't want to be seen with 'em, not anymore, because it makes it that much harder for me to try to fit in with good people." He shook his head. "But my opinion of what constitutes good people and bad people can be a little fluid."

He saw a hint of sympathy in Ivy's dark eyes. "Did you press Luke about who tried to hire him?"

"Not at the time. I hadn't connected it to the Davenports then. I was trying to keep my nose clean, stay out of messes, and I didn't want to know anything more." He felt a sharp pang of guilt. "If I'd pushed a little harder, maybe I could have stopped it. But I just wanted to stay clear of trouble."

"You should have told us," Antoine agreed. "Do you have any idea how to find this Luke person again?"

"I tried to find him a few weeks ago, but he wasn't anywhere around. I talked to some mutual acquaintances and they told me Luke had gone to Atlanta for a while to see if he could get any work down there."

"What kind of work did he do?"

Seth shot Antoine a pointed look.

"The kind of work you used to do?"

"Yeah, he runs cons when he can. If you can get your hands on Atlanta area mug shots from bunco arrests in the past three weeks, I could maybe pick him out of a lineup."

"We'll look into that," Ivy said. "Meanwhile, there's the issue of the photos you took of the funeral."

"I told you what that was about."

"And conveniently, your so-called contact at the FBI is out of pocket."

"Not very damned convenient for me," Seth disagreed. "And how many times do we have to go back over this same ground? You do realize you've left Rachel Davenport by herself, unprotected, in order to chase me around in circles for no good reason?"

Ivy and Antoine exchanged looks. As if they'd reached a silent agreement, Antoine got up and exited the interview room, leaving Ivy alone with Seth.

"Where's he going?"

"He'll get someone to check on Ms. Davenport."

"Look, Ivy—Detective." He couldn't help but make a little face as he corrected himself, a picture in his mind of Ivy Hawkins as a snub-nosed thirteen-year-old with shaggy hair, skinned knees and a crooked grin. It was hard to take her seriously as a police officer when he'd known her as a tagalong for so many years. "I know why you have to bring me in and ask me these questions. I'm trying to be patient and cooperative. I am. But you and Sutton painted a really bad picture of me for Rachel. I've been trying to help her, not hurt her. And it's got to be hard for her to trust anyone, especially someone like me—"

Ivy's eyes widened. "Oh my God. Are you involved with her?"

He sat back in consternation.

"Oh my God." Ivy sat back, too, staring across the table at him through widened eyes. "What exactly did we interrupt this afternoon?"

He made himself as opaque as he could and didn't answer.

"Oh my God."

"Will you please stop saying that?" he asked.

Ivy brought her hand up to her mouth, covering it as if it were the only way to keep from blurting out her shock again. The resulting image would have been comical if Seth hadn't been so worried.

A knock on the door drew Ivy out of her seat. A uniformed officer told her something, and she turned to Seth. "Stay here. I'll be right back."

"Is something up?"

"I'll be back in a minute." Ivy left the interview room, closing the door behind her.

Seth put his head in his hands, frustrated by the delay. Rachel probably thought the worst of him right now. And who could blame her? He'd kept things secret, as usual, not trusting her with the full measure of truth. He talked a good game about trying to earn her trust, but when it came right down to it, he hadn't trusted her enough to be completely honest.

And now, he had to pay for it. He just prayed Rachel didn't have to pay for it, as well. Because she'd already been alone in that house for too long, without anyone to protect her from whoever wanted to do her harm.

"You should have told me about all of this." Paul gave Rachel a stern look softened slightly by the sympathy in his brown eyes. "Why did you try to go through all of this alone?"

"I wasn't alone."

"And trusting a man like Seth Hammond is even crazier."

"He was very kind to me. He's taken some risks to help me out," she defended Seth, wondering why she was bothering. Paul would look at the evidence and assume the worst. Seth had tried to warn her that's how it would be. To anyone on the outside, all the evidence would seem to point to Seth's playing games with her. If she hadn't spent the past few days getting to know Seth intimately, she might concur.

Intellectually, she could see the warning signs, but she couldn't connect them to the Seth Hammond she knew. He had been nothing but kind to her, even when telling her a few hard truths. He'd been genuinely remorseful about the ways he'd hurt people in the past. He'd told her the truth when a lie would have served him better.

"Why would someone do all of this to you?" Paul asked her.

"I think it must have something to do with Davenport Trucking. Or, more specifically, my job there."

Paul's brow furrowed. "In what possible way?"

"Paul, what do you know about my father's will?"

He shrugged. "Only what scuttlebutt at the office says. Your father wanted you to be CEO when he died, and so you will be."

"Have you ever heard anyone speculating about what might happen if I weren't able to take the job?"

"Not that, exactly." Paul pressed his mouth into a thin line. "I guess people are wondering why you'd want the job. You always loved being a librarian. I think some people thought George was being unfair to ask you to take over his dream by leaving your own dream behind."

She'd felt the same way, at first. And felt a hell of a lot of guilt about it, considering her father's deteriorating condition. "I need them to realize I'm doing this job because I want to, not because I feel obligated to."

"Is that really how you feel?" Paul looked unconvinced.

"At least for the next few years."

"And then?"

"And then we'll see." She had a feeling she'd go back to the library sooner or later. But not before she was certain her father's legacy was in the best hands possible. She owed her father's memory that much.

He was silent for a long moment. "It would be easier on you if you stepped down."

"I'm not going to let someone scare me away from a job I've decided to do." She lifted her chin.

"You really think these murders are about you?"

"I know it sounds crazy."

"It sounds narcissistic," he said.

"It's neither. It's just what the evidence is pointing to. You think I want to believe people have been murdered to get to me? Believe me, I don't."

"But you've been listening to Seth Hammond. He's not exactly the most reliable of tale-tellers. What if he's playing his own game with you?"

"I've thought about that." She'd thought about it a lot, especially over the past hour, testing her faith in him against the logic her father had taught her. "I just don't see what he gets out of it."

"Do you know how he used to make a living?"

"He was a con man."

"He was a particular kind of con man. He preyed on vulnerable women. Convinced them that he wanted them, that he loved them. That they should trust him. He bilked them, and then he was gone."

She didn't answer, knowing he wasn't telling her anything that Seth would deny.

"You're not falling for him, are you?"

"I know what he is," she answered. Her cell phone rang. She dug it from her pocket and saw an unfamiliar local number.

Was it Seth? He might be stuck at the police station, using his one phone call to get in touch with her. She punched the button and answered the call.

It wasn't Seth. It was a police officer. "Ms. Davenport, this is Jerry Polito with the Bitterwood Police Department. Detective Antoine Parsons asked me to check on you, see if you're okay there by yourself."

"I'm not by myself, Officer," she answered with a look at Paul. "My stepbrother is here."

"Good." The policeman sounded relieved. "Detective Parsons suggested you might want to have someone stay with you, given all that's been happening to you."

"Thank you." She hung up and turned to Paul. "The police. They were concerned about having left me here alone."

"You're not alone." Paul put his hand on her shoulder. "I'll stick around tonight, okay?"

He had stayed there plenty of times during his mother's marriage to her father, but she couldn't shake the feeling that she'd prefer to be alone than to have Paul stick around for the night. Maybe it was as simple as wanting to be free from scrutiny or unwelcome pity for a while.

And, if she was being honest with herself, she was hoping Seth would be released soon and come back to finish what they'd started that morning.

God, she needed to talk to him. She needed to hear his voice, to make sure he was okay.

"Why don't I make you some tea?" Paul suggested,

nudging her toward the kitchen. "You still have some of that honey chamomile stuff you and my mom like so much?"

"I think so." She followed him into the warm room at the back of the house, trying not to remember the time she'd spent in there with Seth just that morning.

But the kitchen was no worse than the den, where she'd begun her earnest seduction of the most dangerous man she knew. Or the hallway, where they'd kissed up against the wall for a long, breathless moment before finding their way to the bedroom.

Even after her shower, she'd imagined she could still smell him on herself, a rich, musky male scent that made her toes curl and her heart pound. She wanted him there with her. Where he belonged. If he walked through the front door that very minute, she knew she'd tell Paul to go home and leave her alone with Seth. To hell with what Paul thought about it.

To hell with what anyone thought.

"Paul Bailey has a record," Ivy told Antoine. She spoke too quietly for Seth to hear her from his seat at the interview table, but he'd long ago learned how to read lips. Cleve had pounded into him the importance of equipping himself with all the tools necessary to do a thorough con job.

Being able to tell what people were discussing while out of earshot was just one of his skills. Another was reading body language. And Ivy Hawkins's body language screamed anxiety.

Antoine Parsons looked at the folder Ivy showed him, his brow furrowed. The anxiety seeped from her body into his, setting up a low, uneasy vibration in the room.

Seth couldn't stand the wait. "Why did you look at Paul Bailey's record?"

Both of the detectives turned to look at him as if they'd forgotten he was still in the room. "We've been looking at everyone at Davenport Trucking." Antoine sounded distracted. "The records from Mississippi just came through. He had some gambling problems when he was working casinos there. It's how he lost his job— skimming and setting up some cheats for money."

Seth sat back in his chair, surprised. He'd never thought of Paul Bailey as a possible suspect. The guy didn't seem interesting enough to earn suspicion.

"Even if he has a gambling problem, I'm not sure how taking control of Davenport Trucking could help him," Ivy answered. "I did some looking into the company back during the murder investigation. The CEO position's compensation package isn't all that large. Most of the profits are funneled back into the company. If Paul were to be made CEO, at most his pay would go up a hundred thousand."

"That's a lot of money," Antoine murmured.

"It can't just be about money," Seth said. "If he's the guy behind it, he was out there offering twenty grand for the hit. If he's so money-strapped, how can he pay twenty grand?"

Ivy and Antoine exchanged looks. "If it's not about money, what's it about?"

"I never said it wasn't about money. I said it's not *just* about money." Seth stood up from the interview table, bracing himself for one or both of the detectives to tell him to sit back down. But they didn't, so he continued, "I've been trying to figure out why anyone would target Rachel Davenport in the particular way they have, and it's got to be about Davenport Trucking, right? All the evidence points in that direction."

Ivy nodded slowly. "Agreed."

"Whoever targeted Rachel didn't kill her, because killing her creates a different set of events than just getting her out of contention for the job."

"What different set of events?" Antoine asked.

Seth outlined what he'd learned about the triggers that came into play depending on how the CEO job came to be vacated. "If she's dead, control of the company goes to her uncle Rafe, and he makes all the decisions without input from the trustees. But if she's merely incapacitated, the trustees make a decision based on recommendations already in place. There's a list of preapproved candidates for CEO. Paul Bailey, by the way, is one of those preapproved candidates."

"Does he know he's one of the candidates?"

"Probably. His mama is one of the trustees, and they seem to have a close relationship. Plus, from what Rachel's told me, Paul hasn't always been gung ho about working for the company, so I figure there must have been discussions between George Davenport and Paul for the old man to feel okay about including him on that list of candidates."

"But if the compensation's not that much better—" Antoine began.

"That's what's been bugging the hell out of me," Seth admitted. "But while I was waiting for y'all to get back in here, I started thinking about what the job would entail besides just money. It's long hours and a lot of stress, because you've got dozens of trucks at your command and you're responsible for where they go, what they haul, what fines have to be paid if you screw things up, what repairs and regular maintenance have to be done, and suddenly it hit me that I needed to stop thinking about it as a businessman and start considering how I might use it if I had criminal intentions."

Ivy shot him an amused look. "What a stretch for you."

He made a face at her. "If I was criminally inclined these days, there's a hell of a lot I could do with a fleet of trucks. I could move drugs back and forth. Illegal arms. Hell, I could traffic in people. Sex slaves, illegals, anything and everything. I could haul a dirty bomb from Central America to Washington, D.C., if I had my own fleet of trucks."

"I'm glad you don't," Antoine murmured.

"My point is, control of the trucks is control of a lot of potential income. If someone was inclined to use even a tenth of the fleet for illicit purposes—"

"They could make a fortune," Ivy finished for him.

There was a knock on the interview room door. Antoine grimaced at the interruption and went to answer the knock.

"If Paul Bailey still has a gambling problem, maybe he owes somebody very bad a lot of money," Ivy said grimly.

"It could be the mob, the Redneck Mafia, South American money launderers—"

"Could be anyone who wants to control a fleet of trucks for the small price of forgiving Paul Bailey's gambling debt," Ivy said. "Good God."

"And he's there with Rachel right now," Antoine said from the doorway, his expression dark. A uniformed policeman stood behind him.

Seth snapped his gaze up. "What?"

"Jerry just talked to her on the phone. Her step-brother is there with her. She said he was going to stay there so she wouldn't be alone."

"Damn it!" Seth started toward the door, ready to bowl them both over if they tried to stop him.

Neither of them did.

Chapter 16

The chamomile tea was a little sweet for her taste, but Rachel wasn't going to complain. After the day she'd just survived, she wasn't about to be picky when someone gave her a little uncomplicated pampering.

Paul settled into the chair across from her at the kitchen table and sipped his own cup of tea. "I closed off that trapdoor to the attic while the tea was brewing."

"Yes, I know. I heard the hammering." She smiled.

"Speaking of the attic, I was actually planning to come here today before I talked to Jim Hallifax. Feel up to a little scavenger hunt?"

She raised her eyebrows over her cup of tea. "Scavenger hunt?"

"Mother called from Wilmington. She meant to take her wedding album with her to her sister's place but left it behind. I was planning to carry it with me when I visit her later this week, but I have no idea where she kept the album. She said she thought it might be in the attic?"

Rachel grimaced at the thought of going up there again. "I'm sure it's probably in an obvious place."

Paul gave her a teasing smile. "Oh, right, you're scared of high places, aren't you? Still haven't outgrown that?"

"It's not that, exactly." She stopped short of telling him what her phobia was really about. Funny, she thought, how she'd been able to share that deep, dark secret with Seth but balked at telling a man who was practically family. "And you're right. I should have outgrown it by now. Did Diane give you any idea where in the attic it might be?"

Paul smiled helplessly. "She said something about a box on the top of a bookshelf?"

Oh great, Rachel thought. *A high place within a high place.*

But this was a good test for her to prove, to herself if no one else, that she wasn't going to let her past define her any longer.

She put down her cup and pushed to her feet. "Fine. But you're coming with me to hold the stepladder."

"I knew you weren't involved with this." Delilah told Seth as they sped along the twists and turns of Copperhead Road, part of a three-vehicle rescue mission. Ivy's Jeep was in the lead, with Antoine right behind her. Delilah and Seth took up the rear, to his dismay, forced to go only as fast as the vehicles ahead of them.

"You knew?" He shot her a skeptical look.

"Okay, I wanted to believe." She looked apologetic. "I'm in this to help Rachel."

"I know. I'm sorry I didn't see it sooner."

"There was a lot you had to look past first." He tamped down a potent mixture of frustration and fear as he tried Rachel's cell phone again. It went directly to voice mail. "Why the hell isn't she answering?"

"Did you try the home phone?"

"Yeah. I get a busy signal."

Delilah didn't respond, but he could tell from the grim set of her jaw that she was worried.

"I think I love her," he said, even though he'd meant to say something entirely different.

Delilah's gaze flicked toward him. "What?"

"I think I love Rachel." He shook his head and corrected himself. "I know I love her."

"Oh my God."

"Why do people keep saying that? You think I'm not capable of loving someone?"

"I didn't say that. It's just—surprising."

He slammed his hand against the dashboard. "Can't we go faster?"

"These mountain roads are treacherous at normal speeds," Delilah said. "At high speeds, we could all end up dead, and how's that going to help Rachel?"

His heart felt as if it were going to pound right out of his chest. "I shouldn't have let y'all leave there without her. I should've protected her better. Damn it!"

"When did this happen? This thing with Rachel?"

He stared at her. "We're going to talk about my love life in the middle of all this?"

"You brought it up."

"I don't know," he growled. "I always thought she was pretty, of course. And I guess when I started suspecting the murders had something to do with Davenport Trucking, I started paying more attention to her."

"You suspected a connection all along?"

"After the second murder, when it was clear that both of the dead women had worked at Davenport, yeah. I did."

"This is so crazy. Her stepbrother."

"If he's in debt to the mob or someone connected like that, his life is on the line. He's already proved he's willing to kill to stay alive. He's not going to stop just because his stepsister is next on the list." He tried to keep his voice calm, but inside he was raging.

If, God forbid, they arrived too late—

"Oh, no," Delilah murmured.

He looked at her and found her gazing through the windshield ahead, her brow furrowed. He followed her gaze and saw what she had.

Smoke, rising in a black column over the treetops.

Something straight ahead was on fire.

And the only thing straight ahead was Rachel's house.

The slamming of the attic door had caught Rachel by surprise. Already nervous, she'd jumped and whirled at the sound, ready to scold Paul for scaring the wits out of her.

But Paul wasn't there.

"Paul?" She'd been certain he was right behind her on the ladder. She'd felt his footfalls on the rungs below her, making her cling all the more tightly to the ladder as she climbed.

He hadn't answered, but she'd heard noise on the other side of the door. Reaching down to push the attic door open again, she'd discovered it wouldn't budge. "Paul, damn it! This isn't funny!"

More sounds of movement had come from below, but Paul hadn't answered.

Then she'd smelled it. The pungent odor of gasoline. "Paul?"

She'd heard a faint hiss, then a louder crackling noise on the other side of the door. The smell of smoke mixing with the fuel odor had spurred her into full-blown panic mode.

She'd grabbed the metal hasp of the attic door again to give it a tug and found it hot as blazes, making her snatch her hand back with a hiss of pain.

Fire. The house is on fire.

She wasn't sure how long she'd stood frozen in place after that, trying to think. Long enough to realize there was more than just panic going on. Her brain seemed oddly sluggish, as if it took thoughts a longer time than usual to make it from idea to action.

Had she been drugged? Had he given her something in the chamomile tea? Something to slow her reaction time, to muddy her thinking so that she couldn't escape his trap?

She needed help. She needed—

She needed her phone. Digging in the pocket of her jeans, she'd expelled a soft sigh of sheer relief at finding it there. But when she tried to make a call, there was no signal.

That's crazy, she'd thought, trying to quell her rising fear long enough to think past the cottony confusion swirling in her brain. The house was one of the few places in Bitterwood where there was almost never any trouble getting a signal.

Unless, she realized, someone had a jammer.

Paul. Oh, no. It couldn't be.

Okay, okay. Think. She obviously couldn't get out the way she'd come in. Smoke already poured into the attic through the narrow seams in the door. Even if Paul hadn't wedged it shut behind her somehow, the fire would make getting out that way impossible.

But there was another trap door by the window.

She was halfway there before she remembered that Paul had already nailed it shut. Stumbling over the last few steps, she came to a stop against the window frame, sagging in despair.

He'd planned this, she realized. He'd come here today not to protect her but to kill her.

But why? Did he want to run Davenport Trucking so badly that he'd kill her for it? How did that make any sense? He'd never seen the job as anything more than a paycheck. He didn't even go to Christmas parties or participate in any of the interoffice morale projects.

But his interest had picked up in the past few months, hadn't it?

Why?

She felt certain the answer was somewhere just beyond the mists in her brain, so close she could almost feel it.

She banged her hand against the wall in frustration. "Paul!" she shouted, wondering if he could hear her over the rising din of crackling flames. "Paul, if you want the CEO job, I'll give it to you. Right now. In writing. Paul!"

Hell, he was probably nowhere near the house by now. The police knew he'd been there as recently as thirty minutes ago. He was probably already gone, off to set up an alibi for himself.

She turned and looked out the window, staring down the dizzying twenty-five-foot drop to the flagstone patio below.

Paul was gone, and she was trapped in her worst nightmare.

A dark sedan swept past them on Copperhead Road, traveling in the opposite direction. So intent was Seth on the expanding column of smoking rising ahead of them that he almost ignored the passing motorist.

But a faint flicker of recognition sparked in his brain as the sedan reached them and passed. "That's Paul Bailey's car!"

Delilah's head twisted as the other vehicle passed. She shoved her cell phone at Seth. "Hit the *S* button. Sutton's on my speed dial."

Sutton answered on the first ring. "What?"

"The dark blue Toyota Camry that just passed us going south—that's Paul Bailey's car. Go after him."

A moment later, Ivy's Jeep pulled a sharp U-turn and headed off after the sedan. Antoine's department sedan braked and turned, as well. He slowed as they started to pass, and Delilah put on the brakes, rolling down the window at his gesture.

"I've called in Fire and Rescue, but they're across town. It may be up to y'all to get her out." He gunned the engine and swept off in pursuit of Ivy's Jeep and Bailey's Toyota.

Delilah pressed the accelerator to the floor, forcing Seth to grab the dashboard and hang on.

The house almost looked normal at first glance, but

smoke was pouring from somewhere on the second floor, rising over the slanted eaves to coil like a slithering snake in the darkening sky. Seth jumped out of the truck before it stopped rolling, racing for the front door at a clip.

Delilah's footsteps pounded behind him on the flagstone walkway. "You don't have any protective gear!"

He ignored her, not letting himself think about what lay on the other side of the door. Tried not to smell the smoke or hear the crackle of the fire's hissing taunts. The heat was greater the closer he got, but he pretended he didn't feel it, because if he let himself feel it, if he let himself picture the licking flames and skin-searing heat, he wasn't sure he could do what he had to do.

"Rachel!" he shouted, taking the porch steps two at a time. He reached for the door handle.

"No!" Delilah's small, compact body slammed into him, knocking him to the floor of the porch. He struggled with her, but she was stronger than he remembered, pinning him against the rough plank floor. "Stop. There could be a back draft if you open the door right now! We have to do this right."

He stared at her, his heart hammering against his sternum, each thud laced with growing despair. "What if she's already dead?"

Delilah's gaze softened. "We'll find a way in. I promise."

She let him up, holding out her hand to help him to his feet. He gingerly put his hand on the doorknob and found it sizzling hot to the touch. Fear gripped him, a cold, tight fist squeezing his intestines until he felt light-headed. He could see the flicker of flames already climbing the curtains of the front windows and tried not to collapse into complete panic.

"Maybe the fire hasn't reached the back," Delilah said, her hand closing around his arm.

The back. Of course. If the fire hadn't gotten to the back of the house—

He forced his trembling legs into action, speeding back down the porch steps and around the corner of the house.

The back of the house showed no sign of fire yet. Even if the rest of the house was in flames, if Rachel was holed up somewhere the fire hadn't reached, he might be able to get her out through the trapdoors in the mudroom and closet.

But to do that, he had to go inside.

Where the fire was.

"Seth!" Delilah caught up with him and grabbed his arm, pointing up.

He followed her gaze and saw a pale face gazing down at him through the open attic window. Smoke slithered out around her, coiling her in its sinister grasp.

"Rachel," he breathed. She was alive.

"The trapdoor's nailed…shut…" She swayed forward, grabbing the window frame in time to keep from toppling out. "I think…I'm drugged."

"We need a ladder," Delilah said urgently. "A tall one."

"Rachel, do you have a ladder? A long one?"

"No ladders!" She shook her head, sagging against the window frame. "No ladders. Please, no ladders." The last came out weakly, and she disappeared from the window.

"She's terrified of heights," he told Delilah. "But that

may be the only way to get her. Go check the shed over there for a ladder."

"What are you going to do?" she asked, her dark eyes wide.

"I'm going to see if I can undo whatever Paul did to the trapdoors and get her out that way." It would still involve ladders, but shorter ones, not a rickety steel nightmare.

He could spare her that much, couldn't he? Even if it meant facing his own worst nightmare?

"You're really going into the fire?" Delilah stared at him as if she were seeing him for the first time.

"I have to," he answered, and put his hand on the back doorknob. It was only mildly warm to the touch. Taking care, he opened the door. Heat billowed out to greet him, but it didn't trigger any sort of combustion. He looked at his sister. "Go find a ladder, in case I fail."

She gave him a final, considering look before jogging off to the shed.

He entered the mudroom and tried the trapdoor, surprised but relieved to find it unlocked. He climbed into the second-floor bedroom closet, coughing as smoke seeped in under the bedroom door and burned his lungs.

It was a lot hotter in the closet, but he didn't let himself think about it. He turned on the closet light, which made the thick cloud of smoke in the small room all the more visible. Covering his mouth with his sleeve, he reached for the ladder to the attic trapdoor and stopped, gazing up in dismay. The door wasn't just nailed closed. It had been anchored in place with at least two dozen long nails. Even if he had a hammer—which he didn't— it would take long, precious minutes to pull out all those nails. And the police had confiscated his Swiss Army knife.

Painfully aware of the ticking clock, he reversed course and went back through the mudroom door. The heat here was stronger, pouring around him in slick, greasy waves. The odor of gasoline wafted toward him, and he realized there was an open container sitting right by the back door.

He set it outside quickly and looked toward the shed. The door was open and Delilah was inside, digging around. "I need a hammer!" he called to her. "Can you see a hammer?"

She emerged from the shed a moment later, carrying a large, old-looking claw-head hammer. He met her halfway to get it.

"The fire is spreading," he told her breathlessly as he took the hammer. "Even if I get up to her, we may not have any choice but to get down by ladder. The sooner the better. I'm not sure we can wait for the fire trucks to arrive. Have you found a ladder?"

"I spotted it in the back. I have to dig for it. You get into the attic. I'll get the ladder." She squeezed his arm, encouragement shining in her dark eyes. Warmth spread through his whole body like a booster shot of hope.

"See you on the other side of the window," he said.

He raced back into the burning house, dismayed to discover that in the few brief seconds he'd been outside, fire had licked closer to the mudroom. He could see flames dancing through the kitchen doorway, spreading inexorably closer. By the time he made it into the attic, the mudroom exit wasn't likely to be a viable escape route.

It was going to be the ladder or nothing.

The heat in the bedroom closet was oppressive, though the door had not yet become engulfed in flames. Still, eerie yellow light flickered through the narrow slit beneath the door, and smoke pouring through the crack limited visibility in the crowded space to inches.

He pulled down the trapdoor ladder as far as it would go with the door nailed shut and hauled himself up on the rungs, praying the wood was sturdy enough to hold his weight while he worked. So far, the electricity in the house was still on, giving him enough light to see the nails he had to remove.

"Rachel?" he called, wondering if she could hear him on the other side of the trapdoor. Was she even conscious anymore?

"Seth?" Her faint voice sounded remarkably close, as if she was just on the other side.

"I'm right here, sugar. I'm pulling out the nails. But you have to get off the door or you'll fall through, and I won't be able to catch you."

He heard scraping noises above him, then silence.

"Rachel, are you off the door now?"

When her voice came, it was faint. "You have to go. The fire…"

"You think I'm going to leave you up there alone?"

"It was Paul. Paul did this. I think he did everything."

"That's right, we know who it is now, so it's going to be okay. We'll get him, and then you'll be safe."

"You must hate me."

He smiled at the plaintive tone. "Never."

"I didn't listen to you."

"Yeah, you did," he said, his voice coming out in a soft grunt as he struggled with a particularly difficult nail. "I told you I was trouble, and you listened. Smart girl."

"I didn't believe you—"

"I know. It's okay."

"No!" Her voice rose a little, her obvious fear tempered with frustration. "Listen to me. I didn't believe... you did it."

His fingers faltered on the hammer, nearly dropping it. "You didn't?"

"I know you. Who you are when you're not being a defensive jackass."

A helpless smile curved his lips. "You do, do you?"

She didn't answer.

His gut tightened, and he attacked the final nails with fierce determination, so focused that he didn't realize until the ladder dropped to open the trapdoor that the fire had finally breached the closet door, the crackling flames waiting for him as he dropped. Fire snapped at his pant legs and singed his shoes as he scrambled up the ladder and into the attic.

Rachel lay on her side a few feet away, her eyes closed and her breathing labored. Her face was sooty from the smoke rising through the rough slat flooring into the attic. He crouched beside her, his heart pounding.

Her pale eyes flickered open, and her soot-stained mouth curved into a weak smile. "I knew you were a hero."

He cradled her smudged face. "Yeah, well, we can debate that later. Right now, we're going to get you out of here. Okay?" He helped her to her feet and crossed to the open window, praying Delilah had come through.

She was standing below on the flagstone patio, locking the extension ladder into position. Struggling with the unwieldy contraption, she positioned it against the wall beneath the attic window. It didn't reach the windowsill, ending about five feet beneath.

Damn it. Seth gazed at the gap between himself and freedom.

"You'll have to climb down to it," Delilah called. "I've seen you monkey your way up a fir tree. You can do it!"

He could do it, but what about Rachel? She'd have to climb out of that window into nothing but her trust in his ability to keep her from falling.

Could she do that?

"Rachel?"

Her eyes fluttered up to meet his, her pupils dark and wide. "What?"

"I have to go out the window to the ladder."

She shook her head fiercely. "No ladder."

"We have to go out this way. The closet below is already on fire."

Her chin lifted. "Then you have to go without me."

"No," he said firmly. "We live together or we die together. Your choice. But I'm not going out there without you."

Chapter 17

"Please, Seth. I can't do it." Panic sizzled in Rachel's veins, driving out anything but fear, as black and deadly as the smoke filling the room at her back. "You go. Now."

His hands closed around her face, forcing her to look up at him. His face was soot-smudged and dripping sweat, but in his clear green eyes she saw a blaze of emotion that sucked the air right out of her aching lungs.

"I will not go without you." Each word rang with fierce resolve. His hands clutched her more tightly in place, as if he planned to drag her out the window with him, whatever the consequences.

"Okay." She peeled his hands from her face and gave him a little push toward the window. "Be careful!" she added with a rush of panic as he hauled himself onto the windowsill.

He disappeared over the side, only his fingers on the windowsill remaining in sight. After a harrowing moment, his face appeared over the sill again. "Okay, sugar. Your turn."

Terror gripped her gut, and she almost turned around and ran toward the trapdoor, preferring to take her chance with the fire. But his hand snaked over the side, grabbing her wrist as if he'd read the panic in her expression.

"You can do this. I braved the fire. You brave the heights."

Fly, baby. You can fly. Her mother's voice rang in her ears, a fierce, mean whisper of madness.

No. I won't fly.

I'll climb down like a sane person.

She closed her eyes a moment, mentally working her way through the next few seconds. She'd get settled on the windowsill, get her balance. Seth would be just below. He wouldn't let her fall.

He'd never let her fall.

She swung one trembling leg over the windowsill, clinging to the frame until she was straddling it, more or less balanced. But her imagination failed her. She couldn't visualize a way to get her other leg over the sill without plunging out the window.

"Take my hands, Rachel." Seth's voice gathered the scattered threads of her unraveling sense and tied them together. "Just take my hands and swing your leg over the edge."

She caught his hands. Fierce strength seemed to flow through his fingers into hers, and she swung her leg out of the window. She was hunched in an uncomfortable position, but she maintained her balance.

"This is the hardest point. Get this right, and we're home free." Seth released one of her hands and braced his against the wall. "I want you to slide off the ledge and onto my arm, turning around to face the wall as you do it. Okay?"

She stared at him. "That's your plan?"

He grinned up at her. "Take it or leave it."

She realized, in that scary, crazy moment, that she was helplessly in love with Seth Hammond. Faults and all. Any fire-phobic man who'd haul a drugged, acro-phobic basket case out of a burning house was a man in a million. Whatever had driven him in his sin-laden past, he was a hell of a man in the present.

And if he thought he was going to talk her out of what she was feeling, then he had one hell of a surprise coming to him.

"Remember what we did this afternoon?" she asked, sliding her butt off the sill and into the curve of his arm.

His green eyes snapped up to meet hers. "Yes," he answered warily.

She slid the rest of the way into his grasp, anchoring her fingers on the ladder rungs. The hard heat of his body behind her felt like solid ground.

"As soon as I sober up, we're doing that again. Understood?"

She felt his body shake lightly behind her as laughter whispered in her ear. "Understood."

Step by careful step, they reached the safety of the patio together just as the fire trucks pulled into the driveway.

"There's not much to salvage, I'm afraid." Delilah kept her voice low as she crossed to where Seth sat next to Rachel's hospital bed. The E.R. doctor had insisted she stay overnight for observation, given how much smoke she'd inhaled. But he was optimistic that she'd be fine in a day or two.

"I know she'll hate losing the mementos of her family," he murmured, brushing his thumb against the back of her hand where it lay loosely in his palm. "But I don't think she'll miss that damned attic."

"You're right about that." Rachel's voice, thick with sleep, drew his attention back to the bed. Her eyes fluttered open. "So, we lived, huh?"

He squeezed her hands. "Yes, we did."

She rubbed her reddened eyes. "I feel like I swallowed a smokestack."

"You nearly did."

The door of the hospital room opened, and Rafe Hunter breezed into the room on the sheer force of his personality, his wife, Janeane, bringing up the rear. Rafe nudged Seth aside and grabbed his niece's hands. "Rachel, darling, are you all right?"

Rachel gave Seth a quick look over her uncle's shoulder.

"I'll be back in a little while," he promised her, backing out of the room to let her family have time with her. Delilah came with him, laying her hand on his arm as he started to slump against the wall.

"There's a waiting room down at the end of the hall," she said, hooking her arm through his. "Ivy and Sutton need to talk to you."

Seth didn't like the bleak tone of Delilah's voice. "What's going on?" he asked as she led him into the small waiting area at the end of the corridor.

Inside were a handful of hospital visitors scattered

among the rows of chairs and benches. At the far end, near the big picture window looking out on the eastern side of Maryville, Sutton Calhoun and Ivy Hawkins had their heads together with a grim-looking Antoine Parsons.

All three turned when he and Delilah walked up. "What's happened?" Seth asked, his gut tight with dread.

"Paul Bailey is dead."

Seth stared at Antoine. "I thought you caught him and took him into custody."

"We did. We booked him, and he was waiting in his cell for his lawyer. The guard near his cell had to go referee a fight between a couple of drunks down the hall, and, when he got back, Bailey was dead."

"Murdered?"

"We're not sure." Antoine sounded apologetic. "We don't know if he ingested something or what. The coroner's got the body already and should have the autopsy done in a few days."

"He didn't do all of this by himself," Seth said firmly. "Someone was pulling his strings."

"That's what we think, too," Ivy assured him. "This case isn't over."

Seth ran his hand over his jaw, his palm rasping over the day's growth of beard. "Is Rachel still in danger?"

"Probably not," Sutton said gently. "Paul Bailey was clearly the link. If he was in charge of the company, then whoever had control of him had access to the trucks. Without him, there's no entry point. Whoever did this will just look for another fool to manipulate."

"So the man behind the curtain just gets away with five murders and weeks of tormenting Rachel?" Rage burned in Seth's gut, as hot and destructive as the fire that had licked at his heels in Rachel's house.

"He won't get away with it if we don't let him," Delilah said. "I've been thinking about what you told us. About Adam Brand."

There was an odd tone to his sister's voice that he hadn't heard before. A vulnerability that she'd never really shown, not even as a girl. He looked at her and saw anxiety shining in her dark eyes.

"What about him?" he asked.

"I've been trying to reach him, going around the obvious channels. I called some people we both knew back in the day. And that story about his being on vacation? It's bull. It's just the official story, at least for now."

"What's the real story?" Sutton asked curiously.

Delilah's expression went stony. "The real story is that he's gone AWOL. And the FBI is investigating him for espionage."

Seth shook his head firmly. "No way. Not Brand."

His sister's eyes blazed at him. "Something's really wrong, Seth. Because there's no way in hell Adam Brand would do anything to hurt this country. And now I'm wondering if what's going on with him has anything to do with his reason for having you follow Rachel."

"How?" Seth asked, not sure how to connect the two ideas together.

"I don't know," Delilah admitted. "I can't see an obvious connection." Her chin lifted. "But I'm going to find out."

She pulled out her cell phone and walked over to an empty spot on the other side of the room.

Sutton's gaze followed her movement briefly, then turned back to Seth. "I guess we owe you an apology."

Seth shook his head. "Not yet. Let me get a few more years of the straight and narrow under my belt and then maybe you'll owe me."

"You're really out of the life?" Ivy asked, more curious than disbelieving. "I hear it has a way of sucking you right back in."

"I don't want the guilt," he said simply. "It's not a life you can live if you have any sort of conscience, and apparently my daddy didn't blow mine up in that explosion after all."

Sutton looked at him through thoughtful eyes and gave a brief nod. "Good for you, Hammond. Prove everybody wrong."

"Speaking of daddies, you talked to yours recently?" Seth asked.

"I went by to see him once I was back in the country," Sutton answered. "He's getting back a lot more of his functions than I think he ever believed he would."

"I should have insisted he keep up with the therapy," Seth said with regret. "I'm sorry."

"He wasn't ready then. You couldn't have made him." Sutton shrugged. "You went above and beyond. I owe you."

"Not yet," Seth repeated with a faint smile.

He waited a few more minutes, giving Rachel time with her family, until he could stand it no longer. He left the waiting room and headed back down the hall to her room.

Her aunt and uncle had gone, but Rachel was still awake. "Where's the family?" he asked as she smiled sleepily at him.

"I asked them to call Diane," she told him, her smile fading. "To let her know what's going on with Paul."

She didn't know Paul was dead, he realized. He was tempted to keep that information from her until she felt better.

But that wasn't fair, was it? Keeping things from her would only convince her she couldn't trust him. He'd damned near been burned—literally—by his secrets. If he was serious about the straight and narrow, serious about becoming a man who could deserve a woman like Rachel Davenport, he had to start by telling the truth, even when it was unpleasant.

Even when it hurt.

He pulled up a chair by her bed and took her outstretched hand. "I just talked to Ivy and Antoine about Paul."

Her fingers tightened around his. "He's in really bad trouble, isn't he? That's why I wanted Uncle Rafe to talk to Diane. She's always liked him. He'll break it to her gently."

"I don't know how to say this but just say it. Paul is dead."

Her fingers went suddenly limp in his. "Dead? How?"

He told her what he knew. "It's possible he smuggled something into the jail. If we're right about someone pulling his strings, it may be that he found death preferable than whatever his puppet master had in store for him."

"He used to gamble in college—Diane used to bail him out all the time—but he went to rehab for it."

"Sometimes—a lot of the time—good intentions aren't enough. Sometimes, rehab doesn't stick."

Silence fell between them as they each considered the double meaning of his words. Rachel spoke first.

"Someone made Paul do this. I don't think he'd have done anything this terrible if he wasn't under extreme pressure."

Seth wasn't as inclined to give Paul Bailey's motives the benefit of the doubt, but he couldn't argue with her logic. "The police are looking into Paul's background, trying to figure out who he owed. If we figure that out, we'll be able to protect you better."

"So you think I'm still in danger?" She sounded deflated.

"Not the way you were, no. We don't think so. Paul was the leverage to get a foothold in the trucking company. Without him, whoever was pulling his strings can't get control over the trucks, and we're pretty sure that's what he wanted."

"You don't have any idea why he wanted control of the trucks?"

"Obviously the idea is to use them to ship some sort of contraband. We just don't know what."

"Couldn't they buy their own trucks?"

"Probably not without greater scrutiny."

"So he might already be under investigation?"

Seth thought about Adam Brand. Had the FBI agent tugged the tail of the wrong tiger? "Probably. We just have to match the suspect to the crime."

"We do?" She quirked an eyebrow at him. "You've joined the Bitterwood P.D. now, hero?"

He smiled at the thought at first, but his smile quickly faded. It was a surprisingly tempting idea, he realized. And if he hadn't burned his reputation to the ground, maybe he'd have had a chance to try his hand at being one of the good guys. "No, but I'm interested in the outcome of the case."

Her lips curved again. "Because of me?"

Helpless to say no, he nodded. "Because of you."

Her smile widened briefly but quickly faded. Tears welled in her eyes, and she brushed them away with an angry swipe of her fingers. "Poor Diane. She's lost everyone."

"She didn't lose you. Right?"

Her fingers tightened around his. "Thanks to you."

He kissed her knuckles. "There were a few minutes there I thought I was going to have to stay in that attic with you until the fire got us."

"I wouldn't have let that happen," she said firmly.

He smiled at her confident tone. "Yeah, you say that now."

"I meant what I said up there."

Heat flushed through him as he remembered what she'd said, but he didn't want to assume they remembered the same thing. She'd been drugged, after all. "Which part?"

Her lopsided smirk reassured him that they *were* thinking of the same thing. "You know which part."

He shook his head. "What am I going to do with you?"

Her smirk grew into a full grin. "You need me to remind you?"

"I'm still a risky bet, Rachel. Not everyone's going to be able to see beyond my past. They're going to think you're crazy for wanting to be with me...."

She pushed herself upright in the bed, leaning toward him to place her hand on his cheek. "I'm a big girl. I can take it. What I can't take is life without you in it."

Gazing into her shining blue eyes, he realized she meant every word she was saying.

He closed his hand over hers where it lay on his cheek. "I'm going to do everything I can to make sure you never regret your decision. I promise."

She leaned closer, brushing her lips against his. "That's a good, solid start. Don't you think?"

He wrapped his arms around her, careful not to get tangled in her IV tube. "Yeah, it is," he growled in her ear, breathing in the smoky sweet smell of her, letting it fill him with hope. "It's a very good start."

* * * * *

Five years of memories didn't compare an ounce to the man
they'd been made about. Not when he seemingly materialized
out of midair, wrapped in a uniform that fit nicely, topped
with a cowboy hat his daddy had given him and carrying
some emotions behind clear blue eyes.

Eyes that, once they found Mel during her attempt to flee
the hospital, never strayed.

Not that she'd expected anything but full attention when
Sterling Costner found out she was back in town.

Though, silly ol' Mel had been hoping that she'd have more
time before she had this face-to-face.

Because, as much as she was hoping no one else would
catch wind of her arrival, she knew the gossip mill around
town was probably already aflame.

"I'm glad this wasn't destroyed," Mel said lamely once
she slid into the passenger seat, picking up her suitcase in the
process. She placed it on her lap.

She remembered leaving her apartment with it, but not
what she'd packed inside. At least now she could change out
of her hospital gown.

Sterling slid into his truck like a knife through butter.

The man could make anything look good.

"I didn't see your car, but Deputy Rossi said it looked like someone hit your back end," he said once the door was shut. "Whoever hit you probably got spooked and took off. We're looking for them, though, so don't worry."

Mel's stomach moved a little at that last part.

"Don't worry" in Sterling's voice used to be the soundtrack to her life. A comforting repetition that felt like it could fix everything.

She played with the zipper on her suitcase.

"I guess I'll deal with the technical stuff tomorrow. Not sure what my insurance is going to say about the whole situation. I suppose it depends on how many cases of amnesia they get."

Sterling shrugged. He was such a big man that even the most subtle movements drew attention.

"I'm sure you'll do fine with them," he said.

She decided talking about her past was as bad as talking about theirs, so she looked out the window and tried to pretend for a moment that nothing had changed.

That she hadn't married Rider Partridge.

That she hadn't waited so long to divorce him.

That she hadn't fallen in love with Sterling.

That she hadn't—

Mel sat up straighter.

She glanced at Sterling and found him already looking at her.

She smiled.

It wasn't returned.

Love Harlequin romance?

DISCOVER.

Be the first to find out about promotions,
news and exclusive content!

Facebook.com/HarlequinBooks

Twitter.com/HarlequinBooks

Instagram.com/HarlequinBooks

Pinterest.com/HarlequinBooks

YouTube.com/HarlequinBooks

ReaderService.com

EXPLORE.

Sign up for the Harlequin e-newsletter and
download a free book from any series at
TryHarlequin.com

CONNECT.

Join our Harlequin community to
share your thoughts and connect
with other romance readers!
Facebook.com/groups/HarlequinConnection

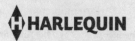

HSOCIAL2021